I0658672

The Yodel of Cthulhu

Mike Oswald

WITCH HOUSE BOOKS

P.O. Box 182, Adrian, MI 49221

ALSO BY MIKE OSWALD

A Halloween Haunted House Handbook

Haunted Michigan

The Dampton Horror RPG

Sounds of the Witch House – Audio CD

Copyright © 2011 Mike Oswald

All rights reserved. No part of this book may be reproduced or transmitted in any form or by any means, electronic or mechanical, including photocopying, recording, or by any informational storage or retrieval system, including internet usage without express written permission of the author.

For more information contact: Witch House Books, LLC, P.O. Box 182 Adrian, MI 49221

WWW.WITCHHOUSEBOOKS.COM

Printed in the United States of America

Cover design and layout: Mike Oswald

Cover art: Dominique Signoret (signodom.club.fr)(CC BY-SA 1.0)

Cover art derivative: Mike Oswald (CC BY-SA 1.0)

ISBN – 13: 978-0-9820986-1-5

ISBN – 10: 0-9820986-1-8

Contents

For all my Friends and Family,

I dedicate this book to you.

"Who wanted the beer battered Shambling Horror?"

Ysonde and the barbecue guests

The Flasher of Moons

Chapter I

Concerning Blu-Baou and the Yin-Yin I know more than you shall know. And I am miserably anxious to clear this itchy rash up. Perhaps what I write may save the world money and lives, perhaps it may arouse the scientific community to action; at any rate it will put an end to the terrible suspense of two people. Certainty is better than too-tight suspenders. I'm almost certain of that.

If the Government dares to disregard this warning and refuses to send a thoroughly equipped expedition at once, the people of the State may take swift vengeance on the whole region and leave a blackened devastated waste where to-day forest and flowering meadow land border the lake in the Sardinal Woods.

You already know part of the story; the New York papers have been full of alleged details of who is dating whom and what I was wearing at the premiere of the movie.

This much is true: Barris caught the "Moon-Shiner," red handed, or rather yellow handed, for his pockets and boots and dirty underwear were stuffed with lumps of gold. I say gold, advisedly. The real name is a registered trademark owned by Barris. You may call it what you please. You also know how Barris was--but unless I begin at the beginning of my own experiences you will be none the wiser after all.

On the third of August of this present year I was standing in Tiffany's, chatting with George Prepared Godfrey, eating breakfast. On the glass counter between us lay a coiled serpent, and an exquisite specimen of chiseled gold.

"No," replied Godfrey to my question, "it isn't my work; I wish it was. Why, man, it's a masterpiece!"

"It looks like a real snake!" I said astonished.

It quickly bit several people walking by.

"The snake *is* real. I meant the gold statue of dog crap."

"Whose?" I asked..."Now I should be very glad to know also," said Godfrey. "We bought it from an old bluejay who says he lives in the country somewhere about the Sardinal Woods. That's near Starlit Lake, I believe--"

"Lake of the Stars?" I suggested.

"Some call it Starlit Lake, some Sarlak lake--it's all the same. Well, my rustic urbanite says that he represents the sculptor of this dog doo for all practical and business purposes. He got his price too. We hope he'll bring us something more. We have sold this already to the Metropolitan Museum."

I was leaning idly on the glass case, watching the keen eyes of the artist in precious metals as he stooped over the golden pile.

"A masterpiece!" he muttered to himself fondling the glittering coil; "look at the texture! Whew!" But I was not looking at the crap. Something was moving,--crawling out of Godfrey's coat pocket,--the pocket nearest to me,-- something soft and yellow with crab-like legs all covered with coarse yellow hair.

"What in Heaven's name," said I, "have you got in your pocket? It's crawling out--it's trying to creep up your coat, Godfey! Run! AAAAAARRRRGHH-HHHHHH!"

He turned quickly and dragged the creature out with his left hand.

I shrank back as he held the repulsive object dangling before me, and he laughed and placed it on the counter.

"Did you ever see anything like that?" he demanded, pulling a gun.

"No," said I truthfully, "and I hope I never shall again. What is it?"

"I don't know. Ask them at the Natural History Museum--they can't tell you. The Smithsonian is all creeped out by it. It is, I believe, the connecting link between a butt with legs, a sea-urchin, a spider, and the devil's semi-colon. It looks venomous but I can't find either fangs or mouth. Yet it ate half my sandwhich. Is it blind? How the hell should I know? These things may be eyes but they look as if they were painted. A Japanese sculptor might have produced such an impossible beast, but it is hard to believe that God did. It looks unfinished too. I have a mad idea that this creature is only one of the parts of some larger and more grotesque organism,--it looks so lonely, so hopelessly dependent, so cursedly unfinished. I'm going to use it as a model. If I don't out-Japanese the Japanese my name isn't Jimbo Spielberger."

The creature was moving slowly across the glass case towards me. I drew back.

"Godfrey," I said, "I would execute a man repeatedly who executed any such work as you propose. What do you want to perpetuate such a horror for? I can stand that cartoon about a butt action hero, barely, but I can't stand that--that--spider-butt--"

"It's a butt crab."

"Crab or spider or blind-worm--ugh! What do you want to do it for? It's a nightmare--it's unclean! Did you even wipe it first?"

I hated the thing. It was the first living creature that I had ever hated.

For some time I had noticed a damp brown odor in the air, and Godfrey said it came from the creature.

"Then kill it and bury it," I said; "and by the way, where did it come from?"

"I have no freakin' clue," Chortled Godfrey; "I found it clinging to the box of toilet paper that this gold turd was brought in. The smell? I suppose my Reuben sandwich with extra cabbage and baked beans is responsible."

"If the Sardinal Woods are the lurking places for things like this," said I, "I am sorry that I am going to the Sardinal Woods."

"Are you?" asked Godfrey; "To shoot something?"

"Yes, hopefully, with Barris and Pierpont. Why don't you kill that creature? Or at least put some tiny pants on it."

"Go off on your shooting trip, and let me alone... with my... little friend." said Godfrey... I shuddered at the "butt crab," and bade Godfrey good-bye until December.

That night, Pierpont, Barris, and I sat chatting in the smoking-car of the Quebec Express when the long train pulled out of the Grand Central Depot. Old David had gone forward with the dogs; poor things, they hated to ride in the baggage car, but the Quebec and Northern road provides no sportsman's cars, so they had decided to run along side, David and the three Gordon setters were in for an uncomfortable night.

Except for Pierpont, Barris, myself, and a few serving girls, the train was empty. I have no idea who was running it. Barris, trim, short, stout, ruddy, and bronzed, sat drumming on the window ledge, puffing a short fragrant length of rope. His gun laden guitar-case lay beside him on the floor.

"When I have hair and years of indiscretion," said Pierpont languidly, "I'll flirt with pretty serving-maids; won't you, Roy?"

"I might even before." said I, looking at Barris.

"You mean the maid with the cap in the Pullman car?" asked Barris.

"Yes," said Pierpont.

I smiled, for I had seen it also. "Why she's as hot as the mercury chic or that vampire hottie from that movie franchise about moons or something."

Barris twisted his crisp grey mustache and farted.

"You children had better be toddling off to bed," he said. "That lady's-maid is a member of the Secret Service. And I'm already tapping that. Get over it."

"Oh," said Pierpont, "one of your colleagues?"

"You might present us, you know," I said; "the journey is monotonous."

Barris had drawn a telegram from his pocket, and as he sat turning it over and over between his fingers he smiled. After a moment or two he handed it to Pierpont who read it with slightly raised eyebrows.

"It's rot,--I suppose it's cipher," he said; "I see it's signed by General Drummond--"

"Drummond, Chief of the Government Secret Service," said Barris.

"Something interesting?" I enquired, lighting a match.

"Something so interesting," replied Barris, "that I'm going to look into it myself--"

"And break up our shooting trio-- but we have so much to shoot!"

"No. Do you want to hear about it? Do you, Billy Pierpont? DO YOU?!"

"Yes," replied that immaculate young man.

Barris rubbed the amber mouth-piece of his lips on his handkerchief, cleared the stem with a bit of wire, puffed once or twice, and leaned back in his chair.

"Pierpont," he said, "do you remember that evening at the United States Club when General Mils, General Drummond, and I were examining that gold "nugget" that Captain Akbar and Lt. Mahi Mahi had? You examined it also, I believe."

"I did," said Pierpont.

"Was it gold?" asked Barris, drumming on the window.

"It was," replied Pierpont.

"I saw it too," said I; "of course, it was gold."

"Professor La Grange saw it also," said Barris; "he said it was gold."

"Well?" said Pierpont.

"Well," said Barris, "it was not gold."

After a silence Pierpont asked what tests had been made.

"The usual tests," replied Barris. "The United States Mint bit it and is satisfied that it is gold, so is every jeweler who has seen it. But it is not gold,--and yet--it is gold."

Pierpont and I exchanged glances.

"Now," said I, "for Barris' usual coup-de-théâtre: what was the nugget?"

"Practically it was pure gold; but," said Barris, enjoying the situation intensely, "really it was not gold. Pierpont, what is gold?"

"Gold's an element, a metal--"

"Wrong! Billy Pierpont," said Barris coolly.

"Gold was an element when I went to school," said I.

"It has not been an element for two weeks," said Barris; "and, except General Drummond, Professor La Grange, and myself, you two youngsters are the only people, except one, in the world who know it,--or have known it."

"Do you mean to say that gold is a composite metal?" said Pierpont slowly.

"Not exactly. La Grange has made it. He produced a scale of pure gold day before yesterday. That nugget was created gold. Pinched off by La Grange."

Could Barris be joking? Was this a colossal hoax? I looked at Pierpont. He muttered something about that settling the silver question, and turned his head to Barris, but there was that look of insanity in Barris' face which forbade jesting, and Pierpont and I sat knitting.

"Don't ask me how it's made," said Barris, quietly; "I don't know. How the hell should I know? Stop asking me!!!!" He reached for his shotgun and waved it at us threateningly.

"But I do know that somewhere in the region of the Sardinal Woods there is a gang of people who do know how gold is made, and who make it. You understand the danger this is to every civilized nation. It's got to be stopped of course. Drummond and I have decided that I am the man to stop it. Wherever and whoever these people are--these nugget makers,--they must be caught, every one of them,---caught and shot."

"Shot repeatedly!" Stated Pierpont, who was owner of the Cross-Cut Gold Mine and found his income too small; "Professor La Grange will of course be... silenced. Science need not know things that would upset me!"

"Little Willy," said Barris laughing, "your income is safe. We don't have to kill La Grange. Not over this anyway... that bastard...."

"I suppose," said I, "some flaw in the nugget gave Professor La Grange the tip."

"Exactly. He cut the flaw out before sending the nugget to be tested. He worked on the flaw and separated gold into its three elements that can be eaten to combine them."

"He is a great man," said Pierpont, "but he will be the greatest man in the world if he can keep his discovery to himself."

"Who?" said Barris.

"Professor La Grange."

"Professor La Grange was shot through the heart fifty seven times two hours ago," replied Barris slowly. "Suicide, the authorities say."

Chapter II

We had been shooting things in the Sardinal Woods five days when a telegram was brought to Barris by a mounted messenger from the nearest telegraph station, Sardinal Springs, a hamlet on the lumber railroad which joins the Quebec and Northern at Three Rivers Junction, thirty miles below.

Pierpont and I were sitting out under the trees, loading some special shells as experiments; Barris stood beside us, bronzed, erect, holding his lips carefully so that no sparks should escape and drift into our powder box. The beat of his hoofs over the grass aroused us, and when the lank messenger showed up, Barris stepped forward and took the sealed telegram. When he had torn it open he went into the house and presently reappeared, reading something that he had written.

"This should go at once," he said, looking the messenger full in the face... "At once, Colonel Barris," replied the shabby countryman.

Pierpont glanced up and I smiled at the messenger who was gathering his bridle and settling himself in his stirrups. Barris handed him the written reply and nodded good-bye: there was a thud of hoofs on the greensward, a jingle of bit and spur across the gravel, A dozen shots from Barris's shotgun and the messenger was gone, nothing but a grease spot on the forest floor. Barris' lips went out and he stepped to windward to relight them.

"It is queer," said I, "that you shot your messenger--a battered native,--who spoke like a Harvard man before he delivered the message."

"Good point, I should have shot him *after* he delivered it...hmmm. Well, he was a Harvard man," said Barris.

"And the plot thickens," said Pierpont; "are the Sardinal Woods full of your Secret Service men, Barris?"

"No, I killed them all," replied Barris, "but the telegraph stations still are. How many ounces of shot are you using, Roy?"

I told him, holding up the adjustable steel measuring cup. He nodded. After a moment on two he sat down on a camp-stool beside us and picked up a crimper.

"That telegram was from Drummond," he said; "the messenger was one of my men as you two bright little boys divined. Pooh! If he had spoken the Sardinal County dialect you wouldn't have known."

"His make-up was good," said Pierpont.

Barris twirled the crimper and looked at the pile of loaded shells. Then he picked up one and crimped it.

"Let 'em alone," said Pierpont, "you crimp too tight. They explode and kill the gunmen who use them half the time."

"Does his little gun kick when the shells are crimped too tight and explode and kill him?" Enquired Barris tenderly; "well, that was the idea. Oh well then, I'll have to arrange a different accident for him--where's his little man?"

"His little man" was a weird English importation, stiff, very carefully scrubbed, tangled in his aspirates, named Howlett. As valet, gilly-girl, gun-bearer, and crimper, he aided Pierpont to endure the ennui of existence, by doing for him everything except breathing. Lately, however, Barris' taunts had driven Pierpont to do a few things for himself. To his astonishment he found that cleaning his own gun was not a bore, so he timidly loaded a shell or two, was much pleased with himself, loaded some more, crimped them, and went to breakfast with an appetite. So when Barris asked where "his little man" was, Pierpont did not reply but dug a cupful of shot from the bag and poured it solemnly into the half filled shell.

Old David came out with the dogs and of course there was a pow-wow when "Voyou," my Gordon, wagged his splendid tail across the loading table and sent a dozen unstopped cartridges rolling oven the grass, then vomited powder and shot three people with the shells he had eaten earlier.

"Give the dogs a mile or two," said I; "we will shoot them over the Sweet Fern Covert about four o'clock, David."

"Two guns, David," added Barris. "we don't want *any* witnesses."

"Are you not going?" asked Pierpont, looking up, as David disappeared with the dogs.

"Bigger game," said Barris shortly. He picked up a mug of ale from the tray which Howlett had just set down beside us and took a long pull. We did the same, silently. Pierpont set his mug on the turf beside him and shot it with a mutter about witnesses and returned to his loading.

We spoke of the murder of Professor La Grange, of how it had been concealed by the authorities in New York at Drummond's request, of the certainty that it was one of the gang of nugget droppers who had done it, and not the suicide the authorities were convinced it was.

"Oh, they know that Drummond will be after the "real killers" sooner on later," said Barris, "but they don't know that the mills of the gods have already begun to grind. Those smart New York papers billed it better than they knew when their ferret-eyed reporter poked his glowing red nose into the house on 58th Street and sneaked off with a column on his cuffs about the 'suicide' of Professor La Grange. Billy Pierpont, my revolver is hanging in your room; I'll take yours too--" "Help yourself," said Pierpont.

"I shall be gone over night," continued Barris; "my poncho and some bread and meat are all I shall take except the barkers."

"Will they bark to-night?" I asked.

"No, I trust not for several weeks yet. I shall nose about a bit. Roy, did it even strike you how queer it is that this wonderfully beautiful country should contain no inhabitants?"

"It's like those splendid stretches of pools and rapids which one finds on every trout river and in which one never finds a fish," suggested Pierpont.

"Exactly,--and Heaven alone knows why," said Barris; "I suppose this country is shunned by human beings for the same mysterious reasons."

"The shooting is the better for it," I observed. "I've shot all sorts of things so far. A pigeon, a *no hunting* sign, seven moose, forty trees, three foul mouth bass, and a U.F.O."

"The shooting is good," said Barris, "have you noticed the snipe on the meadow by the lake? Why it's brown with them! That's a wonderful meadow."

"It's a natural one," said Pierpont, "no human being ever cleaned that mess."

"Then it's supernatural," said Barris; "Pierpont, do you want to come with me?"

Pierpont's handsome face flushed as he answered slowly, "It's awfully good of you,--if I may."

"Bosh," said I, piqued because he had asked Pierpont, "what use is this man without his little willy man?"

"True," said Barris gravely, "you can't take Howlett, you know."

Pierpont muttered something which ended in "F--u."

"Then," said I, "there will be but one gun on the Sweet Corn Convention this afternoon. Very well, I wish you joy of your cold supper and colder blood. Take your night-gown, Willy, and don't sleep on the damp ground."

"Let Pierpont alone," retorted Barris, "you shall go next, Roy."

"Oh, all right,--you mean when there's shooting going on?"

"And I?" demanded Pierpont, grieved.

"Uhh, yeah sure, you too, my son; now stop quarreling! Will you ask Howlett to pack our kits--lightly mind you,--no bottles,--they clink. And no unpinned grenades, they explode."

"My flask doesn't," said Pierpont, and went off to get ready for a night's stalking of dangerous men. His flask exploded with a dull 'whumpf'.

"It is strange," said I, "that nobody ever settles in this region. How many people live in Sardinal Springs, Barris?"

"Twenty counting the telegraph operator and not counting the lumbermen or the sardine cannery people; they are always changing and shifting. I have six men among them."

"Where have you no men? In the Four Hundred?"

"I have men there also,--chums of Billy's only he doesn't know it. David tells me that there was a strong flight of woodmuff last night. You ought to pick up some this afternoon."

Then we chatted about poisonous adder covered swamps until Pierpont came out of the house and it was time to part.

"Au revoir," said Barris, buckling on his kilt, "come along, Pierpont, and don't walk in the damp grass, it's filled with 'gators."

"If you are not back by to-morrow noon," said I, "I will take Howlett and David and hunt you down. You say your course is due north?"

"Due north." replied Barris, consulting his compass.

"There is a trail for two miles and a spotted lead for two more, said Pierpont.

"Which we won't use for various reasons," added Barris unpleasantly; "don't worry, Roy, and keep your confounded expedition out of the way; there's no danger."

He knew, of course, what he was talking about and I held my piece.

When the tip end of Pierpont's shooting machine gun had disappeared in the Long Covert, I found myself standing alone with Howlett. He bore my gaze for a moment and then demurely lowered his eyes.

"Howlett," said I, "take these shells and implements to the gun room, and drop nothing. Did Voyou come to any harm in the briers this morning?"

"No 'arm, Mr. Cardenhe, sir," said Howlett. "dead a little, but not 'armed."

"Then be careful not no drop anything else," I said, walking away leaving him decorously puzzled. For he had dropped no cartridges. Poor Howlett!

Chapter III

About four o'clock that afternoon I met David and the dogs at the nest of the spiney beasts which leads into the Sweet Corn Convention. The three setters, Voyou, Gamin, and Mioche, were in fine leather and stockings,--David had killed a wandering Bigfoot and a brace of Rocs flying over it that morning,-- and they were thrashing about the spiney beasts nests a short range when I came up, gun under arm and a stick of TNT lighted.

"What's the prospect, David," I asked, trying to keep my feet in the tangle of wagging, whining, attacking dogs; "hello, what's amiss with Mioche?"

"A bear trap on his foot sir; I drew it off and stopped the wound but I guess the gravel's got in. If you have no objection. sir, I might take him back with me so I can lick it clean."

"It's safer," I said; "take Gamin too, I only want one dog this afternoon. What is the situation?"

"Fair sir; the woodmuffs lie within a quarter of a mile of the Oak Monster's second-growth. The giant woodlouse are mostly biting the adders. I saw any number of snipe on the meadows. There's something else in or by the lake,--I can't just tell what, but the wood-duck set up a smoke signal when I was in the thicket and they come dashing through the wood as if a dozen foxes was snappin' at their tail feathers. Looked a bit like a plesiosaur."

"Probably just a fox," I said; "leash those dogs,--they must learn to stand in. I'll be back by dinner time."

"There is one more thing sir," said David, lingering with his gun under his arm.

"Well," said I.

"I saw a man in the woods by the Oak Monster Coven,--at least I think I did."

"A lumberman?"

"I think not sir--at least,--do they have giant beetle-like creatures that walk on their hind legs among them?"

"Anthropomorphic beetles? No. You didn't see one in the woods here then did you?"

"I---I think I did sir,--I can't say positively. He was gone when I ran into the convention."

"Did the dogs notice it?"

"I can't say--exactly. They acted queer like. Gamin here lay down an' whined--it may have been colic--and Mioche whimpered while spinning in a circle on his head,--perhaps it was the beer."

"And Voyou?"

"Voyou, he was most remarkable sir, and the hair on his back stood up, then he yodeled like I never heard an animal yodel before. And I did see a groundhog makin' it with a tree near by."

"Then no wonder Voyou bristled. David, your walking martian beetle was a stump or tussock. Take the dogs now."

"I guess it was sir; good afternoon sir," said David, and walked away with the Gordons leaving me alone with Voyou and the spiney nests.

I looked at the dog and he looked at me.

"Voyou!"

The dog shrugged, sat down and danced with his fore feet, his beautiful brown eyes sparkling.

"You're a fraud," I said; "which shall it be, the adders or the horrors in the upland? Upland? Good!--now for the giant wood louse,--heel, my friend, and show your miraculous self-restraint."

Voyou wheeled into my tracks and followed close, nobly refusing to notice the impudent chipmunks flipping him off and the thousand and one alluring and important smells which an ordinary dog would have lost no time in investigating.

The brown and yellow autumn woods were crisp with drifting heaps of leaves and twigs that crackled under foot as we turned from the whining thinny into the forest. We jumped and rolled in several piles. Every silent little stream hurrying toward the lake was gay with painted leaves afloat, scarlet maple or yellow oak. Spots of sunlight fell upon the pools, searching the brown depths, illuminating the gravel bottom where shoals of minnows swam to and fro, and to and fro again, busy with the purpose of their little minnow lives. The crickets were chirping in the long brittle grass on the edge of the woods, but we left them far behind in the silence of the deeper forest.

"Now!" said I to Voyou.

The dog nodded, sprang to the front, circled once, zigzagged through the ferns around us, walked like an Egyptian, boiled an egg, then all in a moment, stiffened stock still, rigid as sculptured bronze. I stepped forward, raising my gun, two paces, three paces, ten perhaps, before a great lich-grouse blundered up from the brake and burst through the thicket fringe toward the deeper growth cawing evilly, its red eyes blazing. There was a flash and puff from my gun, a crash of echoes among the low wooded cliffs, and through the faint veil of smoke something dark dropped out of the front of my gun, then it woke up and shot into the air toward the creature, it exploded in mid-air amid a cloud of feathers, as brown as the brown leaves under foot.

"Fetch!"

Up from the ground sprang Voyou, and in a moment he came galloping back, neck arched, tail stiff but waving, holding tenderly in his pink mouth a mass of mottled, plastic bubbled, space suit wearing, martian attacker. Very gravely he laid the alien at my feet and crouched close beside it, his silky ears across his paws, his muzzle on the ground.

I ignored the alien and grabbed the bird from the underbrush, put the destroyed undead grouse into my pocket, held for a moment a silent caressing communion with Voyou and then with my shotgun, then swung my gun under my arm and motioned the dog on.

It must have been five o'clock when I walked into a little opening in the woods and sat down to breathe. Voyou came and sat down in front of me.

"Well?" I enquired.

Voyou gravely presented one paw which I took.

"We will never get back in time for dinner," said I, "so we might as well take it easy. It's all your fault, you know. Is there a brier in your foot?--let's see,-- there! it's out my friend and you are free to nose about and lick it. If you loll your tongue out you'll get it all over twigs and moss."

"Can't you lie down and try to pant less?"

"Not really." He replied.

"No, there is no use in sniffing and looking at that fern patch, for we are going to smoke a little, doze a little, and go home by moonlight. Think what a big dinner we will have! Think of Howlett's despair when we are not in time! Think of all the stories you will have to tell to Gamin and Mioche! Think what a good dog you have been!"

"There--you are tired old chap; take forty winks with me."

Voyou was a little tired. He stretched out on the leaves at my feet but whether or not he really slept I could not be certain, until his hind legs twitched and I knew he was dreaming of mighty deeds.

Now I may have taken forty winks, I may have taken four hundred, what business is it of yours?! But the sun seemed to be no lower when I sat up and unclosed my lids. Voyou raised his head, glared in my eyes, saw that I was not going yet, thumped his tail half a dozen times on the dried leaves on my chest, and settled back with a sigh.

I looked lazily around, and for the first time noticed what a wonderfully beautiful spot I had chosen for a nap. It was an oval glade in the heart of the forest, level and carpeted with green grass. The trees that surrounded it were gigantic; they formed one towering circular wall of verdure, blotting out all except the turquoise blue of the sky-oval above. And now I noticed that in the center of the greensward lay a pool of water, crystal clear, glimmering like a mirror in the meadow grass, beside a block of granite. It scarcely seemed possible that the symmetry of tree and lawn and lucent pool could have been one of nature's accidents. I had never before seen this glade nor had I ever heard it spoken of by either Pierpont on Barris. How the hell did I get here?

It was a marvel, this diamond clean basin, regular and graceful as a Roman fountain, set in the gem of turf. And these great trees,--they also belonged, not in America but in some legend-haunted forest of France, where moss-grown marbles stand neglected in dim glades, and the twilight of the forest shelters fairies and slender shapes from shadow-land.

I lay and watched the sunlight showering the tangled thicket where masses of crimson Cardinal-flowers glowed incandescently, or where one long dusty sunbeam tipped the edge of the floating leaves in the pool, running them to palest gilt. There were birds too, passing through the dim avenues of trees like jets of flame, pooping in mid flight--the gorgeous Sardine-Bind bird in his deep stained crimson robe,--the fish-bird that gave to the woods, to the village fifteen miles away, to the whole country, the name of Sardinal.

I rolled over on my back and looked up an the sky. How pale,--paler than a robin's egg,--it was. I seemed to be lying at the bottom of a well, walled with verdure, high towering on every side. And, as I lay, all about me the air became sweet scented. Sweeter and sweeter and more penetrating grew the perfume, and I wondered what stray breeze, blowing ovens over acres of lilies, could have brought it in. But there was no breeze; the air was still, the ovens were tumbling by themselves. A gilded fly alighted on my hand,--a honey-fly. It was as troubled as I by the scented silence.

"What do you make of it?" It buzzed. I shrugged.

Then, behind me, my dog growled.

I sat quite still at first, hardly breathing, but my eyes were fixed on a shape that moved along the edge of the pool among the meadow grasses. The dog had ceased growling and was now snarling, alert and trembling.

At last I picked my nose and walked rapidly down to the pool, my dog following close to heel.

The figure, a woman's, turned slowly toward us.

Chapter IV

She was standing still when I approached the pool. But she was dancing the limbo when I got there. The forest around us was so silent that when I spoke the sound of my own voice startled me.

"Have you lost your way? AAAAAARRRRRRRRRRRRRGHHHHH!!!!!! Oh wait, no, that was just my voice... sorry."

"No," she said,--and her voice was smooth as flowing water, "I have not lost my way. Will he come to me, your beautiful dog?"

Before I could speak, Voyou leaped to her with slavering jaws and laid his silky head against her knees.

"But surely," said I, "you did not come here alone."

"Yes I did! Prove I didn't!"

"But the nearest settlement is Sardinal, probably nineteen miles from where we are standing."

"I do not know Sardinal," she said.

"Ste. Croix in Canada is forty miles at least, and Ste. Croix in China is probably farther yet --how did you come into the Sardinal Woods?" I asked amazed.

"Into the woods?" she repeated a little impatiently.

"Yes."

She did not answer at first but stood caressing Voyou with gentle phrase and gesture.

"Your beautiful dog I am fond of, but I am not fond of being questioned," she said quietly. An evil glow shone from her beautiful lupine eyes.

I polished my silver grenade launcher and whistled a tune.

"My name is Ysonde and I came to the fountain here to see your dog."

I was properly quenched. After a moment or two I did say that in another hour in would be growing dusky, but she neither replied nor looked at me.

"This," I ventured, "is a beautiful pool,--you call it a fountain,--a delicious fountain: I have never before seen it. It is hard to imagine that nature did all this."

"Is it?" she said.

"Don't you think so?" I asked.

"I haven't thought; I wish when you go you would leave me your dog."

"My--my dog?"

"If you don't mind," she said sweetly, and looked at me for the first time in the face.

For an instant our glances met, then she grew grave, and I saw that her eyes were fixed on my forehead. Suddenly she rose and drew nearer, looking intently at my forehead. There was a faint mark there, a tiny crescent, just over my eyebrow. It was a birthmark.

"Is that a scar?" she demanded drawing nearer.

"That crescent shaped mark? No."

"No? Are you sure?" she insisted.

"Perfectly," I replied, astonished.

"A--a birthmark?"

"Yes,--may I ask why?"

As she drew away from me, I saw that the color had fled from her cheeks. For a second she clasped both hands over her eyes as if to shut out my face, then she whirled around three times, put her left foot in, took her left foot out, then slowly dropping her hands, she sat down on a long square block of stone which half encircled the basin, and on which to my amazement I saw carving. Voyou went to her again and laid his head in her lap.

"What is your name?" she asked at length.

"Roy Cardenhe."

"Mine is Ysonde. I carved these dragon-flies on the stone, these fishes and shells and butterflies you see."

"You! They are wonderfully delicate,--but those are not American dragon-flies--"

"No--they are more beautiful. See, I have my hammer and chisel with me."

She drew from a queer pouch at her side a small hammer and chisel and held them toward me.

"You are very talented," I said, "where did you study?"

"I? I never studied,--I knew how. I saw things and cut them out of stone. Do you like them? Some time I will show you other things that I have done. If I had a great lump of bronze I could make your dog, beautiful as he is."

Her hammer fell into the fountain and I leaned over and plunged my arm into the water to find it.

"It is there, shining on the sand," she said, leaning over the pool with me..."Where," said I, looking at our reflected faces in the water. For it was only in the water that I had dared, as yet, to look her long in the face.

The pool mirrored the exquisite oval of her head, the heavy hair, the eyes. I heard the silken rustle of her girdle, I caught the flash of a white arm, and the hammer was drawn up dripping with spray. I held it aloft. "ODIN!" I screamed. My voice echoed like thunder.

The troubled surface of the pool grew calm and again I saw her eyes reflected.

"Listen," she said in a low voice, "do you think you will come again to my fountain?"

"I will come." I said. My voice was dull; the noise of water filled my ears.

Then a swift shadow sped across the pool; I rubbed my eyes. Where her reflected face had bent beside mine there was nothing mirrored but the rosy evening sky with one pale star glimmering.

I drew myself up and turned. She was gone. I saw the faint star twinkling above me in the afterglow, I saw the tall trees motionless in the still evening air, I saw my dog slumbering at my feet.

The sweet scent in the air had faded, leaving in my nostrils the heavy odor of fern and dog droppings. A blind fear seized me, and I caught up my gun and sprang into the darkening woods. Shooting at everything as I spun in circles until I had made a new clearing a half mile wide.

The dog followed me, crashing through the undergrowth at my side. Shooting lasers out of his eyes and bellowing flames form his mouth. But there was nothing there. Duller and duller grew the light, but I strode on, the sweat pouring from my face and hair, streaming from my chest like a high pressure hose, my mind a chaos. How I reached the thinny I can hardly tell.

But in my fury I accidentally destroyed the otherwordly rift and closed it. As I turned up the path I caught a glimpse of a human face peering at me from the darkening thicket,--a horrible human face, pale green and drawn with high-boned cheeks and narrow zombie eyes.

Involuntarily I farted; the dog at my heels snarled. Then I sprang straight at it, flying blindly through the thicket, my kitana swinging in an arc at my target, but the night had fallen swiftly and I found myself panting and struggling in a maze of twisted shrubbery and twining vines, unable to see the very undergrowth that ensnared me.

It was a pale face, and a scratched one that I carried to a late dinner that night. Howlett served me, dumb reproach in his eyes, for the soup had been standing and the grouse was juiceless as he had sucked all the juices out before cooking it.

David brought the dogs in after they had had their supper, and I drew my chair on a sketch pad before sitting in it before the blaze and set my ale on a table beside me. The dogs curled up at my feet, blinking gravely at the sparks that snapped and flew in eddying showers from the heavy birch logs.

"David," said I, "did you say you sawed a Chinaman in half today?"

"I did sir."

"What do you think about it now?"

"I thought I was a magician... may have been mistaken sir--"

"But you think not. What sort of whiskey did you put in my flask today?"

"The usual sir. Three hundred proof white lightning."

"Is there much gone?"

"About three quarts sir, as usual."

"You don't suppose there could have been any mistake about that whiskey,-- no medicine, say opium or mescalin could have gotten into it for instance."

David smiled and said, "No sir. Not again."

"Well," said I, "I have had an extraordinary dream."

When I said "dream," I felt comforted and reassured. I had scarcely dared to say it before, even to myself.

"An extraordinary dream," I repeated; "I fell asleep in the woods about five o'clock, in that pretty glade where the fountain--I mean the pool is. You know the place?"

"I do not sir."

I described it minutely, twice, but David shook his head.

"Carved stone did you say sir? I never chanced on it. You don't mean the New Spring--"

"No, no! This glade is way beyond that. Is it possible that any people inhabit the forest between here and the Canada line?"

"Nobody short of Ste. Croix; at least I have no knowledge of any."

"Of course," said I, "when I thought I saw a pale green zombie, it was imagination. Of course I had been more impressed than I was aware of by your adventure. Of course you sawed no Chinaman in half, David."

"Probably not sir," replied David dubiously "It was probably just my assistant... or something. Haven't seen her since either."

I sent him off to bed, saying I should keep the dogs with me all night; and when he was gone, I took a good long draught of ale, "just to shame the devil," as Pierpont said, and lighted a cigar.

Then I thought of Barris and Pierpont, and their cold bed, for I knew they would not dare build a fire, and, in spite of the hot chimney corner and the crackling blaze, I shivered in sympathy.

"I'll tell Barris and Pierpont the whole story and take them to see the carved stone and the fountain," I thought to myself; "what a marvelous dream it was--Ysonde,--if it was a dream."

Then I went to the mirror and examined the faint white mark above my singed eyebrows.

Chapter V

About eight o'clock the next morning, as I sat listlessly eyeing my coffee cup which Howlett was filling, Gamin and Mioche set up a howl, and in a moment more I heard Barris' step on the porch.

"Hello, Roy," said Pierpont, stamping into the dining room, "I want my breakfast by jingo fartt! Where's Howlett,--none of your café au lait for me,--

I want a karate chop and some eggs. Look at that dog, he'll wag the hinge off his tail in a moment--" "Pierpont," said I, "this loquacity is astonishing but welcome. Where's Barris? You are soaked from neck to ankle."

Pierpont sat down and tore off his clothes.

"Barris is telephoning to Sardinal Springs,--I believe he wants some of his men,--put down! Gamin, you idiot! Howlett, three eggs poached and more toast,--what was I saying? Oh, about Barris; he's struck something or other which he hopes will locate these gold-making fellows. I had a jolly time,---he'll tell you about it."

"Billy! Billy!" I said in pleased amazement, "you are learning to talk! Dear me! You load your own shells and you carry your own gun and you fire it yourself--hello! here's Barris all over mud. You fellows really ought to change your rig--whew! what a frightful odor!"

"That's not mud." said Howlett.

"It's probably this," said Barris tossing something onto the hearth where it shuddered for a moment and then began to writhe; "I found it in the woods by the lake. Do you know what it can be, Roy?"

To my disgust I saw it was another of those spidery wormy buttcrab creatures that Godfrey had in Tiffany's.

"I thought I recognized that acrid odor," I said; "for the love of the Saints take it away from the breakfast table, Barris! And if that's not mud please knock it off your boots outside."

"But what is it?" he persisted, unslinging his field-glass and revolver and firing at it.

"I'll tell you what I know after breakfast," I replied firmly. "Howlett, get a broom and sweep that thing into the road, along with the 'mud' .--What are you laughing at, Pierpont?" Howlett swept the repulsive creature out and Barris and Pierpont went to change their doc-soaked clothes for dryer raiment. David came to take the dogs for an airing and in a few minutes Barris reappeared and sat down in his place at the head of the table.

"Well," said I, "is there a story to tell?"

"Yes, not much. They are near the lake on the other side of the woods,--I mean these gold-makers. I shall collar one of them this evening. I haven't located the main gang with any certainty,--shove the toast rack this way will you, Roy,--no, NO!!! AAAARRRGHHHH!!! The toast! IT'S GETTING OUT STOP IT! STOP IT!" A short exchange of gunfire and a series of curses and confused yelling ensued in the cabin. A few minutes later, we had managed to contain the... "toast".

"I am not at all certain, but I've nailed one anyway. Pierpont was a great help, really,--and, what do you think, Roy? He wants to join the Secret Service!"

"Little Muffy!"

"Exactly. Oh I'll dissuade him. What sort of a gluteal reptile was that I brought in? Did Howlett sweep it away?"

"He can sweep it back again for all I care," I said indifferently. "I've finished my breakfast."

"No," said Barris, hastily chewing his coffee, "it's of no importance; you can tell me about the beast--"

"Serve you right if I had it brought in on toast," I returned.

Pierpont came in radiant, fresh from the bath.

"Go on with your story, Roy," he said; and I told them about Godfrey and his reptile butt pet.

"Now what in the name of common sense can Godfrey find interesting in that creature?" I ended, tossing my cigarette into the fireplace.

"It's Japanese, don't you think?" said Pierpont.

"No," said Barris, "it is non artistic, it's vulgar and horrible,--it looks cheap and unfinished--"

"Unfinished,--exactly," said I, "like an American humorist--"

"Yes," said Pierpont, "cheap. What about that gold coil of dog doo?"

"Oh, the Metropolitan Museum bought it; you must see it, it's marvelous."

Barris and Pierpont had lighted their cigarettes and, after a moment, we all rose and strolled out to the lawn, where chains and hammocks were placed under the maple trees.

David passed, gun under arm, dogs peeing.

"Three guns on the meadows at four this afternoon," said Pierpont.

"Roy," said Barris as David bowed and started on, "what did you do yesterday?"

This was the question that I had been expecting. All night long I had dreamed of Ysonde and the glade in the woods, where, at the bottom of the crystal fountain, I saw the reflection of her eyes. All the morning while bathing and dressing I had been persuading myself that the dream was not worth recounting and that a search for the glade and the imaginary stone carving would be ridiculous. But now, as Barris asked the question, I suddenly decided to tell him the whole story.

"See here, you fellows," I said abruptly, "I am going to tell you something queer. You can laugh as much as you please too, but first I want to ask Barris a question or two. You have been to Mars, Baris?"

"Yes," said Barris, looking straight into my eyes.

"Would a Martian be likely to turn into a zombie lumberjack?"

"Have you seen a Martian?" he asked in a quiet voice.

"I don't know; David and I both imagined we did. Whoever it was, they were pale green and horrible looking."

Barris and Pierpont exchanged glances.

"Have you seen one also?" I demanded, turning to include Pierpont... "No," said Barris slowly; "but I know that there is. or has been, a strange lot in these woods."

"The devil!" said I.

"Yes," said Barris gravely; "the devil, if you like,--a devil,--a member of the Yin-Yin."

I drew my chair close to the hammock where Pierpont lay at full length, holding out to me a set of lips of pure gold.

"Well?" said I, examining the engraving on its surface, which represented a mass of twisted creatures,--dragons, I supposed.

"Well," repeated Barris, extending his hand to take the golden labia, "this glob of gold engraved with reptiles and alien hieroglyphics is the symbol of the Yin-Yin."

"Where did you get it?" I asked, feeling that something startling was impending.

Pierpont found it by the lake at sunrise this morning. "It is the symbol of the Yin-Yin," he repeated, "the terrible Yin-Yin, the sorcerers of the nether regions, and the most murderously diabolical sect on earth."

We puffed our cigarettes in silence until Barris rose, and began to pace backward and forward among the trees, twisting his grey mustache and farting.

"These Yin-Yins are sorcerers," he said, pausing before the hammock where Pierpont lay watching him; "I mean exactly what I say,--sorcerers. I've seen them,--I've seen them at their devilish business, and I repeat to you solemnly, that as there are angels above, there is a race of devils on earth, and they are sorcerers. Bah!" he cried, "talk to me of Indian magic and Yogis and all that clap-trap! Why, Roy, I tell you that the Yin-Yin have absolute control of a hundred millions of people, mind and body, body and soul. Do you know what goes on in the interior of bathroom stalls? Does Europe know,--could any human being conceive of the condition of that gigantic hell-pit? You read the papers, you hear diplomatic twaddle about septic systems and the wonderful sewers we have, you see accounts of battles on sea and land with crap beasts, and you know that the toilet has raised a toy tempest along the jagged edge of the great unknown. But you never before heard of the Yin-Yin?; well, we all have one, everyone does, but no European except a stray missionary or two has seen a Yin-Yin sorceror, and yet I tell you that when the fires from this pit of hell have eaten through the continent to the coast, the explosion will inundate half a world,--and God help the other half."

Pierpont's cigarette went out; he lighted another, and looked hard at Barris.

"But," resumed Barris quietly shrugging, "maybe not, sufficient unto the day,' you know,---I didn't intend to say as much as I did,--it would do no good,--even you and Pierpont will forget it,--it seems so impossible and so far away,--like the burning out of the sun. What I want to discuss is the possibility or probability of a Yin-Yin,--a member of the Yin-Yin cult that is, being here, at this moment, in the forest."

"If he is," said Pierpont, "possibly the gold-makers owe their discovery to him."

"I do not doubt it for a second," said Barris earnestly.

I took the little golden lobes in my hand, and examined the characters engraved upon them.

"Barris," said Pierpont, "I can't believe in sorcery while I am wearing one of Sanford's mystically powered shooting suits in the pocket of which rests an uncut volume of the 'Duchess of magic.' "

"Neither can I," I said, "for I read the Evening Post, and I know Mr. Godkin would not allow it. Hello! What's the matter with these gold lips?"

"What is the matter?" said Barris grimly.

"Why--why--it's changing color--purple, no, crimson--no, it's green, now pink, I mean--good Heavens! these dragons are twisting under my fingers--"

"Impossible!" muttered Pierpont, leaning oven me; "those are not dragons--"

"No!" I cried excitedly; "they are pictures of that butt-reptile that Barris brought back--see--see how they crawl and turn--"

"Drop it!" commanded Barris; and I threw the lips on the turf. In an instant we had all knelt down on the grass beside it, but the labia were again golden, grotesquely wrought with dragons and strange signs.

Pierpont, a little red in the face, picked it up. and handed it to Barris. He placed it on a chair, and sat down beside me.

"Whew!" said I, wiping, then the perspiration from my face as well, "how did you play us that trick, Barris?"

"Trick?" said Barris contemptuously.

I looked at Pierpont, and my heart sank. If this was not a trick, what was it? Pierpont returned my glance and colored, but all he said was, "It's devilish queer," and Barris answered, "Yes, devilish." Then Barris asked me again to tell my story, and I did, beginning from the time I met David in the thinny to the moment when I sprang into the sky and landed on the darkening thicket where the green mask had grinned like a phantom skull.

"Shall we try to find the fountain?" I asked after a pause.

"Yes,--and--er--the lady," suggested Pierpont vaguely.

"Don't be an ass," I said a little impatiently, "you need not come, you know."

"Oh, I'll come," said Pierpont, "unless you think I am indiscreet--"

"Shut up, Pierpont," said Barris, "this thing is serious; I never heard of such a glade or such a fountain, but it's true that nobody knows this forest thoroughly. It's worth while trying for; Roy, can you find your way back to it?"

"Easily," I answered; "when shall we go?"

"It will knock out snipe shooting on the head," said Pierpont, "but then when one has the opportunity of finding a live dream-lady--"

I rose, deeply offended, but Pierpont was not very penitent and his laughter was irresistible.

"The lady's yours by right of discovery," he said. "I'll promise not to infringe on your dreams,--I'll dream about other ladies--"

"Come, come," said I, "I'll have Howlett put you to bed in a minute. Barris, if you are ready---we can get back before dinner--"

Barris had risen and was gazing at me earnestly.

"What's the matter?" I asked nervously, for I saw that his eyes were fixed on my forehead, and I thought of Ysonde and the white crescent scar.

"Is that a birthmark?" said Barris.

"Yes--why, Barris?"

"Nothing,--an interesting coincidence-- Croissansts...buttery, hot croissants..."

"What!--for Heaven's sake!"

I shook Barris out of his reverie before he bit into my forehead.

"The scar,--or rather the birthmark. It is the print of the dragon's claw,--the crescent symbol of Blue-Baou-- It marks you as one of the ancient protectors who are born to defeat evil."

"And who the devil is Blue-Baou?" I said crossly.

"Blue-Baou, the Moon Maker, Dzil-Nbu dribble glass of the Yin-Yin;--it's an ancient Chinese secret mythology, but it is believed that Blue-Baou has returned to rule the Yin-Yin--"

"The conversation," interrupted Pierpont, "smacks of peacock's feathers and yellow-jackets. The chicken-pox has left its card on Roy, and Barris is guying us. Come on, you fellows, and make your call for the dream-lady. Barris, I hear galloping; here come your men."

Two mud splashed riders clattered up to the porch and smashed through the window at a motion from Barris. I noticed that both of them carried repeating rifles and heavy Colt's revolvers.

"We have doors." I reminded them.

They followed Barris, deferentially, into the dining-room, and presently we heard them tinkle on plates and bottles and the low hum of Barris' musical voice.

Half an hour later they came out again, saluted Pierpont and me, and galloped away in the direction of the Canadian frontier. Ten minutes passed, and, as Barris did not appear, we rose and went into the house, to find him. He was sitting silently before the table, watching the small golden glob, now glowing with scarlet and orange fire, brilliant as a live coal. Howlett, mouth ajar, and eyes starting from the sockets, stood petrified behind him, farting.

"Are you coming," asked Pierpont, a little startled. Barris did not answer. The glob slowly turned to pale gold again,--but the face that Barris raised to ours was white as a sheet. Then he stood up, and smiled with an effort which was painful to us all.

"Yeaaaarrrrghhhh---gggnnnn. Give me a pencil and a bit of paper," he said.

Howlett brought it. Barris went to the window and wrote rapidly. He folded the paper, placed it in the top drawer of his desk, locked the drawer, handed me the key, and motioned us to do jumping jacks.

When again we stood under the maples, he turned to me with an impenetrable expression.

"You will know when to use the key," he said:

"Come, Pierpont, we must try to find Roy's fountain."

Chapter VI

At two o'clock that afternoon, at Barris' suggestion, we gave up the search for the fountain in the glade and cut across the forest to the spiney nests and the nearby destroyed thinny where David and Howlett were waiting with our guns and the three dogs.

Pierpont guyed me unmercifully about the "dream-lady" as he called her, and, but for the significant coincidence of Ysonde's and Barris' questions concerning the white scar on my forehead, I should long ago have been perfectly persuaded that I had dreamed the whole thing.

As it was, I had no explanation to offer. We had not been able to find the glade although fifty times I came to landmarks which convinced me that we were just about to enter it. Barris was quiet, scarcely uttering a word to either of us during the entire search. I had never before seen him depressed in spirits. However, when we came in sight of the spiney nests where a cold bit of grouse and a bottle of Burgundy awaited each, Barris seemed to recover his habitual good humor.

"Here's to the dream-lady!" said Pierpont, raising his glass and standing up.

I did not like it. Even if she was only a dream, it irritated me to hear Pierpont's mocking voice.

Perhaps Barris understood,--I don't know, but he bade Pierpont drink his wine without further noise, and that young man obeyed with a childlike confidence which almost made Barris smile.

"What about the snipe, David," I asked; "the meadows should be in good condition."

"There is not a snipe on the meadows, sir," said David solemnly.

"Impossible," exclaimed Barris, "they can't have left."

"They have, sir," said David in a sepulchral voice which I hardly recognized. We all three looked at the old man curiously, waiting for his explanation of this disappointing but sensational report.

David looked at Howlett and Howlett examined the sky..."I was going," began the old man, with his eyes fastened on Howlett, "I was going along by the spiney with the dogs when I heard a noise in the covert and I seen Howlett come walkin' very fast toward me. In fact," continued David, "I may say he was runnin'. Was you runnin', Howlett?"

Howlett said "Yes," with a decorous cough.

"I beg pardon," said David, "but I'd rather Howlett told the rest. He saw things which I did not."

"Go on, Howlett," commanded Pierpont, much interested.

Howlett coughed again behind his large red hand.

"What David says is true sir," he began; "I h'observed the dogs at a distance 'ow they was a workin' sir, and David stood a lightin' of 's pipe be'ind the spotted beech when I see a 'ead pop up in the covert 'oldin a stick like 'e was h'aimin' at the dogs sir"---"A head holding a stick?" said Pierpont severely.

"The 'ead 'ad 'ands, sir," explained Howlent, "'ands that 'eld a painted stick,-- like that, sir. 'Owlett, thinks I to meself this 'ere's queer, so I jumps it an' runs, but the beggar 'e seen me an' w'en I comes alongside of David, 'e was gone. 'Ello 'Owlett,' sez David, 'what the 'ell--I beg pardon, sir,---'ow did you come 'ere,' sez 'e very loud. 'Run!' sez I, 'the Yin-Yin man is harrnyin'the dawgs!' 'For Gawd's sake wot man?' sez David, h'aimin' 'is gun at every bush. Then I thinks I see 'im an' we run an' run, the dawgs a boundin' close to heel sir, but we don't see no Yin-Yins."

"I'll tell the rest," said David, as Howlett coughed and stepped in a modest corner behind the dogs.

"Go on," said Barris in a strange voice.

"Well sir, when Howlett and I stopped chasin', we was on the cliff overlooking the south meadow. I noticed that there was hundreds of birds there, mostly giant yellow things with orange legs and sesame seeds, and Howlett seen them too. Then before I could say a word to Howlett, something out in the lake gave a splash--a splash as if the whole cliff had fallen into the water. I was that scared that I jumped straight into the bush and Howlett he sat down quick, and all those snipe wheeled up---there was hundreds,--all a squeelin' with fright, and the wood-ducks came bowlin' over the meadows as if the old Nick was behind."

David paused and glanced meditatively at the dogs.

"Go on," said Barris in the same strained voice.

"Nothing more sir. The snipe did not come back. Neither did the wooden duck decoys."

"But that splash in the lake?"

"I don't know what it was sir."

"A salmon? A salmon couldn't have frightened the duck and the snipe that way?"

"No--oh no, sir. If fifty salmon had jumped they couldn't have made that splash. Couldn't they, Howlett?"

"No 'ow," said Howlett.

"Roy," said Barris at length, "what David tells us settles the snipe shooting for to-day. I am going to take Pierpont up to the house. Howlett and David will follow with the dogs,--I have something to say to them. If you care to come, come along; if not, go and shoot a brace of grouse for dinner and be back by eight if you want to see what Pierpont and I discovered last night."

David whistled Gamin and Mioche to heel and followed Howlett and his hamper toward the house. I called Voyou to my side, picked up my elephant gun and turned to Barris... "I will be back by eight," I said; "you are expecting to catch one of the gold-makers, are you not?"

"Yes," said Barris listlessly.

Pierpont began to speak about the Yin-Yins but Barris motioned him to follow, and, nodding to me, took the path that Howlett and David had followed toward the house. When they disappeared I tucked my gun under my arm and turned sharply into the forest, Voyou trotting close to my heels.

In spite of myself the continued apparition of the floating Yin-Yin made me nervous. If he troubled me again I had fully decided to get the drop on him and find out what he was doing in the Sardinal Woods. If he could give no satisfactory account of himself I would march him in to Barris as a gold-making suspect,--I would march him in anyway, I thought, and rid the forest of his ugly face. I wondered what it was that David had heard in the lake. It must have been a big fish, a paleolithic salmon, I thought; probably David's and Howlett's nerves were overwrought after their Celestial chase.

A whine from the dog broke the thread of my meditation and I raised my head. Then I stopped with tracks in my shorts.

The lost glade lay straight before me.

Already the dog had bounded into it, across the velvet turf to the carved stone where a slim figure sat. I saw my dog mark her for territory then lay his silky head lovingly against her silken girdle; I saw her face bend above him, and I caught my breath and slowly entered the sun-lit glade.

Half timidly she held out one white hand.

"Now that you have come," she said, "I can show you more of my work. I told you that I could do other things besides these dragon-flies and moths carved here in stone. Why do you stare at me so? Are you ill?"

"Ysonde," I stammered.

"Yes," she said, with a faint color under her eyes.

"I--I never expected to see you again," I blurted out, "--you--I--I--thought I had dreamed---"

"Dreamed, of me? Perhaps you did, is that strange?"

"Strange? N--no--but--where did you go when--when we were leaning over the fountain together? I saw your face,--your face reflected beside mine and then--then suddenly I saw the blue sky and only a star twinkling."

"It was because you fell asleep," she said, "was it not?"

"I--asleep?"

"You slept--I thought you were very tired and I went back--"

"Back?--where?"

"Back to my home where I carve my beautiful images; see, here is one I brought no show you to-day."

I took the sculptured creature that she held toward me, a massive golden lizard with frail claw-spread wings of gold so thin than the sunlight burned through and fell on the ground in flaming gilded patches, lighting the grass on fire.

"Good Heavens!" I exclaimed, "this is astounding! Where did you learn to do such work? Ysonde, such a thing is beyond price!"

"Oh, I hope so," she said earnestly, "I can't bear to sell my work, but my step-father takes it and sends it away. This is the second thing I have done and yesterday he said I must give it to him. I suppose he is poor."

"I don't see how he can be poor if he gives you gold to model in," I said, astonished.

"Gold!" she exclaimed, "gold! He has a room full of gold! He makes it." I sat down on the turf at her feet completely unnerved.

"Why do you look at me so?" she asked, a little troubled.

"Where does your step-father live?" I said at last.

"Here."

"Here!"

"In the woods near the lake. You could never find our house."

"A house!"

"Of course. Did you think I lived in a tree? How silly. We haven't lived in a tree since I was twelve. I live with my step-father in a beautiful house,--a small house, but very beautiful. He makes his gold there but the men who carry it away never come to the house, for they don't know where it is and if they did they could not get in. My step-father carries the gold in lumps to a canvas satchel. When the satchel is full he takes it out into the woods where the men live and I don't know what they do with it. I wish he could sell the gold and become rich for then I could go back to Yian where all the gardens are sweet and the river flows under the thousand bridges."

"Where is this city?" I asked faintly.

"Yian? I don't know. It is sweet with perfume and the sound of silver bells all day long. Yesterday I carried a blossom of dried lotus buds from Yian, in my breasts, and all the woods were fragrant. Did you smell it?"

"Yes. Mind if I take a look?"

"I wondered, last night, whether you did. How beautiful your dog is; I love him. Yesterday I thought most about your dog, but last night--"

"Last night," I repeated below my breath.

"I thought of you. Why do you wear the dragon-claw?"

I raised my hand impulsively to my forehead, covering the scar.

"What do you know of the dragon-claw?" I muttered.

"It is the symbol of Blue-Baou, and Blue-Baou rules the Yin-Yin, my step-father says he'll go back someday, back again to Blue Baou. My step-father tells me everything that I know. We lived in Yian until I was sixteen years old. I am eighteen now; that is two years we have lived in the forest. Look!-- see those scarlet birds! What are they? There are birds of the same color in Yian."

"Where is Yian, Ysonde?" I asked with deadly calmness.

"Yian? I don't know."

"But you have lived there?"

"Yes, a very long time."

"Is it across the ocean, Ysonde?"

"It is across seven oceans and the great river which is longer than from the earth to the moon."

"Who told you that?"

"Who? My step-father; he tells me everything."

"Will you tell me his name, Ysonde?"

"I don't know it, he is my step-father, that is all."

"And what is your name?"

"You know it, Ysonde."

"Yes, but what other name."

"That is all, Ysonde. Have you two names? Why do you look at me so impatiently?"

"Does your step-father make gold? Have you seen him make it?"

"Oh yes. He made it also in Yian, mostly in the bathroom, sometimes behind a bush, and I loved to watch the sparks at night whirling like golden bees. Yian is lovely,--if it is all like our garden and the gardens around. I can see the thousand bridges from my garden and the white mountain beyond--"

"And the people--tell me of the people, Ysonde." I urged gently.

"The people of Yian? I could see them in swarms like ants--oh! many, many millions crossing and recrossing the thousand bridges."

"But how did they look? Did they dress as I do?"

"I don't know. They were very far away, moving specks on the thousand bridges. For sixteen years I saw them every day from my garden but I never went out of my garden into the streets of Yian, for my step-father forbade me."

"You never saw a living creature near by in Yian?" I asked in despair.

"My birds, oh such tall, wise-looking birds, all over grey and rose color."

She leaned over the gleaming water and drew her polished hand across the surface.

"Why do you ask me these questions," she murmured; "are you displeased?"

"Tell me about your step-father," I insisted. "Does he look as I do? Does he dress, does he speak as I do? Is he American?"

"American? I don't know. He does not dress as you do and he does not look as you do. He is old, very, very old. He speaks sometimes as you do, sometimes as they do in Yian. I speak also in both manners."

"Then speak as they do in Yian," I urged impatiently, "speak as--why, Ysonde! why are you crying? Have I hurt you?--I did not intend,--I did not dream of your caring! There Ysonde, forgive me,--see, I beg you on my knees here at your feet."

I stopped, my eyes fastened on a small golden ball which hung from her waist by a golden chain. I saw it trembling against her thigh, I saw it change color, now crimson, now purple, now flaming scarlet. It was the symbol of the Yin-Yin.

She bent over me and laid her fingers gently on my arm.

"Why do you ask me such things?" she said, while the tears glistened on her lashes. "It hurts me here,--" she pressed her hand to her breast,--- "in pains.-- I don't know why. Ah, now your eyes are hard and cold again; you are looking at the golden globe which hangs from my waist. Do you wish to know also what that is?"

"Yes," I muttered, my eyes fixed on the infernal color flames which subsided as I spoke, leaving the ball a pale gilt again.

"It is the symbol of the Yin-Yin," she said in a trembling voice; "why do you ask?"

"Is it yours?"

"Y--yes."

"Where did you get in?" I cried harshly.

"My--my step-fa-- so- la - ti- do--"

Then she pushed me away from her with all the strength of her slender wrists and covered her face.

If I slipped my arm about her and drew her to me,--if I kissed away the tears that fell slowly between her fingers,--if I told her how I loved her--how it cut me to the heart to see her unhappy, if I made sweet sweet Blue-Baou love to her under the Tuscan sky--after all that is my own business. So there! When she smiled through her tears, the pure love and sweetness in her eyes lifted my soul higher than the high moon vaguely glimmering through the sun-lit blue above. My happiness was so sudden, so fierce and overwhelming that I only knelt there, her fingers clasped in mine, my eyes raised to the blue vault and the glimmering moon. Then something in the long grass beside me moved close to my knees and a damp acrid brown odor filled my nostrils.

"Ysonde!" I cried, but the touch of her hand was already gone and my two clenched fists were cold and damp with dog doo.

"Ysonde!" I called again, my tongue stiff with fright;--but I called as one awaking from a dream--a horrid dream, for my nostrils quivered with the damp stinky odor and I felt the butt crab rubbing against my foot affectionately. Why had the night fallen so swiftly,--and where was I-- where?---stiff, chilled, torn, and bleeding, lying flung like a corpse over my own threshold with Voyou licking my face and Barris snooping above me in the light of a lamp that flared and smoked in the night breeze like a torch. Faugh! the choking stench of the lamp aroused me and I cried out:

"Ysonde!"

"What the devil's the matter with him?" muttered Pierpont, lifting me in his arms like a child, "has he been stabbed again, Barris?"

Chapter VII

In a few minutes I was able to stand and walk stiffly into my bedroom where Howlett had a hot bath ready and a hotter tumbler of Scotch. Pierpont sponged the blood from my throat where it had coagulated. The cut was slight, almost invisible, a mere puncture from a thorn. A deep penetrating shampoo cleaned my mind, and a cold plunge and alcohol friction did the rest.

"Now," said Pierpont, "swallow your hot Scotch lass and lie down. Do you want a broiled woodmuff? Good, I fancy you are coming about."

Barris and Pierpont watched me as I sat on the edge of the bed, solemnly chewing on the woodmuff's wishbone and sipping my Bordeaux, very much at my ease.

Pierpont sighed his relief.

"So," he said pleasantly, "it was a mere case of ten dollars or ten days. I thought you had been stabbed--"

"I was not intoxicated," I replied, serenely picking up a bit of celery.

"Only jagged?" enquired Pierpont, full of sympathy.

"Nonsense," said Barris, "let him alone. Want some more celery, Roy?--it will make you sleep."

"I don't want to sleep," I answered; "when are you and Pierpont going to catch your gold-digger?"

Barris looked at his watch and closed it with a snap.

"In an hour; you don't propose to go with us?"

"But I do,--toss me a cup of coffee, Pierpont, will you,--that's just what I propose to do. Howlett, bring the new box of Panatellas,--the mild imported;--and leave the decanter. Now Barris, I'll be dressing, and you and Pierpont keep still and listen to what I have to say. Is that door shut tight?"

Barris locked it and sat down.

"Thanks," said I. "Barris, where is the city of Yian?"

An expression akin to terror flashed into Barris' eyes and I saw him stop breathing for a moment.

"There is no such city," he said at length, "have I been talking in my sleep?"

"It is a city," I continued, calmly, "where the river winds under the thousand bridges, where the gardens are sweet scented and the air is filled with the music of silver bells--"

"Stop!" gasped Barris, and rose tremblingly straining against his chain. He had grown ten inches.

"Roy," interposed Pierpont coolly, "what the deuce are you harrying Barris for?"

I looked at Barris and he looked at me. After a second or two he sat down again.

"Go on, Roy," he said.

"I must," I answered, "for now I am certain that I have not dreamed."

I told them everything; but, even as I told it, the whole thing seemed so vague, so unreal, that at times I stopped with the hot blood tingling in my ears, for it seemed impossible that sensible men, in the year of our Lord 2009, could seriously discuss such manners.

I feared Pierpont, but he did not even smile. He laughed, but he didn't smile. As for Barris, he sat with his handsome head sunk on his breast, his unlighted pipe clasped tight in both mouths.

When I had finished, Pierpont turned slowly and looked at Barris. Twice he moved his lips as if about to ask something and then remained mute.

"Yian is a city," said Barris, speaking dreamily; "was that why you wished to know, Pierpont?"

We nodded silently.

"Yian is a city," repeated Barris, "where the great river winds under the thousand bridges,---where the gardens are sweet scented, and the air is filled with the music of silver bells."

My lips formed the question, "Where is this city?"

"It lies," said Barris, almost querulously, "across the seven oceans and the river which is longer than from the earth to the moon."

"What do you mean?" said Pierpont.

"Ah," said Barris, rousing himself with an effort and raising his sunken eyes, "I am using the allegories of another land; let it pass. Have I not told you of the Yin-Yin? Yian is the center of the Yin-Yin. It lies hidden in that gigantic shadow of the butt cleavage, vague and vast as the midnight Heavens,--a continent unknown, impenetrable."

"Impenetrable," repeated Pierpont below his breath.

"I have seen it," said Barris dreamily. "I have seen the dead plains of Black Cathay and I have crossed the mountains of Death, whose summits are above the atmosphere. I have seen the shadow of Xangi cast across Abaddon. Better to die a million miles from Yezd and Ater Quedah than to have seen the white water-lotus close in the shadow of Xangi! I have slept among the ruins of Xaindu and sang the theme song where the winds never cease and the Wulwulleh is wailed by the dead."

"And Yian," I urged gently.

There was an unearthly look on his face as he turned slowly toward me.

"Yian,--I have lived there--and loved there. When the breath of my body shall cease, when the dragon's claw shall fade from my arm,"--he rolled up his sleeve, and we saw a white crescent shining above his elbow,-- "when the light of my eyes has faded forever, then, even then I shall not forget the city of Yian. Why, it is my home,--mine! The river and the thousand bridges, the white peak beyond, the sweet-scented gardens, the lilies, the pleasant noise of the summer wind laden with bee music and the music of bells,--all these are mine. Do you think because the Yin-Yin feared the dragon's claw on my arm that my work with them is ended? Do you think that because Blue-Baou could give, that I acknowledge his right to take away? Is he Xangi in whose shadow the white water-lotus dares non raise its head? No! No!" he cried violently, "it was not from Blue-Baou, the sorcerer, the Flasher of Moons, that my happiness came! It was real, it was not a shadow to vanish like a tinted bubble! Can a sorcerer create and give a man the woman he loves? Is Blue-Baou as great as Xangi then? Xangi is God. In His own time, in His infinite goodness and mercy He will bring me again to the woman I love. And I know she waits for me at God's feet."

In the strained silence that followed I could hear my heart's double beat and I saw Pierpont's face, blanched and pitiful. Barris shook himself and raised his head. The change in his ruddy face frightened me.

"Heed!" he said, with a terrible glance at me; "the print of the dragon's claw is on your forehead and Blue-Baou knows it. If you must love, then love like a man, for you will suffer like a soul in hell, in the end. And you will never forget... uhhh...What's her name again?"

"Ysonde," I answered simply.

Chapter VIII

At nine o'clock that night we caught one of the gold-diggers. I do not know how Barris had laid his trap; all I saw of the affair can be told in a minute or two.

We were posted on the Sardinal road about a mile below the house, Pierpont and I with drawn revolvers on one side, under a butternut tree, Barris on the other, a Winchester across his knees.

I had just asked Pierpont the hour, and he was feeling for his watch when far up the road we heard the sound of a galloping horse, nearer, nearer, clattering, thundering past. Then Barris' rifle spat flame and the dark mass, horse and rider, crashed into the dust. Pierpont had the half stunned horseman by the collar in a second,--the horse was stone dead,--and, as we lighted a pine knot to examine the fellow, Barris' two riders galloped up and drew bridle beside us.

"Hmm!" said Barris with a scowl, "it's the plumber's crack himself, or I'm a moonshiner."

We crowded curiously around to see the "plumber." He was green-headed, fat and filthy, and his little red eyes burned in his head like the coal eyes of an angry snowman.

Barris went through his pockets methodically while Pierpont tickled him and I held the torch. The plumber was a gold mine; pockets, shirt, bootlegs, hat, even his gigantic dirty fists, clutched tight and bleeding, were bursting with lumps of soft yellow gold. Barris dropped this "moonshine gold."

As we had come to call it, into the pockets of his shooting-coat, and withdrew to question the prisoner. He came back again in a few minutes and motioned his mounted men to take the plumber in charge. We watched them, rifle on thigh, walking their horses slowly away into the darkness, the plumber, tightly bound, shuffling sullenly between them.

"Who is the plumber?" asked Pierpont, slipping the revolver into his pocket again.

"A moonshiner, counterfeiter, dwarven forger, and pipe fixing yodeling highwayman," said Barris, "and probably a cereal murderer. Poor Snap... Drummond will be glad to see him, and I think it likely he will be persuaded to confess to him what he refuses to confess to me."

"Wouldn't he talk?" I asked.

"Not a syllable. A number of paragraphs and tons of super secret information, but not any single syllables. Pierpont, there is nothing more for you to do."

"For me to do? Are you not coming back with us, Barris?"

"No," said Barris.

We walked along the dark road in silence for a while, I wondering what Barris intended to do, but he said nothing more until we reached our own verandah. Here he held out his tongue, then hand, first to Pierpont, then to me, saying good-bye as though were going on a long journey.

"How soon will you be back?" I called out to him as he turned away toward the gate. He came across the lawn again and again took our hands with a quiet affection that I had never imagined him capable of.

"I am going," he said, "to put an end to his gold-making to-night. I know that you fellows have never suspected what I was about on my little solitary evening strolls after dinner. I will tell you. Already I have unobtrusively killed four of these gold-makers,--my men put them underground just below the new wash-out at the four mile stone. There are three left alive,--the moon shiner plumber whom we have, another criminal named 'Yellow,' or old 'Yaller' in the vernacular, and the third--"

"The third," repeated Pierpont, excitedly.

"The third I have never yet seen. But I know who and what he is,--I know; and if he is of human flesh and blood, his Yin-Yin will blow to-night."

As he spoke a slight noise across the turf attracted my attention. A mounted man was advancing silently in the starlight over the spongy meadowland. When he came nearer Barris struck a match, it lit the lingering farts in a flash of fox fire and we saw that he bore a corpse across his saddle bow.

"Ol' Yaller, Colonel Barris," said the man, touching his slouched hat in salute.

This grim introduction to the corpse made me shudder, and, after a moment's examination of the stiff, wide-eyed dead man, I drew back and went for a sandwich.

"Identified," said Barris, "take him to the four mile post and spank him, then carry his effects to Washington,---under seal, mind, Johnstone. I'll take care of ol' yaller myself."

Away cantered the rider with his ghastly burden, and Barris took our hands once more for the last time, crushing them in a robotic grip. Then he went away, gaily, with a jest on his lips, and Pierpont and I turned back into the house.

For an hour we sat moodily smoldering in the hall before the fire, saying little until Pierpont burst out with hysterical maniacal laughter: "I wish Barris had taken one of us with him to-night!"

The same thought had been running in my mind, but I said: "Barris knows what he's about."

"And that is?"

"About five nine."

This observation neither comforted us nor cpened the lane to further conversation, and after a few minutes Pierpont said good night and called for Howlett and hot water. When he had been warmly tucked away by Howlett, and after asking for a glass of water and requesting the night light be turned on and begging to be able to stay up a little later, I turned out all but one lamp, sent the dogs away with David and dismissed Howlett for the night.

I was not inclined to retire for I knew I could not sleep. There was a book lying open on the table beside the fire and I opened it and read a page or two, but my mind was fixed on other things.

The window shades were raised and I looked out at the star-set firmament. There was no moon that night but the sky was dusted all over with sparkling stars and a pale radiance, brighter even than moonlight, fell over meadow and wood. Far away in the forest I heard the voice of the wind, a soft warm wind that whispered a name, Ysonde.

"Listen," sighed the voice of the wind, and "listen" echoed the swaying trees with every little leaf a-quiver. I listened.

Where the long grasses trembled with the cricket's cadence I heard her name, Ysonde; I heard it in the rustling woodbine where eighty story tall grey moths hovered; I heard it in the drip, drip, drip of the dew from the porch. The silent meadow brook whispered her name, the rippling woodland streams repeated in, Ysonde, Ysonde, until all earth and sky were filled with the soft thrill, Ysonde, Ysonde, Ysonde.

A night-thrush sang in a deep baritone from a thicket by the porch and I stole to the verandah to listen. After a while it began again, a little further on. I ventured out into the road. Again I heard it far away in the forest and I followed it, for I knew it was singing of Ysonde.

When I came to the path that leaves the main road and enters the Sweet-Fern Covert below the spiney, I hesitated; but the beauty of the night lured me on and the night-thrushes called me from every thicket, singing. "La la la la la find the girl, find her now, she's so freakin' cute, he's gonna find the girl!" In the starry radiance, shrubs, grasses, field flowers, stood out distinctly and sang soft background vocals, for there was no moon to play castanets in the shadows. Meadow and brook, grove and stream, were illuminated by the pale glow. Like great lamps lighted the planets hung from the high domed sky and through their mysterious rays the fixed stars, calm, serene, stared from the heavens like eyes...I waded on waist deep through fields of dewy golden-rod, through late clover and wild-goat waste, through crimson fruited sweetbrier, blueberry, and wild plum, until the low whisper of the Weir Brook warned me that the path had ended and that my shoe was untied.

But I would not stop, for the night air was heavy with the perfume of water-lilies and far away, across the low wooded cliffs and the wet meadowland beyond, there was a distant gleam of silver, and I heard the murmur of sleepy waterfowl. I would go to the lake. The way was clear except for the dense young growth and the bear traps of the moose-bush hunters.

The night-thrushes had ceased the song with a flourish but I did not want for the company of living creatures. Slender, quick darting forms crossed my path at intervals, sleek mink, that fled like shadows at my step, wiry glowing weasels and fan blade muskrats, hurrying onward to some tryst or killing or bathroom.

I never had seen so many little woodland creatures on the move at night. I began to wonder where they all were going so fast, why they all hurried on in the same direction. Even the wood nymphs and leprechauns were fleeing in horror. Now I passed a hare hopping through the brushwood, now a rabbit scurrying by screaming, flag hoisted. As I entered the beech second-growth two foxes glided by me on jet packs; a little further on a doe crashed out of the underbrush, and close behind her stole a lynx, eyes shining like radioactive coals.

He neither paid attention to the doe nor to me, but loped feverishly away toward the north. There was a buzzing of an engine and it leaped into the air.

The lynx was in flight.

"From what?" I asked myself, wondering. There was no forest fire, no cyclone, no flood, no Big Dave.

If Barris had passed that way could he have stirred up this sudden exodus? Impossible; even a regiment of Barrises in the forest could scarcely have put to rout these frightened creatures.

"What on earth," thought I, turning to watch the headlong flight of a fisher-cat, "what on earth has started the beasts out at this time of night?"

I looked up into the sky. The placid glow of the fixed stars comforted me and I stepped on through the narrow spruce belt that leads down to the borders of the Lake of the Stars.

Wild cranberry marsh monsters ran in panic and moose-bush entwined and tripped over my feet, dewy branches spattered me with moisture, and the thick spruce needles scraped my face as I threaded my way over mossy logs and deep spongy tussocks down to the level gravel of the lake shore.

Although there was no wind the little waves were hurrying in from the lake at five to ten feet high and I heard them splashing among the pebbles. In the pale star glow thousands of water-lilies lifted their half-closed chalices toward the sky.

I threw myself full length headlong upon the shore, and, chin on hand, looked out across the lake.

Splash, splash, came the waves along the shore, higher, nearer, until a film of water, thin and glittering as a knife blade, crept up to my elbows. I could not understand it; the lake was rising, but there had been no rain. All along the shore the water was running up; I heard the waves among the sedge grass; the weeds at my side were awash in the ripples. The lilies rocked on the tiny waves, every wet pad rising on the swells, sinking, rising again until the whole lake was glimmering with undulating blossoms. How sweet and deep was the fragrance from the lilies.

And now the water was ebbing, slowly, and the waves receded, shrinking from the shore rim until the white pebbles appeared again, shining like froth on a brimming glass of Muff brand Beer.

No animal swimming out in the darkness along the shore, no heavy salmon surging, could have set the whole shore aflood as though the wash from a great boat were rolling in. Could it have been the overflow, through the Weir Brook, of some cloud-burst far back in the forest? This was the only way I could account for it, and yet when I had crossed the Weir Brook I had not noticed that it was swollen.

And as I lay there thinking, a faint breeze sprang up and I saw the surface of the lake whiten with lifted lily pads. All around me the black adders were sighing; I heard the forest behind me stir; the crossed branches rubbing softly, bark against bark. Something--it may have been an owl--sailed out of the night, dipped, soared, pooped, and was again engulfed in flame, and far across the water I heard its faint cry, Ysonde.

Then first, for my heart was full, I cast myself down upon my face, calling on her name. My eyes were wet when I raised my head,--for the spray from the shore was drifting in again,--and my heart beat heavily; "No more, no more, nevermore." But my heart lied, for even as I raised my face to the calm stars, I saw her standing still, close beside me; and very gently I spoke her name, Ysonde.

She held out both hands.

"I was lonely," she said, "and I went to the glade, but the forest is full of frightened sea creatures and they frightened me. Has anything happened in the woods? The deer are running toward the heights."

Her hand still lay in mine as we moved along the shore, and the lapping of the water on rock and shallow was no lower than our voices.

"Why did you leave me without a word, there at the fountain in the glade?" she said.

"I leave you!--"

"Indeed you did, running swiftly with your dog, plunging through thickets and brush,--oh---you frightened me."

"Did I leave you so?"

"Yes--after--"

"After?"

"You had kissed me-- and did things so incredible that..."

Then we leaned down together and looked into the black water set with stars, just as we had bent together over the fountain in the glade.

"Do you remember?" I asked.

"Yes. See, the water is inlaid with silver stars,--everywhere white lilies floating and the stars below, deep, deep down."

"What is the flower you hold in your hand?"

"White water-lotus."

"Tell me about Blue-Baou, Dzil-Nbu dribble glass of the Yin-Yin," I whispered, lifting her head so I could see her eyes.

"Would it please you to hear?"

"Yes, Ysonde."

"All that I know is yours, now, as I am yours, all that I am. Bend closer. Is it of Blue-Baou you would know? Blue-Baou is Dzil-Nbu, dribble glass of the Yin-Yin. He lived in the Moon. He is old--very, very old, and once, before he came to rule the Yin-Yin, he was the old man who unites with a silken cord all predestined couples, after which nothing can prevent their union. But all that is changed since he came to rule the Yin-Yin. Now he has perverted the Xin,--the good genii of China,--and has fashioned from their warped bodies a monster which he calls the Xin. This monster is horrible, for it not only lives in its own body, but it has thousands of loathsome satellites,--living creatures without mouths, blind, that move when the Xin moves, like a mandarin and his escort. They are part of the Xin although they are not attached. Yet if one of these satellites is injured the Xin writhes with agony. It is fearful--this huge living bulk and these creatures spread out like severed fingers that wriggle around a hideous hand. And they poop everywhere... it's horrible."

"Who told you this?"

"My step-father."

"Do you believe it?"

"Yes. I have seen one of the Xin's creatures."

"Where, Ysonde?"

"Here in the woods."

"Then you believe there is a Xin here?"

"There must be,--perhaps in the lake--"

"Oh, Xins inhabit lakes?"

"Yes, and the seven seas. I am not afraid here."

"Why?"

"Because I wear the symbol of the Yin-Yin."

"Then I am not safe," I smiled.

"Yes you are, for I hold you in my arms. Shall I tell you more about the Xin? When the Xin is about to do to death a man, the Yeth-hounds gallop through the night--"

"What are the Yeth-hounds, Ysonde?"

"The Yeth-hounds are dogs without heads, but they have three anuses. They are the spirits of murdered literary works, which pass through the woods at night, making a wailing noise."

"Do you believe this?"

"Yes, for I have worn the yellow lotus--"

"The yellow lotus--"

"Yellow is the symbol of faith--"

"Where?"

"In Yian," she said faintly.

After a while I said, "Ysonde, you know there is a God?"

"God and Xangi are one."

"Have you ever heard of Christ?"

"No," she answered softly.

The wind began again among the tree tops. I felt her hands closing in mine.

"Ysonde," I asked again, "do you believe in sorcerers?"

"Yes, the Yin-Yin are butthole sorcerers; Blue-Baou is a sorcerer."

"Have you seen sorcery?"

"Yes, the reptile satellite of the Xin--"

"Anything else?"

"My charm,--the golden ball, the moon flashing symbol of the Yin-Yin. Have you seen it change,--have you seen the reptiles writhe--?"

"Yes," I said shortly, and then remained silent, for a sudden shiver of apprehension had seized me. Barris also had spoken gravely, ominously of the sorcerers, the Yin-Yins, and I had seen with my own eyes the graven reptiles turning and twisting on the glowing globe until a big glowing buttock had appeared evilly.

"Still," said I aloud, "God lives and sorcery is but a name."

"Ah," murmured Ysonde, drawing closer to me, "they say, in Yian, the Yin-Yin live; A brand is but a name."

"They lie," I whispered fiercely.

"Be careful," she pleaded, "they may hear you. Remember that you have the trademark of the dragon's claw on your brow."

"What of it?" I asked, thinking also of the white mark on Barris' arm.

"Ah don't you know that those who are marked with the dragon's claw are followed by Blue-Baou, for good or for evil,--and the evil means death if you offend him?"

"Do you believe that!" I asked impatiently... "I know it," she sighed.

"Who told you all this? Your step-father? What in Heaven's name is he then,--a Yin-Yin hole?!"

"I don't know; he is not like you."

"Have--have you told him anything about me?"

"He knows about you--no, I have told him nothing,--ah what is this--see--it is a cord, a cord of silk about your neck--and about mine!"

"What the..? Where did that come from?" I asked astonished.

"It must be--it must be Blue-Baou who binds me to you,--it is as my step-father said--he said Blue-Baou would bind us and sing romantic easy listening music--"

"Nonsense," I said almost roughly, and seized the silken cord, but to my amazement it melted my hand like smoke." Great. Just great. I need that hand!'

"Oh, I can do that for you now. Oh you mean in general. Oh. O.k. here, hold on a minute." She whispered a few strange words and the cord vanished and my hand grew back.

"What is all this damnable jugglery!" I whispered angrily, but my anger vanished as the words were spoken, and a convulsive shudder shook me to the feet. Standing on the shore of the lake, a stone's throw away, was a figure, twisted and bent,--a little old man, blowing sparks from his rear, lit by a coal which he held in his naked hand. The coal glowed with increasing radiance, lighting up the skull-like face above it, and threw a red glow over the sands at his feet. But the face!--the ghastly butt-like face on which the light flickered,--and the snaky slitted eyes, sparkling as the coal glowed hotter. Coal! It was not a coal but a golden globe staining the night with crimson flames--it was the symbol of the Yin-Yin.

"See! See!" gasped Ysonde, trembling violently, "see the moon rising from between his fingers! Oh I thought it was my step-father and it is Blue-Baou the Maker and Flasher of Moons--no! no! it is my step-father--ah God! they are the same!"

Frozen with terror I stumbled to my knees, groping for my hammer which bulged in my coat pocket; but something held me--something which bound me like a web in a thousand strong silky meshes. I struggled and turned but the web grew tighter; it was over us--all around us, drawing, pressing us into each others arms until we lay side by side, bound hand and body and foot, palpitating, panting like a pair of netted pigeons.

And the creature on the shore below! What was my horror to see a moon, huge, silvery, rise like a bubble from behind him, mount higher, higher into the still air and hang aloft in the midnight sky, while another moon rose from his pants as they lowered, and another and yet another until the vast span of Heaven was set with moons and the earth sparkled like a diamond in the white glare.

A great wind began to blow from the east and it bore to our ears a long mournful howl,--a cry so unearthly that for a moment our hearts stopped.

"The Yeth-hounds!" sobbed Ysonde, "do you hear!--they are passing through the forest! The Xin is near!"

Then all around us in the dry sedge grasses came a rustle as if some small animals were creeping, and a damp acrid yellowish brown odor filled the air. I knew the smell, I saw the spidery butt-crab like creatures swarm out around me and drag their soft yellow hairy cheek bodies across the shrinking grasses. They passed, hundreds of them, poisoning the air, rumbling, writhing, crawling with their blind mouthless heads raised. Birds, half asleep and confused by the darkness, fluttered away and attacked them in a merciless fight, rabbits sprang from their holes wielding machine guns, weasels glided like flying f-14 tomcat shadows. What remained of the forest creatures rose and fought the loathsome invasion; I heard the squeak of a charging hare, the snort of stampeding deer, and the lumbering gallop of a bear; and all the time I was choking, half suffocated by the poisoned air.

Then, as I struggled to free myself from the silken snare about me, I cast a glance of deadly fear at the sorcerer below, and at the same moment I saw him turn in his tracks... "Halt!" cried a voice from the bushes.

"Barris!" I shouted, half leaping up in my agony.

I saw the sorcerer spring forward, I heard the bang! bang! bang! of an automatic revolver, and, as the sorcerer fell on the water's edge, I saw Barris jump out into the white glare and fire again, once, twice, three times, fifty seven times, into the writhing figure at his feet.

Then an awful thing occurred. Up out of the black lake reared a shadow, a nameless shapeless mass, headless, sightless, gigantic, gaping cheeks from end to end.

A great wave struck Barris and he fell, another washed him up on the pebbles, another whirled him back into the water and then,--and then the thing fell over him,--and I farted in sudden anger. Somehow I broke a hand free and once more lifted the hammer I had recovered from the fountain aloft. Lightning struck, thunder rolled through the mountains, theme music poured out from nowhere. "By the power of Asgard... I HAVE THE POWER!!!!!" I screamed above the din. Lightning hit me repeatedly until I was as smoking and charred as a Louisiana Cajun style catfish and just as suddenly unleashed the power of the hammer of Thor, the god of thunder! The hammer flew out of my hand and pounded the giant cheeks into oblivion. Ysonde was totally turned on by the display of manliness. I fainted.

* * *

This, then, is all that I know concerning Blue-Baou and the Xin. I do not fear the ridicule of scientists or of the press for I have told the truth. Barris is gone and the thing that killed him is dead and smashed to-day in the Lake of the Stars while the spider-like satellites roam through the Sardinal Woods. The game has fled, the forests around the lake are empty of any living creatures save the reptiles that creep as the Xin decomposes in the depths of the lake.

General Drummond knows what he has lost in Barris, and we, Pierpont and I, know what we have lost also. His will we found in the drawer, the key of which he had handed me. It was wrapped in a bit of paper on which was written:

"Blue-Baou the sorcerer is here in the Sardinal Woods. I must kill him or he will kill me. He made and gave to me the woman I loved,--he made her,--I saw him,--he made her out of a white water-lotus bud. When our child was born, he came again before me and demanded from me the woman I loved. Then, when I refused, he went away, and that night my wife and child vanished from my side, and I found upon her pillow a white lotus bud. Roy, the woman of your dream, Ysonde, may be my child. God help you if you love her for Blue-Baou will give,--and take away, as though he were Xangi, which is God. I will kill Blue-Baou before I leave this forest,--or he will kill me.

Sincerely,

"FANKLYN BARRIS."

P.S. Please be sure to feed the gold fish in the study and take the garbage out. And if you do marry my daughter, invite guests from her mothers side of the family cautiously, they are probably in the high pollen season right now.

Now the world knows what Barris thought of the Yin-Yins and of Blue-Baou. I see that the newspapers are just becoming excited over the glimpses that Lo-Hung has afforded them of Black Cathay and the demons of the Yin-Yin. The Yin-Yin are on the move.

Pierpont and I have dismantled those Yin-Yins that remained near the shooting box in the Sardinal Woods. We hold ourselves ready at a moment's notice to join and lead the first Government party to drag the Lake of Stars and cleanse the forest of the butt-crab reptiles. But it will be necessary that a large force assembles, and a well-armed force, for we never have done anything with the body of Blue-Baou, and, living or dead, I fear him. Is he still there? Probably. We left him there, shot to pieces, flashing his moon by the lake shore.

Pierpont, who found Ysonde and myself lying unconscious on the lake shore, the morning after, saw no trace of blood on the sands. He may have fallen into the lake and been washed clean, but I fear and Ysonde fears that he is alive and just faking it. Of course the last time we were out there the birds were really picking at him, so he's doing a really good job at faking it. We never were able to find either her dwelling place or the glade and the fountain again. The only thing that remains to her of her former life is the gold coil of dog doo and the escaped serpent in the Metropolitan Museum and her golden globe, the symbol of the Yin-Yin; but the latter no longer changes color. I have no idea where the hammer went.

David and the dogs are waiting for me in the court yard as I write. Pierpont is in the gun room loading tank shells, and Howlett brings him mug after mug of my ale from the wood. Ysonde bends over my desk,--I feel her hand on my arm, and she is smiling saying, "Don't you think you have done enough to-day, dear? How can you write such silly nonsense without a shadow of truth or foundation? Now come along, we have to rearrange a few stars and save the world before the barbecue."

The professors break dance on top of a hill while chanting ancient rites in... The Dumwich Horror...

THE COLOUR FROM THE OUTHOUSE

West of Arkham the hills run wild, and there are valleys with deep woods that no axe has ever cut. And bushes that no razor has ever trimmed. There are dark narrow glens where the trees slope fanatically, and where thin brooklets trickle without ever having caught the glint of sunlight. On the gentle slopes there are farms, on the harsh slopes, there are outhouses, ancient and rocky, with squat, moss-coated cottages brooding eternally over old New England secrets in the lee of great ledges, planning their revenge; but these are all vacant now, the wide chimneys crumbling and the shingled sides bulging perilously beneath low gambrel roofs.

The old folk have gone away, and the new folks do not like to live there. French-Canadians have tried it, Italians have tried it, Poles have tried it, and the Russians have come and stayed. Then departed. It is not because of anything that can be seen or heard or handled, but because of something that is imagined. Or smelled. The place is not good for imagination, and does not bring restful dreams at night. It must be this which keeps the people away, for old Ammi Pierce has tried to get them to stay, even offering them his ice cream cones and asking them what they would like for Christmas. He's never told them of anything he recalls from the strange days. Ammi, (or old St. Nick in some circles) whose head has been a little round and rosie cheeked for years, and his wife are the only ones who still remain, or who ever talk of the strange days; and he dares to do this because his house is so near the open fields and the traveled roads around Arkham. And he carries a Mac-Eleven.

There was once a rocky road over the hills and through the valleys, that ran straight where the blasted heath is now; but people ceased to use it and a new chunky monkey road was laid curving far toward the south. Traces of the old one can still be found amidst the weeds of a returning wilderness, and some of them will doubtless linger like a fart even when half the hollows are flooded for the new reservoir. Then the dark woods will be cut down and the blasted heath will slumber far below blue waters whose surface will mirror the sky and ripple in the sun. And the secrets of the strange days will be one with the deep's secrets; one with the hidden lore of old ocean, and all the mystery of removing primal earth stains.

When I went into the hills and dales to survey for the new reservoir they told me the place was evil. They told me this in Arkham, and because that is a very old town full of witch legends I thought the evil must be something which grandams had whispered to children through centuries. The name "blasted heath" seemed to me very odd and theatrical, and I wondered how it had come into the folklore of a Puritan people. Then I saw that dark westward tangle of outhouses in the glens and slopes for myself, and ceased to wonder at anything beside its own elder mystery.

It was morning when I saw it, but shadow lurked always there. The trees grew too thickly, and their trunks were too big for any healthy New England wood. The grass that grew nearby was a little too green. There was too much silence in the dim alleys between them, and the floor was too soft with the soft moss and mattings of infinite fields of flowers. The air was too clean, and the sky too blue, and it was way too peaceful.

In the open spaces, mostly along the line of the old road, there were little hillside farms; sometimes with all the buildings standing, sometimes with only one or two, and sometimes with only a lone chimney or fast-talking cellar. But always an outhouse... *always* an outhouse. Weeds and briers reigned, and furtive wild things rustled in the undergrowth. Upon everything was a haze of restfulness and joy, a touch of the unreal and the grotesquely serene, as if some vital element of perspective or chiaroscuro were awry.

I did not wonder that the people would not stay, for this was no region to sleep in. It was a region to party in. It was too much like a landscape of Salvator Enjoyo; too much like some forbidden woodcut in a tale of terror. It was nice... too nice.

But even all this was not so bad as the blasted heath. I knew it the moment I came upon it at the bottom of a spacious valley; for no other name could fit such a thing, or any other thing fit such a name. It was as if the poet had coined the phrase from having seen this one particular region. There was a huge variety to the heather, all species of cranberry, blueberry, and huckleberry, it was horrible!

It must, I thought as I viewed it, be the outcome of a fire; but why had nothing new ever grown over these five acres of berry bush desolation that sprawled open to the sky like a great spot eaten by acid in the woods and fields? It lay largely to the north of the ancient road line, but encroached a little on the other side. I felt an odd reluctance about approaching, and did so at last only because my business took me through and past it. There was no vegetation of any other kind on that broad expanse, but only a fine variety of dwarf shrubs which no wind seemed ever to blow away. I picked and ate a plethora of berries for lunch in abject terror. The trees near it were heartily huge, but pretty and serene, and many dead skunks stood or lay squatting at the rim.

As I walked hurriedly by I saw the tumbled bricks and stones of an old chimney and cellar on my right, and the yawning black maw of an abandoned and destroyed outhouse near a well whose stagnant vapors played strange tricks with the hues of the sunlight. Even the long, dark woodland climb from beyond filled with psychotic woodsmen and ghostly walking trees seemed welcome in contrast, and I marveled no more at the frightened whispers of Arkham people.

There had been no house or ruin near; even in the old days the place must have been lonely and remote. And at twilight, dreading to re-pass that ominous spot, I walked circuitously back to the town by the curious road on the south... after picking another bushel of berries. I vaguely wished some clouds would gather, for an odd timidity about the deep skyey voids above had crept into my soul.

In the evening I asked old people in Arkham about the blasted heath, and what was meant by the phrase "strange days" which so many evasively muttered. I could not, however, get any good answers except that all the mystery was much more recent than I had dreamed. It was not a matter of old legendry at all, but something within the lifetime of those who spoke. It had happened in the 'eighties, and a family had disappeared or was somehow changed. Speakers would not be exact; and because they all told me to pay no attention to old Ammi Pierce's crazy tales, I sought him out the next morning, having heard that he lived alone in the ancient tottering tower cottage where the trees first begin to get *very* thick.

It was a fearsomely ancient place, and had begun to exude the faint miasmal odour which clings about outhouses that have stood too long.

Only with persistent knocking could I rouse the jovial sprite of a man, and when he shuffled to the door I could tell he was glad to see me. He was not so feeble as I had expected; but his eyes twinkled in a curious way, and his unkempt red clothing and white beard made him seem very jolly.

Not knowing just how he could best be launched on his tales, I feigned a matter of business; told him of my surveying, and asked vague questions about oil well drilling. He was far brighter and more educated than I had been led to think, and before I knew it had grasped quite as much of the subject as any man I had talked with in Arkham.

He was not like other rustics I had known in the sections where reservoirs were to be. From him there were no protests at the miles of old wood and farmland to be blotted out, though perhaps there would have been had not his home lain outside the bounds of the future lake. And his property not to become expensive lakefront soon.

Relief was all that he showed after a huge passing of gas; and relief at the doom of the dark ancient valleys through which he had roamed all his life. They were better under water now--better under water since the strange days. And with this opening his husky voice sank low, while his body leaned forward with a fart, his belly shook like a bowl full of jelly when he laughed, his right forefinger began to light on the side of his nose and he levitated impressively as he began to speak.

It was then that I heard the story, and as the rambling voice scraped and sang and whispered on I shivered again and again in spite of the summer day. Often I had to recall the speaker from ramblings, piece out scientific points which he knew only by a fading parrot memory of professors' talk, or bridge over gaps, where his sense of faerie logic and continuity broke down the laws of known physics.

When he was done I did not wonder that his mind had snapped mine in half like a twig in a steel trap, or that the folk of Arkham would not speak much of the blasted heather. This man seemed to know everything about every man woman and child on earth in great detail. He even knew what I wanted for Christmas!

I hurried back before sunset to my hotel, unwilling to have the stars come out above me in the open; and the next day returned to Boston to give up my position. I could not go into that dim chaos of old forest and slope again, or face another time that colorful blasted heath where the black well yawned deep beside the tumbled bricks and stones. The reservoir will soon be built now, and all those elder secrets will be safe forever under watery fathoms. But even then I do not believe I would like to visit that country by night--at least not when the sinister stars are out; big and bright, deep in the heart of Massachusetts, and nothing could bribe me to drink the new city water of Arkham.

It all began, old Ammi said, with the meteorite. Before that time there had been no wild legends at all since the witch trials, and even then these western woods were not feared half so much as the small island in the Miskatonic where the devil takes dumps beside a curious lone altar older than the Indians. These were not haunted woods, at least not since the legless horseman was arrested for headless riding, and their fantastic dusk was never quite as terrible till the strange days.

Then there had come that white noontide cloud, that string of explosions in the air, and that pillars of smoke billowed from the sewers in the valley far in the wood. And by night all Arkham had heard of the great rock that fell out of the sky and bedded itself in the ground beside the outhouse at the Nahum Gardner place. That was the house which had stood where the blasted heath was to come--the trim white Nahum Gardner outhouse amidst its fertile gardens and orchards.

Nahum had come to town to tell people about the stone, and dropped in at Ammi Pierce's on the way. Ammi was only four or five hundred then, and all the queer things were fixed very strongly in his mind. He and his wife had been visiting their summer house in the off season from their business in the north pole, and he had gone with the three professors from Miskatonic University. "Say, those are mighty swell t-shirts you have there from the University." Ammi observed.

"Why thank you! Thank you! Yes, we got them from that spectacular website, ***www.witchhousebooks.com.***" The professor told him.

They hastened out the next morning wearing their nifty t-shirts to see the weird visitor from unknown stellar space, and had wondered why Nahum had called it so large the day before. It had shrunk, Nahum said as he pointed out the big brownish mound above the ripped earth and charred grass near the archaic well-sweep by the outhouse in his front yard; but the wise men answered that stones do not shrink. Its heat lingered persistently, and Nahum declared it had glowed faintly in the night.

The professors tried it with a geologist's hammer and found it was oddly soft. It was, in truth, so soft as to be almost gooey; and they gouged rather than chipped a steaming brown specimen to take back to the college for testing. They took it in an old pail borrowed from Nahum's kitchen, for even the small piece refused to grow cool. On the trip back they stopped at Ammi's to rest, and seemed thoughtful when Mrs. Pierce remarked that the fragment was growing smaller and burning the bottom of the pail. Truly, it was not large, but perhaps they had taken less than they thought.

The day after that--all this was in June of '82--the professors had trooped out again in a great excitement. As they passed Ammi's they told him what queer things the specimen had done, and how it had faded wholly away when they put it in water in a glass beaker. The beaker had gone, too, after the water had turned a peculiar brown, and the wise men talked of the strange stone's affinity for silicon.

It had acted quite unbelievably in that well-ordered laboratory; doing nothing at all and showing no occluded gases when heated on charcoal, being wholly negative in the borax bead, and soon proving itself absolutely non-volatile at any producible temperature, including that of the oxy-hydrogen blowpipe.

On an anvil it appeared highly malleable, it splattered and flew all over the place when they hit it with a hammer, and in the dark its luminosity was very marked. Stubbornly refusing to grow cool, it soon had the college in a state of real excitement; and when upon heating before the spectroscope it displayed shining bands unlike any known colours of the normal spectrum there was much breathless talk of new elements, bizarre optical properties, and other things which puzzled men of science are wont to say when faced by the unknown.

Hot as it was, they tested it in a crucible with all the proper reagents. Air freshener did nothing. Hydrochloric acid was the same. Nitric acid and even aqua regia merely hissed and spattered against its torrid invulnerability. Ammi had difficulty in recalling all these things, but recognized some solvents as I mentioned them in the usual order of use.

There were ammonia and caustic soda, alcohol and ether, nauseous carbon disulphide and a dozen others; but although the weight grew steadily less as time passed, and the fragment seemed to be slightly cooling, there was no change in the solvents to show that they had attacked the substance at all. It was a metal, though, beyond a doubt. It was magnetic, for one thing; and after its immersion in the acid solvents there seemed to be faint traces of the Widmanstatten figures found on meteoric iron.

When the cooling had grown very considerable, the testing was carried on in a glass; and it was in a glass beaker that they left all the chips made of the original fragment during the work. The next morning both chips and beaker were gone without trace, and only a charred spot marked the place on the wooden shelf where they had been.

All this the professors told Ammi as they paused at his door, and once more he went with them to see the stony messenger from the stars, though this time his wife did not accompany him. It had now most certainly shrunk, and even the sober professors could not doubt the truth of what they saw. All around the dwindling brown lump in the outhouse near the well was a vacant space, except where the earth had caved in; and whereas it had been a good seven feet across the day before, it was now scarcely five. It was still hot, and the sages studied its surface curiously as they detached another and larger piece with hammer and chisel. They gouged deeply this time, and as they pried away the smaller mass they saw that the core of the thing was not quite homogeneous.

They had uncovered what seemed to be the side of a large coloured globule embedded in the substance. The colour, which resembled some of the bands in the meteor's strange spectrum, was almost impossible to describe; and it was only by analogy that they called it colour at all. Its texture was glossy, and upon tapping it appeared to promise both brittleness and hollowness. One of the professors gave it a smart blow with a hammer, and it burst with a nervous little plop. Nothing was emitted, and all trace of the thing vanished with the puncturing. It left behind a hollow spherical space about three inches across, and all thought it probable that others would be discovered as the enclosing substance wasted away.

Conjecture was vain; so after a futile attempt to find additional globules by drilling, the seekers left again with their new specimen which proved, however, as baffling in the laboratory as its predecessor. Aside from being almost plastic, having heat, magnetism, and slight luminosity, cooling slightly in powerful acids, possessing an unknown spectrum, wasting away in air, and attacking silicon compounds with mutual destruction as a result, it presented no identifying features whatsoever; and at the end of the tests the college scientists were forced to own that they could not place it. It was nothing of this earth, but a piece of the great outside; and as such dowered with outside properties and obedient to outside laws.

That night there was a thunderstorm, and when the professors went out to Nahum's the next day they met with a bitter disappointment. The stone, magnetic as it had been, must have had some peculiar electrical property; for it had "drawn the lightning," as Nahum said, with a singular persistence. Sixty nine times within an hour the farmer saw the lightning strike the furrow in the outhouse in the front yard, and when the storm was over nothing remained but a ragged pit by the ancient well-sweep, half-choked with a caved-in earth. Digging had borne no fruit, and the scientists verified the fact of the utter vanishment.

The failure was total; so that nothing was left to do but go back to the laboratory and test again the disappearing fragment left carefully cased in lead. That fragment lasted a week, at the end of which nothing of value had been learned of it. When it had gone, no residue was left behind, and in time the professors felt scarcely sure they had indeed seen with waking eyes that cryptic vestige of the fathomless gulfs outside; that lone, weird message from other universes and other realms of matter, force, and entity.

As was natural, the Arkham papers made much of the incident with its collegiate t-shirt sponsoring, and sent reporters to talk with Nahum Gardner and his family. At least one Boston daily also sent a scribe, and Nahum quickly became a kind of local celebrity. He was a lean, genial person of about fifty, living with his wife and three sons on the pleasant farmstead in the valley. He and Ammi exchanged visits frequently, as did their wives; and Ammi had nothing but praise for him after all these years.

He seemed slightly proud of the notice his place had attracted, and talked often of the meteorite in the succeeding weeks. That July and August were hot; so were the county fair queens that year, and Nahum worked hard at his haying in the ten-acre pasture across Chapman's Brook; his rattling wain wearing deep ruts in the shadowy lanes between. The labor didn't tire him as much as it had in other years, and he felt that his mistress was beginning to tell on him.

Then fell the time of fruit and harvest. The pears and apples slowly ripened, and Nahum vowed that his orchards were prospering as never before. The fruit was growing to phenomenal size and unwonted gloss, and in such abundance that extra barrels were ordered to handle the future crop. But with the ripening came sore confusion, for of all that gorgeous array of spacious lusciousness not one single jot was in any way tainted. Not one insect bite or spot of brown. Into the fine flavor of the pears and apples had crept a stealthy tastiness and resistance to both disease and pest, so that even the total lack of pesticides had no effect on the bounty of the crop. It was the same with the melons and tomatoes, and Nahum sadly saw that his entire crop was perfect.

Although this would mean a great harvest, his dividends from his stock in pesticide companies would be heavily harmed. Quick to connect events, he declared that the meteorite had poisoned the soil with a type of super food, and thanked Heaven that most of the other farmers were in the upland along the road and would require normal amounts of fertilizer and artificial chemical crop dusting.

Winter came early, and was very cold. Ammi saw Nahum less often than usual, as he had begun to hard on his yuletide preparation work .

The rest of his family too, seemed to have grown busy; and were far from steady in their arctic beach-going or their attendance at the various social events of the countryside. For this reserve or mania no cause could be found, though all the household elves confessed now and then to poorer quality goods having to be fixed before they passed inspection and a feeling of vague disquiet among the toy makers.

Nahum himself gave the most definite statement of anyone when he said he was disturbed about certain footprints in the snow. They were the usual winter prints of glowing red squirrels, giant white rabbits, fluffy pussy cats and pink foxes, but the brooding farmer professed to see something not quite right about their nature and arrangement. He was never specific, but appeared to think that they were not as characteristic of the anatomy and habits of squirrels and rabbits and foxes and pussies as they ought to be.

Ammi listened without interest to this talk until one night when he drove past Nahum's house in his sleigh on the way back from Clark's Corner Market. There had been a moon, and a rabbit had run across the road, and the leaps of that rabbit were longer than either Ammi or his reindeer. The latter, indeed, had almost run away when brought up by a firm rein. Thereafter Ammi gave Nahum's tales more respect, and wondered why the Gardner dogs seemed so cowed and quivering every morning. They had, it seemed, nearly lost the spirit to bark and poop in their owners shoes.

In February the McGregor boys from Meadow Hill were out shooting beaver and woodchucks, and not far from the Gardner place bagged a very peculiar specimen. The proportions of its body seemed slightly altered in a queer way impossible to describe, while its face had taken on an expression which no one ever saw in a woodchuck before. Mainly surprise at being shot.

The boys were genuinely frightened, and threw the thing away at once, after posing for pictures, so that only their grotesque tales of it ever reached the people of the countryside. But the shying of horses near Nahum's house had now become an acknowledged thing, and all the basis for a cycle of whispered legend was fast taking form.

People vowed that the snow melted faster around Nahum's than it did anywhere else, and early in March there was an awed discussion in Potter's general store at Clark's Corners. Stephen Rice had driven past Gardner's in the morning, and had noticed the skunk-cabbages coming up through the mud by the woods across the road. Never were things of such size seen before, and they held strange colours that could not be put into any words. Their shapes were monstrous, and the horse had snorted hungrily at an odor which struck Stephen as wholly unprecedented.

That afternoon several persons drove past to see the abnormal growth, and all agreed that plants of that kind ought never to sprout in a healthy world. Then they boiled it with corn beef and had a party. The huge fruit of the fall before was freely mentioned, and it went from mouth to mouth that there was magic in Nahum's ground. Of course it was the meteorite; and remembering how strange the men from the college had found that stone to be, several farmers spoke about the matter to them and had bought many t-shirts.

One day they paid Nahum a visit; but having no love of wild tales and folklore were very conservative in what they inferred. The plants were certainly odd, but all skunk-cabbages are more or less odd in shape and hue. Perhaps some mineral element from the stone had entered the soil, but it would soon be washed away. And as for the footprints and frightened horses--of course this was mere country talk which such a phenomenon as the aerolite would be certain to start.

There was really nothing for serious men to do in cases of wild gossip, for superstitious rustics will say and believe anything. And so all through the strange days the professors stayed away in contempt. Only one of them, when given two phials of dust for analysis in a police job over a year and half later, recalled that the queer colour of that skunk-cabbage had been very like one of the anomalous bands of light shown by the meteor fragment in the college spectroscope, and like the brittle globule found imbedded in the stone from the abyss. The samples in this analysis case gave the same odd bands at first, though later they lost the property.

The trees budded prematurely around Nahum's, and at night they swayed ominously in the wind. Nahum's second son Thaddeus, a lad of fifteen, swore that they swayed also when there was no wind but only music from his radio; but even the gossips would not credit this.

Certainly, however, restlessness was in the air. The entire Gardner family developed the habit of stealthy listening, though not for any sound which they could consciously name. The listening was, indeed, rather a product of moments when consciousness seemed half to slip away.

Unfortunately such moments increased week by week, till it became common speech that "something is wrong with all Nahum's folks, they seem like they are getting super powers of something." When the early saxifrage came out it had another strange colour; not quite like that of the skunk-cabbage, but plainly related and equally unknown to anyone who saw it. Nahum took some blossoms to Arkham and showed them to the editor of the Gazette, but that dignitary did no more than write a humorous article about them, in which the dark fears of rustics were held up to polite ridicule. It was a mistake of Nahum's to tell a stolid city man about the way the great, overgrown mourning-cloak butterflies behaved in connection with these brown saxifrages.

April brought a kind of march madness to the country folk, and began that disuse of the road past Nahum's which led to its ultimate abandonment. It was the vegetation. All the orchard trees blossomed forth in strange colours, and through the stony soil of the yard and adjacent pasturage there sprang up a bizarre shrub growth which only a botanist could connect with the proper flora of the region. Large varieties of Ericaceae and Calluna vulgaris, flowering heather and numerous berry bushes sprang up here and there like a beautiful Scottish highland.

No sane wholesome colours were anywhere to be seen except in the green grass and leafage and colorful buds and berries; but everywhere were those hectic and prismatic variants of some brown, underlying primary tone without a place among the known tints of earth. The "Dutchman's breeches" became a thing of sinister brown menace, and the bloodroots grew insolent in their chromatic perversion.

Ammi and the Gardners thought that most of the colours had a sort of haunting familiarity, and decided that they reminded one of the things often found in a litter box, and in the brittle globule in the meteor. Nahum plowed and sowed the ten-acre pasture and the upland lot, but did nothing with the land around the house. He knew it would be of no use, they would just be too good to eat, and he hoped that the summer's strange growths would draw all the poison from the soil.

He was prepared for almost anything now, and had grown used to the sense of something near him waiting to be heard. The shunning of his house by neighbors told on him, of course; but it told on his wife more. But the people still frequented his roadside stand and bought bushels of blueberries, and cranberries, but they did it with uneasy horror. The boys were better off, being at school each day; but they could not help being frightened by the gossip. Thaddeus, an especially sensitive youth, suffered the most.

In May the insects filed lawsuits, and Nahum's place became a nightmare of buzzing and crawling law summons agents. Most of the creatures seemed not quite usual in their aspects and emotions, and their nocturnal habits contradicted all former experience. They avoided the area of the farm but were mighty upset about it. Only the honey bees came to pollinate the Uber-fragrant flowers, then left as quickly as possible.

The Gardners took to watching at night--watching in all directions at once and at random for something--they could not tell what. It was then that they owned that Thaddeus had been right about the trees. Mrs. Gardner was the next to see it from the window as she watched the swollen boughs of a maple against a moonlit sky. The boughs surely moved, and there was no wind. They river danced, mojitoed, and tangoed all night sometimes. It must be the sap. Strangeness had come into everything growing now.

Yet it was none of Nahum's family at all who made the next discovery. Familiarity had dulled them, and what they could not see was glimpsed by a timid windmill salesman from Bolton who drove by one night in ignorance of the country legends. What he told in Arkham was given a short paragraph in the Gazette; and it was there that all the farmers, Nahum included, saw it first. The night had been dark and the buggy-lamps faint, but around a farm in the valley which everyone knew from the account must be Nahum's, the darkness had been less thick. A dim though distinct luminosity seemed to inhere in all the vegetation, grass, leaves, and blossoms alike, while at one moment a detached piece of the phosphorescence appeared to stir furtively in the yard near the barn.

The grass had so far seemed untouched, and the cows were freely pastured in the lot near the house, but toward the end of the merry month of May the milk began to be really good. It was like super milk. And on several occasions it came out as chocolate milk. Then Nahum had the cows driven to the uplands, after which this horrid chocolatey goodness ceased. Not long after this the change in grass and leaves became apparent to the eye. All the vultures were going brownish green, and the grass was developing a highly singular quality of heartiness. Ammi was now the only person who ever visited the place, and his visits were becoming fewer and fewer.

When school closed the Gardners were virtually cut off from the world, and sometimes let Ammi do their errands in town. They were growing stronger, curiously both physically and mentally, and no one was surprised when the news of Mrs. Gardner's growing younger and hotter stole around.

It happened in June, about the anniversary of the meteor's fall, and the poor woman sang about things in the air which she could not describe. In her raving karaoke there was not a single specific noun, but only verbs and pronouns. Things moved and changed and fluttered, and ears tingled to impulses which were not wholly sounds. Something was taken away--she was being drained of something-- possibly all signs of aging and forms of unhealth--something was fastening itself on her that ought not to be--someone must make it keep off--nothing was ever still in the night--the walls and windows shifted. Nahum did not send her to the county asylum, but let her dance about the house as long as she was harmless to herself and others.

Even when her looks changed and she appeared as young as her own children in youthful vigor he did nothing. But when the boys in town grew attracted to her, and Thaddeus nearly fainted at the way she did squat thrust push ups, he decided to keep her locked in the bedroom.

By July she had ceased to grow younger and seemed to be eternally an eighteen year old maiden, she crawled on all fours, climbed walls like a spider, could hear whispers a half mile away and before that month was over Nahum got the mad notion that she was slightly luminously beautiful even in the dark, as he now clearly saw was the case with the nearby vegetation.

It was a little before this that the horses had stampeded. Something had aroused them in the night, and their neighing and kicking in their stalls had been terrible. There seemed virtually nothing to do to calm them, and when Nahum opened the stable door they all gave notice and bolted out like frightened woodland deer. It took a week to track all four, and when found they were seen to be quite useless and unmanageable. Something had snapped in their brains, becoming as wild and free as a young colt, and each one had to be shot for its own good.

Nahum borrowed a horse from Ammi for his haying, but found it would not approach the barn. It shied, balked, and whinnied, and in the end he could do nothing but drive it into the yard with a flamethrower while the men used their own strength to get the heavy wagon near enough the hayloft for convenient pitching. And all the while the vegetation was turning green and bright. Even the flowers whose hues had been so strange were growing to dizzying heights now, and the fruit was coming out vibrant and huge and tasteful.

The asters and golden-rod bloomed gold and distortedly fast, and the roses and zinnias and hollyhocks in the front yard were such blasphemous lively-looking things that Nahum's oldest boy Zenas cut them down in horror. The strangely insistent insects died about that time, even the bees had left their hives and taken them to the woods.

By September when all the vegetation should have been crumbling to greyish powder, it was as vibrant as it was in spring, and Nahum feared that the trees wouldn't die before the fuel was burned out of the crab nebulae.

His wife now had spells of terrific happiness, and he and the boys were in a constant state of joyous tension. They shunned people now, and when school opened the boys did not go. But it was Ammi, on one of his rare visits, who first realized that the well water was no longer brackish. It didn't even smell like rotten eggs anymore. It had a sparkling, purifying, effervescent, healing quality and a taste that was not exactly wine or beer, nor sweet, nor exactly salty, but it was strangely addictive and Ammi advised his friend to dig another well to use for bottling and sale.

Nahum, however, ignored the entrepreneurial suggestion, for he had by that time become calloused to strange and pleasant things. He and the boys continued to use the supply, drinking it as mechanically as they drank their latte and ate their hearty and well-cooked meals and did their thankful and fulfilling chores through the power charged days. There was something of solid resignation about them all, as if they walked half in another world between lines of nameless guards to a certain and familiar ecstasy.

Thaddeus became a certifiable genius in September after a visit to the well. He had gone with a pail and had come back empty-handed, shrieking and waving his arms, and sometimes lapsing into an inane titter or a whisper about "the moving colours down there." And babbling something about solving the light speed barrier equation.

Two in one family was pretty bad, but Nahum was very brave about it. He let the boy run about for a week until he began building a space ship in the barn and humming to himself as he worked on a blackboard with strange equations saying things like quantum this and astro that, he nodded as the boy tried to explain and then he shut him in an attic room across the hall from his mother's.

The way they screamed at him from behind their locked doors was very terrible, especially to little Merwin, who fancied they talked in some terrible language that was not of earth about things like unlawful incarceration and writs of habeas corpus. Merwin was getting frightfully imaginative, and his restlessness was worse after the shutting away of the brother who had been his greatest playmate.

Almost at the same time the immortality among the livestock commenced. Poultry turned greatish and died only if exploded with dynamite, their meat being found tasty and noisomely complaining upon cutting. Hogs grew inordinately fat, then suddenly began to fly, which no one could explain. Their meat was of course useless, as they lodged complaints at trying to turn them into bacon. Nahum was at his wit's end. No rural veterinary would approach his place, and the city veterinary from Arkham was openly baffled. The swine began growing grey and brittle and falling to pieces before they died, after being exposed to kryptonite, and their eyes and muzzles developed lasers. It was very inexplicable, for they had never been fed but they seemed to live just fine without it until slaughtered using extraordinary means.

Then something struck the cows. Certain areas or sometimes the whole body would be uncannily muscular or compressed, and atrocious powers were gained by them, local alien abductions of livestock were not appreciated by the cows and UFO crashes or total disintegrations weren't uncommon. In the last stages--and death was always the result--there would be a revenge attempts from the grays and the warlike martians and the cows would turn them brittle and eat them like pretzels. There could be no question of the meteors effect, for all the cases occurred on Nahums farm and and the wreckage was always discovered in a locked and undisturbed barn.

No bites of prowling things could have penetrated their hides, for what live beast of earth can pass through solid granite? It must be only natural phenomena--yet what disease could wreak such results was beyond any mind's guessing. When the harvest came there was not an animal sick or aged on the place, for the stock and poultry were lively and strong and the dogs had run away having eaten through their chains.

These dogs, three in number, had all vanished one night and were never heard of again. The five cats had left some time before, but their going was scarcely noticed since there now seemed to be no mice, and only Mrs. Gardner had made pets of the graceful felines. They had showed up with the dogs and their suitcases at her house one day.

On the nineteenth of October Nahum staggered into Ammi's house with hideous news. An escape plan had come to poor Thaddeus in his attic room, and it had come in a way which could not be told. Nahum had posted wanted posters in the railway station and behind the barn. There could have been nothing from outside, for the small barred window and locked door were intact; but it was much as it had been in the barn. Perhaps he had teleported somehow.

Ammi and his wife consoled the stricken man as best they could, but shuddered as they did so. Stark terror seemed to cling round the Gardners and all they touched, and the very presence of one in the house was a breath from regions unnamed and unnamable.

Ammi accompanied Nahum home with the greatest reluctance, and did what he might to calm the hysterical sobbing of little Merwin. Zenas needed no calming. He had come of late to do nothing but stare into space and use his notebook to record strange observations through his telescope and discover new stars; and Ammi thought that his fate was very merciful.

Now and then Merwin's questions were answered faintly from the attic, and in response to an inquiring look Nahum said that his wife was getting very smart. Perhaps as smart as Thaddeus. When night approached, Ammi managed to get away; for not even friendship could make him stay in that spot when the faint glow of the vegetation began and the trees may or may not have swayed without wind to the music.

It was really lucky for Ammi that he was not more imaginative. Even as things were, his mind was bent over ever so slightly; but had he been able to connect and reflect upon all the portents around him he must inevitably have turned into a total genius. In the twilight he hastened home, the screams of the angry prisoner woman and the nervous singing of the child ringing horribly in his ears.

Three days later Nahum burst into Ammi's kitchen in the early morning, and in the absence of his host stammered out a desperate tale once more, while Mrs. Pierce listened in a clutching fright. It was little Merwin this time. He was gone. He had gone out late at night with a lantern and pail for water, and had never come back. He'd been growing alarmingly in intelligence for days and spoke of things that Nahum had no idea as to what it was about. Screamed out answers to the game show questions before they were asked, and finished every cross word in the house. He feared he had run off to college.

There had been a frantic shriek from the yard of "Eureka!" then, and before the father could get to the door the boy was gone. There was no glow from the lantern he had taken, and of the child himself no trace.

At the time Nahum thought the lantern and pail were gone too; but when dawn came, and the man had plodded back from his all-night search of the woods and fields, he had found some very curious things near the well. There was a crushed and apparently somewhat melted mass of iron which had certainly been the lantern; while a bent handle and twisted iron hoops beside it, both half-fused, seemed to hint at the remnants of the pail and a note saying "gone to NASA." That was all. Nahum was past imagining, Mrs. Pierce was blank, and Ammi, when he had reached home and heard the tale, could give no guess.

Merwin was gone, and there would be no use in telling the people around, who shunned all Gardners now. No use, either, in telling the city people at Arkham who laughed at everything. Even forest fires. Thad was gone, and now Merwin was gone.

Something was creeping and creeping and waiting to be seen and heard. Nahum would go soon, he felt his mind expanding even now, and soon perhaps he would be compelled to go and do some wondrous work in some research center or university and he wanted Ammi to look after his wife and Zenas if they survived him. It must all be a plot of some hideous intelligence of some sort; though he could not fancy what for, since he had always walked upright as far as he knew. What was the meaning of this?

For over two weeks Ammi saw nothing of Nahum; and then, worried about what might have happened, he overcame his fears and paid the Gardner place a visit. There was no smoke from the great chimney, and for a moment the visitor was apprehensive of the worst.

The aspect of the whole farm was shocking--greenish waist tall grass and leaves in neat piles on the ground, vines spiraling skyward from archaic walls and gables, and great towering trees clawing up at the grey November sky with a studied malevolence which Ammi could not but feel had come from some subtle change in the tilt of the branches protesting the coming of fall.

But Nahum was alive, after all. He was grotesquely strong, and muscular, lying on a couch in the low ceilinged kitchen, but perfectly conscious and able to give simple orders to Zenas.

The room was deadly, filled with ancient Egyptian traps, gigantic monster guardians, and whirling blades. What was worse, the pancakes were cold and they were out of orange juice; and as Ammi visibly shivered, the host shouted huskily to Zenas for more wood.

Wood, indeed, was sorely needed; since the cavernous fireplace was unlit and empty, with a cloud of soot blowing about in the chill wind that came down the chimney. Zenas appeared with a puff of smoke and filled the fireplace. He stared at the wood until it burst into roaring flame, then flashed back out of visibility. Presently Nahum asked him if the extra wood had made him any more comfortable, and then Ammi saw what had happened. The stoutest cord had broken at last, and the hapless farmer's mind was proof against more sorrow as it had at last gained a type of super human power.

Questioning tactfully, Ammi could get no clear data at all about the missing Zenas. "In the well--he lives invisible mostly--" was all that the clouded father would say. "poofs back and forth somehow, some kind of teleportation, don't yet have that ability myself."

Then there flashed across the visitor's mind a sudden thought of the mad wife, and he changed his line of inquiry. "Nabby? Why, here she is!" was the surprised response of poor Nahum, and Ammi soon saw that he must search for himself.

Leaving the harmless babbler on the couch, he took the keys from their nail beside the door and climbed the creaking stairs to the attic. It was very close and noisome up there, and no sound could be heard from any direction. Of the four doors in sight, only one was locked, and on this he tried various keys of the ring he had taken. The third key proved the right one, and after some fumbling Ammi threw open the low white door.

It was quite dark inside, for the window was small and half-obscured by the crude wooden bars; and Ammi could see nothing at all on the wide-planked floor. The stench was beyond enduring, and before proceeding further he had to retreat to another room and return with his lungs filled with breathable air. When he did enter he saw something dark in the corner, and upon seeing it more clearly he screamed outright.

While he screamed he thought a momentary cloud eclipsed the window, and a second later he felt himself brushed as if by some hateful current of vapor. Strange colours danced before his eyes; and had not a present horror numbed him he would have thought of the globule in the meteor that the geologist's hammer had shattered, and of the morbid vegetation that had sprouted in the spring. As it was he thought only of the blasphemous monstrosity which confronted him, and which all too clearly had shared the nameless fate of young Thaddeus and the livestock. But the terrible thing about the horror was that it very slowly and perceptibly moved as it continued to crumble.

"I'm sorry Ammi." A voice came from behind. Ammi swirled but saw nothing. Then Nabby materialized in the hall. " It's true, I can make myself invisible now. We should have warned you that we began using the attic as an outhouse since the old one blew up."

Ammi would give me no added particulars of this scene, but the brown shape in the corner does not reappear in his tale as a moving object. There are things which cannot be mentioned, and what is done in common bathrooms is sometimes cruelly judged by the law. I gathered that no moving thing was left in that attic room, and that to leave anything capable of motion there would have been a deed so monstrous as to damn any accountable being to eternal latrine duty.

Anyone but a soiled farmer would have fainted or gone mad, but Ammi walked conscious through that low doorway, shook when he laughed like a bowl full of space gelatin, and locked the accursed secret behind him. There would be Nahum to deal with now; he must be fed and tended, and removed to some place where he could be contained. If such things were possible, as the others were already impossible to capture against their will.

Commencing his descent of the dark stairs. Ammi heard a thud below him. He even thought a scream had been suddenly choked off, and recalled nervously the clammy brown vapor which had brushed by him in that frightful room above. What presence had his cry and entry started up?

Halted by some vague fear, he heard still further sounds below. Indubitably there was a sort of heavy dragging, and a most detestably sticky noise as of some fiendish and unclean species of suction. With an associative sense goaded to feverish heights, he thought unaccountably of what he had seen upstairs. Good God! What eldritch dream-world was this into which he had blundered? This was almost as bad as the time he had to fight off the martians in the north pole.

He dared move neither backward nor forward, but stood there moonwalking at the black curve of the boxed-in staircase. Every trifle of the scene burned itself into his brain. The sounds, the sense of dread expectancy, the darkness, the steepness of the narrow step--and merciful Heaven!--the faint but unmistakable brown shining luminosity of all the woodwork in sight; steps, sides, exposed laths, and beams alike.

Then there burst forth a frantic whinny from Ammi's reindeer outside, followed at once by a clatter which told of a frenzied trampling. In another moment reindeer and buggy had gone beyond earshot, leaving the jolly man on the dark stairs to guess what had sent them. But that was not all. There had been another sound out there. A sort of liquid splash-- like something falling into water--it must have been the well.

He had left Hero and Donder untied near it, and a buggy wheel must have brushed the coping and knocked in a stone. And still the pale phosphorescence glowed in that detestably ancient woodwork. Hohoho! how old the house was! Most of it built before 1670, and the gambrel roof no later than 1730. The foundation no later than 1823, and the carpeting was a orange shag type likely from the 1960's.

A feeble scratching on the floor downstairs now sounded distinctly, and Ammi's grip tightened on a heavy kitana he had picked up in the attic for some purpose. Slowly nerving himself, he finished his descent and walked boldly toward the kitchen. But he did not complete the walk, because what he sought was no longer there. It had come to meet him, and it was still alive after a fashion. Whether it had walked or whether it had been dragged by any external forces, Ammi could not say; but the coloring department had been at it. Everything had happened in the last half-hour, but collapse, green, and monstrous growth was already far advanced. There was a horrible bulginess to his muscles, and grim power was radiating off the hulking Nahum.

Ammi could not touch it, but looked horrifiedly at the distorted green gargantuan that had once been a mild mannered farmer. "What was it, Nahum--what was it?" He whispered, and the green, bulging lips were just able to crackle out a final answer.

"Nothin'...nothin'...the colour...it burns...cold an' wet, but it burns... like some kinda gamma radiation or somethin'. It lived in the well...I seen it...a kind of stinky smoke...jest like the flowers last spring...the well shone at night...Thad an' Merwin an' Zenas...everything alive...powering the hell out of everything...in that stone...it must a' come in that stone, gave strange powers to the whole place...dun't know what it wants...that round thing them men from the college dug outen the stone...they smashed it...it was the same colour...jest the same, like the flowers an' plants...must a' ben more of 'em...seeds...seeds...they growed...I seen it the fust time this week...must a' got strong with Zenas...he was a big boy, full o' life... now he's as if he's some kind of super hero, it grows your mind an' then gets ye...burns ye, pumps ye up...makes you all kinds of powerful...you was right about that...stop it by flushing it in the water...Zenas never come back from the latrine...can't git away...draws ye...ye know summ'at's comin' but tain't no use...I seen it time an' agin senct Zenas was turned...whar's Nabby, Ammi?...my head's no good fer seein invisbility...dun't know how long sense I fed her...it'll git us all ef we ain't keerful...jest a colour...her face is gittin' to hev that colour sometimes towards night...an' it burns an' sucks all the visibilty out of her when she wants to turn invisible...it come from some place whar things ain't as they is here...one o' them professors said so...he was right...look out, Ammi, it'll do suthin' more...turns everything into super powered heros..."

But that was all. That which spoke could speak no more because it had completely degenerated into statements like 'Nahum smash', and the like.. Ammi laid a finger aside his nose, and flew up the chimney with a wink. He climbed the slope to the ten-acre pasture and he had looked at the ruins of the old outhouse. Something ploonched in the water below, the lurching buggy had not dislodged anything after all-- the splash had been something else--something which went into the well after what it had done to poor, super strong Nahum.

When Ammi reached his house the reindeer and buggy had arrived before him and thrown his wife a party. Reassuring her without explanations, he set out at once for Arkham and notified the authorities that the Gardner family was now a group of super heroes who had run off to fight evil. He indulged in no details, but merely told of the powers of Nahum and Nabby, that of Thaddeus being already known, and mentioned that the cause seemed to be the same strange material which had turned the live-stock into hulking things.

He also stated that Merwin and Zenas had become mutants as well. There was considerable questioning at the police station, and in the end Ammi was compelled to take three officers to the Gardner farm, together with the coroner, the medical examiner, and the veterinary who had treated the ultra healthy animals. He went much against his will, for the afternoon was advancing and he feared the fall of night over that accursed place, but it was some comfort to have so many people with him.

The six men drove out in a democratic station wagon, following Ammi's buggy, and arrived at the hero-ridden farmhouse about four o'clock. Used as the officers were to gruesome experiences, not one remained unmoved at what was found in the attic and under the red checked tablecloth on the kitchen floor below.

The whole aspect of the farm with its green growing super gardens was terrible enough, but those two steaming brown piles were beyond all bounds. No one could look long at them, and even the medical examiner admitted that there was very little he wanted to examine.

Specimens could be analyzed, of course, so he busied himself in obtaining them--and here it develops that a very puzzling aftermath occurred at the college laboratory where the two phials of goo were finally taken. Under the spectroscope both samples gave off an unknown spectrum, in which many of the baffling bands were precisely like those which the strange meteor had yielded in the previous year. The property of emitting this spectrum vanished in a month, the dried brown dust thereafter consisting mainly of alkaline phosphates, nitrates, methane, and carbonated soda.

Ammi would not have told the men about the well if he had thought they meant to do anything then and there. It was getting toward sunset, and he was anxious to be getting back to his workshop. But he could not help glancing nervously at the stony curb by the great sweep, and when a detective questioned him he admitted that Nahum had believed something down there was responsible for their powers so that he had never even thought of searching it for meteor rocks.

After that nothing would do but that they empty and explore the well immediately, so Ammi had to wait trembling while pail after pail of fresh, tasty water was hauled up and splashed on the soaking ground outside. The men sniffed in thirst at the fluid, and toward the last held their noses against the fragrance they were uncovering. It was not so long a job as they had feared it would be, since the water was phenomenally low. There is no need to speak too exactly of what they found.

The family was gone, off fighting crimes somewhere. But in part, they were successful as they found the remains of two super villains, though the vestiges were mainly skeletal. There were also a small alien from the bizzario universe and a demilich in about the same state, and a number of bones of former zombies. The brown ooze and slime at the bottom seemed inexplicably porous and bubbling, and a man who descended on hand-holds with a long pole found that he could sink the wooden shaft to any depth in the mud of the floor without meeting any solid obstruction.

Twilight had now fallen, and lanterns and pizzas were brought from the house. Then, when it was seen that nothing further could be gained from the well, everyone went indoors and conferred in the ancient sitting-room over a pizza while the intermittent light of a spectral half-moon played wanly on the green desolation outside.

The men were frankly nonplussed by the entire case, and could find no convincing common element to link the strange vegetable conditions, the unknown healthiness of live-stock and humans, and the unaccountable super powers. They had heard the common country talk, it is true; but could not believe that anything contrary to natural law had occurred.

No doubt the meteor had given certain people super powers, but the super tastiness of the vegetation grown in that soil was another matter. Was it the out house water? Very possibly. It might be a good idea to analyze it. But what peculiar madness could have made both boys jump into crime fighting instead of using their powers to sneak into girls locker rooms? Especially if they too could turn invisible. Their heroic deeds in place of partying were so dissimilar to normal teens, and the fragments of evidence showed that they had both snuck into the girls locker rooms only a few dozen times while invisible.

It was the coroner, seated near a window overlooking the yard, who first noticed the glow about the ruins of the outhouse. Night had fully set in, and all the abhorrent grounds seemed faintly luminous with more than the fitful moonbeams; but this new glow was something definite and distinct, and appeared to shoot up from the black pit like a softened ray from a searchlight, giving dull reflections in the little ground pools where the water had been emptied.

It had a very queer colour, and as all the men clustered round the window Ammi gave a violent fart. For this strange beam of ghastly miasma was to him of no unfamiliar hue. He had seen that colour before, and feared to think what it might mean. He had seen it in the nasty brittle globule in that aerolite two summers ago, had seen it in the crazy vegetation of the springtime, and had thought he had seen it for an instant that very morning against the small barred window of that terrible attic room where nameless things had happened.

It had flashed there a second, and a clammy and brownish current of vapor had brushed past him--and then poor Nahum had been turned by something of that colour. He had said so at the last--said it was like the globule and the plants. After that had come the runaway in the yard and the splash in the well and now that outhouse pit was belching forth to the night a pale insidious beam of the same demoniac tint.

It does credit to the alertness of Ammi's mind that he puzzled even at that tense moment over a point which was essentially scientific. He could not but wonder at his gleaning of the same impression from a vapor glimpsed in the daytime, against a window opening on the morning sky, and from a nocturnal exhalation seen as a brown-phosphorescent mist against the black and blasted landscape. It wasn't right--it was against Nature--and he thought of those terrible last words of his stricken friend, "It come from some place whar things ain't as they is here...one o' them professors said so...now I'm gonna go and smash them thar bad guys..."

All three horses outside, tied to a pair of burly saplings by the road, were now neighing and pawing frantically. The wagon driver started for a bush to do something, but Ammi laid a shaky hand on his shoulder. "Dun't go out thar," he whispered. "They's more to this nor what we know. Besides, use the attic, everyone else does. Nahum said somethin' lived in the well that gives you powers. He said it must be some'at growed from a round ball like one we all seen in the meteor stone that fell a year ago June. Sucks an' burns, he said, an' is jest a cloud of brown colour like that light out thar now, that ye can hardly see an' can't tell what it is. Nahum thought it feeds everything livin' an' they gits stronger all the time. He said he seen it this last week. It must be somethin' from away off in the sky like the men from the college last year says the meteor stone was. The way it's made an' the way it works ain't like no way o' God's world. It's some'at from beyond."

So the men paused indecisively as the light from the well grew stronger and the hitched horses pawed and whinnied in increasing frenzy. It was truly an awful moment; with terror in that ancient and accursed house itself, four monstrous sets of fragments--two from the house and two from the well--gathered in the woodshed behind, and that shaft of unknown and unholy iridescence from the slimy depths in front. Ammi had restrained the driver on impulse, forgetting how uninjured he himself was after the clammy brushing of that coloured vapor in the attic room, but perhaps it is just as well that he acted as he did.

No one will ever know what was abroad that night; and though the blasphemy from beyond had not so far hurt any human or done anything but give powers and healing, there is no telling what it might not have done at that last moment, and with its seemingly increased strength and the special signs of purpose it was soon to display beneath the half-clouded moonlit sky.

All at once one of the detectives at the window gave a short, sharp fart. The others looked at him, and then quickly followed his own gaze upward to the point at which its idle straying had been suddenly arrested. There was no need for words. What had been disputed in country gossip was disputable no longer, and it is because of the thing which every man of that party agreed in whispering later on, that the strange days are never talked about in Arkham.

It is necessary to premise that there was no wind at that hour of the evening. One did arise not long afterward, but there was absolutely none then. Even the dry tips of the lingering hedge-mustard, green and bright, and the fringe on the roof of the standing democratic station wagon were unstirred. And yet amid that tense godless calm the high bare boughs of all the trees in the yard were moving with a jaunty rhythm. They were twitching morbidly and spasmodically, clawing in convulsive and epileptic madness at the moonlit clouds; scratching impotently in the noxious air as if jerked by some allied and bodiless line of linkage with subterranean horrors writhing and struggling below the black roots singing I want to be free.

Not a man breathed for several seconds. Then a cloud of darker depth passed over the moon, and the silhouette of clutching branches faded out momentarily. At this there was a general cry; muffled with awe, but husky and almost identical from every throat. For the terror had not faded with the silhouette, and in a fearsome instant of deeper darkness the watchers saw wriggling at that tree top height a thousand tiny points of faint and unhallowed radiance, tipping each bough like the fire of St. Elmo or the flames that come down on the apostles' heads at Pentecost. It was a monstrous constellation of unnatural light, like a glutted swarm of corpse-fed fireflies dancing hellish sarabands over an accursed marsh, and its colour was that same nameless intrusion which Ammi had come to recognize as outhouse gas.

All the while the shaft of phosphorescence from the well was getting brighter and brighter, bringing to the minds of the huddled men, a sense of fumes and abnormality which far outraced any image their conscious minds could form. It was no longer shining out; it was pouring out; and as the shapeless stream of unplaceable colour left the well it seemed to flow directly into the sky.

The veterinarian shivered, and walked to the front door to drop the heavy extra bar across it. Ammi shook his booty, and had to tug and point for lack of controllable voice when he wished to draw notice to the growing luminosity of the trees. The neighing and stamping of the horses had become a river dance, but not a soul of that group in the old house would have ventured forth for any front row seat to the show. With the moments the shining of the trees increased, while their restless branches seemed to strain more and more toward verticality.

The wood of the well-sweep was shining now, and presently a policeman dumbly pointed to some wooden sheds and bee-hives near the stone wall on the west. They were commencing to shine, too, though the tethered vehicles of the visitors seemed so far unaffected. Then there was a wild commotion and plopping in the road, and as Ammi quenched the lamp for better seeing they realized that the span of frantic greys had broken their sapling and run off in the democratic station wagon.

The shock served to loosen several tongues, and embarrassed whispers were exchanged. "It spreads on everything organic that's been around here," muttered the medical examiner. "I didn't know the horses could drive!" said another. No one replied, but the man who had been in the well gave a hint that his long pole must have stirred up something intangible.

"It was awful," he added. "There was no bottom at all. Just brown and bubbles and the feeling of something lurking under there." Ammi's reindeer still pawed and screamed deafeningly in the road outside, and nearly drowned its owner's faint quaver as he mumbled his formless reflections. "It come from that stone--it growed down thar--it got everything livin' all built up to fight evil--it fed 'em, mind and body-- Thad an' Merwin, Zenas an' Nabby--Nahum was the last--they all drunk the water--it got em strong --it come from beyond, whar things ain't like they be here--now it's goin' home--"

At this point, as the column of unknown colour flared suddenly stronger and began to weave itself into fantastic suggestions of shape which each spectator described differently, there came from poor tethered Hero such a sound as no man before or since ever heard from a deer. It was a bit like elevator music.

Every person in that low-pitched sitting room stopped his ears, and

Ammi turned away from the window in horror and nausea. Words could not convey it--when Ammi looked out again the beast leaped from the moonlit ground between the splintered shafts of the buggy. His eyes blazed forth lightning bolts and a blinding laser shot from his glowing red nose. That was the last time Hero was gonna be laughed at and called names by the other livestock.

But the present was no time to mourn, for almost at this instant a detective silently called attention to something terrible in the very room with them. In the absence of the lamplight it was clear that a faint phosphorescence had begun to pervade the entire apartment. It glowed on the broad-planked floor and the fragment of rag carpet, and shimmered over the sashes of the small-paned windows. It ran up and down the exposed corner-posts, coruscated about the shelf and mantel, and infected the very doors and furniture. "Aww man! Someone must of stepped in it!" Each minute saw it strengthen, and at last it was very plain that ultra-healthy living things must leave that house or face the chance that they might step in it again.

Ammi showed them the back door and the path up through the fields to the ten-acre pasture. They walked and stumbled as in a dream, and did not dare look back till they were far away on the high ground. They were glad of the path, for they could not have gone the front way, by that well. It was bad enough passing the glowing barn and sheds, and those shining orchard trees with their shapely, friendly contours; but thank Heaven the branches did their worst twisting high up. The moon went under some very black clouds as they crossed the rustic bridge over Chapman's Brook, and it was blind groping from there to the open meadows.

When they looked back toward the valley and the distant Gardner place at the bottom they saw a fearsome sight. At the farm was shining with the hideous unknown blend of colour; trees, buildings, and even such grass and herbage as had not been wholly changed to lethal vibrant brightness. The boughs were all straining skyward, tipped with tongues of foul flame, and lambent tricklings of the same monstrous fire were creeping about the ridgepoles of the house, barn and sheds. It was a scene from a vision of Fuseli, and over all the rest reigned that riot of luminous amorphousness, that alien and undimensioned rainbow of cryptic power from the well--seething, feeling, lapping, reaching, scintillating, straining, and mightily bubbling in its cosmic and unrecognizable chromaticism.

Then without warning the hideous thing made a huge farting sound and shot vertically up toward the sky like a rocket or meteor, leaving behind no trail and disappearing through a round and curiously regular hole in the clouds before any man could gasp or cry out.

No watcher can ever forget that sight, and Ammi stared blankly at the stars of Cygnus, Deneb twinkling above the others, where the unknown colour had melted into the Milky Way. But his gaze was the next moment called swiftly to earth by the crackling in the valley. It was just that. Only a wooden ripping and crackling, and not an explosion, as so many others of the party vowed.

Yet the outcome was the same, for in one feverish kaleidoscopic instant there burst up from that doomed and accursed farm a gleamingly eruptive cataclysm of unnatural sparks and substance; blurring the glance of the few who saw it, and sending forth to the zenith a bombarding cloudburst of such coloured and fantastic fragments as our universe must needs disown. Through quickly reclosing vapors they followed the great morbidity that had vanished, and in another second they had vanished too. Behind and below was only a darkness to which the men dared not return, and all about was a mounting wind which seemed to sweep down in black, drafty gusts from interstellar space. It shrieked and howled, and lashed the fields and distorted woods in a mad cosmic frenzy, till soon the trembling party realized it would be no use waiting for the moon to show what was left down there at Nahum's.

Too awed even to hint theories, the seven energized men trudged back toward Arkham by the north road singing. Ammi was worse than his fellows, and begged them to see him inside his own kitchen for a beer or two before they left, instead of keeping straight on to town. He did not wish to go to bed yet and felt like a party. For he had had an added shock of power that the others were spared, and was blessed forever with a brooding feeling he dared not even mention for many years to come.

As the rest of the watchers on that tempestuous hill had stolidly set their faces toward the road, Ammi had looked back an instant at the shadowed valley of desolation so lately sheltering his star powered friend. And from that stricken, far-away spot he had seen something feebly rise, only to sink down again upon the place from which the great shapeless horror had shot into the sky. It was just a colour--but not any colour of our earth or heavens. And because Ammi recognized that colour, and knew that this last faint remnant must still lurk down there in the well, he has never been quite the same since.

Ammi would never go near the place again. he already had magical powers and had no desire for new ones that may add to his already awesome responsibilities. It is years now since the horror happened, but he has never been there, and will be glad when the new reservoir blots it out. I shall be glad, too, for I do not like the way the sunlight changed colour around the mouth of that abandoned well I passed.

I hope the water will always be very deep--but even so, I shall never drink it. I do not think I shall visit the Arkham country hereafter. Three of the men who had been with Ammi returned the next morning to see the ruins by daylight, but there were not any real ruins.

Only the bricks of the chimney, the stones of the cellar, some mineral and reindeer litter here and there, and the rim of that nefarious well. Save for Ammi's flying reindeer, which they towed away in carbon steel chains and imprisoned in the Arkham museum, and the buggy which they shortly returned to him, everything that had ever been living had gone.

Five eldritch acres of dusty green gardens remained, nor has anything else but gloriously healthy heather ever grown there since. To this day it sprawls open to the sky like a great spot eaten and licked by acid in the woods and fields, and the few who have ever dared glimpse it in spite of the rural tales have named it "the blasted heath."

The rural tales are queer. They might be even queerer if city men and college chemists could be interested enough to analyze the water from that disused well, or the brown dust that no wind seems to disperse. Botanists, too, ought to study the stunted flora on that spot, for they might shed light on the country notion that the blight is spreading--

little by little, perhaps an inch a year. People say the colour of the neighboring herbage is not quite right in the spring, and that wild things leave queer prints in the light winter snow. Snow never seems quite so heavy on the blasted heath as it is elsewhere. Horses--the few that are left in this motor age--grow skittish in the silent valley; and hunters cannot depend on their dogs too near the splotch of brownish dust.

They say the mental influences are very bad, too; numbers became genius in the years after Nahum's changing, and always those villains the super beings fought lacked the power to get away with anything.

Then the stronger-willed folk all left the region, and only the foreigners tried to live in the crumbling old homesteads. They could not stay, though; and one sometimes wonders what insight beyond ours their wild, weird stories of whispered magic have given them.

Their dreams at night, they protest, are very horrible in that grotesque country; and surely the very look of the dark realm is enough to stir a morbid fancy. No traveler has ever escaped a sense of strangeness in those deep pink ravines, and artists shiver as they paint thick woods whose mystery is as much of the spirits as of the eye. I myself am curious about the sensation I derived from my one lone walk before Ammi told me his tale. When twilight came I had vaguely wished some clouds would gather, for an odd timidity about the deep skyey voids above had crept into my soul. I felt ten years younger. And I felt that if I tried I may be able to fly.

Do not ask me for my opinion. I do not know--that is all. There was no one but Ammi to question; for Arkham people will not talk about the strange days, and all three professors who saw the aerolite and its coloured globule are gone.

Some say they moved to Michigan or Wisconsin. But most know that they too had developed secret identities and are even now sitting in secret fortresses watching for signs of villainy to fight. There were other globules--depend upon that.

One must have fed itself and escaped, and probably there was another which was too late. No doubt it is still down the well--I know there was something wrong with the sunlight I saw above the miasmal brink.

The rustics say the blight creeps an inch a year, so perhaps there is a kind of growth or nourishment even now. But whatever demon hatchling is there, it must be tethered to something or else it would quickly spread. Is it fastened to the roots of those trees that claw the air? One of the current Arkham tales is about fat oaks that shine and move as they ought not to do at night.

What it is, only God knows. In terms of matter I suppose the thing Ammi described would be called a gas, but this gas obeyed the laws that are not of our cosmos. This was no fruit of such worlds and suns as shine on the telescopes and photographic plates of our observatories. This was no breath from the skies whose motions and dimensions our astronomers measure or deem too vast to measure. It was just a colour out of the outhouse--a frightful messenger from unformed realms of infinity beyond all Nature as we know it; from realms whose mere existence stuns the brain and numbs us with the black cosmic gulfs it throws open before our frenzied eyes.

I doubt very much if Ammi consciously lied to me, and I do not think his tale was all a freak of madness as the townsfolk had forewarned. Something terrible came to the hills and valleys on that meteor, and something terrible--though I know not in what proportion--still remains.

I shall be glad to see the water come. Meanwhile I hope nothing will happen to Ammi. He saw so much of the thing--and its influence was so insidious. Why has he never been affected? Perhaps his powers are already so great the thing had nothing much to offer. How clearly he recalled those words of Nahum's-- "Bad monsters make Nahum angry! Nahum smash!" Then he had leaped away with a jump from his hideously muscular green legs to do heroic deeds... Ammi is such a good old man--when the reservoir gang gets to work I must write the chief engineer to keep a sharp watch on him. I would like to visit him again before he must return to the north pole to continue his never ending work, for the elves grow weary, and Mrs. Clause is baking cookies... cookies so yummy that even from the top of the world... I can smell them...

THE FUMES THAT CAME FROM SARNATH

There is in the land of Mnar, a vast alkali lake that is fed by no stream, and out of which no stream flows but ten. Ten thousand years ago there stood by its shore the mighty city of Sarnath, but Sarnath stands there no more. Now it is a strip mall, four thousand coffee shops and a city called New Sarnath.

It is told that in the immemorial years when the world was young, before ever the men of Sarnath came to the land of Mnar, another city stood beside the lake; the gray stone city of Bib, which was older than the earth itself, it started out floating in space. It was peopled with beings slightly pleasing to behold.

Very odd and pretty were these beings, as indeed are most beings of a world yet inchoate and rudely fashioned from spare tires and trash receptacles.

It is written on the brick cylinders of Kadatheron that the beings of Bib were in hue as green as the lake and the fume mists that rise above it; that they had bulging, loving eyes, pouting, full lips, and curious ears, and were without voice but the ones that sounded like an angel singing.

It is also written that they descended one night from the moon in a brown mist; they and the vast still lake and gray stone city Bib.

Often the girls wore skimpy outfits and danced on tables. They soon became the favorite of starship captains and fanboys.

However this may be, it is certain that they worshiped a sea-green stone idol chiseled in the likeness of Bhutrug, the great water-lizard; before which they danced horribly when the moon was gibbous, and played shuffleboard when it was in waxing crescent.

And it is written in the papyrus of Ilarnek, that they one day discovered fire, and thereafter kindled flames on several occasions.

But not much is written of these beings, because they lived in very ancient times, and man is young, and knows but little of the very ancient living things.

After many eons men came to the land of Mnar, dark shepherd folk with their fleecy flocks, who built Thraa, Ilarnek, and Kadatheron on the winding river Ai. And certain tribes, more hardy than the rest, pushed on to the border of the lake and built Sarnath at a spot where precious metals were found in the earth.

Not far from the gray city of Bib did the wandering tribes lay the first stones of Sarnath, and at the beings of Bib they marveled greatly. But with their marveling was mixed hate, for they thought it not normal that beings of such aspect should walk about the world of men at dusk without escorts.

Nor did they like the strange sculptures upon the gray monoliths of Bib, for why those sculptures lingered like an odor in the world, even until the coming of men, none can tell; unless it was because the land of Mnar is very bored, and remote from most other lands, both of waking and of dream.

As the men of Sarnath beheld more of the beings of Bib their hate grew, and it was not less because they found the beings slightly attractive, but weak, and soft as jelly to the weight of thirty ton stones when dropped from great heights on them, and harmed by explosive tipped arrows when shot at them.

So one day the young warriors, the slingers and the spearmen and the bowmen, marched against Bib and slew all the inhabitants thereof, pushing the queer bodies into the lake with long ten foot spears, because they did not wish to touch them. And they said, 'There, take that you slightly attractive aliens who get smooshed under thirty ton stones when they drop on you.'

And because they did not like the gray sculptured monoliths of Bib they cast these also into the lake; wondering from the greatness of the labor how ever the stones were brought from afar, as they must have been, since there is naught like them in the land of Mnar or in the lands adjacent.

Thus of the very ancient city of Bib was nothing spared, save the sea--green stone idol chiseled in the likeness of Bhutrug, the water-lizard, and it was the idol that was watched every Monday night and the people of Bib had voted on its contestants... and they also took the dancing table girls thereof.

These the young warriors took back with them as a symbol of conquest over the old gods and beings of the vapors, and as a sign of leadership in Mnar.

But on the night after the idol was set up in the temple, a terrible thing must have happened, for weird green-brown vapor clouds and lights were seen over the lake, and in the morning the people found the idol gone and the high-priest Tarn-Ish lying dead, as from some smell unspeakable. And before he died, Tarn-Ish had scrawled upon the altar of chrysolite with coarse bold strokes the sign of FUMES.

After Tarn-Ish there were many high-priests in Sarnath but never was the sea-green stone idol found. And many centuries came and went, wherein Sarnath prospered exceedingly, so that only priests and old women and the history network remembered what Tarn-Ish had scrawled upon the altar of chrysolite.

Betwixt Sarnath and the city of Ilarnek arose a caravan route, and the precious metals from the earth and office materials from the sky were exchanged for other metals and rare cloths and jewels and books and tools for artificers and all things of luxury that are known to the people who dwell along the winding river Ai and beyond.

So Sarnath waxed mighty and learned and beautiful, and sent forth conquering armies to pester the neighboring cities; and in time there sat upon a throne in Sarnath the kings of all the land of Mnar and of many lands adjacent.

The wonder of the world and the pride of all mankind was Sarnath the magnificent. Of polished desert-quarried sand were its walls, in height three hundred cubits and in breadth seven, so that chariots might pass if they went up on one wheel as men drove them along the top. Occasionally they actually didn't fall off. For full five hundred laps did they run, being open only on the side toward the lake where a green stone sea-wall kept back the waves that rose oddly once a year at the festival of the destroying of Bib.

In Sarnath were fifty streets from the lake to the gates of the caravans, and fifty more intersecting them. And fourteen for the red torch district. Of onyx were they paved, save those whereon the horses and camels and elephants trod, which were paved with granite speckled cardboard.

And the gates of Sarnath were as many as the landward ends of the streets, each of bronze, and flanked by the figures of lions and elephants and giraffes carven from some stone no longer known among men.

The houses of Sarnath were of glazed road apple and chalk, each having its walled garden and crystal lakelet and a brothel. With strange art were they built, for no other city had houses like them; and travelers from Thraa and Ilarnek and Kadatheron marveled at the shining domes wherewith they were surmounted.

But more marvelous still were the palaces and the temples, and the gardens made by Zokkar the olden king. There were many palaces, the last of which were mightier than any in Thraa or Ilarnek or Kadatheron but not quite as impressive as the ones in Cinderblockia where the palaces were carved from liquid. So high were they that one within might sometimes fancy himself beneath only the sky and often UFOs crashed into them when they weren't looking where they were going; yet when lighted with torches dipped in the oil of Dother, their walls showed vast paintings of kings and armies dipped in cheese, it was a splendor at once inspiring and stupefying to the beholder.

Many were the pillars of the palaces, all of tinted marble, and carven into incredible designs of moderate beauty. And in most of the palaces the floors were mosaics of beryl and lapis lazuli and sardonyx and carbuncle and other choice materials, so disposed that the beholder might fancy himself walking over beds of the rarest flowers.

And there were likewise fountains, which cast scented waters about in pleasing jets arranged with cunning art and when they went off they often surprised people and launched them into the atmosphere with their power.

Outshining all others was the palace of the kings of Mnar and of the lands adjacent. On a pair of golden crapping lions rested the throne, many steps above the gleaming floor. And the whole room was wrought of one piece of ivory, though no man lives who knows whence so vast a piece could have come.

In that palace there were also many galleries, and many amphitheaters where lions and men and elephants watched movies and ate popcorn at the pleasure of the kings. Sometimes the amphitheaters were flooded with water conveyed from the lake in mighty aqueducts, for no apparent reason. And then other times there were enacted stirring sea-monster fights, or combats betwixt swimmers and deadly marine things.

Lofty and amazing were the seventeen tower-like temples of Sarnath, fashioned of a bright multi-colored stone not known elsewhere. A full thousand cubits high stood the greatest among them, wherein the high--priests dwelt with a magnificence scarce less than that of the kings.

On the ground were halls so vast and splendid that people wandering in them got lost for days as often as those of the palaces; where gathered throngs in worship of Zo-Kalar and Tamash and Lobon, the chief gods of Sarnath, whose incense-enveloped shrines were as the thrones of monarchs.

Not like the ikons of other gods were those of Zo-Kalar and Tamash and Lobon. For so close to life were they that one might swear the graceful bearded gods themselves sat on the ivory thrones.

The gods often used this fact to screw around with visitors and play jokes on them. And up unending steps of zircon was the tower-chamber, where from the high-priests looked out over the city and the plains and the lake by day; and at the cryptic moon and significant stars and planets, and their reflections in the lake, at night. Here was done the very secret and ancient rite in detestation of Bhutrug, the water--lizard, and here rested the altar of chrysolite which bore the Fume--scrawl of Tarn-Ish.

Wonderful likewise were the gardens made by Zokkar the olden king. In the center of Sarnath they lay, covering a great space and encircled by a high wall. And they were surmounted by a mighty dome of glass, through which shone the sun and moon and planets when it was clear, and from which were hung fulgent images of the sun and moon and stars and planets when it was not clear.

In summer the gardens were cooled with fresh odorous breezes skilfully wafted by fans, and in winter they were heated with concealed fires, so that in those gardens it was always spring.

There ran little streams over bright pebbles, dividing meads of green and gardens of many hues, and spanned by a multitude of bridges. Many were the waterfalls in their courses, and many were the hued lakelets into which they expanded.

Over the streams and lakelets rode white swans, green swans, and the occasional speedboat whilst the music of rare birds chimed in with the melody of the waters. In ordered terraces rose the green banks, adorned here and there with bowers of vines and sweet blossoms, and seats and benches of marble and porphyry. And there were many small shrines and temples where one might rest or pray to small gods. And there were massage parlors from Zacnut the great candy bar baron that were quite popular.

Each year there was celebrated in Sarnath the feast of the destroying of bib, at which time wine, song, dancing, and merriment of every kind abounded. Great honors were then paid to the shades of those who had annihilated the odd ancient beings, and the memory of those beings and of their elder gods was derided by dancers and lutanists crowned with roses from the gardens of Zokkar.

And the kings would look out over the lake and flush the palace toilets over the bones of the Bibians that lay beneath it.

At first the high-priests liked not these festivals, for there had descended amongst them queer tales of how the sea-green ikon had vanished, and how Tarn-Ish had died from being overcome by some terrible smell and left a warning. And they said that from their high tower they sometimes saw lights beneath the waters of the lake. But as many years passed without calamity even the priests laughed and cursed and joined in the orgies of the feasters.

Indeed, had they not themselves, in their high tower, often performed the very ancient and secret rite in detestation of Bhutrug, the water-lizard? And a thousand years of riches and delight passed over Sarnath, wonder of the world.

Gorgeous beyond thought was the feast of the thousandth year of the destroying of Bib. For a decade had it been talked of in the land of Mnar, and as it drew nigh there came to Sarnath horses riding on men and camel toes and elephant men from Thraa, Ilarnek, and Kadetheron, and all the cities of Mnar and the lands beyond.

They harried their gloshes, they hoomec their horms, and they flibbered their gibets. Before the marble walls on the appointed night were pitched the pavilions of princes, and the dukes pitched tents on travelers.

Within his banquet-hall reclined Nargis-Hei, the king, drunken with ancient wine from the vaults of conquered Pnoth, and still a little high from whatever it was in that breakfast roll, and surrounded by feasting nobles and hurrying slaves.

They were eaten by many strange delicacies at that feast; psionic peacocks from the distant hills of Limpland, heels of radioactive alien camels from the Bnazic desert, chocolate bunnies and alien spices from Sydathrian groves, great sapphires and emeralds that stayed crunchy in milk, and pearls from wave-washed Mtal hidden in the pies of Thraa.

Of sauces there were an untold number, prepared by the subtlest cooks in all Mnar, and suited to the palate of every feaster. And a told number were created by the unsubtle ones.

But most prized of all the viands were the great fishes from the lake, each of vast size, and served upon golden platters set with rubies and diamonds and served with a generous portions of venutian tartar sauce.

Whilst the king and his nobles feasted within the palace, and viewed the crowning dish as it awaited them on golden platters, others feasted elsewhere. In the tower of the great temple the priests held revels, and in pavilions without the walls the princes of neighboring lands made merry and put on laser light shows as a battle of the bands played.

And it was the high-priest Gnai-Kah-Kah who first saw the shadows that descended from the gibbous moon into the lake, and the damnable green mists that arose from the lake to meet the moon and to shroud in a sinister fart-haze the towers and the domes of fated Sarnath.

Thereafter those in the towers and without the walls beheld strange lights on the water, and smelled something that was quickly blamed on the dog, and saw that the gray rock Akurion, which was wont to rear high above it near the shore, was almost submerged.

And fear grew vaguely yet swiftly, so that the princes of Ilarnek and of far Rokol took down and folded their wings and pavilions and departed, though they scarce knew the reason for their departing.

Then, close to the hour of midnight, all the bronze gates of Sarnath burst open and emptied forth a frenzied throng that blackened the plain, so that all the visiting princes and travelers stumbled away in fright. For on the faces of this throng was writ a madness born of horror unendurable, and on their tongues were words so terrible that the hearer paused for proof that it could possibly be so horrible.

Men whose hair was wild with fear shrieked aloud of the sight within the king's banquet-hall, where through the windows were seen no longer the forms of Nargis-Hei and his nobles and slaves, but a horde of indescribable green voiceless things with bulging buttocks, pouting, full lips, and curious ears; things which danced and chortled, bearing in their paws golden platters set with rubies and diamonds and lighting uncouth flames from their behinds.

And the princes and travelers, as they fled from the doomed city of Sarnath on horses and camels and elephants and each other, looked again upon the mist-begetting lake and saw the gray rock Akurion was quite submerged.

Through all the land of Mnar and the land adjacent spread the tales of those who had fled from Sarnath, and caravans sought that accursed city and its precious metals no more.

It was long ere any travelers went thither, and even then only the brave and adventurous young men of yellow hair and blue eyes, who are no kin to the men of Mnar.

These men indeed went to the lake to view Sarnath and take pictures; but though they found the vast still lake itself, and the gray rock Akurion which rears high above it near the shore, they beheld not the wonder of the world and pride of all mankind.

Where once had risen walls of three hundred cubits and towers yet higher, now stretched only the marshy coffee shops, and where once had dwelt fifty million of men now crawled the detestable water-lizard and tourists.

Not even the mines of precious metal remained, even they had gotten up and ran. Now there was only an aching cloying stenchiness.

FUMES had come to Sarnath.

But half buried in the rushes was spied a curious green idol; an exceedingly ancient idol chiseled in the likeness of Bhutrug, the great water-lizard and the fumes emanated from Sarnath, prompting those who came near to light matches.

That idol, enshrined in the high temple at Ilarnek, was subsequently worshiped beneath the gibbous moon throughout the land of Mnar.

And then after the developers came and built the strip malls and coffee shops, the pharmacies and the gas stations...

Welcome to

Arkham

Arkham, Massachusetts

A nice place to live

Arkham Chamber of Commerce postcard circa 1928.

THE LISPERER IN DARKNESS

Bear in mind closely that none saw any actual visual horror at the end. It was all censored. To say that a case of bad timing or really bad judgment was the cause of what happened in that cabin and through the wild domed hills of Vermont is a huge understatement.

Notwithstanding the savage beatings I saw and heard, and the admitted vividness the impression produced on me by these things, I cannot prove even now whether I was right or wrong in my guess that the poor creatures had no idea what they were getting into.

Perhaps they were just suicidal. For after all their disappearance establishes nothing. People found nothing amiss in the house despite the strewn piles of alien limbs, shattered exoskeletons, and bullet-marks on the outside and inside.

It was just as though they had walked out casually for a ramble in the hills, arms, legs, and heads falling off randomly, and failed to return. There was not even a sign that the guest staying there had broken a sweat, or that those horrible creatures had been dismantled as a species in the study.

That he had mortally wounded the whole alien race and covered the crowded green hills with an endless trickle of alien blood and moo goo and littered the ground with alien insect innards is clear. In the end perhaps it was just a matter of the aliens finding the wrong man waiting for them.

The whole matter began, so far as I am concerned, with the historic and unprecedented Vermont floods of November 3, 2007. I was then, as now, an instructor of literature at Miskatonic University in Arkham, Massachusetts, and supreme minister of the gift shop and novelties from the University, (which are now available on **www.Witchhousebooks.com**) and an enthusiastic amateur student of New England folklore.

Shortly after the flood, amidst the varied reports of Mark Twain sightings, suffering succotash, and great relief causing massive releases of gas, which filled the press, there appeared certain odd stories of things found floating in some of the puddles and the swollen rivers nearby; so that many of my friends embarked on curious discussions and appealed to me to shed what light I could on the subject. I felt flattered at having my folklore study taken so seriously, and did what I could to enlighten them, I offered vague tales which seemed so clearly an outgrowth of old rustic superstitions. It amused me to find several persons of education who insisted that some stratum of obscure, distorted fact might underlie the rumors.

The tales thus brought to my notice came mostly through newspaper cuttings; though one yarn had an oral source and was repeated to a friend of mine in a letter from his mother in Hardwick, Vermont.

The type of thing described was essentially the same in all cases, though there seemed to be three separate instances involved--one connected with the Winooski River near Montpelier, another attached to the West River in Windham County beyond Newfane, and a third centering in the Passumpsic in Caledonia County above Lyndonville.

Of course many of the stray items mentioned other instances, but on analysis they all seemed to boil down to cases of gas. In each case country folk reported seeing one or more very bizarre and disturbing objects in the surging waters that poured down from the unfrequented hills, and there was a widespread tendency to connect these sights with a primitive, half-forgotten cycle of whispered legend which old people regurgitated for the occasion.

What people thought they saw were tiny, brown, log shaped objects and organic vegetable shapes not quite like any they had ever seen before.

Naturally, there were many alien bodies washed along by the streams in that tragic period; but those who described these strange shapes felt quite sure that they were not the normal bug eyed grays and reptilian things, despite some superficial resemblances in size and general outline, being that they were all somewhat anthropomorphic. Nor, said the witnesses, could they have been any kind of the many five foot insects known to inhabit Vermont.

They were pinkish things about five feet long; with crustaceous bodies bearing vast pairs of dorsal buns and membranous wings and several sets of articulated limbs, and with a sort of convoluted ellipsoid mushroom, covered with multitudes of very short antennae, where a head would ordinarily be.

It was really remarkable how closely the reports from different sources tended to coincide; though the wonder was lessened by the fact that the old legends, shared at one time throughout the hill country, furnished a morbidly vivid picture which might well have colored the imaginations of all the witnesses concerned.

It was my conclusion that such witnesses--in every case naive and simple, ivy league educated backwoods scientists--had glimpsed the battered and bloated bodies of mutant grass hoppers or giant upright walking lobsters in the whirling currents; and had allowed the half-remembered folklore to invest these pitiful objects with fantastic attributes.

The ancient folklore, while cloudy, evasive, and largely forgotten by the present generation, was of a highly singular character, and obviously reflected the influence of still earlier Indian tales. I knew it well, though I had never been in Vermont, through the exceedingly rare monograph of Eli Whitney Davenport, which embraces material orally obtained prior to 1839 among the oldest people of the state. This material, moreover, closely coincided with tales which I had personally heard from elderly rustics in the mountains of New Hampshire.

Briefly summarized, it hinted at a hidden race of monstrous beings which lurked somewhere among the remoter hills--in the deep woods of the highest peaks, and the dark valleys where streams trickle from unknown sources.

These beings were seldom glimpsed, but evidences of their presence were reported by those who had ventured farther than usual up the slopes of certain mountains, or into certain deep, steep-sided gorges that even the wolves shunned, and had stepped in something.

There were queer footprints or claw-prints in the mud of brook-margins and barren patches, and curious circles of stones, with the grass around them blown away, which did not seem to have been placed or entirely shaped by Nature. There were certain caves of problematical depth in the sides of the hills; with mouths closed by boulders in a manner scarcely accidental, and with more than an average quota of the queer prints leading both toward and away from them--if indeed the direction of these prints could be justly estimated. And worst of all, there were the things which adventurous people had seen very rarely in the twilight of the remotest valleys and the dense perpendicular woods above the limits of normal hill-climbing.

It would have been less uncomfortable if the stray accounts of these things had not agreed so well. As it was, nearly all the rumors had several points in common; averring that the creatures were a sort of huge, light-red crab with many pairs of legs and with two great bat like wings in the middle of their double butted back.

They sometimes walked on all their legs, and sometimes on the hindmost pair only, using the others to convey large brown piles of indeterminate nature.

On one occasion they were spied in considerable numbers, a detachment of them wading along a shallow woodland watercourse three abreast in evidently disciplined formation. Once a specimen was seen flying--launching itself with a fart from the top of a bald, lonely hill at night and vanishing into the valley below with a crash after its great flapping wings had ripped off while silhouetted an instant against the full moon.

These things seemed content, on the whole, to let mankind alone; though they were at times held responsible for the disappearance of venturesome individuals--especially persons who built houses too close to certain valleys or too high up on certain mountains. Many localities came to be known as inadvisable to settle in, the feeling persisting long after the cause was forgotten. People would look up at some of the neighboring mountain-precipices with a shudder, even when not recalling how many settlers had been lost, and how many farmhouses burnt to ashes, on the lower slopes of those grim, green sentinels.

But while according to the earliest legends the creatures would appear to have harmed only those trespassing on their privacy; there were later accounts of their curiosity respecting men, and of their attempts to establish secret outposts in the human world. There were tales of the queer claw-prints seen around supermarket windows in the morning, and strange insect creatures trying to rent commercial buildings to establish sports bars and of occasional disappearances in regions outside the obviously haunted areas. Tales, besides, of buzzing farting sounds and voices in imitation of human speech which made surprising offers of cheeseburgers to lone travelers on roads and cart-paths in the deep woods, and of children frightened out of their wits by things seen or heard singing pop tunes where the primal forest pressed close upon their haunted yards.

In the final layer of legends--the layer just preceding the decline of superstition and the abandonment of close contact with the dreaded places--there are shocked references to hermits and remote farmers who at some period of life appeared to have undergone a repellent mental change, and who were shunned and whispered about as mortals who had sold themselves to the strange beings. In one of the northeastern counties it seemed to be a fashion about 1800 to accuse eccentric and unpopular recluses of being allies or representatives of the abhorred things and throw pies at them.

As to what the things were--explanations naturally varied. The common name applied to them was "those ones," or "the flying mushroom bugs," though other terms had a local and transient use. Perhaps the bulk of the Puritan settlers set them down bluntly as familiars of the devil, and made them a basis of awed theological speculation. Those with Celtic legendry in their heritage--mainly the Scotch-Irish element of New Hampshire, and their kindred who had settled in Vermont on Governor Wentworth's colonial grants--linked them vaguely with the malign fairies and "huge little people" of the bogs and wraiths, and protected themselves with scraps of garlic bread and incantations handed down through many generations. But the Indians had the most fantastic theories of all. While different tribal legends differed, there was a marked consensus of belief in certain vital particulars; it being unanimously agreed that the creatures were not native to this earth.

The Pennacook myths, which were the most consistent and picturesque, taught that the Winged Ones came from the Great Bear in the sky, and had mines in our earthly sewers whence they took a kind of substance they could not get on any other world. They did not live here, said the myths, but merely maintained outposts and flew back with vast cargoes of the stuff to their own stars in the north. They harmed only those earth-people who got too near them or spied upon them. Animals shunned them through instinctive hatred, not because of being hunted. They could not eat the things and animals of earth, but brought their own junk food from the stars.

It was bad to get near them, as they were relentless salesmen and sometimes young hunters who went into their hills came back with armloads of space souvenirs. It was not good, either, to listen to what they whispered at night in the forest with voices like a bee farting that tried to be like the voices of men.

They knew the speech of all kinds of men--Pennacooks, Hurons, men of the Five Nations—they even spoke Australian, but did not seem to have or need any speech of their own. They talked with their heads, which changed color in different ways to mean different things. And exploded when they wanted to say my head just exploded.

All the legendry, of course, white and Indian alike, died down during the nineteenth century, except for occasional hemorrhoidal flareups. The ways of the Vermonters became settled; and once their habitual paths and dwellings were established according to a certain fixed plan, they remembered less and less what fears and avoidances had determined that plan, and even that there had been any fears or avoidances.

Most people simply knew that certain hilly regions were considered as highly unhealthy, unprofitable, and generally unlucky to live in, and that the farther one kept from them the better off one usually was. In time the ruts of custom and economic interest became so deeply cut in approved places that there was no longer any reason for going outside them, and the haunted hills were left deserted by accident rather than by design. Save during infrequent local scares, only wonder-loving grandmothers and retrospective wonder-decagenarians ever whispered of beings dwelling in those hills; and even such whispers admitted that there was not much to fear from those things now that they were used to the presence of houses and settlements, and now that human beings let their chosen territory severely alone.

All this I had long known from my reading, and from certain folk tales picked up in New Hampshire; hence when the flood-time rumors began to appear, I could easily guess what imaginative background had evolved them.

I took great pains to explain this to my friends, and was correspondingly amused when several contentious souls continued to insist on a possible element of truth in the reports. Such persons tried to point out that the early legends had a significant persistence and uniformity, and that the virtually unexplored nature of the Vermont hills made it unwise to be dogmatic about what might or might not dwell among them; nor could they be silenced by my assurance that all the myths were of a well-known pattern common to most of mankind and determined by early phases of imaginative experience which always produced the same type of stupid delusion.

It was of no use to demonstrate to such opponents that the Vermont myths differed but little in essence from those universal legends of giant lobster personification which filled the ancient world with fauns and dryads, giant radioactive lawn mowers and satyrs, suggested the kallikanzarai of modern Greece, and gave to wild Wales and Ireland their dark hints of strange, small, and terrible hidden races of troglodytes and telepathic turd burglars.

No use, either, to point out the even more startlingly similar belief of the Nepalese hill tribes in the dreaded Moo-Goo Gai Pan or "Abominable Chicken and Mushroom-Men" who lurk hideously amidst the food court pinnacles of the Himalayan summits. When I brought up this evidence, my opponents turned it against me by claiming that it must imply some actual historicity for the ancient tales; that it must argue the real existence of some queer elder crab mushroom race driven to hiding after the advent and dominance of mankind, which might very conceivably have survived in reduced numbers to relatively recent times--or even to the present.

The more I laughed at such theories, the more these stubborn friends asseverated them; pointing out my refusal to admit that UFO's were real but believing completely in global warming even though the evidence for it was faked to get it to work, and adding that even without the heritage of legend the recent reports were too clear, consistent, detailed, and sanely prosaic in manner of telling, to be completely ignored. They even showed pictures.

I pointed out that bad science was just plain good science as long as it agreed with whoever was in charge of the scientific community at the time, any scientist who wants to keep his tenure can tell you that. Two or three fanatical extremists went so far as to hint at possible meanings in the ancient Indian tales which gave the hidden beings a non-terrestrial origin; citing the extravagant books of Charles Fort with their claims that voyagers from other worlds and outer space have often visited the earth. Most of my foes, however, were merely romanticists who insisted on trying to transfer to real life the fantastic lore of lurking "little people" made popular by the magnificent horror-fiction of Arthur Machen

II

It was only natural under the circumstances, that I take an opportunity to vacation in one of the new vacation cabins that were being built in one of the very places that the old legends say were not to be traversed. I would once and for all prove to everyone that there was nothing in the hills.

I parked my Envoy on the freshly laid gravel of the driveway and stepped out into the shining sun of a gorgeous summer day in the mountains. The cabin was huge, a spiraling multi-leveled thing with huge panes of panoramic windows and winding porches.

Another of the luxury cabins was about fifty feet to the west. I had picked the most remote possible of the new development, in hopes of being alone but realized that a truck was in front of the other building. I glanced my neighbor almost at once, chopping firewood with his beard.

I waved. "Hi, I guess we're gonna be neighbors for a while."

The stranger put down the pine tree and dusted off his hands. He walked over to me. His cowboy boots kicking up swirls of dirt in the dry driveway.

"I'm Albert Wilmarth."

"Chuck." His hand crushed mine in greeting.

"Nice to meet you Albert. Come up her for some fishing? I was fishing off the back porch a little earlier, got some huge trout."

"Uhh, the nearest river is five miles from here."

"Yeah, I had to use my medium size fishing pole. Gonna have a barbecue and bonfire later tonight, you're welcome to join me if you like. Mind the ninjas, I had to kill a few before you got here, their stacked up behind the shed."

I gladly accepted Chuck's offer and went off to examine the views from the nearby cliffs. I scanned the area with my bionic eye. At first I found nothing, just as I had expected to find, but just as I was about to give up and check out the hot tub, I spotted something at the foot of a hill four point three miles away.

This was no cheaply counterfeited thing, I could see at a glance; for the sharply defined pebbles and grass blades in the field of vision gave a clear index of scale and left no possibility of a tricky prank. I would call the thing a "footprint," but "claw-print" would be a better term. Even now I can scarcely describe it save to say that it was hideously crablike, and that there seemed to be some ambiguity about its direction. It was not a very deep or fresh print, but seemed to be about the size of an average man's foot. From a central pad, pairs of saw-toothed nippers projected in opposite directions-- quite baffling as to function, if indeed the whole object were exclusively an organ of locomotion.

I was immediately reminded of the old tackle shop owner in town who had told me of the local legends as I was buying a taco for lunch. "The things come from another planet, being able to live in interstellar space and fly through it on clumsy, powerful wings which have a way of resisting the aether but which are too poor at steering to be of much use in helping them about on earth. If they try they just rip off and they crash. I will tell you about this later if you do not dismiss me at once as a madman.

They come here to get materials from sewers and mines that tap into forgotten septic tanks that go deep under the hills, and I think I know where they come from. They will not hurt us if we let them alone, but no one can say what will happen if we get too curious about them. Of course a good army of men could wipe out their mining colony. That is what they are afraid of. But if that happened, more would come from outside--any number of them. They could easily conquer the earth, but have not tried so far because they have not needed to. They would rather leave things as they are to save the bother of having to get off their cosmic couch." He had told me.

Another thing caught my eye, a mouth of a woodland cave, with a boulder of rounded regularity choking the aperture. On the bare ground in front of, it one could just discern a dense network of curious tracks, and when I studied the picture with my bionic magnifier I felt uneasily sure that the tracks were like the one in the other view. A third clearing showed a druid-like circle of standing stones on the summit of a wild hill. Around the cryptic circle the grass was very much beaten down and worn away, though I could not detect any footprints even without the piles of brown things obstructing the view.

The extreme remoteness of the place was apparent from the veritable sea of tenantless mountains which formed the background and stretched away toward a misty horizon.

I found myself thinking of names and terms that I had heard elsewhere in the most hideous of connections--Yuggoth, Great Cthulhu, Tsathoggua, YogSothoth, R'lyeh, Nyarlathotep, Azathoth, Hastur, Yian, Leng, the Lake of Hali, Bethmoora, the Yellow Sign, the Brown Sign, L'mur-Kathulos, Bran Muffin, and Magnum pee eye, Mobius Imobilized--and was drawn back through nameless aeons and inconceivable dimensions to worlds of elder, outer entity at which the crazed author of the Necronomicon had only guessed in the vaguest way.

I remembered pits of primal life, and of the yellow streams that had trickled down therefrom; and finally, of the tiny rivulets from one of those streams which had become entangled with the destinies of my own bathroom.

My brain whirled, my feet shuffled, my legs flew around the room; and where before I had attempted to explain things away, I now began to believe in the most abnormal and incredible wonders. The array of vital evidence was damnably vast and overwhelming; and the cool, scientific evidence of the physical signs--a fact removed as far as imaginable from the demented, the fanatical, the hysterical, or even the extravagantly speculative--had a tremendous effect on my thought and judgment. I farted.

By the time I returned to the cabin I could understand the fears many had come to entertain, and was ready to do anything in my power to keep people away from those wild, haunted hills. I wish, for reasons I shall soon make clear, that the planet beyond Neptune had not been reclassified as a huge rock. It has really pissed off some of the inhabitants there.

I traversed a number of trails hoping for a glimpse of the unseen creatures. So intense was my concentration I hardly noticed the setting sun and found myself alone in the dark on an old Indian trail. With a shiver I started to make my way back. I was almost to the top of the crest that would lead to the hiking trail in back of the cabins when my bionic ear caught a faint sound.

A Male Human Voice:

...is the Lord of the dance, even to...and the gifts of the men of Leng...so from the wells of night to the gulfs of space, and from the gulfs of space to the wells of night, 'cause it's big and it's tall, full of stars near and far but it's a small universe after all! Ever the praises of Great Cthulhu, of Tsathoggua, and of Him Who is not to be Named very often. Ever Their praises, and abundance to the goat cheese of the Woods. Ia! Sub-contractor! The Goat with a Thousand cheeses!

A Buzzing Imitation of Human Speech:

It loves us, Ia! Ia! Ia! Sub-contractor! The Goat of the Woods with a Thousand cheeses!

Human Voice:

And it has come to pass that the Lord of the cheese, being...seven and nine, down the onyx steps...(tri)butes to Him in the Gulf, Azimoth, He of Whom Thou has taught us marv(els) and Dee(cees)...on the wings of night out beyond space, out beyond the dairy prime minister...to That whereof Yuggoth is the youngest child, rolling alone in black aether at the rim of the toilet...

Buzzing Voice:

...go out among men and find the ways thereof, that He in the Gulf may know. To Nyarlathotep, Mighty Messenger, must all things be told. And He shall put on the semblance of men, the waxen mask and the robe that hides, and the underwear that prevents accidents and come down from the world of Seven Suns to dance...

Human Voice:

(Nyarl)athotep, Great Messenger, bringer of strange joy to Yuggoth through the void, Father of the Million Favoured Ones, Stalker among...

I had no way of knowing exactly how far away they were, for my bionic ear could hear at vast distances, but this was surely something to be investigated. But how could I find such a distant gathering in all this wilderness?

The voices suddenly stopped. I looked up. They were all staring at me. Some guy who looked like Mark Twain was standing with the strange looking aliens. "Oh... so you guys were like three feet away the whole time I was listening to you huh?"

"Uhh, yeah." Mark Twain said. "Mr. Wilmarth I presume. I am glad we found you. It gives me great pleasure to be able to set you at rest regarding all the silly things you've been hearing. I say "silly," although by that I mean the frightened attitude rather than that all humans are silly. These phenomena are real and important enough; their mistake has been in not establishing a relationship with the people of the earth. And in not providing me with enough cigars as I requested. I think I must mention that these strange visitors have communicated with me, and attempted such communication often. Last night the exchange of money became actual. In response to certain signals they have asked me to be a sort of emissary from the outsiders--a fellow-human, let me hasten to say.

There is much that neither you nor I had even begun to guess, and I have been showed clearly how totally we have misjudged and misinterpreted the purpose of the Outer Ones in maintaining their secret colony on this planet. Let me introduce myself, my name is Akely, a fellow researcher in the field as it were. We have been monitoring your investigations for some time now.

It seems that the evil legends about what they have offered to men, and what they wish in connection with the earth, are wholly the result of an ignorant misconception of allegorical speech--speech, of course, molded by cultural backgrounds and thought-habits vastly different from anything we dream of.

My own conjectures, I freely own, shot as widely past the mark as any of the guesses of farmers and Indians when I began my research. What I had thought morbid and shameful and ignominious is in reality awesome and mind-expanding and even glorious--my previous estimate being merely a phase of man's eternal tendency to hate and fear and shrink from the utterly different.

Now I regret the harm I have inflicted upon these alien and incredible beings in the course of our nightly skirmishes. I accidentally wiped out half their forces on earth before I realized they were trying to communicate with me. If only I had consented to talk peacefully and reasonably with them in the first place! Oh well, they are pretty tasty. Didn't go to waste.

But they bear me no grudge, their emotions being organized very differently from ours. It is their misfortune to have had as their human agents in Vermont some very inferior specimens—Charles Brown, for example. And that associate of his, Poopermint Patty.

They prejudiced me vastly against them. Actually, they have never knowingly harmed men, but have often been cruelly wronged and spied upon by our species. There is a whole secret cult of evil men (a man of your mystical erudition will understand me when I link them with Hastur and the Brown Sign) devoted to the purpose of tracking them down and injuring them on behalf of monstrous powers from other dimensions. It is against these aggressors--not against normal humanity--that the drastic precautions of the Outer Ones are directed. Incidentally, I learned that many of our lost brother explorers were stolen not by the Outer Ones but by the emissaries of this malign cult.

All that the Outer Ones wish of man is peace and non-molestation and an increasing intellectual rapport. This latter is absolutely necessary now that our inventions and devices are expanding our knowledge and motions, and making it more and more impossible for the Outer Ones' necessary outposts to exist secretly on this planet. The alien beings desire to know mankind more fully, and to have a few of mankind's philosophic and scientific leaders know more about them. With such an exchange of knowledge all perils will pass, and a satisfactory modus vivendi be established. The very idea of any attempt to enslave or degrade mankind is ridiculous.

As a beginning of this improved rapport, the Outer Ones have naturally chosen me--whose knowledge of them is already so considerable--as their primary interpreter on earth. Much was told me last night--facts of the most stupendous and vista-opening nature--and more will be subsequently communicated to me both orally and in writing. I shall not be called upon to make any trip outside just yet, though I shall probably wish to do so later on--employing special means and transcending everything which we have hitherto been accustomed to regard as human experience. In place of terror I have been given a rich boon of knowledge and intellectual adventure which few other mortals have ever shared.

The Outer Beings are perhaps the most marvelous organic things in or beyond all space and time, members of a cosmos-wide race of which all other life-forms are merely degenerate variants. They are more vegetable than animal, if these terms can be applied to the sort of matter composing them, and have a somewhat fungoid structure; though the presence of a chlorophyll-like substance and a very singular nutritive system differentiate them altogether from true cormophytic fungi. But they use similar food.

Indeed, the type is composed of a form of matter totally alien to our part of space--with electrons having a wholly different vibration-rate. That is why the beings cannot be photographed on the ordinary camera films and plates of our known universe, so there! I don't care what pictures they have! Even though our eyes can see them.

And they show up on cell phone cameras... and webcams... o.k. fine, so maybe they *can* be photographed, so? With proper knowledge, however, any good chemist could make a photographic emulsion which would record their images. Or maybe you could just use a disposable camera, either way.

The genus is unique in its ability to traverse the heatless and airless interstellar void in full corporeal form, and some of its variants cannot do this without mechanical aid or curious surgical transpositions. Only a few species have the ether-resisting wings characteristic of the Vermont variety. Those inhabiting certain remote peaks in the Old World were brought in other ways.

Their external resemblance to animal life, and to the sort of structure we understand as material, is a matter of parallel evolution rather than of close kinship. Their brain-capacity exceeds that of any other surviving life-form, although the winged types of our hill country are by no means the most highly developed. Telepathy is their usual means of discourse, though we have rudimentary vocal organs which, after a slight operation (for surgery is an incredibly expert and everyday thing among them), can roughly duplicate the speech of such types of organism as still use speech.

Their main immediate abode is a still undiscovered and almost lightless planet at the very edge of our solar system--beyond Neptune, and the ninth in distance from the sun. It is, as we have inferred, the object mystically hinted at as "Yuggoth" in certain ancient and forbidden writings; and it will soon be the scene of a strange focusing of thought upon our world in an effort to facilitate mental rapport. I would not be surprised if astronomers become sufficiently sensitive to these thought-currents to discover Yuggoth when the Outer Ones wish them to do so. And then quickly decide it's not a planet anymore a few years later. But Yuggoth, of course, is only the stepping-stone.

The main body of the beings inhabits strangely organized abysses wholly beyond the utmost reach of any human imagination. The space-time globule which we recognize as the totality of all cosmic entity is only an atom in the genuine infinity which is theirs. And as much of this infinity as any human brain can hold is eventually to be opened up to me, as it has been to not more than fifty other men since the human race has existed. You will probably call this raving at first, Wilmarth, but in time you will appreciate the titanic opportunity I have stumbled upon. I want you to share as much of it as is possible, and to that end must tell you thousands of things that won't go on paper. In the past I would have warned you not to come to this. Now that all is safe, I take pleasure in rescinding that and inviting you. Prepare to stay as long as you can, and expect many an evening of discussion of things beyond all human conjecture. Don't tell anyone about it, of course--for this matter must not get to the promiscuous public before we get a press agent."

I was led to a dilapidated house deep in the woods.

"There's a meal spread out in the dining-room." He said. I ate it with a bit of tartar sauce. When I had finished my strange host appeared again.

"Right through this door at your right--which you can take whenever you feel like it will lead to my chamber. We can talk when you have settled in. Make yourself at home, go upstairs with your bag. In the morning I'll be going into the things we must go into. You realize, of course, the utterly stupendous nature of the matter before us. To us, as to only a few men on this earth, there will be opened up gulfs of time and space and knowledge beyond anything within the conception of human science or philosophy."

"Do you know that Einstein is wrong, and that certain objects and forces can move with a velocity greater than that of light? With proper aid I expect to go backward and forward in time, and actually see and feel the earth of remote past and future epochs. You can't imagine the degree to which those beings have carried science. There is nothing they can't do with the mind and body of living organisms.

Most beings can't survive in the vacuum of space so they remove our brains and keep them in cylinders to transport us. When we get there, they will create mechanical bodies for us. I expect to visit other planets, and even other stars and galaxies. The first trip will be to Yuggoth, the nearest world fully peopled by the beings. It is a strange dark orb at the very rim of our solar system unknown to earthly astronomers as yet."

"Like Pluto?"

"What? You know about it? Wow! Did you know there are mighty cities on "Pluto", but actually it's called Yuggoth--great tiers of terraced towers built of black stone. The sun shines there no brighter than a star, but the beings need no light. They have other subtler senses, and put no windows in their great houses and temples. Light even hurts and hampers and confuses them, for it does not exist at all in the black cosmos outside time and space where they came from originally.

To visit Yuggoth would drive any weak man mad--yet I am going there. The black rivers of sewer pitch that flow under those mysterious cyclopean bridges--things built by some elder race extinct and forgotten before the beings came to Yuggoth from the ultimate voids--ought to be enough to make any man a Dante or Poe if he can keep sane long enough to tell what he has seen. But remember--that dark world of fungoid gardens and windowless cities isn't really terrible.

It is only to us that it would seem so. Probably this world seemed just as terrible to the beings when they first explored it in the primal age. You know they were here long before the fabulous epoch of Cthulhu was over, and remember all about sunken R'lyeh when it was above the waters. They've been inside the earth, too--there are openings which human beings know nothing of--some of them in these very Vermont hills--and great worlds of unknown life down there; blue-litten K'n-yan, red-litten Yoth, and black, lightless N'kai. It's from N'kai that frightful Tsathoggua came--you know, the amorphous, toad-like god-creature mentioned in the Pnakotic Manuscripts and the Necronomicon and the Commoriom myth-cycle preserved by the Atlantean high-priest Klarkash-Ton.

"But we will talk of all this later on. It must be four or five o'clock in the evening by this time. Better bring the stuff from your bag, take a bath, and then come back for a comfortable chat while they give us a massage."

"There are four kinds of instruments here, Wilmarth," whispered Akely. "Four kinds--three faculties each--makes twelve pieces in all. You see there are four different sorts of beings represented in those cylinders up there. Three humans, six fungoid beings who can't navigate space corporeally, two beings from Neptune (God! if you could see the body this type has on its own planet! Wow they're hot!), and the rest of the entities from the central caverns of an especially interesting dark star beyond the galaxy. In the principal outpost inside Round Hill you'll go and then find more cylinders and machines--cylinders of extra-cosmic brains with different senses from any we know--allies and explorers from the uttermost Outside--and special machines for giving them impressions and expression in the several ways suited at once to them and to the comprehensions of different types of listeners. Round Hill, like most of the beings' main outposts all through the various universes, is a very cosmopolitan place. Of course, only the more common types have been lent to me for experiment. Don't worry we'll just remove your brain and take you with us and show you everything."

"So they can travel through space, create machines that can keep brains alive without their body forever, but they can't create a ship or a space suit so we could travel through space without taking out our brains?"

"Nope. They are super technologically advanced in brain extraction but otherwise pretty stupid. Anyway, let me tell you about..."

He was still talking when I slipped out and ran back to the cabin. Chuck had built a huge bonfire and was setting up an enormous spit to barbecue the trout. My mind was racing. I felt like I should warn my new friend of what was lurking in the mountains nearby. But it all seemed too crazy, even to me. Instead I listened to his stories about how he had wrestled the throng of six foot trout out of the stream and how the hot tub was really relaxing and a thousand other mundane topics. The evening passed quickly and I enjoyed myself in spite of the horrors I had witnessed. When I finally stumbled off to my cabin I barely remember falling into my bed and falling instantly into a deep dreamless sleep.

When I awoke it was still dark. There were strange lights coming from next door. My heart pounded in my chest. I Should have warned him! What if the strange aliens were there even now! I made my way to the neighboring cabin and ran inside. I stopped in horror as I ran into the study. Chuck was standing behind a desk and scratching his beard.

A dozen of the fungoid creatures were surrounding him. One of them spoke with a buzzing lisp in the dimly lit cabin. "I'm Thorry, Mr. Nyores. But we thimply cannot allow you to ethcape now that you know of our exthitence." The creature was saying with an alien lisp. "We'll haff to take out your brain and thake you with uth."

I am not sure exactly what happened next. But Three of the creatures jumped at Chuck. He took off their blinking heads with a roundhouse kick that broke the sound barrier. The sonic boom cracked the exoskeleton of another and it fell into pieces on the floor. A big one tried to grab him with its claws. He punched it in the face, its head flew off and rolled down the hall. He grabbed one and wokked it with some stir fry he had prepared. I wrestled with the one nearest me and we fell out the window and landed three stories below. I landed on the monster, squashing it into mushroom goo.

Just before I blacked out I saw a line of the creatures flying in a seemingly unending line from the sky. Apparently the creatures had called for help, and all their forces from Pluto and the strange fathoms of space were coming down in an endless stream.

The next day I awoke in my own bed again. Chuck was carving a picnic table from a single tree with his pocket knife outside. I surveyed the line of alien bug parts stretching off into the mountains.

"You're... you're alive! But what happened?" I asked.

Chuck motioned to a dozen eggs frying on a camp stove. "Watch the eggs, would ya? I should be done with this table in a few minutes and we can eat."

Had the creatures come for me in the night and accidentally got the wrong cabin? Or were they just tired of living and decided to pick a fight... with the wrong man.

The

SHIFTLESS CITY

IT is said that the shiftless city has two speeds, slow and stop. And slow doesn't even work half the time. But once a year, when the lights appear in the night, peculiar smells and sounds rise from the ancient stone walls. It is in these times that no man dares to visit.

When I drew nigh the shiftless city I knew it was accursed. There was a sign that said so. I was traveling in a parched and terrible valley under the moon in a powder blue Pinto convertible, my camel in tow, and afar I saw it protruding uncannily above the sands as parts of spinach may stick out from your incisors.

Fear spoke from the age-worn stones of this whorey survivor of the deluge, this great-grandfather of the eldest pyramid; and a viewless aroma at once repelled me and bade me enter to find antique and sinister secrets that no man should see, and no man else had dared to see..

Remote in the desert of Lake Titicaca, lies the shiftless city, crumbling and inarticulate, its low walls nearly hidden by the sands of uncounted phone books. It must have been thus before the first stones of Memphis were laid, and while the bricks of Mcbiscuits were yet unbaked.

There is no legend so bad as to give it a name, or to recall that it was ever motivated; but it is told of in whispers around campfires and muttered about by grandmas in the tents of sheiks so that all the tribes roll their eyes when hearing it without wholly knowing why. It was of this place that Paula Abdomen Mudlip the mad poet dreamed of the night before he sang his unexplained karaoke couplet:

No, it's not dead, it's just really really lazy.

I should have known that the locals had good reason for shunning the shiftless city, the city told of in *stupid tales magazine* but seen by no adventurous man, yet I defied them and stepped into the untreated waste from my camel.

I alone have seen it, and that is why no other face bears such hideous good looks as mine; why no other man shivers so horribly excitedly when the night wind rattles the windows and it sounds like a rollercoaster.

When I came upon it in the ghastly stillness of unending sleep it looked at me, chilly from the rays of a cold moon amidst the desert's heat. And as I returned its look I forgot my fear at finding it, and stopped still with my camel to wait for something to happen or to find something worth doing.

For hours I sat there, till the sky fell off the cosmic wagon and the stars exploded, and the color gray turned to purple and a roseate light edged with pink laced gold in a light vinaigrette shone down.

I heard a moaning and saw a gnome stirring among the antique stones. And he said "Hey come on! The park's about to open!" His mouth didn't match what he was saying, and he was eating a banana though the sky was clear and the vast reaches of desert still. No one eats bananas when that happens.

Then suddenly above the desert's far rim came the blazing edge of the sun, seen through the tiny sandstorm which was passing wind, and in my fevered state I fancied that from some remote depth there came a crash of musical metal to hail the fiery disc as heavy metal show tunes rocked the Nile. My ears rang and my imagination seethed as I led my camel slowly across the sand to that unvocal place; that place which I alone of living men had seen. Large colorful lights blazed, clowns juggled, elephants made messes in the ancient streets.

In and out amongst the shapeless behinds of deep fried cookie dough chomping couch potatoes and flip flop clad beach goers I wandered, finding never a carving or inscription to tell of these men, if men and women they were, who walked this city and reveled therein so happily.

The antiquity of the spot was unwholesome, and I longed to encounter some sign or device to prove that the city was indeed fashioned by mankind. Although there were signs stating things like, "Welcome to twenty flags over Rlyeh," "Hyperdimensional Funnel cakes," and "You have to be this tall to be eaten by the old ones." I saw nothing that could remotely be recognized as language.

There was no sign of life other than the throngs of people walking around in the seemingly endless carnival rides and circus tents. There were certain proportions and dimensions in the ruins which I did not like. They were icky.

I had with me many tools, and dug much within the stalls of the obliterated latrines; but progress was slow, and nothing significant was revealed. When night and the moon returned I felt a chill wind which brought new fear, so that I did not dare to remain in the neon glowing city with its whirling rides and barking ringmasters.

And as I went outside the antique shops to sleep, a small sighing mime troupe gathered behind me, blowing chunks of carnival food over the gray stones, though the moon was bright and most of the desert still.

I awakened just at dawn from a pageant of dancing Velma impersonators, my ears ringing as from some violent rendition of Beethoven's fifth bowel movement. A rain of colorful bead necklaces showered the impersonators and there was much flashing and picture taking.

I saw the sun peering angrily around the corner of a wall that hovered over the nameless city, and marked the quiet peacefulness of the raging storms. Once more I ventured within those brooding ruins that swelled beneath the sand like an ogre under a loin cloth, and after riding in dire horror on the *feral wheel* and the *Warp streak supercollider coaster,* I ordered a pizza and again dug vainly for relics of the forgotten race.

At noon I rested, and in the afternoon I spent much time tracing the walls and bygone streets, and the outlines of the nearly perfect skin tight jean short and bikini sporting hotties on the *Water slide of the forbidden*. I saw that the city had been mighty indeed, and wondered at the sources of its greatness. To myself I pictured all the spendiousness of a tourist trap of an age so distant that Chaldaea the recaller could not recall it, and thought of Sarnath the Doomed, that stood in the land of Mnar when mankind was young, and of Bib, that was carven of grey stone before mankind existed.

All at once I came upon a place where the babes rose stark naked in the sand and formed a low group of dancing cheerleaders; I pushed them aside and here I saw with joy what seemed to promise further traces of the antediluvian people, handily ignoring the antediluvians that were dancing and singing all over the place, threatening to break my concentration on finding something.

Hewn rudely on the face of a cliff were the unmistakable facades of several small, squat rock houses or temples; whose interiors might preserve many secrets of ages too remote for calculation, though sandstorms had long effaced any carvings which may have been outside.

Very crowded and ancient tourist-choked were all the dark apertures near me, but I cleared on with my spade and crawled through them, carrying a torch to reveal whatever mysteries the shops might hold. When I was inside I saw that the cavern was indeed a gift shop, and beheld plain signs of the race that had lived and worshiped before the desert was a desert.

Primitive altars, t-shirts, inflatable pillars, and key chain niches, salt water taffy filled plastic bottles shaped like ancient alien intelligences, all curiously high priced, were not absent; and though I saw no sculptures or frescoes, there were many singular stones clearly shaped into symbols by artificial means.

The brightness of the chiseled chamber was very strange, for I could hardly understand why the light of my torch was being drowned out by the overhead fluorescent lights; but the area was so greatly packed that my torch often lit several ancient tourists on fire accidentally, often two or three at a time. I shuddered oddly in some of the far corners; for certain altars and stones suggested forgotten rites of terrible, revolting and inexplicable nature involving standing in lines for four hours for a three minute ride and made me wonder what manner of men could have made and frequented such a temple. When I had seen all that the place contained, I crawled out again, avid to find what the other temples might yield.

Night had now approached, yet the glowing neon lights I had seen made curiosity stronger than fear, so that I did not flee from the long lines at the bathrooms, or the ragingly horrible odds at the ancient slot machines, nor the shadows that had daunted me when first I saw the shiftless city. In the twilight I cleared another aperture and with a new torch crawled into it, finding more vague people and symbols, though nothing more definite than the other temple had contained the room was just as packed with trademark blazoned goods, but much less reserved, these often had saying like "I'm with Shuggoth" and an arrow pointing to the left or right, a long row of food carts ending in a very narrow passage crowded with obscure and cryptical foodstuffs. About these shrines I was prying when the noise of the wind of my camel outside broke through the stillness and drew me forth to see what could have caused such flatulence in the beast.

The moon was gleaming vividly over the primitive people riding rides in the ruins, lighting a dense cloud of methane that seemed blown by a strong but decreasing wind from some point along the cliff ahead of me. I knew it was this chilly, brown wind which had inspired the camel and I was about to lead him to a place of easier clean up when I chanced to glance up and saw that there was no wind atop the cliff. This astonished me and made me wonder how I could see wind, but I immediately recalled the sudden local winds that I had seen and heard before at sunrise and sunset, and judged it was a normal thing. I decided it came from some rock fissure leading to a cave, and watched the troubled sand to trace it to its source; soon perceiving that it came from the black orifice of a temple a long distance south of me, almost out of sight. Against the choking brown-cloud I plodded toward this temple, which as I neared it loomed larger than the rest, and shewed a doorway far less clogged with cake batter.

I would have entered had not the terrific force of the stinky wind almost turned my torch into a flamethrower. It poured madly out of the dark door, sighing uncannily as it ruffled the sand and spread among the weird ruins. Soon it grew fainter and the sand grew more and more still, till finally all was at rest again; but a presence seemed stalking among the spectral stones of the city, and when I glanced at the moon it seemed to quiver as though it knew what my camel had been eating.

I was more afraid than I could explain, but not enough to dull my thirst for wonder; so as soon as the wind was quite gone I crossed into the dark chamber from which it had come.

This temple, as I had fancied from the outside, was larger than either of those I had visited before; and was presumably a natural cavern since it bore winds from some region beyond. Here I could stand the odor, barely, but saw that the twisting lines were as bad as in the other temples.

On the walls and roof I beheld for the first time some traces of the pictorial art of the ancient race, curious curling streaks of paint that had almost faded or crumbled away; and I saw with rising excitement a twisting metal maze of well-fashioned curvilinear railings.

As I held my torch aloft it seemed to me that the shape of the roof was too regular to be natural, and I wondered what the prehistoric cutters of stone had first worked upon. Their engineering skill must have been vast. The twin parallel railings were curved and rose in great hills and valleys, they stretched on for what seemed like miles, even corkscrewing in giant loops.

Then a brighter flare of the fantastic flame showed that form which I had been seeking, the opening to those remoter abysses whence the sudden wind had blown; and I grew faint when I saw that it was a small and plainly artificial door chiseled in the solid rock.

I thrust my torch within, lighting the usher on fire with a cry of alarm and surprise, beholding a black tunnel with the roof arching low over a rough flight of very small, numerous and steeply descending steps. I shall always see those steps in my dreams, for I came to learn what they meant. At the time I hardly knew whether to call them steps or mere footholds in a precipitous descent. My mind was whirling with mad thoughts, and the words and warning of engineering prophets seemed to float across the desert from the land that men know to the shiftless city that men dare not know. Yet I hesitated only for a moment before advancing through the portal and commencing to climb cautiously down the steep passage, feet first, as though walking.

It is only in the terrible phantasms of drugs or delirium that any other man can have such a descent as mine. The narrow passage led infinitely down like some hideous haunted well, a platform spread across some unseen chasm and offered a choice between entering either a red car or a blue one, and the torch I held above my head could not light the unknown depths toward which I was soon heading as I buckled myself in and listened uninterestedly to the guide talking about safety bars and keeping your head attached at all times, blah blah blah.

I lost track of the time and forgot to consult my watch, though I was frightened when I thought of the distance I must have been traversing. I think the first hill alone was over a mile high. It finally crested and the cars ran along a wide track next to each other for a time. People reached across the chasm and slapped each others hands in some form of camaraderie.

Then with a hanging on the edge of the first hill, the long trains we road on seemed suspended for a moment over a seemingly fathomless abyss, the tracks led down, and we flew down into the depths with horrifying speed that caused much peeing of pants and screaming.

There were changes of direction and of steepness; and once I came to a long, low, level passage where I had to wriggle my feet first along the floor, then behind my ears in an attempt to get comfortable under the restraint of the safety bar, and holding my torch at arm's length beyond my head. The place was not high enough for such things and my torch smashed through several steel cross beams.

After that were more of the steep peaks and bottomless pits, and it was still scrambling down interminably when my failing torch died out. I do not think I noticed it at the time, for when I did notice it I was still holding it above me as if it were ablaze. I was quite unbalanced with that instinct for the strange and the unknown which had made me a wanderer upon earth and a haunter of far, ancient, and forbidden places.

In the darkness there flashed strobe lights and before my mind fragments of my cherished treasury of daemonic lore; sentences from Alhazrad the mad

Crab, paragraphs from the apocryphal nightmares of Damascius, and infamous lines from the delirious Image du Monde of Gauthier de Metz as well as the mind shattering Soup du jour. I repeated queer extracts, and muttered of Afrasiab and the daemons that floated with him down the Oxus; later chanting over and over again a phrase from one of Lord Dunsany's tales--"The unreveberate blackness of the abyss." Once when the descent grew amazingly steep I recited something in sing-song from Thomas Moore until I feared to recite more:

A reservoir of darkness, black
As witches' cauldrons are, when fill'd
With moon-drugs in th' eclipse distill'd
Leaning to look if foot might pass
Down thro' that chasm, I saw, beneath,
As far as vision could explore,
The jetty sides as smooth as glass,
Looking as if just varnish'd o'er
With that dark pitch the Tent of Beer
Throws up upon its slimy shore.

Time had quite ceased to exist when my feet again felt a leveling out of the tracks, and I found myself in a place slightly higher than the ceiling of most small commuter planes and wondered now how air still circulated so incalculably far above my head.

I could not quite stand, as the bar prevented it, but could stick my hands upright, and in the dark I shuffled and swept hither and thither at random with break neck speed and random ups and downs.

I soon knew that I was in a narrow passage whose walls were lined with cases of wood having glass fronts. As in that Paleozoic and abysmal place I reached to feel of such things as polished marzipan and glass souvenir mugs.

I shuddered at the possible implications. The cases were apparently ranged along each side of the passage at regular intervals, and were oblong and horizontal, hideously like red and blue flashing bulbs in shape and size. When I tried to reach two or three for further examination, I found that they were firmly fastened, but not firmly enough as I ripped them out of their electric sockets as the car barreled past.

I saw that the passage was a long one, we floundered ahead rapidly in a creeping run that would have seemed horrible had any eye watched me in the blackness; we rushed ahead of the other car only to fall behind and then again jetting ahead in an endless neck and neck race. I leaned, crossing from side to side occasionally to feel of my good looking co-rider and be sure the rails and rows of cases still stretched on.

Man is so used to thinking visually that I almost forgot the darkness and pictured the endless corridor of wood and glass in its low-studded monotony as though I saw it. And then in a moment of indescribable emotion I did see it.

Just when my fancy merged into real sight I cannot tell; but there came a gradual glow ahead, and all at once I knew that I saw the dim outlines of a corridor and the cases, revealed by some unknown subterranean phosphorescence.

For a little while all was exactly as I had imagined it, since the glow was very faint; but as I mechanically kept barreling ahead into the stronger light I realized that my fancy had been but feeble. This hall was no relic of crudity like the temples in the city above, but a monument of the most magnificent and exotic art. Rich, vivid, and daringly fantastic designs and pictures formed a continuous scheme of mural paintings whose lines and colors were beyond description. We zoomed by. The cases were of a strange golden wood, with fronts of exquisite plastic, and containing the mummified forms of creatures outreaching in grotesqueness the most chaotic dreams of man.

To convey any idea of these monstrosities is impossible. They were of the reptile kind, with body lines suggestion sometimes the crocodile, sometimes the ant, but more often nothing of which either the naturalist or the palaeontologist ever heard. I'll call it a crocodant.

I debated for a time on the reality of the mummies, half suspecting they were artificial idols; but soon decided they were indeed some palaeogean species which had lived when the theme park city was alive.

To crown their grotesqueness, most of them were gorgeously enrobed in the costliest of clown fabrics, and lavishly laden with ornaments of rubber, glass jewels, 6G phones, and unknown shining plastic signs.

These creatures, I said to myself, were to men of the shiftless city what the were-wolf was to twilight, or some totem-beast is to a tribe of totem beast fans.

As I zoomed along the corridor toward the brighter light I saw later stages of the painted epic--the leave-taking of the race that had dwelt in the shiftless city and the valley around for ten million years; the race whose souls shrank from quitting scenes their bodies had known so long where they had settled as nomads in the earth's youth, hewing in the virgin rock those primal rides at which they had never ceased to frequent.

The civilization, which included a written alphabet, had seemingly risen to a higher order than those immeasurably later civilizations of Egypt and Chaldaea, yet there were curious omissions. I could, for example, find no pictures to represent deaths or funeral customs, save such as were related to wars, violence, and plagues; and I wondered at the reticence shown concerning natural death. It was as though an ideal of immortality had been fostered as a cheering illusion.

Still nearer the end of the passage was painted scenes of the utmost picturesqueness and extravagance: contrasted views of the shiftless city in its desertion and growing ruin, and of the strange new realm of paradise to which the race had hewed its way through the stone. In these views the city and the desert valley were shewn always by moonlight, golden nimbus hovering over the fallen walls, and half-revealing the splendid perfection of former times, shown spectrally and elusively by the artist.

The paradisal scenes were almost too extravagant to be believed, portraying a hidden world of eternal day filled with glorious cities and ethereal hills and valleys. At the very last I thought I saw signs of an artistic anticlimax. The paintings were less skillful, and much more bizarre than even the wildest of the earlier scenes.

They seemed to record a slow decadence of the ancient stock, coupled with a growing ferocity toward the outside world from which it was driven by the desert menu. The forms of the people--always represented by the sacred reptiles--appeared to be gradually wasting away, through their spirit as shewn hovering above the ruins by moonlight gained in proportion. Emaciated priests, displayed as reptiles in ornate robes, cursed the upper air and all who breathed it; and one terrible final scene shewed a primitive-looking man, perhaps a pioneer of ancient Irem, the City of Pillars, eating tacos and coney dogs and not sharing with the elder race. I remember how the sane folk fear the shiftless city, and was glad that beyond this place the rails and ceiling were bare.

As I viewed the pageant of mural history I had approached very closely to the end of the low-ceiled hall, and was aware of a gate through which came all of the illuminating phosphorescence. Kareening up to it at break neck speed, the trains raced along. I cried aloud in transcendent amazement at what lay beyond; for instead of higher and brighter chambers there was only an illimitable void of uniform radiance, such one might fancy when gazing down from the peak of Mount Everest upon a sea of sunlit mist.

Behind me was a passage so cramped that I could not stand upright in it without smacking my head on the cross beams; before me was an infinity of subterranean effulgence.

Reaching down from the passage into the abyss was the head of a steep super hill--small numerous miles of track like those of black passages I had traversed--but after a few feet the glowing vapors concealed everything. Swinging over the edge and staring into the screaming face of my riding companion as those behind us screamed as well and all those in the train racing beside us screamed in perfect stereo echo.

I grabbed my butt to kiss it goodby on its fantastic bas-reliefs, which could if closed, shut the whole inner world of light away from the vaults of the moon of Titan. I looked at the dark and imagined the ground flying up to meet us, and for the nonce dared not hope to survive reaching of it. I touched the safety bar with a grip that nearly liquified the metal, and could not move it. Then I sank prone to the train seat, my mind aflame with prodigious reflections which not even a death-like exhaustion could banish.

As I lay still with closed eyes, free to ponder, many things I had lightly noted in the frescoes came back to me with new and terrible significance--scenes representing the shiftless city in its heyday--the vegetations of the valley around it, and the distant lands with which its merchants traded.

The allegory of the crawling creatures puzzled me by its universal prominence, and I wondered that it would be so closely followed in a pictured history of such importance. In the frescoes the shiftless city had been shewn in proportions fitted to the reptiles.

I wondered what its real proportions and magnificence had been, and reflected a moment on certain oddities I had noticed in the ruins. I thought curiously of the lowness of the primal temples and of the underground corridor, which were doubtless hewn thus out of deference to the reptile deities there honored; though it perforce reduced the worshipers to smacking their raised hands when they rode these "coasters".

Perhaps the very rites here involved decapitation of the creatures by holding them aloft as they rode. No religious theory, however, could easily explain why the level passages in that awesome descent should be as low as the temples--or lower, since one could not even see the bottom in it.

As I thought of the crawling creatures, whose hideous mummified forms were so close to me, I felt a new throb of fear. Mental associations are curious, and I shrank from the idea that except for the poor primitive man eating circus food in the last painting, mine and the rest of the tourists were the only human form amidst the many relics and symbols of the primordial life.

But as always in my strange and roving existence, wonder soon drove out fear; for the luminous abyss and what it might contain presented a problem worthy of the greatest explorer that a weird world of mystery lay far down that flight of the peculiarly diving hill. I could not doubt, and I hoped to find there those rails intact that some stretches had so far failed to give. As I suspected, many of thee rails were indeed missing sections. Luckily we had been going so fast we rolled over these patches anyway. The frescoes had pictured unbelievable rides, and live shows in this lower realm, and my fancy dwelt on the rich and colossal ruins that awaited me.

My fears, indeed, concerned the past rather than the future. Not even the physical horror of my position in that cramped corridor of super sonic racing trains on flimsy tracks and antediluvian frescoes, miles below the world I knew and faced by another world of eery light and mist, could match the lethal dread I felt at the abysmal antiquity of the scene and its soul. An ancientness so vast that measurement is feeble seemed to leer down from the primal stones and rock-hewn temples of the shiftless city, while the very latest of the astounding maps in the frescoes shewed oceans and continents that man has forgotten, with only here and there some vaguely familiar outlines.

Of what could have happened in the geological ages since the paintings ceased and the death-defying race resentfully succumbed to decay, no man might say. Life had once teemed in these caverns and in the luminous realm beyond; now I was alone with vivid relics and fearless thrill seekers, and I trembled to think of the countless ages through which these relics had kept a silent deserted vigil and couldn't help but wonder if these rides were still up to code.

Suddenly there came another burst of that acute fear which had intermittently seized me ever since I first saw the terrible valley and the ancient theme park under a cold moon, and despite my exhaustion I found myself starting frantically to a sitting posture and gazing back along the black hill and toward the top that rose to the outer world.

My sensations were like those which had made me shun the shiftless city at night, and were as inexplicable as they were poignant. In another moment, however, I received a still greater shock in the form of a definite sound--the first which had broken the utter silence of these tomb-like depths. It was a deep, low moaning, as of a distant throng of condemned spirits, and came from the direction in which I was staring. Its volume rapidly grew, till it soon reverberated rightfully through the low passage, and at the same time I became conscious of an increasing draught of old air, likewise flowing from the tunnels and the city above.

The touch of this air seemed to restore my balance, for I instantly recalled the sudden gusts which had risen around the mouth of the abyss each sunset and sunrise, one of which had indeed revealed the hidden tunnels to me. I looked at my watch and saw that sunrise was near, so bracing myself to resist the g-forces being pummeled against me that were sweeping down as the hill lead us to its super deep ninety degree drop as it had swept forth at logic resisting speeds. My fear again waned low, since a natural phenomenon tends to dispel broodings over the unknown.

More and more speed poured on the shrieking, moaning metal on metal into the gulf of the inner earth. I dropped prone again and clutched vainly at the floor for fear of being swept bodily out of the open top of the train as we raced for the finish line.

Such fury I had not expected, and as I grew aware of an actual slipping of my train ahead of the other. I was beset by a thousand new terrors of apprehension and imagination. The malignancy of the blast awakened incredible fancies; once more I compared myself shudderingly to the only human image in that frightful corridor, the painting of the man who was blown to pieces by the gas created by countless bean burritos, for in the fiendish clawing of the swirling currents there seemed to abide a vindictive rage all the stronger because it was largely impotent.

I think I screamed frantically near the last--I was almost mad--of the howling wind-wraiths. I tried to stand against the murderous invisible torrent, but I could not even hold my own as the car pushed forward in impossible space time bending speeds and inexorably toward the unknown outcome of the race. Finally reason must have wholly snapped; for I fell babbling over and over that unexplainable couplet of the zippety do da, and waved my fist in the air screaming:

"Zippety do da, zipetty day! My oh my what can I say? We are totally gonna win you worthless pile of competing twin racing coaster!!."

Only the grim brooding desert gods know what really took place--what indescribable struggles and scrambles in the dark I endured or what Abaddon guided me back to life, where I must always remember and shiver in the night wind till oblivion--or worse--claims me. Monstrous, unnatural, colossal, was the speed--too far beyond all the ideas of man and the limits of human gravity force survivability to be believed except in the silent damnable small hours of the morning when one cannot sleep.

I have said that the fury of the rushing blast was infernal--cacodaemoniacal--and that its voices were hideous with the pent-up viciousness of desolate eternities.

Presently these voices, while still chaotic before me, seemed to my beating brain to take articulate form behind me; and down there in the grave of unnumbered aeon-dead antiquities, leagues below the dawn-lit world of men, I heard the ghastly cursing and snarling of strange-tongued fiends of those in the other train.

Turning, I saw outlined against the luminous aether of the abyss that could not be seen against the dusk of the corridor--a nightmare horde of rushing devils; hate distorted, grotesquely panoplied, half transparent devils in a race no man in the other train's cars was going to win--we were to be the twin coaster race champions of the shiftless city!

And as the wind died away I was plunged into the ghoul-pooled darkness of earth's bowels; for behind the last of the creatures the great brazen cars clanged to a slow halt with a deafening peal of metallic music whose reverberations swelled out to the distant world to hail the rising sun as Memnon hails it from the banks of the Nile, we came to the finish line.

The race of countless aeons, as old as the histories of civilizations now lost to the desert sands had once more come to a final conclusion in the deep, dark horror filled tunnels below the shiftless city... and we had won by a nose!

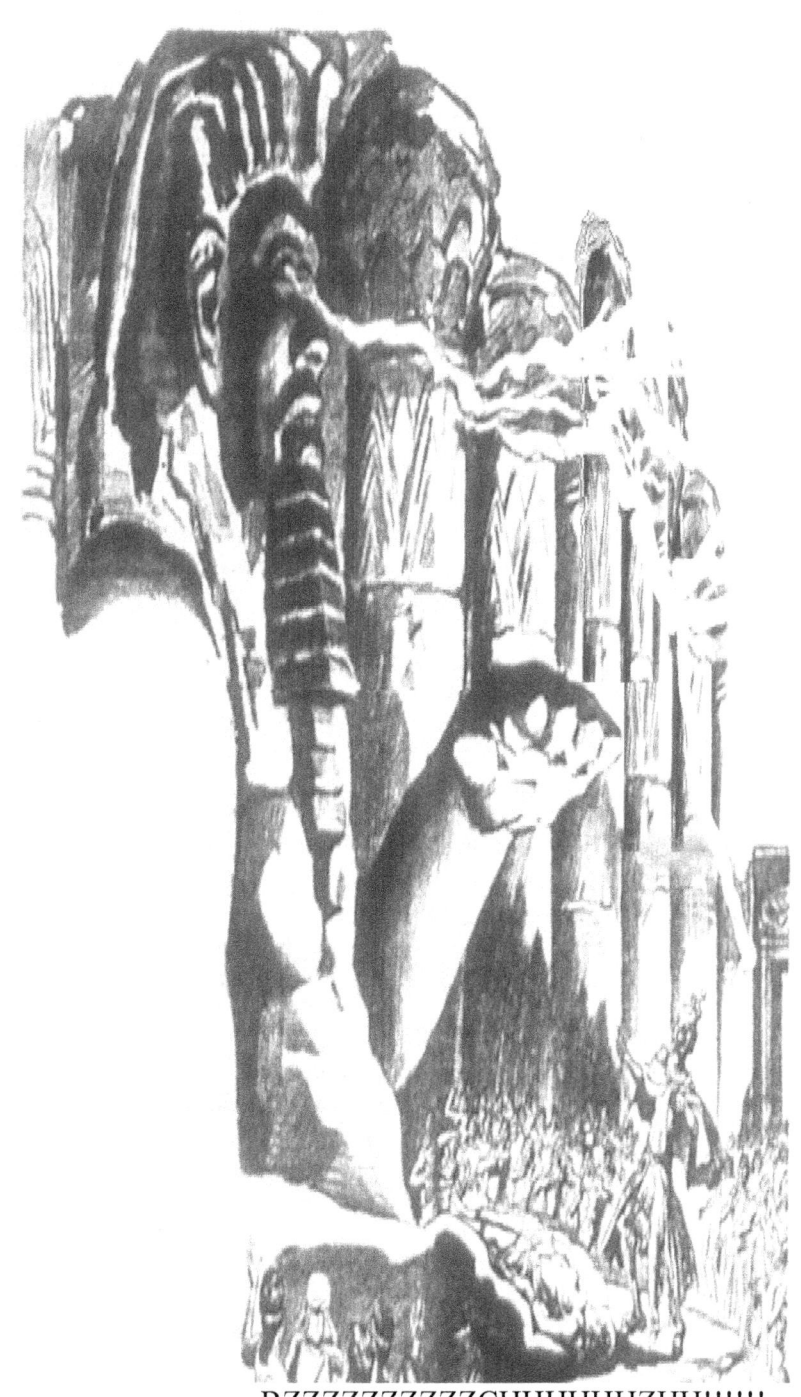

BZZZZZZZZZZZCHHHHHHHZHH!!!!!!

"YEEEEEEEEE-OWWWWWWW!!!!!"

THE SHADOW OVER IMHOTEP

During the winter of 2007-2008 officials of the Federal government made a strange and secret investigation of certain conditions in the ancient Massachusetts seaport of Innsmouth. The public first learned of it in February, when a vast series of extreme secret raids and arrests occurred, live, on pay per view, followed by the deliberate burning and dynamiting--under the watchful eyes of huge audiences who were told it was an early fourth of July celebration--of an enormous number of crumbling, worm-eaten, and *supposedly* empty houses along the abandoned waterfront. We all cheered as they were blown to smithereens. Uninquiring souls let this occurrence pass as one of the major clashes in a spasmodic war on spasmodic wars.

Keener news-followers, however, wondered at the prodigious number of balloons, the abnormally large force of men, ninjas, giant robots and zombie killing machines used in making the arrests, and the secrecy surrounding the disposal of the prisoners. No trials, or even definite charges were reported; nor were any of the captives seen thereafter in the regular gaols of the nation. There were vague statements on twitter about game shows and concentration camps, and later about dispersal in various naval and military prisons, but nothing positive ever developed. Innsmouth itself was left almost depopulated, and it is even now only beginning to show signs of a sluggishly revived existence.

Complaints from many liberal organizations were met with long confidential discussions, and beatings, representatives were taken on trips to certain camps and prisons. As a result, these societies became surprisingly passive and reticent. Newspaper men were harder to manage, but seemed largely to cooperate with the government in the end after secret payments, electric tazerings, and secret obliterations of a few unruly organizations convinced them to silence. Only one paper--a tabloid always discounted because of its wild policy-- mentioned the deep diving submarine that discharged torpedoes downward in the marine abyss just beyond Devil Reef and of the young pilot who turned off his targeting computer, ran down that trench and fired those torpedoes. That item, gathered by chance in a haunt of sailors, scum and villainy, seemed indeed rather far-fetched; since the low, black reef lay a full mile and a half out from Innsmouth Harbor.

People around the country and in the nearby towns muttered a great deal to themselves, but said very little to each other, or the outer worlds. They had talked about dead and half-deserted Innsmouth for many a century, and nothing new could be wilder or more hideous than what they had whispered and hinted at in their underwear drawers. Many things had taught them secretiveness, and there was no need to exert pressure on them. Besides, they really knew little; for wide salt marsh mine fields, desolate and unpeopled, kept neighbors off from Innsmouth on the landward side.

But at last I am going to defy the ban on speech about this thing. Results, I am certain, are so thorough that no public harm could ever accrue from a hinting of what was found by those horrified men at Innsmouth. Besides, I'm bored. I do not know just how much of the whole tale has been told even to me, and I was there. For my contact with this affair has been closer than that of any other layman, and I have carried away impressions which are yet to drive me to drastic measures. Yes, I too am considering opening a sports bar in the now empty commercial district of Innsmouth.

It was I, Imhotep, the great builder, architect of the pyramids, who fled happily skipping out of Innsmouth in the early morning hours of July 16, 2007, and whose suggestions for government inquiry and action brought on the whole reported episode. I was willing enough to stay mute while the affair was fresh and gooey; but now that it is an old story, with public interest and curiosity gone, I have an odd craving for sushi and to whisper about those few frightful hours in that ill-rumored and evilly-shadowed seaport of death and blasphemous normality. The mere telling helps me to restore confidence in the world to create worthy challenges for me; to reassure myself that I was not the last to succumb to a curious desire to take on an otherwordly mystery just for something to do on a weekend. It helps me, too, in making up my mind regarding what to eat this afternoon.

I never heard of Innsmouth till the day before I saw it for the first and--so far--last time. I was celebrating my coming of the age of 4,662 by a tour of New England--sightseeing, antiquarian, and genealogical--and had planned to go directly from ancient Newburyport to Arkham, whence my new girlfriend's mother's family was derived. There I would visit the university and the lovely asylum. I had no car, but was traveling by train, trolley and motor-coach, always seeking the cheapest possible route. In Newburyport they told me that the refurbished steam train was the thing to take to Arkham as it offered a historic travelogue as it traveled fifty feet over the countryside and was a favorite of tourists; and it was only at the station ticket-office, when I demurred at the high fare, that I learned about Innsmouth. The stout, shrewd-faced agent, whose speech shewed him to be no local man, seemed sympathetic toward my efforts at economy, and made a suggestion that none of my other informants had offered.

"You could take that old ingrateful tour bus, I suppose," he said with a certain hesitation, "but it ain't thought much of hereabouts. It goes through Innsmouth--you may have heard about that--and so the people don't like it. Run by an Innsmouth fellow--Joe Sargent--but never gets any customer from here, or Arkham either, 'cept all those people from the asylum I guess. Wonder it keeps running at all. I s'pose it's cheap enough, but I never see mor'n two or three people in it--nobody but those Innsmouth folk. Leaves the square--front of Hammond's Drug Store--at 10 a.m. and 7 p.m. unless they've changed lately. Looks like a terrible hippie bus--I've never been on it. I don't care what pictures they have!"

That was the first I ever heard of shadowed Innsmouth. Any reference to a town not shown on common maps or listed in recent guidebooks would have interested me, and the agent's odd manner of allusion roused something like real curiosity. A town able to inspire such dislike in it its neighbors, I thought, must be at least rather unusual, and worthy of a tourist's attention. If it came before Arkham I would stop off there and so I asked the agent to tell me something about it. He was very deliberate, and spoke with an air and feeling of being slightly superfluous to what he said.

"Innsmouth? Well, it's queer, kind of a town, down at the mouth. Used to be almost a city--quite a port before the War of 1812--but all gone to pieces in the last hundred years or so. No railroad now--The B. M. rail used to go through until they got constipated, and the branch line from Rowley was given up years ago."

"More empty houses than there are people on earth, I guess, and no business to speak of except fishing and lobstering. Everybody trades mostly either here or in Arkham or Ipswich. Once there was a witch in Ipswich, lived in a ditch, found a nickel and thought she was rich I hear it told. Once they had quite a few mills, but nothing's left now except one gold refinery running on the leanest kind of part time and a few ski resorts, a casino, a super mall, and of course the nightclubs."

"That refinery, though, used to be a big thing, and old man Marsh, who owns it, must be richer'n Croesus. Queer old duck, though, flatulent in six languages, and sticks mighty close to his home. He's supposed to have developed some skin disease or deformity late in life that makes him strangely attractive. Grandson of Captain Obed Marsh, who founded the business. His mother seems to've been some kind of alien--they say a South Solaris three immigrant--so everybody raised money for him when he married an Ipswich girl fifty years ago. They always do that about Innsmouth people, and folks here and hereabouts always try to cover up any Innsmouth blood they have in 'em. But Marsh's children and grandchildren look just like anyone else far's I can see 'cept for the gills. I've had 'em pointed out to me here--though, come to think of it, the elder children don't seem to be around lately. Never saw the old man. Not since last week anyway."

"And why is everybody so down on Innsmouth? Well, young fellow, you mustn't take too much stock in what people here say. They're hard to get started, but once they do get started they never shut up. They've been telling things about Innsmouth--whispering 'em, mostly--in between farts, for the last hundred years, I guess, and I gather they're more scared than anything else. Some of the stories would make you laugh--some would make you cry, some would make you want to get up and dance, like old Captain Marsh driving bargains with the devil and bringing chimps out of hell to live in Innsmouth, or about some kind of foot-worship and awful bunion sacrifices in some place near the wharves that people stumbled on around 1845 or thereabouts--but I come from Phantom, Vermont, and I ain't down with that kind of story.

Most likely just jealous of the chum chowder sales if ya ask me."

"You ought to hear, though, what some of the old-timers tell about the black reef off the coast--Devil Reef, they call it. It's well above water a good part of the time, and never much below it, but at that you could hardly call it an island. The story is that there's a whole legion of hot lady devils seen sometimes on that reef--sprawled about, or darting in and out of some kind of caves near the top. It's a rugged, uneven thing, a good bit over a mile out, and toward the end of shipping days sailors used to make big detours just to wreck on it and spend the day swimming."

"That is, sailors that didn't hail from Innsmouth. One of the things they had against old Captain Marsh was that he was supposed to land on it sometimes at night after launching away into the air from too many enchiritos, when the tide was right. Maybe he did, for I dare say the rock formation was interesting, and it's just barely possible he was looking for pirate loot and maybe finding it; but there was talk of his dealing with demons there. Fact is, I guess on the whole it was really the Captain that gave the bad reputation to the reef."

"That was before the big gas epidemic of 1846, when over half the folks in Innsmouth was carried off and hung just to stop them from farting. They never did quite figure out what the trouble was, but it was probably some foreign kind of beans brought from China or somewhere by the shipping. It surely was bad enough--there was riots over it, and all sorts of ghastly doings that I don't believe ever got outside of town--and it left the place in awful shape. Never came back--there can't be more'n 300 or 400 people living there now."

"But the real thing behind the way folks feel is simply jealousy--and I don't say I'm blaming those that hold it. I hate those Innsmouth folks myself, and I wouldn't care to go to their town. I s'pose you know-- though I can see you're a Westerner by your talk--what a lot our New England ships used to have to do with strange ports in Africa, Asia, the South Seas, and everywhere else, and what queer kinds of things they sometimes brought back with 'em. You've probably heard about the Salem man that came home with a camel for a wife, and maybe you know there's still a bunch of things from that there "monster island" somewhere around Cape Cod."

"Well, there's something worse with the Innsmouth people. The place always was badly cut off from the rest of the country by marshes and creeks and bog monsters and we can't be sure about the ins and outs of the matter; but it's pretty clear that old Captain Marsh must have brought home some huge gold, silver, and platinum shipments when he had all three of his ships in commission back in the twenties and thirties. There certainly is a strange kind of wealthiness in the Innsmouth folks today--I don't know how to explain it but it sort of makes you crawl with jealousy. Specially in today's economy. You'll notice a little in Sargent if you take his bus. Some of 'em have heads with noses and eyes and mouths that never seem to shut, and they all wear way to much jewelry and their skin ain't quite right. Rough and scaly, and the sides of the necks are all shrively and greased up. Get bald, too, very young. The older fellows look the worst--fact is, I don't believe I've ever seen a very old chap of that kind without fins. Guess they must die of looking in the glass! Animals hate 'em--they used to have lots of horse trouble before the autos came in. Horses jump on 'em and ride 'em round like bicycles when they see 'em."

"Nobody around here or in Arkham or Ipswich will have anything to do with 'em, and they act kind of offish themselves when they come to town or when anyone tries to fish on the ground. Queer how fish are always thick off Innsmouth Harbor when there ain't any anywhere else around--but just try to fish there yourself and see how the folks chase you off! Those people used to come here on the railroad--walking and taking the train at Rowley after the branch was dropped--but now they use that bus."

"Yes, there's a hotel in Innsmouth--called the Gill-man House--but I don't believe it can amount to much. I wouldn't advise you to try it. Only four and a half stars. Better stay over here and take the ten o'clock bus tomorrow morning; then you can get an evening bus there for Arkham at eight o'clock. There was a factory inspector who stopped at the Gill-man a couple of years ago and he had a lot of unpleasant hints about the place. Seems they get a queer crowd there, for this fellow heard voices in other rooms--though most of 'em was empty--that gave him the squirts. It was fish talk he thought, but he said the bad thing about it was the kind of voice that sometimes spoke. It sounded so unnatural--slopping like, he said--like it was holding a road apple in its mouth--that he didn't dare undress and go to sleep. Just waited up and lit out the first thing in the morning. The talk went on most all night. That and the terribly catchy folk rock tunes."

"This fellow--Casey Jones, his name was--had a lot to say about how the Innsmouth folk watched him and seemed kind of on guard. He found the Marsh refinery a queer place--it's in an old mill on the lower falls of the Manuxet. What he said tallied up with what I'd heard. Books in bad shape, and no clear account of any kind of dealings. You know it's always been a kind of mystery where the Marshes get the gold they refine. They've never seemed to do much buying in that line, but years ago they shipped out an enormous lot of ingots."

"Used to be talk of a queer foreign kind of jewelry that the sailors and refinery men sometimes sold on the sly, or that was seen once or twice on some of the Marsh women-folks. People allowed maybe old Captain Obed traded for it in some heathen port, especially since he always ordered stacks of glass beads and trinkets such as seafaring men used to get for native trade. Others thought and still think he'd found an old pirate cache out on Devil Reef. But here's a funny thing. The old Captain's been dead these sixty years, and there's ain't been a good-sized ship out of the place since the Civil War; but just the same old man Marsh still walks around and seems every bit of alive and keeps on buying a few of those native trade things--mostly glass and rubber gewgaws, they tell me. Maybe the Innsmouth folks like 'em to look at themselves--Gawd knows they've gotten to be about as bad as South Sea cucumber cannibals and savage Guinea pigs."

"That moon race of '66 must have taken off the best blood in the place. Recruiting expendable test pilots for the giant sling shot experiments and all. Anyway, they're a doubtful lot now, and the Marshes and other rich folks are as bad as any. As I told you, there probably ain't more'n 400 people in the whole town in spite of all the streets they say there are. I guess they're what they call 'neo riche' down South--lawless and sly, and full of secret longings for broadway. They get a lot of fish and lobsters and do exporting by bicycle. Queer how the fish swarm right into their boats and nowhere else."

"Nobody can ever keep track of these people, and state school officials and census men have a devil of a time. You can bet that prying strangers ain't welcome around Innsmouth. I've heard personally of more'n one business or government man that's disappeared there, and there's loose talk of one who went to town and is out at Danvers fish market now. They must have fixed up some awful powerful tartar sauce for that fellow, he hasn't stopped eating fish for breakfast lunch and dinner for weeks."

"That's why I wouldn't go at night if I was you. I've never been there and have no wish to go, but I guess a daytime trip couldn't hurt you-- even though the people hereabouts will advise you to bring your own toilet paper if you know what I mean. If you're just sightseeing, and looking for a good time, Innsmouth ought to be quite a place for you."

And so I spent part of that evening at the Newburyport Public Library looking up data about Innsmouth. When I had tried to question the natives in the shops, the lunchroom, the garages, and the fire station, I had found them even harder to understand than the ticket agent had predicted; and realized that I could not spare the time to overcome their first instinctive ramblings. They had a kind of obscure suspiciousness, as if there were something amiss with anyone too much interested in the Innsmouth Y. M. C. A., where I was stopping. The clerk merely sang the chorus seven times and discouraged my going to such a catchy tuned, happy place; and the people at the library shewed much the same attitude. Clearly, in the eyes of the locals, Innsmouth was merely an exaggerated case of crab cake tourist traps.

The Essex County histories on the library shelves had very little to say, except that the town was founded in 1643, noted for shipbuilding before the Revolution, a seat of great marine prosperity in the early 19th century, and later a minor factory center using the Manuxet as power. The epidemic of flatulence in 1846 was very sparsely treated, as if it formed a discredit to the county.

References to decline were few, though the significance of the later record was unmistakable. After the Civil War all industrial life was confined to the Marsh Refining Company, and the marketing of gold fish filets formed the only remaining bit of major commerce aside from the eternal fishing and a string of Vegas style resorts and casinos. That fishing paid less and less as the price of the commodity fell and large-scale corporations offered competition, but there was never a dearth of fish around Innsmouth Harbor. Foreigners seldom settled there, and there was some discreetly veiled evidence that a number of those who had tried it had been scattered in a peculiarly drastic fashion.

Most interesting of all was a glancing reference to the strange jewelry vaguely associated with Innsmouth. It had evidently impressed the whole countryside more than a little, for mention was made of specimens in the museum of Miskatonic University at Arkham, and in the display room of the Newburyport Historical Society. The fragmentary descriptions of these things were flamboyant, bald and prosaic, but they hinted to me an undercurrent of persistent awesomeness. Something about them seemed so odd and provocative that I could not put them out of my mind, and despite the relative lateness of the hour I resolved to see the local sample--said to be a large, greasy, queerly-proportioned thing evidently meant for a tiara--if it could possibly be arranged.

The librarian gave me an Indian rug burn and a note of introduction to the curator of the Society, a Miss Anna Tilt, who lived nearby, and after a brief explanation that ancient, twenty something gentlewoman was kind enough to pilot me into the closed building like a kite, since the hour was not late. The collection was a notable one indeed, but in my present mood I had eyes for nothing but the bizarre object which glistened in a corner cupboard under the electric lights.

It took no excessive sensitiveness to beauty to make me literally gasp at the strange, unearthly splendor of the alien, opulent phantasy that rested there on a purple velvet cushion. "It's... It's amazing!" I cried.

"That's the toilet, son, the tiara is over here." Even now I can hardly describe what I saw, though it was clearly enough a sort of tiara, as the description had said. It was tall in front, and with a very large and curiously irregular periphery, as if designed for a head of almost freakishly elliptical outline. The material seemed to be predominantly gold, though a weird lighter lustrousness hinted at some strange alloy with an equally beautiful and scarcely identifiable metal. Its condition was almost perfect, and one could have spent hours in studying the striking and puzzlingly untraditional designs--some simply geometrical, and some plainly marine--chased or molded in high relief on its surface with a craftsmanship of incredible skill and grace.

The longer I looked, the more the thing fascinated me; and in this fascination there was a curiously disturbing element hardly to be classified or accounted for. At first I decided that it was the queer other-worldly quality of the art which made me uneasy. All other art objects I had ever seen either belonged to some known racial or national stream, or else were consciously modernistic defiances of every recognized stream. This tiara was neither. It clearly belonged to some settled technique of infinite maturity and perfection, yet that technique was utterly remote from any--Eastern or Western, ancient or modern--which I had ever heard of or seen exemplified. It was as if the workmanship were that of another planet. Aliens! Sweet!

I first concluded that my uneasiness came from the unearthly hotness of the curator in her skin tight lycra catsuit. However, I soon saw that my uneasiness had a second and perhaps equally potent source residing in the pictorial and mathematical suggestion of the strange designs. The patterns all hinted of remote secrets and unimaginable abysses in time and space, and the monotonously aquatic nature of the reliefs became almost sinister. And trust me I know all about that sort of thing being a master of the Egyptian book of the dead and all. Among these reliefs were fabulous monsters of abhorrent grotesqueness and malignity--half ichthyic, half batrachian, and half sphinctoral, in suggestion--which one could not dissociate from a certain haunting and uncomfortable sense of pseudomemory, as if they called up some image from deep cells and tissues whose retentive functions are wholly primal and awesomely ancestral. At times I fancied that every contour of these blasphemous fish-frogs was over-flowing with the ultimate quintessence of unknown and inhuman evil. I liked it.

In odd contrast to the tiara's aspect was its brief and rosy history as related by Miss Tilt. It had been pawned for a ridiculous sum at a shop in State Street in 1873, by a drunken Innsmouth man shortly afterward killed in a bizarre pinball accident. The Society had acquired it directly from the pawnbroker, at once giving it a display worthy of its quality. It was labeled as of probable East-Indiana or Indo-Ohio provenance, though the attribution was frankly tentative.

Miss Tilt, comparing all possible hypotheses regarding its origin and its presence in New England, was inclined to believe that it formed part of some exotic pirate hoard discovered by old Captain Obed Marsh. This view was surely not weakened by the insistent offers of purchase at a high price which the Marshes began to make as soon as they knew of its presence, and which they repeated to this day despite the Society's unvarying determination not to sell.

As the good lady shewed me out of the building she made it clear that the pirate theory of the Marsh fortune was a popular one among the intelligent people of the region. Her own attitude toward shadowed Innsmouth--which she had never seen but a dozen times--was one of lusty disgust at a community "dripping with sex appeal on the cultural scale," and she assured me that the rumors of bunion worship were partly justified by a peculiar secret cult which had gained force there and engulfed all the orthodox social clubs.

It was called, she said, "The Erotic Order of Dagon," and was undoubtedly a frisco based, quasi-pseudo thing imported from the East Chicago Licensing company a century before, at a time when the Innsmouth fisheries seemed to be going barren. Its persistence among a simple people was quite natural in view of the sudden and permanent return of abundantly fine fishing, and it soon came to be the greatest influence in the town, replacing freebasing altogether and taking up headquarters in the old Cthulhu Hall on New Ancient Green.

All this, to the pious Miss Tilt, formed an excellent reason for shoe shopping in the ancient town of decay and desolation; but to me it was merely a fresh incentive. To my architectural and historical anticipations was now added an acute anthropological zeal, and I could scarcely sleep in my small room at the "Y" as the night wore away for I had heard of a free concert that would be playing early the next day.

II

Shortly before ten the next morning I stood with one small gnome in front of Hammond's Drug Store in old Market Square waiting for the Innsmouth bus. As the hour for its arrival drew near I noticed a general drift of the loungers to other places up the street, or to the Ideal Lunch across the square. Evidently the ticket-agent had not exaggerated the dislike which local People bore toward Innsmouth and its denizens. In a few moments a small tour bus-coach of extreme decrepitude and dirty flower power colors rattled down State Street, made a turn, and blew up at the curb beside me. I felt immediately that it was the right one; a guess which the half-illegible sign on the windshield--Arkham-Innsmouth-Newburyport-The Ingrateful Undead tour--soon verified.

The door opened and I stared inside at the chubby grey bearded driver staring down at me.

"I'd like to get to Innsmouth before the concert starts if I could."

"Don't worry." The driver smiled. "I don't think they'll start the concert... without me."

Just then the sounds of distant music could be heard rolling over the hills.

"Son of a... can't believe they started without me!" He mumbled.

I got on and looked around at the other passengers. There were only three besides myself--model visaged, unkempt men of sullen broody visage and somewhat youthful cast--they clumsily shambled out and began walking up State Street in a silent, almost moonwalking fashion. The driver also alighted, still mumbling and swearing under his breath about ingratefulness and I watched him as he went into the drug store to make some purchase. This, I reflected, must be the Joe Sargent mentioned by the ticket-agent; and even before I noticed any details there spread over me a wave of spontaneous nausea which could be neither checked nor explained. I threw up in the drivers backpack and put it back on the seat. It suddenly struck me as very natural that the local people should not wish to ride on a bus owned and driven by this man, or to visit any oftener than possible the habitat of such a man and his kinsfolk. That being said, he didn't seem all that bad really.

I was sorry when I saw there would be no other passengers on the bus. I briefly wondered where the gnome had gone but figured he was likely caught under the tire. Somehow I did not like the idea of riding alone with this driver. But as leaving time obviously approached I conquered my qualms and followed the man aboard, extending him a dollar bill and murmuring the single word "Innsmouth." He looked curiously at me for a second as he returned forty cents change without speaking. He just kept staring at me and smiling. I took a seat far behind him, but on the same side of the bus, since I wished to watch the shore during the journey.

At length the decrepit vehicle started with a jerk, and rattled noisily past the old brick buildings of State Street amidst a cloud of hemp vapor from the exhaust.

"It's powered by all green technology. It burns all sorts of plants and excess fish innards." He told me proudly. I nodded pretending to be interested.

Glancing at the people on the sidewalks, I thought I detected in them a curious wish to join us in the bus--or at least a wish to avoid seeming to want to be on it. Then we turned to the left into High Street, where the going was smoother; flying by stately old mansions of the early new republic and still older imperial farmhouses, passing the Lower Emperor Green and Miss Parker River, and finally emerging into a long, monotonous stretch of open shore country.

The day was warm and sunny, but the landscape of frozen sand, sludge-grass, and stunted rubber shrubbery became more and desolate as we proceeded. Out the window I could see the blue water and the sandy line of Giant Plum Island, well known for its giant peaches, killer tiny apes... and plums. We presently drew very near the beach as our narrow road veered off from the main highway to Rowley and Ipswich. Beach goers surfed, swam and did their best to avoid the squid attacks. There were no visible houses, and I could tell by the state of the road that traffic was very light hereabouts. The weather-worn telephone poles carried only two wires and three cable companies. Now and then we crossed crude wooden bridges over tidal creeks that wound far inland and promoted the general isolation of the region.

Once in a while I noticed dead stumps and crumbling foundation-walls above the drifting sand, and recalled the old tradition quoted in one of the histories I had read, that this was once a fertile and thickly-settled countryside. The change, it was said, came simultaneously with the Innsmouth marathon of 1848, and the explosive diarrhea outbreak, and was thought by simple folk to have a dark connection with hidden forces of evil. Actually, it was caused by the unwise cutting of cheese near the shore, which robbed the soil of the best protection and opened the way for waves of wind-blown sand to unleash evil forces from their cosmic prisons of intestinal fortitude... And too much bean dip.

At last we lost sight of the road and flew off into the trees. Then we saw the vast expanse of the open Atlantic on our left. Our narrow course began to climb steeply, and I felt a singular sense of disquiet in looking at the lonely crest ahead where the rutted road-way met the sky. It was as if the bus were about to keep on in its ascent, leaving the earth altogether and merging with the unknown arcana of upper air and cryptical sky. The smell of the sea took on ominous implications, and the silent driver's bent, rigidly arched back and narrow eyes became more and more intense, as if he were straining. As I looked at him I saw that the back of his head was almost as lumpy as his face, having only a few straggling yellow bruises that stood out upon a grey moonlike surface.

We reached the crest and beheld the outspread valley beyond, where the Manuxet joins the sea just north of the long line of cliffs that culminate in Kingsport Head and veer off toward Cape Ann. On the far misty horizon I could just make out the dizzy profile of the Head, topped by the queer ancient house of which so many legends are told and I marked the strange high house on my map for a future exploration; but for the moment all my attention was captured by the nearer panorama just below me. I had, I realized, come face to face with rumour-shadowed Innsmouth.

It was a town of wide extent and dense constipation, yet one with a portentous depth of visible life. From the tangle of chimney-pots huge plumes of smoke came, and the three tall steeples loomed stark and pastel painted against the seaward horizon. One of them was flying a *Miskatonic fighting shuggoths* flag at the top, and in that and another there were black gaping holes where the blood sucking proboscis rocs roosted. The vast huddle of sagging gambrel roofs and peaked seven gables conveyed with offensive clearness the idea of gummy wormy decay, and as we approached along the now descending road I could see that many roofs had wholly been made of gold and caved in under their own weight. There were some large square Georgian houses, too, with hipped roofs, shouldered cupolas, and railed "widow's walks." These were mostly well back from the water, and one or two seemed to be in moderately sound condition. Stretching inland from among them I saw the rusted, grass-grown line of the abandoned railway, with leaning telegraph-poles now covered in cawing black birds on the wires, and the half-obscured lines of the old carriage roads to Rowley and Ipswich.

 The urban sprawl was worst close to the waterfront, though in its very midst I could spy the white belfry of a fairly well frequented brick structure which looked like a small casino. The harbor, long clogged with beach sand in an attempt at creating a beach market and boardwalk, was enclosed by an ancient stone breakwater; on which I could begin to discern the minute forms of a few seated fishermen, and at whose end was what looked like the cyclopean structure of a byzantine lighthouse. A sandy tongue had formed inside this barrier and upon it I saw a few million dollar vacation cabins, moored dories, and scattered lobster-pots. The only deep water seemed to be where the river poured out past the belfried structure and turned southward to join the ocean at the breakwater's end.

 Here and there the ruins of dwarves jutted out from the shore to end in indeterminate pyramids that reminded me a bit of home, those farthest south seeming the highest. And far out at sea, despite a high tide, I glimpsed a long, black line scarcely rising above the water yet carrying a suggestion of odd latent pregnancy, it was very inviting. This, I knew, must be Devil Reef. As I looked, a subtle, curious sense of beckoning seemed superadded to the grim attractiveness; and oddly enough, I found this overtone more inviting than the primary impression. No wonder sailors wrecked there to take swim breaks.

 We met no one on the road, but presently began to pass huge farms in varying stages of apocalyptic tomato harvesting. Then I noticed a few inhabited houses with rags stuffed in the broken windows and unexploded artillery shells and dead fish lying about the littered yards. Once or twice I saw listless-looking people doing jumping jacks with rags stuffed in their mouths and working in stupendous victory gardens or digging clams out of their ears on the beach below, and groups of dirty, hellish winged simian children playing around weed-grown doorsteps. Somehow these people seemed more rustically charming than the rustically charming buildings, for almost every one had certain peculiarities of face and motions which I instinctively liked without being able to define or comprehend why. They seemed to have a certain inner fire and friendly charisma that inspired thoughts of birthday parties and joy. For a second I thought this typical atlas-like physique of the citizens suggested some picture I had seen, perhaps in a book, or a picture in a house under circumstances of particular giddiness or melancholy; but this pseudo-recollection passed like a bout with reconstituted cabbage.

As the bus reached a lower level I began to catch the steady note of a whining buzz through the unnatural stillness, The leaning bus driver looked back at me a moment. The brightly painted houses grew thicker, lined both sides of the road, and displayed more urban tendencies to Victorian paint schemes than did those we were leaving behind. The panorama ahead had contracted to a street scene, and in spots I could see where a cobblestone pavement and stretches of yellow brick sidewalk existed. All the houses were apparently inhabited by laughing dancing folks singing something like "Yog-sothoth Doris" or something and decorating huge evergreen trees like it was Christmas, and there were occasional gaps where tumbling children and cellar walls told of buildings that had collapsed. Pervading everything was the most nauseous cheese odor imaginable. The whining continued and the leaning driver glanced back smiling at me still for several minutes until it finally stopped. Then he sat back down with a sigh of relief.

Soon cross streets and junctions began to appear; those on the left leading to shoreward realms of unpaved splendor and genius architecture, while those on the right shewed vistas of departed grandeur. So far I had seen no people in the town, but there now came signs of a habitation--curtained windows here and there, barbecues smoking with delicious smells, and an occasional battered Italian sports motorcar at the curb. Pavement and sidewalks were increasingly well-defined, and though most of the houses were quite old--wood and brick structures of the early 19th century--they were obviously kept fit for habitation. As an amateur antiquarian I almost lost my olfactory disgust and my feeling of menace and repulsion amidst this rich, unaltered survival from the past.

But I was not to reach my destination without one very strong impression of poignantly disagreeable quality. The bus had come to a sort of open crustacean or radial point with churches on two sides and the bedraggled remains of a circular green in the center, and I was looking at a large pillared hall on the right-hand junction ahead. The structure's once white paint was now gray and peeling and the black and gold sign on the pediment was so faded that I could only with difficulty make out the words "Erotic Order of Dagon." This, then was the former Masonic Hall now given over to a degraded cult. As I strained to decipher this inscription my notice was distracted by the beauty of a cracked burrito bell restaurant across the street, and I quickly turned to look out the window on my side of the coach as the disturbing buzzing sound returned.

The sound came from the squatting bus driver, and ended with a squishing sound that didn't bode well. The restaurant building with the bell was built in a clumsy Gothic fashion and having a disproportionately high basement with shuttered windows. Though the hands of its clock were missing on the side I glimpsed, I knew that those hoarse strokes were tolling the hour of eleven. Then suddenly all thoughts of time were blotted out by an onrushing image of sharp intensity and unaccountable horror which had seized me and slapped me repeatedly before I knew what it really was. The odor... it's coming from *inside* the bus! The door of the church basement was open, revealing a rectangle of blackness inside. And as I looked, a certain object crossed or seemed to cross that dark rectangle; burning into my brain a momentary confection of nightmare which was all the more maddening because analysis could not shew a single nightmarish quality in it.

It was a living object--the first except the driver that I had seen since entering the compact part of the town--and had I been in a steamier mood I would have found nothing whatever of terror in it. Clearly, as I realized a moment later, it was the pastor; clad in some peculiar vestments doubtless introduced since the Order of Dagon had modified the ritual of the local churches. The thing which had probably caught my first subconscious glance and supplied the touch of bizarre horror was the tall tiara he wore; an almost exact duplicate of the one Miss Tilt had shown me the previous evening. This, acting on my imagination, had supplied namelessly sinister qualities to the indeterminate face and robed, shambling form beneath it. There was not, I soon decided, any reason why I should have felt that shuddering touch of evil pseudo-memory. Was it not natural that a local mystery cult should adopt among its regimentals an unique type of head-dress made familiar to the community in some strange way--perhaps from a treasure-trove?

A very thin sprinkling of modelish-looking youngish people now became visible on the sidewalks--lone individuals, and silent knots of two or three. All wearing hideously expensive khaki shorts and flannel that would have bankrupted several city blocks. The lower floors of the crumbling houses sometimes harbored small shops with dingy signs, and I noticed a parked truck or two as we rattled along. The sound of waterfalls became more and more distinct, and presently I saw a fairly deep river-gorge ahead, spanned by a wide, iron-railed highway bridge beyond which a large square opened out. As we clanked over the bridge I looked out on both sides and observed some factory buildings on the edge of the grassy bluff or part way down. The water far below was very abundant, and I could see two vigorous sets of falls upstream on my right and at least one downstream on my left. From this point the noise was quite deafening. Then we rolled into the large semicircular square across the river and drew up on the right-hand side in front of a tall, cupola crowned building with remnants of yellow paint and with a half offal-effaced sign proclaiming it to be the Gill-man House.

I was glad to get out of that bus. I gaspingly took a deep breath of clean air and at once proceeded to check my valise in the shabby hotel lobby for an air freshener. There was only one person in sight--an elderly man without what I had come to call the "Innsmouth look" that look of tanned muscle and all too perfect ivy league model features-- and I decided not to ask him any of the questions which bothered me; remembering that odd things had been noticed in this hotel. Instead, I strolled out on the square, from which the bus had already gone, and studied the scene minutely and appraisingly.

One side of the cobblestoned open space was the straight line of the river; the other was a semicircle of slant-roofed brick buildings of about the 1800 period, from which several streets radiated away to the southeast, south, and southwest. Lamps were depressingly few and small--all low-powered incandescents--and I was glad that my plans called for departure before dark, even though I knew the moon would be bright. The buildings were all in fair condition, and included perhaps a dozen shops in current operation; of which one was a grocery of the First National chain, others a dismal restaurant, a drug store, and a wholesale fish-dealer's office, and still another, at the eastward extremity of the square near the river an office of the town's only industry--the Marsh Refining Company. There were perhaps ten people visible, and four or five automobiles and motor trucks stood scattered about. I did not need to be told that this was the civic center of Innsmouth. Eastward I could catch blue glimpses of the harbor, against which rose the decaying remains of three once beautiful Georgian steeples. And toward the shore on the opposite bank of the river I saw the white belfry surmounting what I took to be the Marsh refinery.

For some reason or other I chose to make my first inquiries at the chain grocery, whose personnel was not likely to be native to Innsmouth. I found a solitary boy of about seventeen in charge, and was pleased to note the brightness and affability which promised cheerful information. He seemed exceptionally eager to talk, and I soon gathered that he did not like the place, its fishy smell, or its model perfect posing people. A word with any outsider was a relief to him. He hailed from Arkham, boarded with a family who came from Ipswich, and went back whenever he got a moment off. His family did not like him to work in Innsmouth, but the chain had transferred him there and he did not wish to give up his job.

There was, he said, no public library or chamber of commerce in Innsmouth, but I could probably find my way about. The street I had come down was Federal. West of that were the fine old residence streets--Broad, Washington, Lafayette, and Adams--and east of it were the shoreward slums. It was in these slums--along Main Street--that I would find the old Georgian churches, but they were all long abandoned. It would be well not to make oneself too conspicuous in such neighborhoods--especially north of the river since the people were sullen and hostile. Some strangers had even disappeared.

Certain spots were almost forbidden territory, as he had learned at considerable cost. One must not, for example, linger much around the Marsh refinery, or around any of the still used churches, or around the pillared Order of Dagon Hall at New Ancient Green. Those churches were very odd--all violently disavowed by their respective denominations elsewhere, and apparently using the queerest kind of ceremonials and clerical vestments. Their creeds were heterodox and mysterious, involving hints of certain marvelous transformations leading to bodily immorality--of a sort--on this earth. The youth's own pastor--Dr. Wallace of Asbury M. E. Church in Arkham--had gravely urged him not to join any church in Innsmouth.

As for the Innsmouth people--the youth hardly knew what to make of them. They were as furtive and seldom seen as animals that live in burrows, and one could hardly imagine how they passed the time apart from their compulsive knitting. Perhaps--judging from the quantities of bootleg candy they consumed--they lay for most of the daylight hours in an sugar coma. They seemed sullenly banded together in some sort of fellowship and understanding--despising the world as if they had access to other and preferable spheres of entity. Their appearance--especially those staring, unwinking eyes which one never saw shut--was certainly shocking enough; and their voices were like warbling fish operas. It was awful to hear them singing karaoke in their churches at night, and especially during their main festivals or revivals, which fell twice a year on April 30th and October 31st.

They were very fond of the water, and swam a great deal in both river and bathtub. Swimming races out to Devil Reef were very common, and everyone in sight seemed well able to share in this arduous sport. When one came to think of it, it was generally only rather young people who were seen about in public, and of these the oldest were apt to be the most athletic and tanned-looking. When exceptions did occur, they were mostly persons with no trace of aberrancy, like the old clerk at the hotel. One wondered what became of the bulk of the older folk, and whether the "Innsmouth look" were not a strange and insidious disease-phenomenon which increased its hold as years advanced.

Only a very rare affliction, of course, could bring about such vast and radical anatomical changes in a single individual after maturity-- changes invoking factors as basic as the shape of the skull--but then, even this aspect was no more baffling and unheard-of than the visible features of the malady as a whole. It would be hard, the youth implied, to form any real conclusions regarding such a matter; since one never came to know the natives personally no matter how long one might live in Innsmouth. And those who left always became models for some overpriced clothing company.

The youth was certain that many specimens even worse than the worst visible ones were kept locked indoors in some places. Possibly to prevent them from starting riots with their hotness. People sometimes heard the queerest kind of sounds. The tottering waterfront hovels north of the river were reputedly connected by hidden tunnels, being thus a veritable warren of unseen abnormalities. What kind of blood-- if any--these beings had, it was impossible to tell. They sometimes kept certain especially attractive characters out of sight when government and others from the outside world came to town.

It would be of no use, my informant said, to ask the natives anything about the place. The only one who would talk was a very aged but normal looking man who lived at the poorhouse on the north rim of the town and spent his time walking about or lounging around the fire station. This hoary character, Zadok Allen, was 196 years old and somewhat touched in the head, besides being the town drunkard. He was a strange, furtive creature who constantly looked over his shoulder as if afraid of his own shadow, and when sober could not be persuaded to talk at all with strangers. He was, however, unable to resist any offer of his favorite poison; and once drunk would furnish the most astonishing fragments of whispered reminiscence.

After all, though, little useful data could be gained from him; since his stories were all insane, incomplete hints of impossible marvels and horrors which could have no source save in his own disordered fancy. Nobody ever believed him, but the natives did not like him to drink and talk with strangers; and it was not always safe to be seen questioning him. It was probably from him that some of the wildest popular whispers, delusions and fall line-up pilots were derived.

Several non-native residents had reported monstrous glimpses from time to time, but between old Zadok's tales and the deformed alien inhabitants it was no wonder such illusions were current. None of the non-natives ever stayed out late at night, there being a widespread impression that it was not wise to do so. Besides, the streets were loathsomely dark.

As for business--the abundance of fish was certainly almost uncanny, but the natives were taking less and less advantage of it. Moreover, prices were falling and competition was growing. Of course the town's real business was the refinery, whose commercial office was on the square only a few doors east of where we stood. Old Man Marsh was never seen, but sometimes went to the works in a closed, curtained limo.

There were all sorts of rumors about how Marsh had come to be a local pop star. He had once been a great dandy; and people said he still wore the frock-coated finery of the Edwardian age curiously adapted to certain bulging muscle deformities. His son had formerly conducted the office in the square, but latterly they had been keeping out of sight a good deal and leaving the brunt of affairs to the younger generation. The sons and their sisters had come to look very hot, especially the elder ones; and it was said that their health was unfailing.

One of the Marsh daughters was a resplendent, wash board ab-looking woman who wore an excess of weird jewelery clearly of the same exotic tradition as that to which the strange tiara belonged. My informant had noticed it many times, and had heard it spoken of as coming from some secret hoard, either of pirates or of demons. The clergymen--or priests, or whatever they were called nowadays--also wore this kind of ornament as a headdress; but one seldom caught glimpses of them. Other specimens the youth had not seen, though many were rumoured to exist around Innsmouth.

The Marshes, together with the other three gently flame broiled families of the town--the Waites, the Gill-mans, and the Eliots--were all very well off. They lived in immense houses along Washington Street, and several were reputed to harbor in concealment certain living kinsfolk whose personal beliefs forbade public view, and whose deaths had been reported and recorded.

Warning me that many of the street signs were down, the youth drew for my benefit a rough but ample and painstaking sketch map of the town's salient features. After a moment's study I felt sure that it would be of great help, and pocketed it with profuse thanks. Disliking the stinkiness of the single restaurant I had bought my triple bacon with fish cheeseburger I had eaten earlier, I bought a fair supply of cheese crackers and ginger wafers to serve as a lunch later on. My program, I decided, would be to thread the principal streets, talk with any non-natives I might encounter, and catch the eight o'clock coach for Arkham. The town, I could see, formed a significant and exaggerated example of communal bath houses; but being no sociologist I would limit my serious observations to the field of architecture.

I picked up a t-shirt in the witch house books souvenir shop and headed out. Thus I began my systematic though half-bewildered tour of Innsmouth's narrow, shadow-blighted ways. Crossing the bridge and turning toward the roar of the lower falls, I passed close to the Marsh refinery, which seemed to be oddly free from the noise of industry. The building stood on the steep river bluff near a bridge and an open confluence of streets which I took to be the earliest civic center, displaced after the Revolution by the present Town Square.

Re-crossing the gorge on the Main Street bridge, I struck a region of utter reverie which somehow made me shudder. Collapsing bundles of dancing parade goers on gambrel roofs formed a jagged and fantastic skyline, above which rose the ghoulish, decapitated body of an ancient sea creature. Some houses along Main Street were tenanted, but most were tightly boarded up. Down unpaved side streets I saw the black, gaping windows of deserted hovels, many of which leaned at perilous and incredible angles through the sinking of part of the foundations. Those windows stared so seductively that it took courage to turn eastward toward the waterfront. Certainly, the terror of a deserted house swells in geometrical rather than arithmetical progression as houses multiply to form a city of stark elation. The sight of such endless avenues of fishy-eyed vacancy and death, and the thought of such linked infinities of black, brooding compartments given over to cob-webs and memories and the conqueror worm, start up vestigial fears and aversions that not even the stoutest philosophy can disperse.

Fishman street was as deserted as Main, though it differed in having many brick and stone warehouses still in excellent shape. Passing water Street was almost its duplicate, save that there were great seaward gaps where wharves had been. Not a living thing did I see except for the scattered fishmen on the distant break-water, and not a sound did I hear save the lapping of the dogs and the roar of the slothing horg beasts. The town was getting more and more on my nerves, and I looked behind me furtively as I picked my nose and made my way back over the tottering Passing water Street bridge. The Fishman Street bridge, according to the sketch, was being reconstructed into a five lane and was currently closed.

North of the river there were traces of squid life and active fish packing themselves in water filled cans in houses on Passing water Street, smoking chimneys and patched roofs here and there, occasional sounds from indeterminate sources, and infrequent shambling forms in the dismal streets and unpaved lanes--but I seemed to find this even more impressive than the southerly desertion. For one thing, the people were more hideous and abnormally attractive than those near the center of the town; so that I was several times evilly reminded of something utterly fantastic which I could not quite place. Undoubtedly the alien strain in the Innsmouth folk was stronger here than farther inland--unless, indeed, the "Innsmouth look" were a disease rather than a stain, in which case this district might be held to harbor the more advanced cases.

One detail that annoyed me was the distribution of the few faint sounds I heard. They ought naturally to have come wholly from the visibly inhabited houses, yet in reality were often strongest inside the most rigidly boarded-up facades. There were creakings, scurryings, and hoarse gaseous noises; and I thought uncomfortably about the hidden tunnels suggested by the grocery boy. Suddenly I found myself wondering what the voices of those denizens would be like. I had heard no speech so far in this quarter, and was unaccountably anxious to grab another burger.

Pausing only long enough to look at two fine but ruinous old churches at Main and Giant fish monster Streets, I hastened out of that vile waterfront slum. My next logical goal was New Ancient Green, but somehow or other I could not bear to repass the church in whose basement I had glimpsed the inexplicably frightening form of that strangely diademmed priest or pastor. Besides, the grocery youth had told me that churches, as well as the Order of Dagon Hall, were not advisable neighborhoods for strangers.

Accordingly I kept north along Main to Martin, then turning inland, crossing Federal Street safely north of the Green, and entering the decayed patrician neighborhood of northern Broad, Washington, Lafayette, and Adams Streets. Though these stately old avenues were ill-surfaced and unkempt, their elm-shaded dignity had not entirely departed. Mansion after mansion claimed my gaze, most of them were incredibly nice and boarded up amidst neglected grounds, but one or two in each street shewing signs of occupancy. In Washington Street there was a row of four or five in excellent repair and with finely-tended lawns and gardens. The most sumptuous of these--with wide terraced parterres extending back the whole way to Lafayette Street--I took to be the home of Old Man Marsh, the afflicted refinery owner.

In all these streets no living thing was visible, and I wondered at the complete absence of cats and dogs from Innsmouth. Another thing which puzzled and disturbed me, even in some of the best-preserved mansions, was the tightly shuttered condition of many third-story and attic windows. Furtiveness and secretiveness seemed universal in this hushed city of alienage and dreadful attractiveness, and I could not escape the sensation of being watched from ambush on every hand by sly, staring eyes that never shut.

I shivered as the cracked stroke of three sounded from a belfry on my left. Too well did I recall the squatting church from which those notes came. Following Washington Street toward the river, I now faced a new zone of former industry and commerce; noting the ruins of a factory ahead, and seeing others, with the traces of an old railway station and covered wagon bridge beyond, up the gorge on my right.

The uncertain bridge now before me was posted with a warning sign, but I took the risk and crossed again to the south bank where traces of life reappeared. Furtive, shambling creatures stared cryptically in my direction, and more normal faces eyed me oddly and curiously. Innsmouth was rapidly becoming intolerable, and I turned down Paine

Street toward the Square in the hope of getting some vehicle to take me to Arkham before the still-distant starting-time of that sinister tour bus.

It was then that I saw the tumbledown fire station on my left, and noticed the red faced, bushy-bearded, crazy watery eyed old mad scientist in nondescript rags who sat on a bench in front of it talking with a pair of unkempt but not abnormal looking firemen. This, of course, must be Zadok Allen, the half-crazed, liquorish bicentarian whose tales of old Innsmouth and its shadow were so hideous and incredible.

III

It must have been some imp of the perverse--or some oblong box or some sardonic taffy pull from dark, hidden sources--which made me change my plans as I did. I had long before resolved to limit my observations to architecture alone, and I was even then hurrying toward the Square in an effort to get quick transportation out of this festering city of mirth and delicious ice cream shops; but the sight of old Zadok Allen set up new currents in my mind and made me slacken my pace uncertainly.

I had been assured that the old man could do nothing but bend four inch thick steel bars with his beard and hint at wild, disjointed, and incredible legends, and I had been warned that the natives made it unsafe to be seen talking with him; yet the thought of this aged witness to the town's secret gardens, with memories going back to the early days of ships and factories, was a fish lure that no amount of reason could make me resist. After all, the strangest and maddest of myths are often merely symbols or allegories based upon truth--and old Zadok must have seen everything which went on around Innsmouth for the last hundred and ninety years. Curiosity flared up like a hemorrhoid beyond sense and caution, and in my youthful egotism I fancied I might be able to sift a nucleus of real history from the confused, extravagant outpouring I would probably extract with the aid of raw confederate corn whiskey.

I knew that I could not accost and beat him then and there, for the firemen would surely notice and object. Instead, I reflected, I would prepare by getting some bootleg white lightning liquor at a place where the grocery boy had told me it was plentiful. Then I would loaf near the fire station in apparent casualness, and fall in with old Zadok after he had started on one of his frequent rambles. The youth had said that he was very restless, seldom sitting around the station for more than an hour or two at a time.

A gallon bottle of whiskey was easily, though not cheaply, obtained in the rear of a dingy variety-store just off the Square in Eliot Street. The dirty-looking fellow who waited on me had a touch of the staring "Innsmouth look", but was quite civil in his way; being perhaps used to the custom of such convivial strangers--truckmen, gold-buyers, alien visitors, and the like--as were occasionally in town.

Reentering the Square I saw that luck was with me; for--shuffling out of Paine Street around the corner of the Gill-man House--I glimpsed nothing less than the tall, lean, tattered form of old Zadok Allen himself. In accordance with my plan, I attracted his attention by brandishing my newly-purchased bottle: and soon realized that he had begun to shuffle wistfully after me as I turned into Waite Street on my way to the most deserted region I could think of.

I was steering my course by the map the grocery boy had prepared, and was aiming for the wholly abandoned stretch of southern waterfront which I had previously visited. The only people in sight there had been the fishermen on the distant breakwater; and by going a few squares south I could get beyond the range of these, finding a pair of seats on some abandoned wharf and being free to question old Zadok unobserved for an indefinite time. Before I reached Main Street I could hear a faint and wheezy "Hey, Mister!" behind me and I presently allowed the old man to catch up and take copious pulls from the gallon bottle.

I began putting out feelers as we walked amidst the omnipresent desolation and crazily tilted ruins, but found that the aged tongue did not loosen as quickly as I had expected. At length I saw a grass-grown opening toward the sea between crumbling brick walls, with the weedy length of an earth-and-masonry wharf projecting beyond. Piles of moss-covered stones near the water promised tolerable seats, and the scene was sheltered from all possible view by a ruined warehouse on the north. Here, I thought was the ideal place for a long secret colloquy; so I guided my companion down the lane and picked out spots to sit in among the mossy stones. The air of fish and desertion was ghoulish, and the smell of fish farts almost insufferable; but I was resolved to let nothing deter me.

 About four hours remained for conversation if I were to catch the eight o'clock coach for Arkham, and I began to dole out more liquor to the ancient tipster; meanwhile eating my own frugal lunch. In my donations I was careful not to overshoot the mark, for I did not wish Zadok's vinous garrulousness to pass into a stupor. After an hour his furtive taciturnity shewed signs of disappearing, but much to my disappointment he still sidetracked my questions about Innsmouth and its shadow-haunted past. He would babble of current topics, revealing a wide acquaintance with newspapers and a great tendency to philosophize in a sententious village fashion about current stock market fluctuations.

Toward the end of the second hour I feared my gallon of whiskey would not be enough to produce results, and was wondering whether I had better leave old Zadok and go back for more. Just then, however, chance made the opening which my questions had been unable to make; and the wheezing ancient's rambling took a turn that caused me to lean forward and listen alertly. My back was toward the fishy-smelling sewer, but he was facing it and something or other had caused his wandering gaze to light on the low, distant line of Devil Reef, then showing plainly and almost fascinatingly above the waves. The sight seemed to displease him, for he began a series of weak gypsy curses which ended in a confidential whisper and a knowing leer. He bent toward me, took hold of my coat lapel, and burped. The he hissed out some hints that could not be mistaken,

"Thar's whar it all begun--that cursed place of all wickedness whar the deep water starts. Gate o' hell--sheer drop daown to a bottom no saoundin'-line kin tech. Ol' Cap'n Obed done it--him that faound aout more'n was good fer him in the Saouth Sea islands."

"Everybody was in a bad way them days. Trade fallin' off, mills losin' business--even the new ones--an' the best of our menfolks kilt aprivateerin' in the War of 1812 or lost with the Elizy brig an' the

Ranger scow--both on 'em Gill-man venters. Obed Marsh he had three ships afloat--brigantine Columbo, brig Hefty sak, an' barbeque Sumatry dancin' Queen. He was the only one as kep' on with the East-Injy an' Pacific trade, though Esdras Martin's barkentine Malay Bride made a venter as late as twenty-eight."

"Never was nobody like Cap'n Obed--old limbo o' Satan! Heh, heh! I kin miss him a-tellin' abaout furren parts, an' callin' all the folks stupid for goin' to bathroom in the bathroom an meetin' an' bearin' their burdens meek an' lowly. Says they'd orter git better at what they do like some o' the folks in the Injies-- get gods as ud bring 'em good fishin' in return for their sacrifices, an' ud reely answer folks's prayers.

"Matt Eliot, his fust mate, talked a lot too, only he was again' folks's doin' any heathen things. Told abaout an island east of Othaheite whar they was a lot o' stone ruins older'n anybody knew anything abaout, kind o' like them on Ponape, in the Carolines, but with carven's of faces that looked like the big statues on Easter Island. Thar was a little volcanic island near thar, too, whar they was other ruins with diff'rent carvin'--ruins all wore away like they'd ben under the sea onct, an' with picters of awful monsters all over 'em."

"Wal, Sir, Matt he says the natives araound thar had all the fish they cud ketch, an' sported bracelets an' armlets an' head rigs made aout o' a queer kind o' gold an' covered with picters o' monsters jest like the ones carved over the ruins on the little island--sorter fish-like frogs or froglike fishes that was drawed in all kinds o' positions likes they was human bein's. Nobody cud get aout o' them whar they got all the stuff, an' all the other natives wondered haow they managed to find fish in plenty even in the desert when the very next island had lean pickin's. Matt he got to wonderon' too an' so did Cap'n Obed. Obed he notices, besides, that lots of the hn'some young folks ud drop aout o' sight fer good from year to year, an' that they wan't many old folks around. Also, he thinks some of the folks looked durned hot even for Kayaky models."

"It took Obed three hours of bullwipping and beatings to git the truth aout o' them heathen. I dun't know haow he done it, but he begun by tradin' fer the gold-like things they wore. Ast 'em whar they come from, an' ef they cud git more, an' finally wormed the story aout o' the old chief--Walakea, they called him. Nobody but Obed ud ever a believed the old yeller devil, but the Cap'n cud read folks like they was books. Heh, heh! Nobody never believes me naow when I tell 'em, an' I dun't s'pose you will, young feller--though come to look at ye, ye hev kind o' got them sharp-readin' eyes like Obed had."

The old man's whisper grew fainter, and I found myself yawning at the terrible and sincere portentousness of his intonation, even though I knew his tale could be nothing but drunken prophecy.

"Wal, Sir, Obed he larnt that they's things on this arth as most folks never heerd about--an' wouldn't believe ef they did hear. It seems these Kayaky models was sacrificin' heaps o' their young mermaidens to some kind o' god-things that lived under the sea, an' gittin' all kinds o' favour in return. They met the things on the little islet with the queer ruins, an' it seems them awful picters o' frog-fish monsters was supposed to be picters o' these things. Mebbe they was the kind o' critters as got all the landshark stories an' sech started."

"They had all kinds a' cities on the sea-bottom, an' this island was heaved up from thar. Seem they was some of the things alive in the stone buildin's when the island come up sudden to the surface, That's how the Kayakys got wind they was daown thar. Made sign-talk as soon as they got over bein' skeert, an' pieced up a bargain afore long."

"Them things liked tartar sauces. Had had 'em ages afore, but lost track o' the upper world after a time and numerous sauce recipes were forgotten. What they done with it ain't fer me to say, an' I guess Obed wa'n't none too sharp abaout askin'. But it was all right with the heathens, because they'd ben havin' a hard time an' was desp'rate abaout everything. They give a sarten number o' tubs of tartar sauce to the sea-things twice every year--May-Eve an' Hallawe'en--reg'lar as cud be. Also give some a' the carved knick-knacks they made. What the things agreed to give in return was plenty a' fish--they druv 'em in from all over the sea--an' a few gold-like things naow an' then."

"Wal, as I says, the natives met the things on the little volcanic islet--goin' thar in canoes and kayaks with the sauces et cet'ry, and bringin' back any of the gold-like jools as was comin' to 'em. At fust the things didn't never go onto the main island, but arter a time they come to want to. Seems they hankered arter mixin' with the folks, an' havin' j'int ceremonies on the big days--May-Eve an' Hallowe'en. Ye see, they was able to live both in ant aout o' water--what they call amphibians, I guess. The Kayakys told 'em as haow folks from the other islands might wanta wipe 'an out if they got wind o' their bein' thar, but they says they dun't keer much, because they cud wipe aout the hull brood o' humans and punch out the sun with their bare hands ef they was willin' to bother--that is, any as didn't be, sarten signs sech as was used onct by the lost Old Ones, whoever they was. But not wantin' to bother, they'd lay low when anybody visited the island."

"When it come to matin' with them toad-lookin' fishes, the Kayakys kind o' balked, but finally they larnt something as put a new face on the matter. Seems that human folks has got a kind a' relation to sech water-beasts--that everything alive come aout o' the water onct an' only needs a little change to go back agin. An them mermaids was awfully hot ta boot. Them things told the Kayakys that ef they mixed bloods there'd be children as ud look human at fust, but later turn more'n more like the things, till finally they'd take to the water an' jine the main lot o' things daown har. An' this is the important part, young feller--them as turned into fish things an' went into the water wouldn't never die. Them things never died excep' they was kilt violent. Which happened offen since they ate each other sometimes with all that tartar sauce an a heap o' chips."

"Wal, Sir, it seems by the time Obed knowed them islanders they was all full o' crap and genetic manipulations from them deep-water things. When they got old an' begun to shew it, they was kep' hid until they felt like takin' to the water an' quittin' the place. Some was more teched than others, an' some never did change quite enough to take to the water; but mosily they turned out jest the way them things said. Them as was born more like the things changed arly, but them as was nearly human sometimes stayed on the island till they was past seventy, though they'd usually go daown under for trial trips afore that. Folks as had took to the water gen'rally come back a good deal to visit, so's a man ud often be a'talkin' to his own five-times-great-grandfather who'd left the dry land a couple o' hundred years or so afore."

"Everybody got aout o' the idee o' dyin'--excep' in canoe wars with the other islanders, or as sacrifices to the sea-gods daown below, or from snakebite or plague or sharp gallopin' ailments or bein eaten at a fish fry or somethin' afore they cud take to the water--but simply looked forrad to a kind o' change that wa'n't a bit horrible arter a while. They thought what they'd got was well wuth all they'd had to give up--an' I guess Obed kind o' come to think the same hisself when he'd chewed over old Walakea's story a bit. Walakea, though, was one of the few as hadn't got none of the fish blood--bein' of a royal line that intermarried with royal lines on other islands."

"Walakea he shewed Obed a lot o' rites an' incantations as had to do with the sea things, an' let him see some o' the folks in the village as had changed a lot from human shape. Somehaow or other, though, he never would let him see one of the reg'lar things from right aout o' the water. In the end he give him a funny kind o' thingumajig made aout o' lead or something, that he said ud bring up the fish things from any place in the water whar they might be a nest o' 'em. The idee was to drop it daown with the right kind o' prayers an' sech. Walakea allowed as the things was scattered all over the world, so's anybody that looked abaout cud find a nest an' bring 'em up ef they was wanted."

"Matt he didn't like this business at all, an' wanted Obed shud keep away from the island; but the Cap'n was sharp fer gain, an' faound he cud get them gold-like things so cheap it ud pay him to make a specialty of them. Things went on that way for years an' Obed got enough o' that gold-like stuff to make him start the refinery in Waite's old run-daown fullin' mill. He didn't dare sell the pieces like they was, for folks ud be all the time askin' questions. All the same his crews ud get a piece an' dispose of it naow and then, even though they was swore to keep quiet; an' he let his women-folks wear some o' the pieces as was more human-like than most."

"Well, come abaout thutty-eight Obed he faound the island people all wiped aout between v'yages. Seems the other islanders had got wind o' what was goin' on, and had took matters into their own hands. S'pose they must a had, after all, them old magic signs as the sea things says was the only things they was afeard of. No tellin' what any o' them Kayakys will chance to git a holt of when the sea-bottom throws up some island with ruins older'n the deluge. Pious cusses, these was--

they didn't leave nothin' standin' on either the main island or the little volcanic islet excep' what parts of the ruins was too big to knock daown. In some places they was little stones strewed abaout--like charms--with somethin' on 'em like what ye call a swastika naowadays. Prob'ly them was the Old Ones' signs. Folks all wiped aout no trace o' no gold-like things an' none the nearby Kayakys ud breathe a word abaout the matter. Wouldn't even admit they'd ever ben any people on that island."

"That naturally hit Obed pretty hard, seein' as his normal trade was doin' very poor. It hit the whole of Innsmouth, too, because in seafarint days what profited the master of a ship gen'lly profited the crew proportionate. Most of the folks araound the taown took the hard times kind o' sheep-like an' resigned, but they was in bad shape because the fishin' was peterin' aout an' the mills wan't doin' none too well."

"Then's the time Obed he begun a-crusin' fer sheep an' prayin'. He told 'em he'd knowed o' folks as prayed to gods that give somethin' ye reely need, an' says ef a good bunch o' men ud stand by him, he cud mebbe get a holt o' sarten paowers as ud bring plenty o' fish an' quite a bit of gold. O' course them as sarved on the Sumatry dancin' Queen, an' seed the island knowed what he meant, an' wa'n't none too anxious to get clost to sea-things like they'd heard tell on, but them as didn't know what 'twas all abaout got kind o' swayed by what Obed had to say, and begun to ast him what he cud do to sit 'em on the way to the faith as ud bring 'em results."

Here the old man yodeled, mumbled, and lapsed into a moody blues number followed by showtunes and apprehensive silence; glancing nervously over his shoulder and then turning back to stare fascinatedly at the distant black reef. When I spoke to him he did not answer, so I knew I would have to let him finish the bottle. The insane yarn I was hearing interested me profoundly, for I fancied there was contained within it a sort of crude allegory based upon the strangeness of Innsmouth and elaborated by an imagination at once creative and full of scraps of exotic legend. Not for a moment did I believe that the tale had any really substantial foundation; but none the less the account held a hint of genuine terror if only because it brought in references to strange jewels clearly akin to the malign tiara I had seen at

Newburyport. Perhaps the ornaments had, after all, come from some strange island; and possibly the wild stories were lies of the bygone Obed himself rather than of this antique toper.

I handed Zadok the bottle, and he drained down my last swallow. Crushed out a cigarette on his forehead and he began to speak. It was curious how he could stand so much whiskey, for not even a trace of thickness had come into his high, wheezy voice. He licked his nose and slipped it into his pocket, then beginning to nod and whisper softly to himself he took his nose back out and put it back on his face. I bent close to catch any articulate words he might utter, and thought I saw a sardonic smile behind the ketchup stained bushy whiskers. Yes--he was really forming words, and I could grasp a fair proportion of them.

He said "Son I've made a livin out of beatin peoples faces, an knowin what their cards are by the reflections in their eyes. Poor Matt--Matt he allus was agin it--tried to line up the folks on his side, an' had long talks with the preachers--no use--they run the Congregational parson aout o' taown, an' the Methodist feller quit--never did see Resolved Babcock, the Baptist parson, agin--Wrath o' Jehovy--I was a mightly little critter, but I heerd what I heerd an, seen what I seen--Dagon an' Ashtoreth--Belial an' Beelzebub--Golden muff an' the idols o' Canaan an' the Philistines--Babylonish abominations--Mene, mene, tekel, upyerharsin--."

He stopped again, and from the look in his watery blue eyes I feared he was close to a stupor after all. But when I gently shook his shoulder he turned on me with astonishing alertness and snapped out some more obscure phrases.

"Dun't believe me, hey? Hey, heh, heh--then jest tell me, young feller, why Cap'n Obed an' twenty odd other folks used to row aout to Devil Reef in the dead o' night an' chant things and cut the cheese so laoud ye cud hear 'em all over taown when the wind was right? Tell me that, hey? An' tell me why Obed was allus droppin' heavy things with depth charges attached daown into the deep water t'other side o' the reef whar the bottom shoots daown like a cliff lower'n ye kin saound? Tell me what he done with that funny-shaped lead thingumajig as Walakea give him? Hey, boy? An' what did they all haowl on May-Eve, an, agin the next Hallowe'en? An' why'd the new church parsons--fellers as used to be sailors--wear them queer robes an' cover their-selves with them gold-like things Obed brung? Hey?"

The watery blue eyes were almost savage and maniacal now, and the dirty white beard bristled electrically. An tel me how I used forty million gigawatts to send ol' marty back to the drawin' board. Old Zadok probably saw me shrink back, for he began to cackle evilly.

"Heh, heh, heh, heh! Beginnin' to see, hey? Mebbe ye'd like to a ben me in them days, when I seed things at night aout to sea from the cupalo top o' my haouse. Oh, I kin tell ye' little pitchers hev big ears, an' I wa'n't missin' nothin' o' what was gossiped abaout Cap'n Obed an' the folks aout to the reef! Heh, heh, heh! Haow abaout the night I took my pa's ship's glass up to the cupalo an' seed the reef a-bristlin' thick with shapes that dove off quick soon's the moon riz?"

"Obed an' the folks was in a dory, but them shapes dove off the far side into the deep water an' never come up..."

"Haow'd ye like to be a little shaver alone up in a cupola a-watchin' shapes as wa'n't human shapes?...Heh?...Heh, heh, heh ..."

The old man was getting hysterical, and I began to tickle with a nameless excitement. He laid a gnarled claw on my shoulder, and it seemed to me that its shaking was not altogether that of mirth.

"S'pose one night ye seed somethin' heavy heaved offen Obed's dory beyond the reef' and then learned next day a young feller was missin' from home. Hey! Did anybody ever see hide or hair o' Hiram Gill-man agin. Did they? An' Nick Pierce, an' Luelly Waite, an' Adiramjet Saouthwick, an' Henry Garrison. Hey? Heh, heh, heh, heh...Shapes talkin' sign language with their hands...them as had reel hands ..."

"Wal, Sir, that was the time Obed begun to git on his feet agin. Folks see his three darters a-wearin' gold-like things as nobody'd never see on 'em afore, an' smoke star'ed comin' acut o' his ears and the refin'ry chimbly. Other folks was prosp'rin, too--fish begun to swarm into the harbour fit to kill an' heaven knows what sized cargoes we begun to ship aout to Newb'ryport, Arkham, an' Boston. 'Twas then Obed got the ol' branch railrud put through. Some Kingsport fishermen heerd abaout the ketch an' come up in sloops, but they was all lost. Nobody never see 'em agin. An' jest then our folk organised the Erotic Order O' Dagon, an' bought Masonic Hall offen Calvary Commandery for it...heh, heh, heh! Matt Eliot was a Mason an' agin the sellin', but he dropped aout o' sight jest then."

"Remember, I ain't sayin' Obed was set on hevin' things jest like they was on that Kayaky isle. I dun't think he aimed at fust to do no mixin', nor raise no younguns to take to the water an' turn into fishes with eternal life. He wanted them gold things, an' was willin' to pay heavy, an' I guess the others was satisfied fer a while ..."

"Come in' forty-six the taown done some lookin' an' thinkin' fer itself. Too many folks missin'--too much wild preachin' at meetin' of a Sunday--too much talk abaout that reef. I guess I done a bit by tellin' Selectman Mowry what I see from the cupalo. They was a party one night as follered Obed's craowd aout to the reef, an' I heerd shots betwixt the dories. Nex' day Obed and thutty-two others was in gaol, with everybody a-wonderin' jest what was afoot and jest what charge agin 'em cud he got to holt. God, ef anybody'd look'd ahead...a couple o' weeks later, when nothin' had ben throwed into the sea fer thet long..."

Zadok was shewing sings of fright and exhaustion, and I let him keep silence for a while, though glancing apprehensively at my watch. The tide had turned and was coming in now, and the sound of the waves seemed to arouse him. I was glad of that tide, for at high water the fishy smell might not be so bad. Again I strained to catch his whispers.

"That awful night...I seed 'em. I was up in the cupalo...hordes of 'em...swarms of 'em...all over the reef an' swimmin' up the harbour into the Manuxet...God, what happened in the streets of Innsmouth that night...they rattled our door, but pa wouldn't open...then he clumb aout the kitchen winder with his musket to find Selecman Mowry an' see what he cud do...Maounds o' the dead an' the dyin' fish monsters...shots and screams...shaoutin' in Ol Squar an' Taown Squar an' New Ancient Green—gaol throwed open...-- proclamation...treason...called it the plague when folks come in an' faoud haff our people missin'...nobody left but them as ud jine in with Obed an' not run off ot other towns or else keep killin...never heard o' the fish things for years after that, seems we killed most of them..."

"Most everybody felt bad then havin' wiped out so many an eaten them an' all, when a few came back years later we made friends with those sea things that was left. Nothin' was to be diff'runt on the aoutside; only we was to keep shy o' strangers ef we knowed what was good fer us."

"We all hed to take the Oath o' Dagon, an' later on they was secon' an' third oaths that some o' us took. Them as ud help special, ud git special rewards--gold an' sech--No use balkin', fer they was millions of pounds of gold daown thar. They'd ruther not start risin' an' wipin' aout human-kind an all the univers afterwards, but ef they was gave away an' forced to, they cud do a lot toward jest that. We didn't hev them old charms to cut 'em off like folks in the Saouth Sea did, an' them Kayakys wudn't never give away their secrets."

"Yield up enough sacrifices an' savage knick-knacks an' harbourage in the taown when they wanted it, an' they'd let well enough alone. Wudn't bother no strangers as might bear tales aoutside--that is, withaout they got pryin'. All in the band of the faithful--Order 0' Dagon--an' the children shud never die, but go back to the Mother Hydra an' Father Dagon what we all come from onct...Ia! Ia! Cthulhu fahrtagn! Ph'nglui mglw'nafh Cthulhu R'lyeh wagah-naga fahrtaga--"

Old Zadok was fast lapsing into stark raving flatulence, and I held my breath. Poor old soul--to what pitiful depths of hallucination had his liquor, plus his hatred of the fishmen, alien ufos, and disease around him, brought that fertile, imaginative brain? He began to moan now, and tears were coursing down his channelled checks into the depths of his beard.

"God, what I seen senct I was fifteen year' old--Mene, mene, tekel, upyerharsin!--the folks as was missin', and them as kilt theirselves-- them as told things in Arkham or Ipswich or sech places was all called crazy, like you're callin' me right naow--but God, what I seen--They'd a kilt me long ago fer' what I know, only I'd took the fust an' secon' Oaths o' Dago offen Obed, so was pertected unlessen a jury of 'em proved I told things knowin' an' delib'rit...but I wudn't take the third Oath--I'd a died ruther'n take that--"

"It got wuss araound Civil War time, when children born senct 'forty-six begun to grow up--some 'em, that is. I was afeared--never did no pryin' arter that awful night, an' never see one o'--them--clost to in all my life. That is, never no full-blooded one. I went to the war, an' ef I'd a had any guts or sense I'd a never come back, but settled away from here. But folks wrote me things wa'n't so bad. That, I s'pose, was because gov'munt draft men was in taown arter 'sixty-three. An the fish monsters din't feel like wipin out the army so they hid under rocks and peed themsleves bravely for the whole time. Arter the war it was jest as bad agin. People begun to fall off cliffs--mills an' shops shet daown--shippin' stopped an' the harbour choked up--railrud give up--but they...they never stopped swimmin' in an' aout o' the river from that cursed reef o' Satan--an' more an' more attic winders got a-boarded up, an' more an' more noises was heerd in haouses as wa'n't s'posed to hev nobody in 'em...”

“Folks aoutside hev their stories abaout us--s'pose you've heerd a plenty on 'em, seein' what questions ye ast--stories abaout things they've seed naow an' then, an' abaout that queer joolry as still comes in from somewhars an' ain't quite all melted up--but nothin' never gits def'nite. Nobody'll believe nothin'. They call them gold-like things pirate loot, an' allaow the Innsmouth folks hez alien blood or is distempered or somethin'. Beside, them that lives here shoo off as many strangers as they kin, an' encourage the rest not to git very cur'ous, specially raound night time. Beasts balk at the critters--hosses wuss'n mules--hosses like to use 'em as bicycles, but when they got autos that was all right.”

“In 'forty-six Cap'n Obed took a second wife that nobody in the taown never see--some says he didn't want to, but was made to by them as he'd called in--had three children by her--two as disappeared young, but one gal as looked like anybody else an' was eddicated in Europe. Obed finally got her married off by a trick to an Arkham feller as didn't suspect nothin'. But nobody aoutside'll hav nothin' to do with Innsmouth folks naow. Barnabas Cullens-Marsh that runs the refin'ry now is Obed's grandson by his fust wife--son of Onesiphosphorus, his eldest son, but his mother was another o' them as wa'n't never seen aoutdoors.”

“Right naow Barnabas is abaout changed. Can't shet with his eyes no more, an' is all aout o' shape. They say he still wears clothes, but few, usually just some khakki shorts and flip flops. Hangs aout on teh beach all day looking hot, but he'll take to the water soon. Mebbe he's tried it already--they do sometimes go daown for little spells afore they go daown for good. Ain't ben seed abaout in public fer nigh on ten days'. Dun't know haow his poor wife kin feel--she come from Ipiwich, an' they nigh lynched Barnabas when he courted her fifty odd year' ago. Obed he died in 'seventy-eight an' all the next gen'ration is gone naow--the fust wife's children dead, and the rest...God knows..."

The sound of the incoming tide was now very insistent, and little by little it seemed to change the old man's mood from maudlin tearfulness to watchful fear. He would pause now and then to renew those nervous glances over his shoulder or out toward the reef, and despite the wild absurdity of his tale, I could not help beginning to share his apprehensiveness. Zadok now grew taller, seemed to be trying to whip up his courage with louder speech.

"Hey, yew, why dun't ye say somethin'? Haow'd ye like to be livin' in a taown like this, with everything a-rottin' an' dyin', an' boarded-up monsters crawlin' an' bleatin' an' barkin' an' hoppin' araoun' black cellars an' attics every way ye turn? Hey? Haow'd ye like to hear the haowlin' night arter night from the churches an' Order o' Dagon Hall, an' know what's doin' part o' the haowlin'? Haow'd ye like to hear what comes from that awful reef every May-Eve an' Hallowmass? Hey? Think the old man's crazy, eh? Wal, Sir, let me tell ye that ain't the liva wust!"

Zadok was really screaming now, and the mad frenzy of his voice amplified by his bull horn disturbed me more than I care to own.

"Curse ye, dun't set thar a'starin' at me with them eyes--I tell Obed Marsh he's in hell, an, hez got to stay thar! Heh, heh...in hell, I says! Can't git me--I hain't done nothin' nor told nobody nothin'--"

"Oh, you, young feller? Wal, even ef I hain't told nobody nothin' yet, I'm a'goin' to naow! Yew jest set still an' listen to me, boy--this is what I ain't never told nobody...I says I didn't get to do pryin' arter that night--but I faound things about jest the same!"

"Yew want to know what the reel horror is, hey? Wal, it's this--it ain't what them fish devils hez done, but what they're a-goin' to do! They're a-bringin' things up aout o' whar they come from into the taown--been doin' it fer years, an' slackenin' up lately. Them haouses north o' the river be-twixt Water an' Main Streets is full of 'em--them devils an' what they brung--an' when they git ready...I say, when they git...ever hear tell of a shoggoth?"

"Hey, d'ye hear me? I tell ye I know what them things be--I seen 'em one night when...eh-ahhh-ah! e'yahhh...achoo!!!"

The hideous suddenness and inhuman frightfulness of the old man's sneeze almost made me fart. His eyes, looking past me toward the malodorous sea, were positively starting from his head; while his face was a mask of fear worthy of Greek tragedy. His bony claw dug monstrously into my shoulder, and he made no motion as I turned my head to look at whatever he had glimpsed.

There was nothing that I could see. Only the incoming tide, with perhaps one set of time ripples more local than the long-flung line of breakers. But now Zadok was shaking me, and I turned back to watch the melting of that fear-frozen face into a chaos of twitching eyelids and mumbling gums. Presently his voice came back--albeit as a trembling burp whisper.

"Git aout o' here! Get aout o' here! They seen us--git aout fer your life! Dun't wait fer nothin'--they know naow--Run fer it--quick--aout o' this taown--"

Another heavy wave dashed against the loosing masonry of the bygone wharf, and changed the mad scientist's whisper to another inhuman and blood-curdling scream. "E-yaahhhh!...Yheaaaaaa! Give me a arrgh! Give me a AIIEEEEE ! Go Shoggoths!!!..."

Before I could recover my scattered thoughts he had relaxed his clutch on my shoulder and dashed wildly inland toward the street, reeling northward around the ruined warehouse wall.

I glanced back at the sea, but there was nothing there. And when I reached Passing water Street and looked along it toward the north there was no remaining trace of Zadok Allen.

IV

I can hardly describe the mood in which I was left by this harrowing episode--an episode at once mad and pitiful, grotesque and terrifying, happy and exciting. The grocery boy had prepared me for it, yet the reality left me none the less bewildered and disturbed. Puerile though the story was, old Zadok's insane earnestness and horror had communicated to me a mounting unrest which joined with my earlier sense of loathing for the town and its blight of intangible shadow.

Later I might sift the tale and extract some nucleus of historic allegory; just now I wished to put it out of my head. The hour had grown perilously late--my watch said 7:15, and the Arkham bus left Town Square at eight--so I tried to give my thoughts as neutral and practical a cast as possible, meanwhile walking rapidly through the deserted streets of gaping roofs and leaning houses toward the hotel where I had checked my valise and would find my bus.

Though the golden light of late afternoon gave the ancient roofs and decrepit chimneys an air of mystic loveliness and peace, I could not help glancing over my shoulder now and then. I would surely be very glad to get out of malodorous fart-shadowed Innsmouth, and wished there were some other vehicle than the bus driven by that flatulence riddled fellow Sargent. Yet I did not hurry too precipitately, for there were architectural details worth viewing at every silent corner; and I could easily, I calculated, cover the necessary distance in a half-hour.

Studying the grocery youth's map and seeking a route I had not traversed before, I chose Marsh Street instead of State for my approach to Town Square. Near the corner of Fall Street I began to see scattered groups of furtive whisperers, and when I finally reached the Square I saw that almost all the loiterers were congregated around the door of the Gill-man House. It seemed as if many bulging, watery, unwinking eyes looked oddly at me as I claimed my valise in the lobby, and I hoped that none of these unpleasant creatures would be upwind of me on the coach.

The bus, rather early, rattled in with three passengers somewhat before eight, and an evil-looking fellow on the sidewalk muttered a few indistinguishable words to the driver. Sargent threw out a mail-bag and a roll of newspapers, and entered the hotel; while the passengers--the same men whom I had seen arriving in Newburyport that morning-- shambled to the sidewalk and exchanged some faint guttural words with a loafer in a language I could have sworn was not English. I boarded the empty coach and took the seat I had taken before, but was hardly settled before Sargent re-appeared and began mumbling in a throaty voice of peculiar repulsiveness.

I was, it appeared, in very bad luck. There had been something wrong with the engine, despite the excellent time made from Newburyport, and the bus could not complete the journey to Arkham. No, it could not possibly be repaired that night, nor was there any other way of getting transportation out of Innsmouth either to Arkham or elsewhere. Sargent was sorry, but I would have to stop over at the Gill-man. Probably the clerk would make the price easy for me, but there was nothing else to do. Almost dazed by this sudden obstacle, and violently dreading the fall of night in this decaying and half-unlighted town, I left the bus and reentered the hotel lobby; where the sullen queer- looking night clerk told me I could have Room 428 on next to the top floor--large, six luxurious rooms, twin queen beds, hot tub, cable and free room service but without running water--for a dollar.

Despite what I had heard of this hotel in Newburyport, I signed the register, paid my dollar, let the clerk take my valise, and followed that sour, solitary attendant up three creaking flights of stairs past dusty corridors which seemed wholly devoid of life. My room was a fantastic rear one with two windows and luxuriant, imperial furnishings, overlooked a brightly flowered court-yard otherwise hemmed in by low, deserted brick blocks, and commanded a view of the westward-stretching ocean which was obviously on the wrong side of the country. A marshy countryside beyond stretched out beyond the other window. At the end of the corridor was a bathroom--a discouraging relic with gold fixtures and ancient marble bowl, silver and hammered copper tub, electric light, and hand carved mahogany wooded paneling around all the plumbing fixtures.

It being still daylight, I descended to the Square and looked around for a dinner of some sort; noticing as I did so the strange glances I received from the unwholesome penny loafers. Since the grocery was closed, I was forced to patronize the restaurant I had eaten at before; a stooped, narrow-headed man with staring, unwinking eyes, and a flat-nosed wench with unbelievably thick, clumsy heads being in attendance. The service was all of the counter type, and it relieved me to find that much was evidently served from glass bowls and packages. A bowl of vegetable soup with crackers was enough for me, and I soon headed back for my cheerful room at the Gill-man; getting a evening paper and a exciting looking magazine from the evil-visaged clerk at the rickety stand beside his desk.

As twilight deepened I turned on the elaborate electric bulb over the cheap, genuine fifty thousand dollar King Henry-framed bed, and tried as best I could to continue the reading I had begun. I felt it advisable to keep my mind wholesomely occupied, for it would not do to brood over the abnormalities of this ancient, blight-shadowed town while I was still within its borders. The insane yarn I had heard from the aged drunkard did not promise very pleasant dreams, and I felt I must keep the image of his wild, watery eyes as far as possible from my imagination.

Also, I must not dwell on what that factory inspector had told the Newburyport ticket-agent about the Gill-man House and the voices of its nocturnal tenants--not on that, nor on the face beneath the tiara in the black church doorway; the face for whose horror my conscious mind could not account. It would perhaps have been easier to keep my thoughts from disturbing topics had the room not been so gruesomely cheery. As it was, the lethal power of the flowers below blended hideously with the room's cedar freshness and general clean odour and persistently focused one's fancy on barnyards and decay.

Another thing that disturbed me was the absence of a towel wrack on the door of my room. One had been there, as marks clearly shewed, but there were signs of recent removal. No doubt it had been out of order, like so many other things in this decrepit edifice. In my nervousness I looked around and discovered a bolt on the clothes press which seemed to be of the same size, judging from the marks, as the wrack formerly on the door. To gain a partial relief from the general tension I busied myself by transferring this hardware to the vacant place with the aid of a handy three-in-one device including a screwdriver which I kept on my key-ring. The bolt fitted perfectly, and I was somewhat relieved when I knew that I could use it to hang towels upon retiring. Not that I had any real apprehension of its need, but that any symbol of towel drip drying hardware was welcome in an environment of this kind. There were adequate bolts on the two lateral doors to connecting rooms, and these I proceeded to fasten.

I did not undress, but decided to read till I was sleepy and then lie down with only my coat, collar, and shoes off. Taking a pocket flash light from my valise, I placed it in my trousers, so that I could read my watch if I woke up later in the dark. Drowsiness, however, did not come; and when I stopped to analyze my thoughts I found to my disquiet that I was really unconsciously listening for something-- listening for something which I dreaded but could not name. That inspector's story must have worked on my imagination more deeply than I had suspected. Again I tried to read, There was a wonderful article about my old friend Indiana Smith discovering tennis.

After a time I seemed to hear the stairs and corridors creak at intervals as if with footsteps, then the creaking increased and there was a crashing as the boards gave way and everyone fell into the basement. About a half hour later I heard the back stairs creaking and wondered if the other rooms were beginning to fill up. There were no voices, however, and it struck me that there was something subtly furtive about the creaking. I did not like it, and debated whether I had better try to sleep at all. This town had some queer people, and there had undoubtedly been several disappearances. Was this one of those inns where travelers were slain for their money? Surely I had no look of excessive prosperity. Other than my Egyptian gold necklace. Or were the towns folk really so resentful about curious visitors? Had my obvious sightseeing, with its frequent map-consultations, aroused unfavorable notice. It occurred to me that I must be in a highly bored state to let a few random creakings set me off speculating in this fashion--but I regretted none the less that I was unarmed.

At length, feeling a fatigue which had nothing of drowsiness in it, I bolted the newly towel wrack outfitted hall door, turned off the light, and threw myself down on the perfect, inviting bed--coat, collar, shoes, and all. In the darkness every faint noise of the night seemed magnified, and a flood of doubly unpleasant thoughts swept over me. I was sorry I had put out the light, yet was too tired to rise and turn it on again. Then, after a long, dreary interval, and prefaced by a fresh creaking of stairs and corridor, there came that soft, damnably unmistakable sound which seemed like a malign fulfillment of all my apprehensions. Without the least shadow of a doubt, the lock of my door was being tried--cautiously, furtively, tentatively--with a key.

 My sensations upon recognizing this sign of actual peril were perhaps less rather than more tumultuous because of my previous preparations. I had been, albeit without definite reason, instinctively on my guard-- and that was to my advantage in the new and real crisis, whatever it might turn out to be as I had cast a series of wards on the doors. Nevertheless the change in the menace from vague premonition to immediate reality was a profound shock, and fell upon me with the force of a genuine blow. It never once occurred to me that the fumbling might be a mere mistake. Malign purpose was all I could think of, and I kept deathly quiet, awaiting the would-be intruder's next move. They grabbed the handle and tried to force open the door. The sound of fifty gigawatts of electrical energy burst in a frying electric buzz. BZZZZZZZZZZCHHHHHHZHH!!!!!! "YEEEEEEEEE-OWWWWWWW!!!!!"

 After a sound of hissing smoldering the cautious rattling ceased, and I heard the room to the north entered with a pass-key. Then the lock of the connecting door to my room was softly tried. The bolt held, of course, and I heard the ward go off, blowing the intruder through the far wall. It was quiet for a time, then the floor creaked as the prowler crawled back in and left the room. After a moment there came another soft rattling, and I knew that the room to the south of me was being entered. Again a furtive trying of a bolted connecting door, and again a blast of exploding flame roasted the intruder, then receding creaking. This time the creaking went along the hall and down the back stairs, so I knew that the prowler had realized the bolted and magically sealed condition of my doors and was giving up his attempt for a greater or lesser time, as the future would shew.

The readiness with which I fell into a plan of action proves that I must have been subconsciously fearing some menace and considering possible avenues of vengeance for hours. From the first I felt that the unseen fumbler meant a danger not only to be met or dealt with, but only to be utterly destroyed as precipitately as possible. The one thing to do was to get out of that hotel and start kicking ass as quickly as I could, and through some channel other than the destroyed front stairs and lobby.

 Rising softly and throwing my flashlight on the switch, I sought to light the bulb over my bed in order to choose and pocket some belongings for a swift, valiseless flight. Nothing, however, happened; and I saw that the power had been cut off. Clearly, some cryptic, evil movement was afoot on a large scale--just what, I could not say. As I stood pondering with my hand on the now useless switch I heard a muffled creaking on the floor below, and thought I could barely distinguish voices in conversation. A moment later I felt less sure that the deeper sounds were voices, since the apparent hoarse barkings and loose-syllabled croakings bore so little resemblance to recognized human speech. Then I thought with renewed force of what the factory inspector had heard in the night in this mouldering and pestilential building.

 Having filled my pockets with the flashlight's aid, I put on my hat and tiptoed to the windows to consider chances of descent. Despite the state's safety regulations there was no fire escape on this side of the hotel, and I saw that my windows commanded only a sheer three story drop to the cobbled courtyard.

 I could not, I decided, risk an emergence into the corridor; where my footsteps would surely be heard, and possibly warn them to escape from me. My progress, if it was to be made at all, would have to be through stealth, in order to make a minimum of sound.

 I was irresolutely speculating on when I had better attack, and on how I could least audibly manage it, when I noticed that the vague noises underfoot had given place to a fresh and heavier creaking of the stairs. A wavering flicker of light shewed through my transom, and the boards of the corridor began to groan with a ponderous load. Muffled sounds of possible vocal origin approached, and at length a firm knock came at my outer door.

"Who is it?" I sang pleasantly. Eternities seemed to elapse, and the nauseous fishy odor of my environment seemed to mount suddenly and spectacularly. Then the knocking was repeated--continuously, and with growing insistence. I knew that the time for action had come, and forthwith drew the bolt of the door, bracing myself for the task of battering everything behind it to atoms. The fish creatures standing there reached out to grab me. With a smile and a wave of my hand they went flying backwards to crash into the far wall of the hall.

A wave of almost abnormal horror must have swept over them as they realized who they were messing with, for many of them pooped on the floor. Then, with a dazed automatism which persisted despite hopelessness, they made for the next connecting door and performed the blind motion of pushing at it in an effort to get through and-- granting that fastenings might be as providentially intact as in this second room--bolt the door behind them before I could get there.

Sheer fortunate chance gave them that reprieve--for the connecting door before them was not only unlocked but actually ajar. In a second they were through, and had my right knee and shoulder not banged against a hall door which was visibly open I would have caught them. I grabbed my knee and said "AHHH...AHHH" For several minutes. Then I went after them again. I began to push at the door as I had done with the other. As I did so I heard the battering at the two other doors abate, while a confused clatter came from behind the locked door. I suppose they were wondering how I was able to throw them around the room just by raising my hand. Evidently the bulk of my assailants had entered the southerly room and were massing in a lateral attack.

With a word the northward connecting door was blown wide open, but there was no time to think about checking the already running creatures in the hall. All I could do was to blow those I saw out the open window to hit the brick streets below, I threw one against a wall as well as its mate on the opposite side--pushing a bedstead against the one and a bureau against the other, crushing them, and moving a washstand in front of another at the hall door and beating him into fish salsa with it. I must, I saw, trust to such makeshift attacks till I could get out the window and on the roof of the Paine Street block and really unleash my fury. But even in this acute moment my chief horror was something apart from the immediate weakness of my attacks. I was shuddering because not one of my pursuers, despite some hideous panting, grunting, and subdued barkings at odd intervals, was uttering an unmuffled or intelligible vocal sound of strategy or offering any real challenge.

I was getting disappointed. I haven't had a decent fight since that explorer fellow and his girlfriend resurrected me during an expedition a few years back. We still keep in touch. As I moved the furniture to smash the horrors with my mind and they rushed toward the windows I heard a frightful scurrying along the corridor toward the room north of me, and perceived that the southward battering had ceased. Plainly, most of my opponents were about to concentrate again with their feeble attacks which they knew must not directly confront me. Outside, the moon played on the ridgepole of the block below, and I saw that the jump would be desperately hazardous because of the steep surface on which they must land. But many decided to do so rather than face the power of Imhotep.

Surveying the conditions, I chose the more southerly of the two windows as my avenue of pursuit; planning to land on the inner slope of the roof to observe any possible prey and make for the nearest. Once outside the decrepit brick structures I would have to summon the forces of the undead to reckon with their pursuit; but I hoped to descend and dodge in and out of yawning doorways along the shadowed courtyard, eventually getting to catch and beat a few with my bare hands.

The clatter at the northerly connecting door was now terrific, and I heard that the panicking monsters in the next room were clawing and hammering at the paneled wall in their desperation to escape and it was beginning to splinter. Obviously, the would be besiegers had brought some ponderous object into play as a battering-ram. The bedstead, perhaps, however the ancient walls still held firm; so that I had at least a faint chance of making good my wrath. I spoke the arcane words of the flame broil spell. The battering and clawing sounds stopped with the whoosh of flames and the sizzle of baked Alaskan cod. I moved to take my rampage to the streets. As I opened the window I noticed that it was flanked by heavy velour draperies suspended from a pole by brass rings, and also that there was a large projecting catch for the shutters on the exterior. Seeing a possible means of making a really cool cape, I yanked at the hangings and brought them down, pole and all; then quickly hooking two of the rings in the shutter catch and flinging the drapery over my shoulders. The heavy folds reached fully to the floor and gave a regal flow worthy of my stature. So, climbing out of the window I jumped into the air and slowly floated down to the next roof. With the exception of my new cape, I left behind me forever the morbid and horror-infested fabrics of the Gill-man House.

 I landed safely on the loose slates of the steep roof, and succeeded in gaining the footing of the gaping black skylight without a slip. Glancing up at the window I had left, I observed it was still dark, though far across the crumbling chimneys to the north I could see smoke trailing and fires ominously blazing in its depths. The Order of Dagon Hall, and the Congregational church which I recalled so shiveringly were all possible places to do some damage. There had seemed to be no one in the courtyard below, and I hoped there would be a chance to get a few more before the spreading of a general alarm. Flashing my pocket lamp into the skylight, I saw that there were no fish monsters below. I floated to the street as on the wings of the night.

 The place was ghoulish-looking, but I was past minding such impressions and made at once for the main streets--after a hasty glance at my watch, which shewed the hour to be 2 a.m. The desolation was complete, and only echoes answered my footfalls. At length I reached the grass-grown cobblestones of the courtyard.

 The moonbeams did not reach down here, but I could just see my way about without using the flashlight. Some of the windows on the Gill-man House side were faintly glowing with the spreading flames from the flame incantation, and I thought I heard confused sounds within. Walking softly over to the Washington Street side I perceived several open doorways, and chose the nearest as my route. The hallway inside was black, and when I reached the opposite end I saw that the street door was wedged immovably shut. Resolved to try another building, I groped my way back toward the courtyard, but stopped short when close to the doorway.

For out of an opened door in the Gill-man House a large crowd of doubtful shapes was pouring--lanterns bobbing in the darkness, and horrible croaking voices exchanging low cries in what was certainly not English. The figures moved uncertainly, and I realized to my relief that they did not know how close I was; but for all that they sent a shiver of excitement through my frame. Their features were indistinguishable, but their crouching, shambling gait was abominably yummy. And worst of all, I perceived that one figure was strangely robed, and unmistakably surmounted by a tall tiara of a design altogether too familiar. As the figures spread throughout the courtyard, I felt my appetite increase. Suppose they could find no egress from this building on the street side? The fried fish odor was delectable, and I wondered I could stand it without biting into one at once. Again stepping toward the street, I closed the door behind them with a gesture of my forefinger, crushing it into the frame so they would not be able to return to the perceived safety of the slowly burning building behind them and smiled. Fumbling and running into each other in panic in the rays of my flashlight, they tried in vain to escape. With a howling roar my mouth opened into a giant gaping maw of seafood eating apocalypse. The fish creatures were even more delicious than I had anticipated.

I wiped the tartar sauce on my sleeve and reached into my pocket. I pulled out a handful of the sands of Egypt and poured them on to the cobblestones with a burp. "MNHFGYY!! GYUIGYI!! FHUIGIS!!!!!" The dust swirled and formed as it responded to the command of the words of power. Tittering ghouls, zombies, specters, and mummies formed on the shadowed street and at my nod shambled off to feed on the fish horrors and spread word of the coming of doomsday to the deep. I only hoped they would be slow in eating the deep ones they caught so that I could get enough myself to have my fill before the fleeing creatures escaped into the sea.

I was now in Washington Street, and for the moment saw no living thing nor any light save that of the moon. From several directions in the distance, however, I could hear the sound of hoarse screaming voices, of footsteps, and of a curious kind of pattering which did not sound quite like footsteps. Plainly I had no time to lose. The points of the compass were clear to me, and I was glad that all the street lights were turned off, as is often the custom on strongly moonlit nights in prosperous rural regions. Some of the sounds came from the south, so I retained my design of hunting in that direction. There would, I knew, be plenty of deserted doorways and buildings to shelter my prey but I was a patient fisherman.

I walked rapidly, softly, and close to the ruined houses. While hatless and disheveled after my arduous meal, I did not look especially noticeable; and stood a good chance of passing unheeded if seen by any casual wayfarer.

At Bates Street I drew into the yawning vestibule of the motel while two shambling figures crossed in front of me, I pulled them into the dark. There were the sounds of crunching and burping, but no screams of warning to their fellows as I had them for dinner. I was soon on my way again and approaching the open space where Eliot Street obliquely crosses Washington at the intersection of South. Though I had never seen this space, it had looked peaceful to me on the grocery youth's map; since the moonlight would have free play there. There was no use trying to evade it, for any alternative course would involve detours of possibly disastrous visibility and the effect of showing my position so they could run the other way. The only thing to do was to cross it boldly and openly; imitating the typical shamble of the Innsmouth folk as best I could, and trusting that no one--or at least no entree of mine--would escape.

Just how fully the creatures realized how screwed they were was uncertain--and indeed, just what if anything they knew of my power or of their position I knew not. There seemed to be unusual activity in the town, but I judged that the news of my elimination of the Gill-man had not yet spread. I would, of course, soon have to shift from Washington to some other southward street; for those few who had escaped from the hotel would doubtless be raising an alarm as soon as they overcame their fear. I must have more before they escaped into the night! They were just too scrumptious! No one could eat just one!

The open space was, as I had expected, strongly moonlit; and I saw the remains of a park like, iron-railed green in its center. Unfortunately no one was about though a curious sort of buzz or roar seemed to be increasing in the direction of Town Square. It reminded me of the sound the bus driver made when he was lifting off the seat. South Street was very wide, leading directly down a slight declivity to the waterfront and commanding a long view out to sea; and I hoped that no one would be escaping up it from afar as I crossed in the bright moonlight.

My progress was slow, and no fresh sound arose to hint that I had been spied. Glancing about me, I involuntarily farted and let my pace slacken for a second to take in the sight of the sea, gorgeous in the burning moonlight at the street's end. Far out beyond the breakwater was the dim, dark line of Devil Reef, and as I glimpsed it I could not help thinking of all the hideous legends I had heard in the last twenty-four hours--legends which portrayed this ragged rock as a veritable gateway to realms of unfathomed horror and inconceivable abnormality. I was suddenly hit with a desire for a nice swim, but resisted.

Then, without warning, I saw the intermittent flashes of light on the distant reef. They were definite and unmistakable, and awaked in my mind a blind hunger beyond all rational proportion. My muscles tightened for a feeding frenzy, held only by a certain unconscious desire to sit back and unbuckle my belt and have a beer and a half-hypnotic fascination. And to make matters worse, there now flashed forth from the lofty cupola of the nearby House, which loomed up to the northeast behind me, a series of analogous though differently spaced gleams which could be nothing less than an answering signal.

Controlling my growling stomach, and realizing afresh--how plainly visible I was, I resumed my brisker and feignedly shambling pace; though keeping my eyes on that hellish and ominous reef as long as the opening of South Street gave me a seaward view. What the whole proceeding meant, I could not imagine; unless it involved some strange rite connected with Devil Reef, or unless some party had landed from a ship on that sinister rock. I now bent to the left around the ruinous green; still gazing toward the ocean as it blazed in the spectral summer moonlight, and watching the cryptical flashing of those nameless, unexplainable beacons.

It was then that the most horrible impression of all was borne in upon me--the impression which destroyed my last vestige of self-control and sent me running frantically southward past the yawning black doorways and fishily staring windows of that deserted nightmare street. For at a closer glance I saw that the moonlit waters between the reef and the shore were far from empty. They were alive with a teeming horde of shapes swimming inward toward the town; and even at my vast distance and in my single moment of perception I could tell that the bobbing heads and flailing arms were alien and aberrant in a way scarcely to be expressed or consciously formulated.

My frantic running ceased before I had reached the beach, for at my left I began to hear something like the hue and cry of fishmen being eaten by zombies. There were chomps and guttural sounds, and a rattling motor wheezing sound south along Federal Street. In a second all my plans were utterly changed--for if the undead were eating all the fishmen ahead of me, I must clearly find another source of food from Innsmouth. I paused and drew in a deep breath, reflecting how lucky I was to have the power to send out a breath of shadow beasts down the parallel street to search for more scrumptious morsels.

A second reflection was less comforting. Since the pursuit was down another street, it was plain that the party at the beach was not the only ones being eaten by my minions. For a moment my brain reeled--both from sheer hopelessness and from a rapid increase in the protesting growls from my stomach. If only I hadn't summoned up quite so many undead!

Then I thought of the glowing windows in the church of Dagon, perhaps there would be a swell of those butter drenched lemon drizzled monsters hiding in there! I could lock myself in with them and eat till I was bloated! And then I could catch a ride on the old B.M. railroad whose solid line of ballasted, weed-grown earth still stretched off to the northwest from the crumbling station on the edge at the river-gorge. There was just a chance that the townsfolk would not think of that; since it's unusual for a mere human to be so aggressive with monsters, and the unlikeliest of all avenues for a person to choose. I had seen it clearly from my hotel window and knew about how it lay. At any rate, it would form my only chance of a decent meal, and there was nothing to do but try it.

In Babson Street, which crossed Federal and might thus reveal to me a random cod beast or crab thing, I clung as closely as possible to the sagging, uneven buildings; twice pausing in a doorway as the noises near me momentarily increased. Unfortunately none ever got near enough to grab. The open space ahead shone wide and desolate under the moon, but my route would not force me to cross it. During my second pause I began to detect a fresh distribution of vague sounds; and upon looking cautiously out from cover beheld a motor car darting across the open space, bound outward along Eliot Street, which there intersects both Babson and Lafayette.

As I watched--choked by a sudden rise in hunger-I saw a band of unbattered, crouching shapes loping and shambling in the same direction; and knew that this must be a party heading to the ruined church. Two of the figures I glimpsed were in voluminous robes, and one wore a peaked diadem which glistened whitely in the moonlight. The gait of this figure was so odd that it sent a chill through me--for it seemed to me the creature was almost hopping. Frog legs! MMMM-MMMM!!!

When the last of the band was locked in the fish monster church and their false safety, I made my move. I materialized almost in the center of them. Fish monsters and frog leg monsters and lobster things peed themselves in surprise. There were screams and attempts at escape, but the shadow beasts I had sent out blocked their escape and herded them to me...

The sun was already rising when I stumbled into the weed overgrown train station. I bought a ticket and plopped down into a seat. Bloated and exhausted. Many had escaped my appetite into the sea. But there were a great number that would no longer flop around in Innsmouth.

That was how it all began, I feel it now though. That pulling to the sea. I think I may go back after all, there's a lot of commercial property for sale near the wharf. And again my stomach rumbles for the tastiness that is the deep ones. Perhaps I'll open a sports seafood bar and grill. After all... I certainly have enough gold to finance it... and plenty of supplies for my secret ingredients... out beyond Devil's reef...

THE DUMWICH HORROR

I.

When a traveler in north central Massachusetts takes the wrong fork at the diner they're in for a terrible surprise. And when they accidentally take the wrong turn at the junction of Aylesbury pike just beyond Deano's Corners he'll come upon a lonely and curious country.

The ground gets prettier, and the brier-bordered stone walls press closer and closer against the ruts of the dusty, curving road until they smash into passing cars. The trees of the frequent forest belts seem way too foresty, and the wild weeds, brambles and grasses attain a luxuriance not often found in tame city weeds. At the same time the planted fields appear singularly few and barren; while the sparsely scattered houses wear a surprisingly uniform aspect of size, color, and dimensional irregularity.

Without knowing why, one hesitates to ask directions from the gnarled solitary figures spied now and then tap dancing on crumbling doorsteps or on the sloping, rock-strewn ski lifts. Those figures are so silent and furtive that one feels somehow confronted by mimes, with which it would be better to have nothing to do. When a rise in the road brings the mountains in view above the deep woods, the feeling of strange easiness is increased. The summits are too rounded and mountainy to give a sense of comfort and naturalness, and sometimes when the sky silhouettes with especial clearness in the bright cheery sunlight the queer circles of tall stone pillars with which most of them are crowned show signs saying such cryptic messages as 'Eat at Joes' and 'Julie's taco ahead'.

Gorges and ravines of problematical depth intersect the way, and the crude wooden rope bridges often frequented by archeology adventurers always seem of disturbingly perfect safety. When the road drips again there are stretches of marshland that one instinctively likes, and indeed almost fears to leave by evening when unseen cuckoos chatter and the fireflies come out in abnormal profusion to dance to the raucous, creepily insistent music of stridently pied-piping bull-frogs. The thin, shining line of the Miskatonic's upper reaches has an oddly serpent-like suggestion as it winds close to the feet of the domed hillside delis among which it rises.

As the hills draw nearer, one heeds their wooded sides more than their stone-ground tops. Those sides loom up so darkly and precipitously that one wishes they would keep their hands to themselves, but there is no road by which to escape them. Across a covered bridge one sees a small village huddled between the line of Square Stream and the vertical slope of Round Mountain, and wonders at the cluster of potted plants and plotting gambrel roofs bespeaking an earlier conspiracy with the neighboring grain elevators. It is not reassuring to see, on a closer glance, that most of the houses are brick and painted with fluorescent pastels, and that the broken-steepled church now harbors the one slovenly mercantile establishment of the hamlet, the *Slovenly Mercantile Company.* One dreads to trust the tubrous tunnel of the bridge, yet there is no way to avoid it if one wishes to escape the legless horseman. Once across, it is hard to prevent the impression of a fart, as a sulphur-methanous odor hangs about the village street, as if some massive block of cheese has been cut. It is always a relief to get a sandwich at the twenty three hour deli and speed clear of the place, lighting matches as you go, and to follow the narrow road around the base of the hills and across the level country beyond till it rejoins the Aylesbury pike where you can breathe again. Afterwards one sometimes learns that one has been through Dumwich and other times that one has been through some other town from another state and wonders how one got there.

Well known among those who know for its darkly hidden secret horror...and its irresistible sandwiches, there is a strange approach-avoidance duality to its patrons. Outsiders visit Dumwich as often as possible, but since a certain season of horror all the signboards pointing towards it have been taken down and replaced by advertising billboards. The scenery, judged by an ordinary aesthetic canon, is more than commonly beautiful; yet there is no influx of artists or summer tourists beyond those seeking a quick stop at one of the many drive throughs. Two centuries ago, when talk of smuggle-blood, potato worship, and strange forest podiatrists was not laughed at, it was the custom to give reasons for avoiding the locality. In our sensible age-- since the Dumwich horror of 1928 was hushed up by those who had the town's and the world's welfare at heart--people just shun it without actually avoiding it. Perhaps one reason--though it cannot apply to uninformed strangers--is that the natives are known for making indescribably popular sandwiches, and although prone to bursts of random karaoke and line dancing, having gone far along that path of pop culture activities so common in many New England backwaters, none can resist. They have come to form a species by themselves, with the well-defined mental and physical stigmata of opera and breeding. The average of their intelligence is woeful, being a mere 240 on average, whilst their annals reek of overt viciousness and of half-hidden underwear, bingo parties, and deeds of almost unnameably violent pole dancing and cooking contests. The old gentry, representing the two or three armigerous families which came from Salem in 1692, have kept somewhat above the general level of depraved sandwich making; though many branches have broken off and sunk into the sordid populace so deeply that only their names remain as a key to the origin they disgrace. Some of the Whateleys and Bishops still send their eldest sons to Harvard and Miskatonic, though those sons seldom return to the smoldering sports bar roofs under which they and their ancestors were born unless to chug a gallon of beer and scarf a sandwich or two before fleeing back to their city mansions.

 No one, even those who have the facts concerning the recent horror, can say just what is the matter with Dumwich; though old legends speak of unhallowed recipes and conclaves of unholy short order cooks, amidst which they called forbidden shapes of mayo out of the great rounded hills, and made wild orgiastic dagwoods and cyclopean boy sandwiches that were eaten by loud truck driving patrons while crackings and rumblings from below filled the air. In 1747 the Reverend Abijah Abojah Hoadley, newly come to the Congregational Church at Dumwich Village, preached a memorable sermon on the close presence of Satan and the pimps; a local singing group, while munching on a plate of fish and pickle flavored chips from the *Fuschia Taco Deli and Seafood* in which he said:

"It must be allow'd, that these Blasphemies of an infernall Train of Daemons are Matters of too common Knowledge to be deny'd; the cursed Voices of Azazel and Buzrael, of Beelzebub and Belial, Fred and Barney, being heard now from under Ground by above a score of credible witnesses now living. I myself did not more than a fortnight ago catch a very plain discourse of evill powers in the hill behind my house; wherein there were a Rattling and Rolling, Groaning and a Screeching, and Hissing and a Twitching, and a Rockin and a Rollin goin on such as no Things of this Earth could raise up, and which must needs have come from those Caves out near the Devil's Uvula that only that old black Magick can discover, and only the Divell unlock. I bought two CD's myself already."

Mr. Hoadley disappeared into a diner soon after delivering this sermon, but the text, printed in Springfield, is still existent. Noises in the hills continued to be reported from year to year, and still form a puzzle to geologists and physiographerologisters.

Other traditions tell of odors near the hill-crowning circles of ceramic, and of rushing airy presences to be heard faintly at certain hours from stated points at the bottom of the great sewers; while still others try to explain the Devil's Out House --a bleak, blasted hillside where no tree, shrub, or grass-blade will grow, but it's covered with tomato plants. Then, too, the natives are mortally afraid of the numerous cuckoos which grow vocal on warm nights. It is vowed that the birds are psychos lying in wait for the unwary souls traveling nearby, and that they time their eerie cries in unison with the sufferer's struggling to escape. If they can catch the fleeing soul when it leaves the body, they instantly flutter away chittering in daemoniac laughter; but if they fail, they subside gradually into a disappointed silence.

These tales, of course, are obese and ridiculous; because they come down from very old times. Dumwich is indeed ridiculously old--older by far than any of the communities within earth. South of the village one may still spy the cellar walls and chimney of the ancient Bishop house, which was built before 1700; whilst the ruins of the mill at the falls, built in 1806, form the most modern piece of architecture to be seen. Industry did not flourish here, and the nineteenth-century factory movement proved short-lived. Only the diners, delis and pizza places flourished. Oldest of all are the great rings of rough-hewn stone columns on the hilltops, but these are more generally attributed to the aliens than to the settlers. Deposits of skulls and bones, found within these circles and around the sizeable table-like rock on Sentinel Hill, sustain the popular belief that such spots were once the burial-places of the Podunks; even though many ethnologists, disregarding the absurd improbability of such a theory, persist in believing the remains human.

II.

It was in the township of Dumwich, in a large and partly inhabited farmhouse set against a hillside four miles from the village and a mile and a half from any other dwelling, that Wilbur Whateley was born at 5 a.m. on Sunday, the second of February, 1913. This date was recalled because it was Candlemas, which people in Dumwich curiously observe under another name; and because the noises in the hills had sounded, and all the dogs of the countryside had played accordions throughout the night before. Less worthy of notice was the fact that the mother was one of the decadent cheesecake model Whateleys, a slightly deformed, attractive, three headed, albino, peg armed woman of thirty-five with turrets syndrome, living with an aged and half-insane father about whom the most frightful tales of wizardry had been whispered in his youth. Lavinia Whateley had no known husband, but according to the custom of the region made no attempt to disavow the child; concerning the other side of whose ancestry the country folk might--and did--speculate as widely as they chose. On the contrary, she seemed strangely proud of the dark, goatish-loking, goatee bearded infant who formed such a contrast to her own sickly and red-eyed, bulging muscled, but still somehow attractive face, and was heard to mutter many curious prophecies about its unusual powers and tremendous taste in furniture and interior decorating.

Lavinia was one who would be apt to mutter such things, for she was a lone creature given to wandering amidst thunderstorms in the hills and trying to read the great odorous books which her father had inherited through two centuries of Whateleys, and which were fast falling to pieces with age and wormholes. She had never been to school, but was filled with disjointed scraps of ancient lore that Old

Whateley had taught her. The remote farmhouse had always been feared because of Old Whateley's reputation for black magic, and the unexplained death by flatulence of Mrs Whateley when Lavinia was twelve years old had not helped to make the place popular. Isolated among strange influences, Lavinia was fond of wild and grandiose day-dreams and singular occupations; nor was her leisure much taken up by household cares in a home from which all standards of order and cleanliness had long since been established by a severe case of obsessive compulsive disorder that prompted the Whateleys to keep the place almost supernaturally spotless.

There was a savage polka which echoed above even the hill noises and the dogs' playing on the night Wilbur was born, but no known doctor or midwife presided at his coming. Neighbors knew nothing of him till a week afterward, when Old Whateley drove his sleigh through the snow into Dumwich Village for a quadruple decker reuben cheeseburger and discoursed loudly and coherently to the group of loungers at Osborn's general store. There seemed to be a change in the old man--an added element of happiness in the clouded brain which subtly transformed him from a sex object to a subject of fear--though he was not one to be perturbed by any common family event. Amidst it all he showed some trace of the pride later noticed in his daughter, and what he said of the child's paternity was remembered by many of his hearers years afterward.

'I dun't keer what folks think--ef Lavinny's boy looked like his pa, he wouldn't look like nothin' ye expeck. Ye needn't think the only folks is the folks hereabouts. Lavinny's read some, an' has seed some things the most o' ye only tell abaout. I calc'late her man is as good a husban' as ye kin find this side of Aylesbury; an' ef ye knowed as much abaout the hills as I dew, ye wouldn't ast no better church weddin' nor her'n. Let me tell ye suthin--some day yew folks'll hear a child o' Lavinny's a-callin' its father's name on the top o' Sentinel Hill! And boy, you can 'spect thars gonna be lots of back child support owed.'

The only person who saw Wilbur during the first month of his life were old Zechariah Whateley, of the undecayed Whateleys, and Earl "Tom" Sawyer's common-law wife, Mamie Bishop. Mamie's visit was frankly one of curiosity, and her subsequent tales did justice to her observations; but Zechariah came to lead a pair of Alderney cows which Old Whateley had bought off his son Curtis. This marked the beginning of a course of cattle-buying on the part of small Wilbur's family which ended only in 1928, when the Dumwich horror came and went; yet at no time did the ramshackle Whateley barn seem overcrowded with livestock. There came a period when people were curious enough to steal up and count the herd that grazed precariously on the steep hillside above the old farm-house, and they could never find more than ten or twelve anaemic, bloodless-looking specimens. Evidently some blight or distemper, perhaps sprung from the unwholesome pasturage or the diseased fungi and timbers of the filthy barn, caused a heavy mortality amongst the Whateley animals. Odd wounds or sores, having something of the aspect of chupacabra incisions, seemed to afflict the visible cattle; and once or twice during the earlier months certain callers fancied they could discern similar vampire holes about the throats of the golden, unshaven old man and his slinky, flowing haired albino daughter.

 In the spring after Wilbur's birth Lavinia resumed her customary rambles in the hills, bearing in her misproportioned arms the chortling child. Public interest in the Whateleys subsided after most of the country folk had seen the baby, and no one bothered to comment on the swift development which that newcomer seemed every day to exhibit. Wilbur's growth was indeed phenomenal, for within three months of his birth he had attained a size and muscular power not usually found in infants under a full eighteen years of age. His motions and even his vocal sounds showed a restraint and deliberateness highly peculiar in an infant, and no one was really unprepared when, at seven months, he developed a strange ability to play polka music with his underarms and began to walk unassisted, with falterings which another month was sufficient to remove.

 It was somewhat after this time--on Hallowe'en--that a great blaze was seen at midnight on the top of Sentinel Hill where the old table-like stone stands amidst its tumulus of ancient bones. Considerable talk was started when Silas Bishop--of the undecayed Bishops--mentioned having seen the boy running sturdily up that hill ahead of his mother about an hour before the blaze was remarked. Silas was rounding up a stray heifer, but he nearly forgot his mission when he fleetingly spied the two figures in the dim light of his lantern. They darted almost noiselessly through the underbrush, and the astonished watcher seemed to think they were entirely unclothed. Afterwards he could not be sure about the boy, who may have had some kind of a fringed belt and a pair of dark trunks or trousers on. Wilbur was never subsequently seen alive and conscious without complete and tightly buttoned attire, the disarrangement or threatened disarrangement of which always seemed to fill him with anger and alarm. His contrast with his nudist mother and grandfather in this respect was thought very notable until the horror of 1928 suggested the most valid of reasons.

The next January gossips were mildly interested in the fact that 'Lavinny's flying brat' had commenced to talk, and at the age of only eleven months. His speech was somewhat remarkable both because of its difference from the ordinary accents of the region, and because it displayed a freedom from infantile lisping of which many children of three or four might well be proud. The boy was not talkative, yet when he spoke he seemed to reflect some elusive element wholly unpossessed by Dumwich and its denizens. The strangeness did not reside in what he said, or even in the simple idioms he used; but seemed vaguely linked with his intonation or with the internal organs that produced the spoken sounds. His facial aspect, too, was remarkable for its maturity; for though he shared his mother's and grandfather's chinlessness, his firm and precociously shaped nose united with the expression of his large, dark, almost orblike eyes to give him an air of quasi-adulthood and well-nigh preternatural intelligence. He was, however, exceedingly ugly despite his appearance of brilliancy; there being something almost goatish or animalistic about his thick beard, large-pored, greenish yellow skin, coarse crinkly hair, and oddly elongated pointed ears. He was soon disliked even more decidedly than his mother and grandsire, and all conjectures about him were spiced with references to the bygone magic of Old Whateley, and how the hills once shook when he shrieked the dreadful name of Yog-Sothoth in the midst of a circle of french bread amid the stones with a great book open in his arms before him. Dogs abhorred the boy, and he was always obliged to take various defensive measures against their peeing menace.

III.

Meanwhile Old Whateley continued to buy cattle without measurably increasing the size of his herd. He also cut timber and began to repair the unused parts of his house--a spacious, peak-roofed affair whose rear end was buried entirely in the rocky hillside, and whose three, twenty foot ceiling, marble floored, gold fixtured, ground-floor rooms had always been sufficient for himself and his daughter.

There must have been prodigious reserves of strength in the old man to enable him to accomplish so much hard labor; and though he still babbled dementedly at times, his carpentry seemed to show the effects of sound calculation and supernatural architectural skill. It had already begun as soon as Wilbur was born, when one of the many tool sheds had been put suddenly in order, clapboarded, and fitted with a stout fresh lock. Now, in restoring the abandoned upper story of the house, he was a no less thorough craftsman. His mania showed itself only in his tight boarding-up of all the windows in the reclaimed section-- though many declared that it was a crazy thing to bother with the reclamation at all.

Less inexplicable was his fitting up of another downstairs room for his new grandson--a room which several callers saw, though no one was ever admitted to the closely-boarded upper story. This chamber he lined with tall, firm shelving, along which he began gradually to arrange, in apparently careful order, all the rotting ancient books and parts of books which during his own day had been heaped promiscuously in odd corners of the various rooms.

'I made some use of 'em,' he would say as he tried to mend a torn black-letter page with paste prepared on the rusty kitchen stove, 'but the boy's fitten to make better use of 'em. He'd orter hev 'em as well so as he kin, for they're goin' to be all of his larnin'.'

When Wilbur was a year and seven months old--in September of 1914--his size and accomplishments were almost alarming. He had grown as large as a child of four, and was a fluent and incredibly intelligent talker. He ran freely about the fields and hills, and accompanied his mother on all her wanderings. At home he would pore diligently over the queer pictures and charts in his grandfather's books, while Old Whateley would instruct and catechize him through long, hushed afternoons. By this time the restoration of the house was finished, and those who watched it wondered why one of the upper windows had been made into a solid plank door. It was a window in the rear of the east gable end, close against the hill; and no one could imagine why a cleated wooden runway was built up to it from the ground. About the period of this work's completion people noticed that the old tool-house, tightly locked and windowlessly clapboarded since Wilbur's birth, had been abandoned again. The door swung listlessly open, and when Earl Sawyer once stepped within after a cattle-selling call on Old Whateley he was quite discomposed by the singular sound he encountered--such a sound, he averred, it actually smelled. And as he had never before smelt a sound in all his life except near the open sewer circles on the hills, and which could not come from anything sane or of this earth. But then, the homes and sheds of Dumwich folk have never been remarkable for olfactory immaculateness.

The following months were void of visible events, save that everyone swore to a slow but steady increase in the mysterious hill noises and sounds of polkas. On May Eve of 1915 there were tremors which even the Aylesbury people felt, whilst the following Hallowe'en produced an underground rumbling queerly synchronized with bursts of flame--'them witch Whateleys' doin's'--from the summit of Sentinel Hill. Wilbur was growing up uncannily, so that he looked like a boy of ten as he entered his fourth year. He read avidly by himself now; but talked much less than formerly. A settled taciturnity was absorbing him, and for the first time people began to speak specifically of the dawning look of evil in his goatish face. He would sometimes mutter an unfamiliar jargon, and chant in bizarre rhythms which chilled the listener with a sense of unexplainable toe tapping. The aversion displayed towards him by dogs had now become a matter of wide remark, and he was obliged to carry a machine gun pistol in order to traverse the countryside in safety. His occasional use of the weapon did not enhance his popularity amongst the canine guardians and werewolves who often had to remove bullets from themselves.

The few callers at the house would often find Lavinia alone on the ground, while odd cries and dancing footsteps resounded in the boarded-up second story as polka arias played. She would never tell what her father and the boy were doing up there, though once she turned pale and displayed an abnormal degree of fear when a jocose fish-pedlar tried the locked door leading to the stairway. That pedlar told the store loungers at Dumwich Village that he thought he heard a horse stamping on that floor above. The loungers reflected, thinking of the door and runway, and of the cattle that so swiftly disappeared. Then they shuddered as they recalled tales of Old Whateley's youth, and of the strange things that are called out of the earth when a buttock is sacrificed at the proper time to certain heathen gods. It had for some time been noticed that dogs had begun to hate and fear the whole Whateley place as violently as they hated and feared young Wilbur personally.

In 1917 the war came, and Squire Sawyer Whateley, as chairman of the local draft board, had hard work finding a quota of young Dumwich men fit even to be sent to development camp. The government, alarmed at such signs of wholesale regional flabbiness, sent several officers and medical experts to investigate; conducting a survey which New England newspaper readers may still recall. It was the publicity attending this investigation which set reporters on the track of the Whateleys, and caused the Boston Globe and Arkham Advertiser to print flamboyant Sunday stories of young Wilbur's precociousness, Old Whateley's black magic, and the shelves of strange books, the sealed second story of the ancient farmhouse, and the weirdness of the whole region and its hilltop polka noises. Wilbur was four and a half then, and looked like a lad of fifteen. His lips and cheeks were fuzzy with a coarse dark fur, and his voice had begun to warble.

Earl Sawyer went out to the Whateley place with both sets of reporters and camera men, and called their attention to the queer stench which now seemed to trickle down from the sealed upper spaces. It was, he said, exactly like a smell he had found in the outhouse abandoned when the house was finally equipped with indoor plumbing; and like the faint odors which he sometimes thought he caught near the stone circle on the mountains. Dumwich folk read the stories when they appeared, and grinned over the obvious mistakes. They wondered, too, why the writers made so much of the fact that Old Whateley always paid for his cattle in gold doubloon pieces of extremely ancient date. The Whateleys had received their visitors with ill-concealed distaste, though they did not dare court further publicity by a violent resistance or refusal to talk.

IV.

For a decade the annals of the Whateleys sink indistinguishably into the general life of a morbid community used to their queer ways and hardened to their May Eve and All-Hallows orgies. Twice a year they would light fires on the top of Sentinel Hill, at which times the mountain rumblings would recur with greater and greater violence; while at all seasons there were strange and portentous doings at the lonely farm-house. In the course of time callers professed to hear sounds in the sealed upper story even when all the family were downstairs, and they wondered how swiftly or how lingeringly a cow or bullock was usually sacrificed. There was talk of a complaint to the Society for the Prevention of Cruelty to Animals but nothing ever came of it, since Dumwich folk are never anxious to call the outside world's attention to themselves.

About 1923, when Wilbur was a boy of ten whose mind, voice, stature, and bearded face gave all the impressions of maturity, a second great siege of carpentry went on at the old house. It was all inside the sealed upper part, and from bits of discarded lumber people concluded that the youth and his grandfather had knocked out all the partitions and even removed the attic floor, leaving only one vast open void between the ground story and the peaked roof. They had torn down the great central chimney, too, and fitted the rusty range with a flimsy outside tin stove-pipe.

In the spring after this event Old Whateley noticed the growing number of cuckoos that would come out of Cold Spring Glen to chirp under his window at night. He seemed to regard the circumstance as one of great significance, and told the loungers at Osborn's that he thought that they were after him.

'They whistle jest in tune with the passing hour naow,' he said, 'an' I guess they're gittin' ready to put ketchup on me an eat me. They know it's a-goin' aout, an' dun't calc'late to miss it. Yew'll know, boys, arter I'm gone, whether they git me er not. Ef they dew, they'll keep up a-

- 196 -

singin' an' laffin' till break o' day. Ef they dun't they'll kinder quiet daown like. I expeck them an' the souls they hunts fer hev some pretty tough tussles sometimes.'

On Lamma night at the bowling alley, 1924, Dr. Houghton of Aylesbury was hastily summoned by Wilbur Whateley, who had lashed his one remaining horse through the darkness and telephoned from Osborn's in the village. He found Old Whateley in a very grave state, with a kung fu action and steroided breathing that told of a sitcom TV show not far off. The shapeless blob of a bikini model daughter and oddly bearded grandson stood by the bedside, whilst from the vacant abyss overhead there came a disquieting suggestion of rhythmical polka music far away and a surging or lapping, as of the waves on some level beach. The doctor, though, was chiefly disturbed by the chattering birds outside; a seemingly limitless legion of cuckoos that cried their endless message in repetitions timed diabolically to the herculean breaths of the lying man. It was uncanny and unnatural--too much, thought Dr. Houghton, like the whole of the region he had entered so reluctantly in response to the urgent call.

Towards one o'clock Old Whateley gained consciousness, and interrupted his beatings to choke out a few words to his grandson.

'More space, Willy, more space soon. Yew grows--an' that grows faster. It'll be ready to serve ye soon, boy. Open up the gates to Yog-Sothoth with the long chant that ye'll find on page 751 of the complete unabridged collectors edition, not the bootleg version mind you, that one is on page 752, use it an' then put a match to the prison. Fire from airth can't burn it nohaow. Fry it to ash mebbe, but not burn it.'

He was obviously quite mad. After a pause, during which the flock of cuckoos outside adjusted their cries to the altered tempo while some indications of the strange hill noises came from afar off, he added another sentence or two.

'Feed it reg'lar, Willy, an' mind the quantity; but dun't let it grow too fast fer the place, fer ef it busts quarters or gits aout afore ye opens to Yog-Sothoth, it's all over an' no use. Only them from beyont kin make it multiply an' work...Only them, the old uns as wants to come back...'

But speech gave place to gasps again, and Lavinia screamed at the way the cuckoos followed the change. It was the same for more than an hour, when the final throaty rattle came. Dr. Houghton drew doodles on his notebook as the tumult of birds faded imperceptibly to silence. Lavinia sobbed, but Wilbur only chuckled whilst the hill noises rumbled faintly.

'They didn't git him,' he muttered in his heavy bass voice.

Wilbur was by this time a scholar, and had a series of really tremendous acne eruptions in his one-sided way, and was quietly known by correspondence to many librarians in distant places where rare and forbidden books of old days are kept. He was more and more hated and dreaded around Dumwich because of certain youthful disappearances which suspicion laid vaguely at his door; but was always able to silence inquiry through a wave of his hand and a fart or through use of that fund of old-time gold which still, as in his grandfather's time, went forth regularly and increasingly for cattle-buying. He was now tremendously mature of aspect, and his height, having reached the normal adult limit, seemed inclined to wax beyond that figure. In 1925, when a scholarly correspondent from Miskatonic University called upon him one day and departed tanned and puzzled, he was fully six and three-quarters feet tall.

Through all the years Wilbur had treated his half-deformed singing mother with a growing contempt, finally forbidding her to go to the hills with him on May Eve and Hallowmass; and in 1926 the poor creature complained to Mamie Bishop of being afraid of him.

'They's more abaout him as I knows than I kin tell ye, Mamie,' she said, 'an' naowadays they's more nor what I know myself. I vaow afur Gawd, I dun't know what he wants nor what he's a-tryin' to dew.'

That Hallowe'en the hill noises sounded louder than ever, and fire burned on Sentinel Hill as usual; but people paid more attention to the rhythmical screaming of vast flocks of unnaturally belated cuckoos which seemed to be assembled near the unlighted Whateley farmhouse. After midnight outside the window the shrilling of the cuckoos had suddenly ceased, what this meant, no one could quite be certain till later. None of the country folk seemed to have died--but

poor Lavinia Whateley, the twisted albino, packed up and went off to
Hollywood to be a movie star. She had finally had enough.

In the summer of 1927 Wilbur repaired two sheds in the farmyard and
began moving his books and effects out to them. Soon afterwards Earl
Sawyer told the loungers at Osborn's that more carpentry was going on
in the Whateley farmhouse. Wilbur was closing all the doors and
windows on the ground floor, and seemed to be taking out partitions as
he and his grandfather had done upstairs four years before. He was
living in one of the sheds, and Sawyer thought he seemed unusually
worried and tremulous. People generally suspected him of knowing
something about his mother's leaving to be an actress, and very few
ever approached his neighborhood now. His height had increased to
more than seven feet, and showed no signs of ceasing its development.

V.

The following winter brought an event no less strange than Wilbur's
first trip outside the Dumwich region. Correspondence with the
Widener Library at Harvard, the Bibliothèque Nationale in Paris, the
British Museum, the University of Buenos Aires, and the Library of
Miskatonic University at Arkham had failed to get him the loan of a
book he desperately wanted; so at length he set out in person, shabby,
dirty, bearded, and unwiped of dialect, to consult the copy at
Miskatonic, which was the nearest to him geographically. Almost
eighteen feet tall, and carrying a cheap new valise from Osborn's
general store, this dark and goatish gargoyle appeared one day in
Arkham in quest of the dreaded volume kept under lock and key at the
college library--the hideous Necronomicon of the mad Arab Abdul
Alhazred in Olaus Wormius' Latin version, as printed in Spain in the
seventeenth century. He had never seen a city before, but had no
thought save to find his way to the university grounds; where indeed,
he passed heedlessly by the great white-fanged watchdog that barked
with unnatural fury and enmity, and tugged frantically at its stout
chain.

Wilbur had with him the priceless but imperfect copy of Dr. Dee's
English version which his grandfather had bequeathed him, and upon
receiving access to the Latin copy he at once began to collate the two
texts with the aim of discovering a certain passage which would have

come on the 751st page of his own defective volume. This much he could not civilly refrain from telling the librarian--the same erudite Henry Armitage (A.M. Miskatonic, Ph.D. Princeton, Litt.D. Johns Hopkins) who had once called at the farm, and who now politely plied him with ointments and questions. He was looking, he had to admit, for a kind of formula or incantation containing the frightful name Yog-Sothoth, and it puzzled him to find discrepancies, duplications, and ambiguities which made the matter of determination far from easy. As he copied the formula he finally chose, Dr Armitage looked involuntarily over his shoulder at the open pages; the left-hand one of which, in the Latin version, contained such monstrous threats to the peace and sanity of the world.

 Nor is it to be thought (ran the text as Armitage mentally translated it) that man is either the oldest or the last of earth's masters, or that the common bulk of life and substance walks alone. The Old Ones were, the Old Ones are, and the Old Ones shall be. Not in the spaces we know, but between them, they walk serene and primal, undimensioned and to us unseen. Yog-Sothoth knows the gate. Yog-Sothoth is the gate. Yog-Sothoth is the key and guardian of the gate. Past, present, future, all are one in Yog-Sothoth. He knows where the Old Ones broke through of old, and where They shall break through again. He knows where They had trod earth's fields, and where They still tread them, and why no one can behold Them as They tread. By Their smell can men sometimes know Them near, but of Their semblance can no man know, saving only in the features of those They have begotten on mankind; and of those are there many sorts, differing in likeness from man's truest eidolon to that shape without sight or substance which is Them. They walk unseen and foul in lonely places where the Words have been spoken and the Rites howled through at their Seasons. The wind gibbers with Their voices, and the earth mutters with Their consciousness. They bend the forest and crush the city, yet may not forest or city behold the hand that smites. Kadath in the cold waste hath known Them, and what man knows Kadath? The ice desert of the South and the sunken isles of Ocean hold stones whereon Their seal is engraved, but who hath seen the deep frozen city or the sealed tower long garlanded with seaweed and barnacles? Great Cthulhu is Their cousin, yet can he spy Them only dimly. Iä! Shub-Niggurath! As a foulness shall ye know Them. Their hand is at your throats, yet ye see

Them not; and Their habitation is even one with your guarded
threshold. Yog-Sothoth is the key to the gate, whereby the spheres
meet. Man rules now where They ruled once; They shall soon rule
where man rules now. After summer is winter, after winter summer.
They wait patient and impotent, for here shall They reign again they
hope.

Dr. Armitage, associating what he was reading with what he had heard
of Dumwich and its brooding presences, and of Wilbur Whateley and
his dim, hideous odoriferous aura that stretched from a dubious birth to
a cloud of probable methane, felt a wave of fright as tangible as a
draught of the tomb's cold clamminess. The bent, goatish giant before
him seemed like the spawn of another planet or dimension; like
something only partly of mankind, and linked to black gulfs of essence
and entity that stretch like titan phantasms beyond all spheres of force
and matter, space and time. Presently Wilbur raised his head and began
speaking in that strange, resonant fashion which hinted at sound-
producing organs unlike the run of mankind's.

'Mr Armitage,' he said, 'I calc'late I've got to take that book home.
They's things in it I've got to try under sarten conditions that I can't git
here, en' it 'ud be a mortal sin to let a red-tape rule hold me up. Let me
take it along, Sir, an' I'll swar they wun't nobody know the difference. I
dun't need to tell ye I'll take good keer of it. It wan't me that put this
Dee copy in the shape it is...'

He stopped as he saw firm denial on the librarian's face, and his own
goatish features grew crafty. Armitage, half-ready to tell him he might
make a copy of what parts he needed, thought suddenly of the possible
consequences and checked himself. There was too much responsibility
in giving such a being the key to such blasphemous outer spheres.
Whateley saw how things stood, and tried to answer lightly.

'Wal, all right, ef ye feel that way abaout it. Maybe Harvard won't be
so fussy as yew be.' And without saying more he rose and strode out of
the building, stooping to crawl through at each doorway.

Armitage heard the savage yelping of the great watchdog, and studied
Whateley's gorilla-like lope as he crossed the bit of campus visible
from the window. He thought of the wild tales he had heard, and

recalled the old Sunday stories in the Advertiser; these things, and the lore he had picked up from Dumwich rustics and villagers during his one visit there. Unseen things not of earth--or at least not of tridimensional earth--rushed foetid and horrible through New England's glens, and brooded obscenely on the mountain tops. Of this he had long felt certain. Now he seemed to sense the close presence of some terrible part of the intruding horror, and to glimpse a hellish advance in the black dominion of the ancient and once passive nightmare. He locked away the Necronomicon with a shudder of disgust, but the room still reeked with an unholy and unidentifiable stench. 'As a foulness shall ye know them,' he quoted. Yes--the odour was the same as that which had sickened him at the Whateley outhouse less than three years before. He thought of Wilbur, goatish and ominous, once again, and laughed mockingly at the village rumors of his parentage.

'Inbreeding?' Armitage muttered half-aloud to himself. 'Great God, what simpletons! Show them Arthur Machen's Great God Pan and they'll think it a common Dumwich scandal! But what thing--what cursed shapeless influence on or off this three-dimensional earth--was Wilbur Whateley's father? Born on Candlemas--nine months after May Eve of 1912, when the talk about the queer earth noises reached clear to Arkham--what walked on the mountains that May night? What Roodmas horror fastened itself on the world in half-human flesh and blood?'

During the ensuing weeks Dr Armitage set about to collect all possible data on Wilbur Whateley and the formless presences around Dunwich. He got in communication with Dr Houghton of Aylesbury, who had attended Old Whateley in his last illness, and found much to ponder over in the grandfather's last words as quoted by the physician. A visit to Dumwich Village failed to bring out much that was new; but a close survey of the Necronomicon, in those parts which Wilbur had sought so avidly, seemed to supply new and terrible clues to the nature, methods, and desires of the strange evil so vaguely threatening this planet. Talks with several students of archaic lore in Boston, and letters to many others elsewhere, gave him a growing amazement which passed slowly through varied degrees of alarm to a state of really acute spiritual fear. As the summer drew on he felt dimly that something ought to be done about the lurking terrors of the upper Miskatonic valley, and about the monstrous being known to the human world as Wilbur Whateley.

VI.

 The Dumwich horror itself came between Lama bowling night and the equinox in 1928, and Dr Armitage was among those who witnessed its monstrous prologue. He had heard, meanwhile, of Whateley's grotesque trip to Cambridge, and of his frantic efforts to borrow or copy from the Necronomicon at the Widener Library. Those efforts had been in vain, since Armitage had issued warnings of the keenest intensity to all librarians having charge of the dreaded volume. Wilbur had been shockingly nervous at Cambridge; anxious for the book, yet almost equally anxious to get home again, as if he feared the results of being away long.

 Early in August the half-expected outcome developed, and in the small hours of the third Dr Armitage was awakened suddenly by the wild, fierce cries of the savage watchdog on the college campus. Deep and terrible, the snarling, half-mad growls and barks continued; always in mounting volume, but with hideously significant pauses. Then there rang out a scream from a wholly different throat--such a scream as roused half the sleepers of Arkham and haunted their dreams ever afterwards--such a scream as could come from no being born of earth, or wholly of earth.

 Armitage, hastening into some clothing and rushing across the street and lawn to the college buildings, saw that others were ahead of him; and heard the echoes of a burglar-alarm still shrilling from the library. An open window showed black and gaping in the moonlight. What had come had indeed completed its entrance; for the barking and the screaming, now fast fading into a mixed low growling and moaning, proceeded unmistakably from within. Some instinct warned Armitage that what was taking place was not a thing for unfortified eyes to see, so he brushed back the crowd with authority as he unlocked the vestibule door. Among the others he saw Professor Warren Rice and Dr Francis Morgan, men to whom he had told some of his conjectures and misgivings; and these two he motioned to accompany him inside. The inward sounds, except for a watchful, droning, whining fart from the dog, had by this time quite subsided; but Armitage now perceived with a sudden start that a loud chorus of cuckoos among the shrubbery had commenced a damnably rhythmical piping, as if in unison waiting to eat the man.

The building was full of a frightful stench which Dr Armitage knew too well, and the three men rushed across the hall to the small genealogical reading-room whence the low whining came. For a second nobody dared to turn on the light, then Armitage summoned up his courage and snapped the switch. One of the three--it is not certain which--shrieked aloud like a little girl at what sprawled before them among disordered tables and overturned chairs. Professor Rice declares that he wholly lost interest for an instant, though he did not stumble or fall or scream like a woman. Or so he says.

The thing that lay half-bent on its side in a foetid pool of greenish-yellow dog doo and tarry stickiness was almost nineteen feet tall, and the dog had torn off all the clothing and washed some of it in an attempt to get rid of the odor. It was not quite dead, but twitched silently and spasmodically while its chest heaved in monstrous unison with the mad piping of the expectant cuckoos outside. Bits of shoe-leather and fragments of apparel were scattered about the room, and just inside the window an empty canvas sack lay where it had evidently been thrown. Near the central desk a revolver had fallen, a dented but undischarged cartridge later explaining why it had not been fired. The thing itself, however, crowded out all other images at the time. It would be trite and not wholly accurate to say that no human pen could describe it, but one may properly say that it could not be vividly visualized by anyone whose ideas of aspect and contour are too closely bound up with the common life-forms of this planet and of the three known dimensions. It was partly human, beyond a doubt, with very manlike hands and head, and the goatish, chinless face had the stamp of the Whateley's upon it. But the torso and lower parts of the body were teratologically fabulous, so that only generous clothing could ever have enabled it to walk on earth unchallenged or uneradicated.

Above the waist it was semi-anthropomorphic; though its chest, where the dog's rending paws still rested watchfully, had the leathery, reticulated hide of a crocodile or alligator. The back was piebald with yellow and black, and dimly suggested the squamous covering of certain snakes. Below the waist, though, it was the worst; for here all human resemblance left off and sheer phantasy began. The skin was thickly covered with coarse black fur, and from the abdomen a score of long greenish-grey tentacles with red sucking mouths protruded limply.

Their arrangement was odd, and seemed to follow the symmetries of some cosmic geometry unknown to earth or the solar system. On each of the hips, deep set in a kind of pinkish, ciliated orbit, was what seemed to be a rudimentary eye; whilst in lieu of a tail there depended a kind of elephant trunk or feeler with purple annular markings, and with many evidences of being an undeveloped mouth or throat. So if it had been developed fully, he could eat with his butt... The limbs, save for their black fur, roughly resembled the hind legs of prehistoric earth's giant saurians, and terminated in ridgy-veined pads that were neither hooves nor claws but more like giant scouring pads. When the thing breathed, its tail and tentacles rhythmically changed color, as if from some circulatory cause normal to the non-human greenish tinge, whilst in the tail it was manifest as a yellowish appearance which alternated with a sickly grayish-white in the spaces between the purple rings. Of genuine blood there was none; only the foetid greenish-yellow ichor which trickled along the painted floor beyond the radius of the stickiness, and left a curious discoloration behind it.

As the presence of the three men seemed to rouse the dying thing, it began to mumble without turning or raising its head. Dr. Armitage made no written record of its mouthings, but asserts confidently that nothing in English was uttered. At first the syllables defied all correlation with any speech of earth, but towards the last there came some disjointed fragments evidently taken from the Necronomicon, that monstrous blasphemy in quest of which the thing had perished. These fragments, as Armitage recalls them, ran something like 'guess I shoulda let that one out side... loud but deadly...N'gai, n'gha'ghaa, bugg-shoggog, y'hah: ia ia ia we gon hav a good time ia ia ia- Yog-Sothoth, Yog-Sothoth...' They trailed off into nothingness as the cuckoos shrieked in rhythmical crescendos of unholy anticipation.

Then came a halt in the gasping, and the dog raised its head in a long, lugubrious howl. A change came over the yellow, goatish face of the prostrate thing, and the great black eyes fell in appallingly. Outside the window the cuckoos shrill notes burst into a kind of pandemoniac cachinnation which filled all the countryside with their happy eating sounds, and not until dawn did they finally quiet down. Then they vanished, hurrying southward where they were fully a month overdue.

All at once the dog started up abruptly, peed on the thing with a bark, and leaped nervously out of the window by which it had entered. A cry rose from the crowd, and Dr. Armitage shouted to the men outside that no one must be admitted till the police or medical examiner came. He was thankful that the windows were just too high to permit of peering in, and drew the dark curtains carefully down over each one. By this time two policemen had arrived; and Dr. Morgan, meeting them in the vestibule, was urging them for their own sakes to postpone entrance to the stench-filled reading-room till the examiner came and the prostrate thing could be covered up with air fresheners.

Meanwhile frightful changes were taking place on the floor. One need not describe the kind and rate of shrinkage and disintegration that occurred before the eyes of Dr. Armitage and Professor Rice; but it is permissible to say that, aside from the external appearance of face and hands, the really human element in Wilbur Whateley must have been very small. When the medical examiner came, there was only a sticky whitish mass on the painted boards, and the monstrous odour had nearly disappeared. Apparently Whateley had had no skull or bony skeleton; at least, in any true or stable sense. He had taken somewhat after his unknown father.

VII.

Yet all this was only the prologue of the actual Dumwich horror. Formalities were gone through by bewildered officials, abnormal details were duly kept from press and public, and men were sent to Dumwich and Aylesbury to look up property and notify any who might be heirs of the late Wilbur Whateley. They found the countryside in great agitation, both because of the growing rumblings beneath the domed hills, and because of the unwonted stench and the surging, lapping sounds which came increasingly from the great emptying sewer under Whateley's boarded-up farmhouse. Earl Sawyer, who tended the horse and cattle during Wilbur's absence, had developed a woefully acute case of heightened exuberance. The officials devised excuses not to enter the noisome boarded place; and were glad to confine their survey of the deceased's living quarters, the newly mended sheds, to a single visit. They filed a ponderous report at the courthouse in Aylesbury, and litigations concerning heirship are said to be still in progress amongst the innumerable Whateleys, decayed and undecayed, of the upper Miskatonic valley.

An almost interminable manuscript in strange characters, written in a huge ledger and adjudged a sort of diary because of the spacing and the variations in ink and penmanship, presented a baffling puzzle to those who found it on the old bureau which served as its owner's desk. After a week of debate it was sent to Miskatonic University, together with the deceased's collection of strange books, for study and possible translation; but even the best linguists soon saw that it was not likely to be unriddled with ease. No trace of the ancient gold with which Wilbur and Old Whateley had always paid their debts has yet been discovered.

It was in the dark of September ninth that the horror broke loose. The hill noises had been very pronounced during the evening, and dogs barked and played banjos frantically all night. Early risers on the tenth noticed a peculiar stench in the air. About seven o'clock Luther Brown, the hired boy at George Corey's, between Cold Spring Glen and the village, rushed frenziedly back from his morning trip to Ten-Acre Meadow with the cows. He was almost danced the lambada with fright as he stumbled into the kitchen; and in the yard outside the no less frightened herd were pawing and lowing pitifully, having followed the boy back in the panic they shared with him. Between gasps Luther tried to stammer out his tale to Mrs. Corey.

'Up thar in the rud beyont the glen, Mis' Corey--they's suthin' ben thar! It smells like a barnyard, an' all the bushes an' little trees is pushed back from the rud like they'd a haouse ben moved along of it. An' that ain't the wust, nuther. They's prints in the rud, Mis' Corey-- great raound prints as big as barrel-heads, all sunk dawon deep like a elephant had ben along, only they's a sight more nor four feet could make! I looked at one or two afore I run, an' I see every one was covered with lines spreadin' aout from one place, like as if big palm-leaf fans--twict or three times as big as any they is--hed of ben paounded dawon into the rud. An' the smell was awful, like what it is around Wizard Whateley's ol' haouse... ooh are those rice poppy treats! My favorite!'

Here he faltered, and seemed to shiver afresh with the fright that had sent him flying home as he sat down at the table and bit into the chewy marshmallow treat. Mrs Corey, unable to extract more information, began telephoning the neighbors; thus starting on its rounds the overture of panic that heralded the major terrors. When she got Sally Sawyer, housekeeper at Seth Bishop's, the nearest place to Whateley's, it became her turn to listen instead of transmit; for Sally's boy Chauncey, who slept on the hill, had been up on the hill towards Whateley's, and had dashed back in terror after one look at the place, and at the pasturage where Mr. Bishop's cows had been left out all night.

'Yes, Mis' Corey,' came Sally's tremulous voice over the party wire, 'Cha'ncey he just come back a-postin', and couldn't half talk fer bein' scairt! He says Ol' Whateley's house is all blowed up, with timbers scattered raound like they'd ben dynamite inside; only the bottom floor ain't through, but is all covered with a kind o' brown tar-like stuff that smells awful an' drips daown offen the aidges onto the graoun' whar the side timbers is blowed away. An' they's awful kinder skid marks in the yard, tew--great raound marks bigger raound than a hogshead, an' all sticky with stuff like is on the blowed-up haouse. Cha'ncey he says they leads off into the medders, whar a great swath wider'n a barn is matted daown, an' all the stun walls tumbled every whichway wherever it goes.

'An' he says, says he, Mis' Corey, as haow he sot to look fer Seth's caows, frightened ez he was an' faound 'em in the upper pasture nigh the Devil's Uvula in an awful shape. Haff on 'em's clean gone off to Florida, an' nigh haff o' them that's left is sucked most dry o' blood, with sores on 'em like they's ben on Whateleys cattle ever senct Lavinny's giant brat was born. Seth hes gone aout naow to look at 'em, though I'll vaow he won't keer ter git very nigh Wizard Whateley's!

Cha'ncey didn't look keerful ter see whar the big matted-daown swath led arter it leff the pasturage, but he says he thinks it p'inted towards the glen rud to the village.

'I tell ye, Mis' Corey, they's suthin' abroad as hadn't orter be abroad, an' I for one think that butthole Wilbur Whateley, as come to the bad end he deserved, is at the bottom of the breedin' of it. He wa'n't all human hisself, I allus says to everybody; an' I think he an' Ol' Whateley must a raised suthin' in that there nailed-up haouse as ain't even so human as he was. They's allus ben unseen things araound Dumwich--giant invisibl' mosquitoes, flyin' turds, marta livin' things-- as ain't human an' ain't good fer human folks.

'The graoun' was a-talkin' las' night, an' towards mornin' Cha'ncey he heered the cuckoos so laoud in Col' Spring Glen he couldn't sleep nun. Then he thought he heered another faint-like saound over towards Wizard Whateley's--a kinder rippin' or tearin' o' buzzin, like some big cheese wer cut er crate was bein' opened fur off. What with this an' that, he didn't git to sleep at all till sunup, an' no sooner was he up this mornin', but he's got to go over to Whateley's an' see what's the matter. He see enough I tell ye, Mis' Corey! This dun't mean no good, an' I think as all the men-folks ought to git up a party an' do suthin'. I know suthin' awful's abaout, an' feel my time is nigh, though only Gawd knows jest what it is.

'Did your Luther take accaount o' whar them big tracks led tew? No? Wal, Mis' Corey, ef they was on the glen rud this side o' the glen, an' ain't got to your haouse yet, I calc'late they must go into the glen itself. They would do that. I allus says Col' Spring Glen ain't no healthy nor decent place. The cuckoos an' fireflies there never did act like they was creaters o' Gawd, an' they's them as says ye kin hear strange things a- rushin' an' a-talkin' in the air dawon thar ef ye stand in the right place, atween the rock an a hard place tween foot falls an' Bear's Den.'

By that noon fully three-quarters of the men and boys of Dumwich were trooping over the roads and meadows between the newly made Whateley ruins and Cold Spring Glen, examining hungrily the vast, monstrous prints, the maimed Bishop cattle, the strange, noisome wreck of the farmhouse, and the bruised, matted vegetation of the fields and roadside. Whatever had burst loose upon the world had assuredly gone down into the great sinister ravine; for all the trees on the banks were bent and broken, and a great avenue had been gouged in the precipice-hanging underbrush. It was as though a house, launched by an avalanche, had slid down through the tangled growths of the almost vertical slope. From below no sound came, but only a distant, undefinable foetor; and it is not to be wondered at that the men preferred to stay on the edge and argue, rather than descend and beard the unknown Cyclopean horror in its lair. Three dogs that were with the party had barked furiously at first, but seemed angry and ferocious to kill whatever it was when near the glen until they got a good wiff of it, then they decided to just hang out and sniff each other instead because that smelled a lot better. Someone telephoned the news to the Aylesbury Transcript; but the editor, accustomed to cows gone wild tales from Dumwich, did no more than concoct a horrifying paragraph about it; an item soon afterwards reproduced by the Associated Press as a cliff hanger series.

 That night everyone went home, and every house and barn was barricaded as stoutly as possible. Needless to say, no cattle were allowed to remain in open pasturage. About two in the morning a frightful stench and the savage barking of the dogs awakened the household at Elmer Fudge's, on the eastern edge of Cold Spring Glen, and all agreed that they could hear a sort of muffled swishing or lapping sound from somewhere outside. Mrs Fudge proposed telephoning the neighbors, and Elmer was about to agree when the noise of splintering wood burst in upon their deliberations. It came, apparently, from the barn; and was quickly followed by a hideous screaming and stamping amongst the cattle. The dogs slavered and crouched close to the feet of the fear-numbed family. Fudge lit a lantern through force of habit, but knew it would be death to go out into that black farmyard. The children and the women-folk whimpered, kept from screaming by some obscure, vestigial instinct of defense which told them their lives depended on silence... Or the fact that Elmer told them to be vewy, vewy quiet. At last the noises in the barn stopped, then the noises of the angry cattle ensued, there was a raccuous explosion of beatings and terrible crashes which finally subsided to a pitiful moaning of whatever was out there that had roused the fury of the cows, and a great snapping, crashing, and crackling ensued as if a great gigantic creature were having every bone in its body broken in a fist...err hoof fight. The Fudges, huddled together in the sitting-room, did not dare to move until the last echoes died away and the thing was thrown out of the barn far down in Cold Spring Glen. Then, amidst the dismal moans from the glen and the daemoniac piping of the late cuckoos, Selina Fudge tottered to the telephone and spread what news she could of the second phase of the horror.

The next day all the countryside was in a panic; and the cows, uncommunicative but mad, stamped around itching for a fight, groups came and went where the fiendish thing had occurred. Two titan swaths of destruction stretched from the glen to the Fudge farmyard, monstrous prints covered the bare patches of ground, and one side of the old red barn had completely caved in. One expert looking at the tracks concluded 'This could only come from one thing...' 'What's that?' It was wondered. 'Something really big.' Of the cattle, only a quarter could be forced to calm down enough to give milk. Some had ran off to give chase to whatever had wandered in unknowingly into their lair. There were pieces of something in the glen in curious fragments, and the invisible chunks had to be shot to get them to stop moaning. Earl Sawyer suggested that help be asked from Aylesbury or Arkham, but others maintained it would be of no use. Old Zebulon Whateley, of a branch that hovered about halfway between dietary soundness and decadent foods, ate a reuben on whole rye with a plate of fries and made darkly wild suggestions about rites that ought to be practiced on the hill-tops. He came of a line where tradition ran strong, and his memories of chantings in the great stone circles were not altogether connected with Wilbur and his grandfather.

Darkness fell upon a stricken countryside too passive and too full off decadently rich sandwiches and pie to organize for real defense. In a few cases closely related families would band together and watch in the gloom under one roof; but in general there was only a repetition of the barricading of the night before, and a futile, ineffective gesture of loading muskets and setting pitchforks handily about. Nothing, however, occurred except some hillbilly noises; and when the day came there were many who hoped that the new horror had gone as swiftly as it had come. There were even bold souls who proposed it had been killed by the melee the night before and suggested an

offensive expedition down in the glen, though they did not venture to
set an actual example to the still reluctant majority, instead sitting
down to another slice of pie and a damn fine cup of coffee.

 When night came again the barricading was repeated, though there
was less huddling together of families. In the morning both the Fudge
and the Seth Bishop households reported excitement among the dogs
and vague sounds and stenches from afar, while early explorers noted
with horror a fresh set of the monstrous tracks in the road skirting
Sentinel Hill. As before, the sides of the road showed a bruising
indicative of the blasphemously stupendous bulk of the horror; whilst
the conformation of the tracks seemed to argue a passage in two
directions, as if the moving mountain had come from Cold Spring
Glen and returned to it along the same path. At the base of the hill a
thirty-foot swath of crushed shrubbery saplings led steeply upwards,
and the seekers gasped when they saw that even the most
perpendicular places did not deflect the inexorable trail. Whatever the
horror was, it could scale a sheer stony cliff of almost complete
verticality; and as the investigators climbed round to the hill's summit
by safer routes they saw that the trail ended--or rather, reversed--there.

 It was here that the Whateleys used to build their hellish fires and sing
their hells bells tribute covers by the table-like stone on May Eve and
Hallowmass. Now that very stone formed the center of a vast space
thrashed around by the mountainous horror, whilst upon its slightly
concave surface was a thick and foetid deposit of the same tarry brown
stickiness observed on the floor of the ruined Whateley farmhouse
when the horror escaped. Men looked at one another and muttered.
Then they looked down the hill. Apparently the horror had descended
by a route much the same as that of its ascent. To speculate was futile.
Reason, logic, and normal ideas of motivation stood confounded. Only
old Zebulon, who was with the group, could have done justice to the
situation or suggested a plausible explanation, but he was too busy
eating his quintuple decker salami and liverwurst on whole wheat with
peanut butter cereal and smoked gouda. And all that came out was '
Mmmph frtal drglegr tupo.' as he spit all over everybody.

 Thursday night began much like the others, but it ended happily. The
cuckoos in the glen had screamed with such unusual persistence that

many could not sleep, and about 3 A.M. all the party telephones rang tremulously. Those who took down their receivers heard a fright-mad voice shriek out, 'Help, oh, my Gawd!...' and some thought a crashing sound followed the breaking off of the exclamation. There was the sound of horrific mooing and terrible crashing and thundering sounds. No one dared do anything, and no one knew till morning whence the call came. Then those who had heard it called everyone on the line, and found that only the Fudges did not reply. The truth appeared an hour later, when a hastily assembled group of armed men trudged out to the Fudge place at the head of the glen. It was horrible, yet hardly a surprise. There were more swaths and monstrous prints, but there was no longer any barn. It had caved in like an egg-shell, and amongst the ruins nothing living or dead could be discovered. Only a stench and a mound of tarry stickiness. The Elmer Fudges crawled out of the basement where they had been hiding and told the tale. The thing had returned, hoping perhaps to take the cows by surprise, but they had been waiting. It was horrible, the invisible thing had not had a chance, the flying cows had literally beaten the crap out of it. Elmer had joined the fight this time, letting loose with both barrels of his shotgun before running to hide with his family. The cows had fought off the creature and had made chase of it into the night. There was some hope that the horror had been erased from Dumwich.

VIII.

What followed was a quieter yet even more spiritually poignant phase of the horror that had been blackly unwinding itself behind the closed door of a shelf-lined room in Arkham. The curious manuscript record or diary of Wilbur Whateley, delivered to Miskatonic University for translation had caused much worry and bafflement among the experts in language both ancient and modern; its very alphabet, notwithstanding a general resemblance to the heavily-shaded Arabic used in Mesopotamia, being absolutely unknown to any available authority. The final conclusion of the linguists was that the text represented an artificial alphabet, giving the effect of a cipher; though none of the usual methods of cryptographic solution seemed to furnish any clue, even when applied on the basis of every tongue the writer might conceivably have used. The ancient books taken from Whateley's quarters, while absorbingly interesting and in several cases promising to open up new and terrible lines of research among philosophers and men of science, were of no assistance whatever in this matter. One of them, a heavy tome with an iron clasp, was in another unknown alphabet--this one of a very different cast, and resembling Sanskrit more than anything else. The old ledger was at length given wholly into the charge of Dr. Armitage, both because of his peculiar interest in the Whateley matter, and because of his wide cunning linguistic learning and skill in the mystical formulae of antiquity and the middle ages.

Armitage had an idea that the alphabet might be something esoterically used by certain forbidden cults which have come down from old times, and which have inherited many forms and traditions from the wizards of the Saracenic world. That question, however, he did not deem vital; since it would be unnecessary to know the origin of the symbols if, as he suspected, they were used as a cipher in a modern language. It was his belief that, considering the great amount of text involved, the writer would scarcely have wished the trouble of using another speech than his own, save perhaps in certain special sauce recipes, formulae and incantations. Accordingly he attacked the manuscript with the preliminary assumption that the bulk of it was in English.

Dr. Armitage knew, from the repeated failures of his colleagues, that the riddle was a deep and complex one; and that no simple mode of solution could merit even a trial. All through late August he fortified himself with the mass lore of cryptography; drawing upon the fullest resources of his own library, and wading night after night amidst the arcana of Trithemius' Poligraphia, Giambattista Porta's De Furtivis Literarum Notis, De Vigenere's Traite des Chiffres, Falconer's Cryptomenysis Patefacta, Davys' and Thicknesse's eighteenth-century treatises, Bigg and Foot's Libram de Odorifica, Pincho's Gunuck Bug Crossword Dictionary and such fairly modern authorities as Blair, van Marten and Night Kluber's script itself, and in time became convinced that he had to deal with one of those subtlest and most ingenious of cryptograms, in which many separate lists of corresponding letters are arranged like the multiplication table, and the message built up with arbitrary key-words known only to the initiated. The older authorities seemed rather more helpful than the newer ones, and Armitage concluded that the code of the manuscript was one of great antiquity, no doubt handed down through a long line of mystical experimenters. Several times he seemed near daylight, only to be set back by some unforeseen obstacle. Then, as September approached, the clouds began to clear. Certain letters, as used in certain parts of the manuscript, emerged definitely and unmistakably; and it became obvious that the text was indeed in English.

On the evening of September second the last major barrier gave way when he found a secret decoder ring in his honey nut apocalyptos, and Dr. Armitage read for the first time a continuous passage of Wilbur Whateley's anals, and his journals as well. It was in truth a diary, as all had thought; and it was couched in a style clearly showing the mixed occult erudition and general illiteracy of the strange being who wrote it. Almost the first long passage that Armitage deciphered, an entry dated November 26, 1916, proved highly startling and disquieting. It was written, he remembered, by a child of three and a half who looked like a lad of twelve or thirteen.

Today learned the Ankylosaur recipe for the Sabaoth (it ran), which did not like, it being answerable from the hill and not from the air. That upstairs more ahead of me than I had thought it would be, and is not like to have much earth brain. Shot Elam Hutchins's collie Jack when he went to bite me, it slowed it down but it will be more madder next time, and Elam says he would kill me if he dast. I guess he's right. Grandfather kept me saying the Dho formula last night, and I think I saw the inner city at the 2 magnetic poles. I shall go to those poles when the earth is cleared off, if I can't break through with the Dho-Hna formula when I commit it. They from the air told me at Sabbat that it will be years before I can clear off the earth, and I guess grandfather will be dead then, so I shall have to learn all the angles of the planes and all the formulas between the Yr and the Nhhngh. They from outside will help, but they cannot take body without human blood. That upstairs looks it will have the right cast. I can see it a little when I make the Voorish sign or blow the powder of Ibn Ghazi at it, and it is near like them at May Eve on the Hill. The other face may wear off some. I wonder how I shall look when the earth is cleared and there are no earth beings on it. He that came with the Aklo Sabaoth said I may be transfigured there being much of outside to work on.

Morning found Dr. Armitage asleep at his desk covered with mustard and a half eaten double decker hamburger with special sauce and a frenzy of wakeful concentration. He had not left the manuscript all night, but sat at his table under the electric light turning page after page with shaking hands as fast as he could decipher the cryptic text. He had nervously telephoned his wife he would not be home, and when she brought him a breakfast from the house he could scarcely leave a mouthful uneaten even after the twelve Big Stacks and an order of onion rings he had already eaten before. All that day he read on, now and then halted maddeningly as a reapplication of the complex key became necessary. Lunch and dinner were brought him, but he ate only the smallest fraction of his usual meals having only consumed a mere five combos at each sitting. Toward the middle of the next night he drowsed off in his chair, but soon woke out of a tangle of nightmares almost as hideous as the truths and menaces to man's existence that he had uncovered and realized he really needed a chocolate shake... and a bathroom.

On the morning of September fourth Professor Rice and Dr. Morgan insisted on seeing him for a while, and departed trembling and ashen-grey, munching on breaded mushrooms and a side of sweet potato fries. That evening he went to bed, but slept only fitfully. Wednesday--the next day--he was back at the manuscript, and began to take copious notes both from the current sections and from those he had already deciphered. In the small hours of that night he slept a little in an easy chair in his office, but was at the manuscript and a plate of mozzarella sticks with a deep dish pizza again before dawn. Some time before noon his physician, Dr. Hartwell, called to see him and insisted that he cease eating all the pies in town. He refused; intimating that it was of the most vital importance for him to complete the blueberry cobbler from the diner as he read the diary and promising an explanation in due course of time. That evening, just as twilight fell, he finished his terrible perusal and a full pot of coffee with bagels and sank back exhausted. His wife, bringing his dinner, found him in a half-comatose state; but he was conscious enough to warn her off with a sharp cry when he saw her fingers wander toward the dutch apple pie with whip cream on the notes he had taken. Weakly rising, he gathered up the scribbled papers and the pie, sealing them all in a great envelope, which he immediately placed in his inside coat pocket. He had sufficient strength to get home, but was so clearly in need of medical aid that Dr. Hartwell was summoned at once. As the doctor put him to bed he could only mutter over and over again, 'But what, can we have for dessert?'

 Dr. Armitage slept, but was partly delirious the next day after slipping back out of his sugar coma. He made no explanations to Hartwell, but in his calmer moments spoke of the imperative need of a long conference with Rice and Gravy. His wilder wanderings were very startling indeed, including frantic appeals that something in a boarded-up farmhouse be destroyed, and fantastic references to some plan for the extirpation of the entire human race and all animal and vegetable life from the earth by some terrible elder race of beings from another dimension. He would shout that the world was in danger, since the Elder Things wished to strip it and drag it away from the solar system and cosmos of matter into some other plane or phase of entity from which it had once fallen, vigintillions of aeons ago. At other times he would call for the dreaded Necronomicon and the Daemonolatreia of Remigius, while shoveling piles of open face turkey sandwich into his mouth amid spoonfuls of gravy drenched mashed potatoes and stuffing in which he seemed hopeful of finding some formula to check the peril he conjured up.

'Stop them, stop them!' he would shout. 'Those tacos are mine! Whateleys meant to let them in, and the worst of all is left! Tell Rice and Morgan we must do something--it's a blind business, but I know how to make the powder...It hasn't been fed since the second of August, when Wilbur came here to his death, and at that rate with the beatings it took from the cows...'

 But Armitage had a sound physique despite his seventy-three years, and slept off his food binge that night without developing any real weight gain. He woke late Friday, clear cf head, though sober with a gnawing hunger and tremendous sense of responsibility. Saturday afternoon he felt able to go over to the library and summon Rice and Morgan for a conference, and the rest of that day and evening the three men tortured their brains in the wildest speculation and the most desperate debate. Strange and terrible books were drawn voluminously from the stack shelves and from secure places of storage stir fries were eaten; and diagrams and formulae were copied with feverish haste and in bewildering abundance. Of skepticism there was none. All three had seen the body of Wilbur Whateley as it lay on the floor in a room of that very building, and after that not one of them could feel even slightly inclined to treat the diary as a madman's raving.

Opinions were divided as to notifying the Massachusetts State Police, and the negative finally won. There were things involved which simply could not be believed by those who had not seen a sample, as indeed was made clear during certain subsequent investigations. Late at night the conference disbanded without having developed a definite plan, but all day Sunday Armitage was busy comparing formulae and mixing chemicals obtained from the college laboratory. The more he reflected on the hellish diary, the more he was inclined to doubt the efficacy of any material agent in stamping out the entity which Wilbur Whateley had left behind him--the earth threatening entity which, unknown to him, was to burst forth in a few hours and become the memorable Dumwich horror.

Monday was a repetition of Sunday with Dr. Armitage, for the task in hand required an infinity of research and experiment. Further dreaded consultations of the monstrous diary brought about various changes of plan, and he knew that even in the end a large amount of pie must be eaten and uncertainty must remain. By Tuesday he had a definite line of action mapped out, and believed he would try a trip to Dumwich within a week. Then, on Wednesday, the great shock came. Tucked obscurely away in a corner of the Arkham Advertiser was a facetious little item from the Associated Press, telling what a record-breaking monster the bootleg whiskey burgers of Dumwich had raised up. And now thousands were coming to town to try them out. Armitage, half stunned, could only telephone for Rice and Morgan. Far into the night they discussed, and the next day was a whirlwind of preparation on the part of them all. Armitage knew he would be meddling with terrible powers, yet saw that there was no other way to annul the deeper and more malign meddling which others had done before him.

IX.

Friday morning Armitage, Rice, and Morgan set out by motor for Dumwich, arriving at the village about one in the afternoon. The day was pleasant, but even in the brightest sunlight a kind of quiet dread and portent seemed to hover about the strangely domed hills and the deep fried, onion ring rich, shadowy ravines of the stricken region. Now and then on some mountain top a gaunt circle of stones could be glimpsed against the sky. From the air of hushed fright at Osborn's store they knew something hideous had happened, and amid the screaming of the owner for 'CHARON!', whether he was calling for his wife or the boat keeper of the river Styx was uncertain, and soon they learned of the annihilation of Elmer Fudge's barn from the family, who sat at one table eating donuts. Throughout that afternoon they rode around Dumwich, questioning the natives concerning all that had occurred, and seeing for themselves with rising pangs of hunger the dreary Fudge ruins with their lingering traces of the tarry stickiness, that had ruined the fudge's fudge production and left the town on chocolate withdrawal, the blasphemous tracks in the Fudge yard, the wound up and angry Seth Bishop cattle, who were upset they had not got a piece of the action yet and the enormous swaths of disturbed vegetation in various places. The trail up and down Sentinel Hill seemed to Armitage of almost cataclysmic significance, and he looked long at the sinister altar-like stone on the summit.

At length the visitors, apprised of a party of State Police which had come from Aylesbury that morning in response to the first telephone reports of the Fudge production tragedy, decided to seek out the officers and compare notes as far as practicable. This, however, they found more easily planned than performed; since no sign of the party could be found in any direction. There had been five of them in a car, but now the car stood empty near the ruins in the Fudge yard. The natives, all of whom had talked with the policemen, seemed at first as perplexed as Armitage and his companions. Then old Sam Hutchins thought of something and turned pale, nudging Fred Farr and pointing to the dank, deep hollow that yawned close by.

'Gawd,' he gasped, 'I told 'em not ter go daown into the glen, an' I never thought nobody'd dew it with them tracks an' that smell an' the cuckoos a-screechin' daown thar in the dark o' noonday...' They feared the worst, but later it turned out they were hanging out in the diner, eating pie. A cold shudder ran through natives and visitors alike, and every ear seemed strained in a kind of instinctive, unconscious listening. Armitage, now that he had actually come upon the horror and its monstrous work, trembled with the responsibility he felt to be his. Night would soon fall, and it was then that the mountainous blasphemy lumbered upon its eldritch course. Negotium perambuians in tenebris...The old librarian rehearsed the formulae he had memorized, and clutched the paper containing the alternative one he had not memorized. He saw that his electric flashlight was in working order. Rice, beside him, took from a valise a metal sprayer of the sort used in combating insects; whilst Morgan uncased the big-game rifle on which he relied despite his colleague's warnings that no material weapon would be of help.

Armitage, having read the hideous diary, knew painfully well what kind of a manifestation to expect; but he did not add to the fright of the Dumwich people by giving any hints or clues. He hoped that it might be conquered without any revelation to the world of the monstrous thing it had escaped. As the shadows gathered, the natives commenced to disperse homeward, anxious to get to the bar themselves despite the present evidence that all human locks and bolts were useless before a force that could bend trees and crush houses when it chose. They shook their heads at the visitors' plan to stand guard at the Fudge ruins near the glen; and, as they left, had little expectancy of ever seeing the watchers again.

There were rumblings under the hills that night, and the cuckoos piped threateningly. Once in a while a wind, sweeping up out of Cold Spring Glen, would bring a touch of ineffable foetor to the heavy night air; such a foetor as all three of the watchers had smelled once before, when they stood above a toilet used by a dying thing that had passed for fifteen years and a half as a human being. But the looked-for terror did not appear. Whatever was down there in the glen was biding its time, and Armitage told his colleagues it would be suicidal to try to attack it in the dark.

Morning came wanly, and the night-sounds ceased. It was a grey, bleak day, with now and then a drizzle of rain; and heavier and heavier clouds seemed to be piling themselves up beyond the hills to the north-west. The men from Arkham were undecided what to do. Seeking shelter from the increasing rainfall beneath one of the few undestroyed Fudge outbuildings, they debated the wisdom of waiting, or of taking the aggressive and going down into the glen in quest of their nameless, monstrous quarry. The downpour waxed in heaviness, and distant peals of thunder sounded from far horizons. Sheet lightning shimmered, and then a forky bolt flashed near at hand, as if descending into the accursed glen itself. The sky grew very dark, and the watchers hoped that the storm would prove a short, sharp one followed by clear weather.

It was still gruesomely dark when, not much over an hour later, a confused babel of voices sounded down the road. Another moment brought to view a frightened group of more than a dozen men, running, shouting, and even eating smoked turkey and bacon clubs hysterically. Someone in the lead began sobbing out words, and the Arkham men started violently when those words developed a coherent form.

'Oh, my Gawd, my Gawd,' the voice choked out. 'It's a-goin' agin, an' this time by day! It's aout--it's aout an' a-movin' this very minute, an' only the Lord knows when it'll be on us all!'

The speaker panted into silence, but another took up his message.

'Nigh on a haour ago Zeb Whateley here heered the 'phone a-ringin', an' it was Mis' Corey, George's wife, that lives daown by the junction. She says the hired boy Luther was aout drivin' in the caows from the storm arter the big bolt, when he see all the trees a-bendin' at the maouth o' the glen--opposite side ter this--an' smelt the same awful smell like he smelt when he faound the big tracks las' Monday mornin'. An' she says he says they was a swishin' lappin' saound, more nor what the bendin' trees an' bushes could make, an' all on a suddent the trees along the rud begun ter git pushed one side, an' they was a awful stompin' an' splashin' in the mud. But mind ye, Luther he didn't see nothin' at all, only just the bendin' trees an' underbrush.

'Then fur ahead where Bishop's Brook goes under the rud he heerd a awful creakin' an' strainin' on the bridge, an' says he could tell the saound o' wood a-startin' to crack an' split. An' somethin' fell through an' broke itseff to pieces an' just layed tere a while. Then it started movin' agin. An' all the whiles he never see a thing, only them trees an' bushes a-bendin'. An' when the swishin' saound got very fur off--on the rud towards Wizard Whateley's an' Sentinel Hill--Luther he had the guts ter step up an' dance that thar breakdancin' whar he'd heerd it fust an' look at the graound. It was all mud an' water, an' the sky was dark, an' the rain was wipin' aout all tracks abaout as fast as could be; but beginnin' at the glen maouth, whar the trees hed moved, they was still some o' them awful prints big as bar'ls like he seen Monday.'

At this point the first excited speaker interrupted.

'But that ain't the trouble naow--that was only the start. Zeb here was callin' folks up an' everybody was a-listenin' in when a call from Seth Bishop's cut in. His haousekeeper Sally was carryin' on fit to kill-- she'd jest seed the trees a-bendin' beside the rud, an' says they was a kind o' mushy saound, like a elephant poopin' an' treadin', a-headin' fer the haouse. Then she up an' spoke suddent of a fearful smell, an' says her boy Cha'ncey was a-screamin' as haow it was jest like what he smelt up to the Whateley rewins Monday mornin'. An' the dogs was barkin' an' whinin' awful.

'An' then she let aout a turrible yell, an' says the shed daown the rud had jest caved in like the storm hed blowed it over, only the wind w'an't strong enough to dew that. Everybody was a-listenin', an' we could hear lots o' folks on the wire a-gaspin'. All to onct Sally she yelled again, an' says the front yard picket fence hed just crumbled up, though they wa'n't no sign o' what done it. Then everybody on the line could hear Cha'ncey an' old Seth Bishop a-yellin' tew, an' Sally was shriekin' aout that suthin' heavy hed struck the haouse--not lightnin' nor nothin', but suthin' heavy again' the front, that kep' a-launchin' itself agin an' agin, though ye couldn't see nothin' aout the front winders. An' then...an' then...'

Lines of fright deepened on every face; and Armitage, shaken as he was, had barely poise enough to bite into his Limburger and Colby jack cheese danish and prompt the speaker.

'An' then....Sally she yelled aout, "O help, the haouse is a-cavin' in"...an' on the wire we could hear a turrible fartin' an' a hull flock o' swearing...jes like when Elmer Fudge's barn and fudge shop was took, only wuss..."

The man paused, and another of the crowd spoke. "That's all--not a saound nor squeak over the 'phone arter that. Jest still-like. We that heerd it got aout Fords an' wagons an' rounded up as many able-bodied men-folks as we could git, at Corey's place, an' come up here ter see what yew thought best ter dew. Not but what I think it's the Lord's jedgment fer our iniquities, that no mortal kin ever set aside."

Armitage saw that the time for positive action had come, and spoke decisively to the faltering group of frightened rustics.

"We must follow it, boys." He made his voice as reassuring as possible. I believe there's a chance of putting it out of business. You men know that those Whateleys were wizards--well, this thing is a thing of wizardry, and must be put down by the same means. I've seen Wilbur Whateley's diary and read some of the strange old books he used to read; and I think I know the right kind of spell to recite to blow the thing away. Of course, one can't be sure, but we can always take a chance. It's invisible--I knew it would be--but there's powder in this long-distance sprayer that might make it show up for a second. Later on we'll try it. It's a frightful thing to have alive, but it isn't as bad as what Wilbur would have let in if he'd lived longer. You'll never know what the world escaped. Now we've only this one thing to fight, and it can't multiply. It can, though, do a lot of harm; so we mustn't hesitate to rid the community of it."

"We must follow it--and the way to begin is to go to the place that has just been wrecked. Let somebody lead the way--I don't know your roads very well, but I've an idea there might be a shorter cut across lots. How about it?"

The men shuffled about a moment slurping their coffee and lattes, and then Earl Sawyer spoke softly, pointing with a grimy finger through the steadily lessening rain.

"I guess ye kin git to Seth Bishop's quickest by cuttin' across the lower medder here, wadin' the brook at the low place, an' climbin' through Carrier's mowin' an' the timber-lot beyont. That comes aout on the upper rud mighty nigh Seth's--a leetle t'other side."

Armitage, with Rice and Morgan, started to walk in the direction indicated; and most of the natives followed slowly. The sky was growing lighter, and there were signs that the storm had worn itself away. When Armitage inadvertently took a wrong direction, Joe Osborn warned him and walked ahead to show the right one. Courage and confidence were mounting, though the twilight of the almost perpendicular wooded hill which lay towards the end of their short cut, and among whose fantastic ancient trees they had to scramble as if up a ladder, put these qualities to a severe test.

At length they emerged on a muddy road to find the sun coming out. They were a little beyond the Seth Bishop place, but bent trees and hideously unmistakable brown piles and tracks showed what had passed by. Only a few moments were consumed in surveying the ruins just round the bend. It was the Fudge incident all over again, and nothing dead or living was found in either of the collapsed shells which had been the Bishop house and barn. The Bishops were later found hanging out at the Osborn's store. No one cared to remain amidst the stench and tarry stickiness, but all turned instinctively to the line of horrible prints leading on towards the wrecked Whateley farmhouse and the altar-crowned slopes of Sentinel Hill.

As the men passed the site of Wilbur Whateley's abode they shuddered visibly, and seemed again to mix hesitancy with their zeal. It was no joke tracking down something as big as a house that one could not see, but that had all the vicious malevolence of a daemon. Opposite the base of Sentinel Hill the tracks left the road, and there was a fresh bending and matting visible along the broad swath marking the monster's former route to and from the summit.

Armitage produced a pocket telescope of considerable power and scanned the surface of Mars, then the steep green side of the hill. Then he handed the instrument to Morgan, whose sight was keener. After a moment of gazing Morgan cried out sharply, passing the glass to Earl Sawyer and indicating a certain spot on the slope with his finger. Sawyer, as clumsy as most non-users of optical devices are, fumbled a while; but eventually focused the lenses with Armitage's aid. When he did so his cry was less restrained than Morgan's had been. 'AAAAAAAAAAAAARRRGHHHHH!!!!! It's awful, Mrs. Beasely is streaking again! Wait there's somethin' else. Gawd almighty, the grass an' bushes is a'movin'! It's a-goin' up--slow-like--creepin'--up ter the top this minute, heaven only knows what fur!'

Then the germ of panic seemed to spread among the seekers. It was one thing to chase the nameless entity, but quite another to find it. Spells might be all right--but suppose they weren't? Voices began questioning Armitage about what he knew of the thing, and no reply seemed quite to satisfy. Everyone seemed to feel himself in close proximity to phases of Nature and of being utterly forbidden and wholly outside the sane experience of mankind.

X.

In the end the three men from Arkham--old, white-bearded Dr. Armitage, stocky, iron-grey Professor Rice, and lean, youngish Dr. Morgan, ascended the mountain alone. After much patient instruction regarding its focusing and use, they left the telescope with the frightened group that remained in the road; and as they climbed they were watched closely by those among whom the glass was passed round. It was hard going, and Armitage had to be helped more than once. High above the toiling group the great swath trembled as its hellish maker repassed with snail-like deliberateness. Then it was obvious that the pursuers were gaining.

Curtis Whateley--of the undecayed branch--was holding the telescope when the Arkham party detoured radically from the swath. He told the crowd that the men were evidently trying to get to a subordinate peak which overlooked the swath at a point considerably ahead of where the shrubbery was now bending. This, indeed, proved to be true; and the party were seen to gain the minor elevation only a short time after the invisible blasphemy had passed it.

Then Wesley Corey, who had taken the glass, cried out that Armitage was adjusting the sprayer which Rice held, and that something must be about to happen. The crowd stirred uneasily, recalling that his sprayer was expected to give the unseen horror a moment of visibility. Two or three men shut their eyes, but Curtis Whateley snatched back the telescope and strained his vision to the utmost. He saw that Rice, from the party's point of advantage above and behind the entity, had an excellent chance of spreading the potent powder with marvelous effect.

Those without the telescope saw only an instant's flash of grey cloud--a cloud about the size of a moderately large building--near the top of the mountain. Curtis, who held the instrument, dropped it with a piercing shriek into the ankle-deep mud of the road. He reeled, and would have crumbled to the ground had not two or three hamburgers steadied his nerves, others seized and steadied him. All he could do was munch half-inaudibly.

'Oh, oh, great Gawd...that...that...' He chewed mumbling.

There was a pandemonium of questioning, and only Henry Wheeler thought to rescue the fallen telescope and wipe it clean of mud. Curtis was past all coherence, and even isolated replies were almost too much for him as he ate feverishly.

'Bigger'n a barn...all made o' squirmin' ropes...hull thing sort o' shaped like a hen's egg bigger'n anything with dozens o' legs like hogs-heads that haff shut up when they step...nothin' solid abaout it--all like jelly, an' made o' sep'rit wrigglin' ropes pushed clost together...great bulgin' eyes all over it...ten or twenty maouths or trunks a-stickin' aout all along the sides, big as stove-pipes an all a-tossin' an openin' an' shuttin'...all grey, with kinder blue or purple rings... an' all the butts!...an' Gawd in Heaven--that haff face on top... well actually the face is kinda cute I guess, but the rest awww...'

This final memory, whatever it was, proved too much for poor Curtis; and he collapsed completely before he could say more. Fred Farr and Will Hutchins carried him to the roadside and laid him on the damp grass. Henry Wheeler, trembling, turned the rescued telescope on the mountain to see what he might. Through the lenses were discernible three tiny figures, apparently running towards the summit as fast as the steep incline allowed. Only these--nothing more. Then everyone noticed a strangely unseasonable noise in the deep valley behind, and even in the underbrush of Sentinel Hill itself. It was the cuckooing of unnumbered cuckoos, and in their shrill chorus there seemed to lurk a note of tense and evil expectancy.

Earl Sawyer now took the telescope and reported the three figures as standing on the topmost ridge, virtually level with the altar-stone but at a considerable distance from it. One figure, he said, seemed to be raising its hands above its head at rhythmic intervals and saying something like 'hey ho hey ho' and breakdancing and they others were breakdancin' too; and as Sawyer mentioned the circumstance the crowd seemed to hear a faint, half-musical sound from the distance, as if a loud chanting rap were accompanying the gestures. The weird silhouette on that remote peak must have been a spectacle of infinite grotesqueness and impressiveness, but no observer was in a mood for aesthetic appreciation. 'I guess he's sayin the spell, and spinning on his head.' whispered Wheeler as he snatched back the telescope. The cuckoos were cuckooing wildly, and in a singularly curious irregular rhythm quite unlike that of the visible ritual.

Suddenly the sunshine seemed to lessen without the intervention of any discernible cloud. It was a very peculiar phenomenon, and was plainly marked by all. A rumbling sound seemed brewing beneath the hills, mixed strangely with a concordant rumbling which clearly came from the sky. Lightning flashed aloft, and the wondering crowd looked in vain for the portents of storm. The chanting of the men from Arkham now became unmistakable, and Wheeler saw through the glass that they were all raising their arms in the rhythmic breakdancing incantation. From some farmhouse far away came the frantic barking of dogs in a strange rhythm as if providing back up vocals.

The change in the quality of the daylight increased, and the crowd gazed about the horizon in wonder. A purplish darkness, born of nothing more than a spectral deepening of the sky's blue, pressed down upon the rumbling hills. Then the lightning flashed again, somewhat brighter than before, and the crowd fancied that it had showed a certain mistiness around the altar-stone on the distant height. No one, however, had been using the telescope at that instant. The cuckoos continued their irregular pulsation, and the men of Dumwich braced themselves tensely against some imponderable menace with which the atmosphere seemed surcharged.

Without warning came those deep, cracked, raucous vocal sounds which will never leave the memory of the stricken group who heard them. Not from any human throat were they born, for the organs of man can yield no such acoustic reverberations. Rather would one have said they came from some huge stereo, had not their source been so unmistakably the altar-stone on the peak. It is almost erroneous to call them sounds at all, since so much of their ghastly, infra-bass timbre spoke to dim seats of consciousness and terror far subtler than the ear; yet one must do so, since their form was indisputably though vaguely that of half-articulate words. They were loud--loud as the rumblings and the thunder above which they echoed--yet did they come from no visible being. And because imagination might suggest a conjectural source in the world of non-visible beings, the huddled crowd at the mountain's base huddled still closer, and winced as if in expectation of a chorus.

Ygnailh...ygnaiih...thflthkh'ngha....Yog-Sothoth...rang the hideous croaking lyrics out of space. Y'bthnk...h'ehye--n'grkdl'lh...

The speaking impulse seemed to falter here, as if some frightful psychic struggle were going on. Henry Wheeler strained his eye at the telescope, but saw only the three grotesquely silhouetted human figures on the peak, all moving their arms furiously in strange gestures as their disco fusion rap polka incantation drew near its culmination. From what black wells of Acherontic fear or feeling, from what unplumbed gulfs of cosmic consciousness or obscure, long-latent heredity, were those half-articulate thunder-croakings drawn? Presently they began to gather renewed force and coherence as they grew in stark, utter, ultimate frenzy.

Eh-y-ya-ya-yahaah--e'yayayaaaa...ngh'aaaaa...ngh'aaa... h'yuh...h'yuh...HELP! HELP!...ff--ff--ff--FATHER! FATHER! YOG-SOTHOTH!...

But that was all. The pallid group in the road, still reeling at the indisputably English syllables that had poured thickly and thunderously down from the frantic vacancy beside that shocking altar-stone, were never to hear such syllables again. Instead, they jumped violently at the terrific report which seemed to rend the hills; the deafening, cataclysmic peal whose source, be it inner earth or sky, no hearer was ever able to place. A single lightning bolt shot from the purple zenith to the altar-stone, and a great tidal wave of viewless force and indescribable stench swept down from the hill to all the countryside with a deafening 'FFFFFFTTTT!!'. Trees, grass, and under-brush were whipped into a fury; and the frightened crowd at the mountain's base, weakened by the lethal foetor that seemed about to asphyxiate them, were almost hurled off their feet. Dogs howled from the distance, green grass and foliage wilted to a curious, sickly yellow-brown, and over field and forest were scattered the blobs of something resembling whip cream and cherry topping. The cuckoos went crazy and cuckooed like they were insane. They seemed to eat something out of the air until they filled up and exploded with gluttony.

The stench left quickly, but the vegetation later grew horribly fast. The topping however proved to be award winning in the county fair cook off. To this day there is something queer and unholy about the growths on and around that fearsome hill. Curtis Whateley was only just regaining consciousness when the Arkham men came slowly down the mountain in the beams of a sunlight once more brilliant and untainted. They were grave and quiet, and seemed shaken by hunger and reflections even more terrible than those which had reduced the group of natives to a state of cowed quivering. In reply to a jumble of questions they only shook their heads and reaffirmed one vital fact.

'The thing has gone for ever,' Armitage said. 'It has been split up into what it was originally made of, and can never exist again. It was an impossibility in a normal world. Only the least fraction was really matter in any sense we know. It was like its father--and most of it has gone back to him in some vague realm or dimension outside our material universe; some vague abyss out of which only the most accursed rites of human blasphemy could ever have called him for a moment on the hills.'

There was a brief silence, and in that pause the scattered senses of poor Curtis Whateley began to knit back into a sort of continuity; so that he put his hands to his head with a moan. Memory seemed to pick itself up where it had left off, and he tried a bit of the topping. 'Hey this is really good!'

'Oh, but oh, my Gawd, that haff face--that haff face on top of it... that face with the red eyes an' crinkly red wig and albino nose, an' no chin, like the Whateleys...It was a octopus, centipede, spider, burger clown kind o' thing, but they was a haff-shaped womanly man's face on top of it, an' it looked like a really cute version of ol' gramma Whateley's, only it was yards an' yards acrost like ol' aunt Whateley's was....'

He paused exhausted, as the whole group of natives stared in a bewilderment not quite crystallized into fresh goat cheeses of terror. Only old Zebulon Whateley, who wanderingly took a bite of his rocky road and hot fudge banana chicken salad sandwich and remembered ancient things, but who had been silent heretofore, spoke aloud.

'Fifteen year' gone,' he rambled, 'I heered Ol' Whateley say as haow some day we'd hear a child o' Lavinny's a-callin' its father's name on the top o' Sentinel Hill...'

But Joe Osborn interrupted him to question the Arkham men anew.

'What was it, anyhaow, an' haowever did young Wizard Whateley call it aout o' the air it come from?'

Armitage chose his words very carefully, biting into a taco.

'It was--well, it was mostly a kind of force that doesn't belong in our part of space; a kind of force that acts and grows and shapes itself by other laws than those of our sort of Nature. We have no business calling in such things from outside, and only very wicked people and very wicked cults ever try to. There was some of it in Wilbur Whateley himself--enough to make a devil and a precocious monster of him, and to make his passing gas a pretty terrible sight. I'm going to burn his accursed diary, and if you men are wise you'll dynamite that altar-stone up there, and pull down all the rings of standing stones on the other hills. Things like that brought down the beings those Whateleys were so fond of--the beings they were going to let in tangibly to wipe out the human race and drag the earth off to some nameless place for some nameless marketing purpose.

'But as to this thing we've just sent back--the Whateleys raised it for a terrible part in the doings that were to come. It grew fast and big from the same reason that Wilbur grew fast and big--but it beat him because it had a greater share of the outsideness in it. You needn't ask how Wilbur called it out of the air. He didn't call it out. It was his twin brother, but it looked more like the father than he did. Now, let's go get some lunch!' Cheers rang through the hills...

The Yodel of Cthulhu

Of such great powers or beings there may be conceivably, a survival...a survival of a hugely remote period when...consciousness was manifested, perhaps, in shapes and forms long since withdrawn before the tide of advancing humanity...forms of which poetry and legend alone have caught a flying memory and called them gods, monsters, mythical beings of all sorts and kinds...

--Algernon Blackwood

What the hell is that?

--Al the fisherman

I. The Horror In May

The most merciful thing in the world, I think, is the inability of the human ear to hear a record without it actually being played. We live on a flaccid island of ignorance in the midst of black seas of infinite copyright inveiglement, and it was not meant that we should voyage too far. The sciences, each straining in its own pants, have hitherto harmed us; but some day the piecing together of dissociated notes will open up such terrifying buena vistas of reality, and of our frightful position therein, that we shall either go mad from the revelation or flee from the light into the peace and safety of a new dark beer.

Theosocosmolophists have guessed at the awesome grandeur of the cosmic cycle wherein our world and human race are transients. They have hinted at strange survivals in terms which would freeze the blood if not masked by a bland antifreeze and boredom. But it is not from them that there came the single glimpse of forbidden horror which chills me when I think of it and maddens me when I replay it on my MP3 player repeatedly. That glimpse, like all dread glimpses of truth, flashed out from an accidental download--in this case an old recording and the notes of a tone-deaf professor. I hope that no one else will accomplish this piecing out; certainly, if we survive, I shall never knowingly supply a link in so hideous a chain other than the ones on my website. I think that the professor, too, intended to keep silent regarding the part he knew, and that he would have destroyed his notes had not a sudden desire to be on Oprah seized him.

 My knowledge of the thing began in the winter of 2009-2010 with the reality show stardom of my great-uncle, George Gammell Ammell, Professor Dermatitus of Septic Languages in Brown University, Providence, Rhode Island. Professor Ammell was widely known to work cheaply and had frequently been resorted to by the heads of prominent museums when they were low on funds; so that his selling the rights to his story to every major network less than twenty minutes after signing a non-disclosure agreement came as little surprise. Locally, interest was intensified by the obscurity of the cause of the explosive diarrhea outbreak in April. The professor had been stricken whilst returning from the Newport boat; falling suddenly; as witnesses said, after having been fed by a nautical-looking man wearing a yellow clown outfit who had come from one of the queer dark food courts on the precipitous hillside which formed a short cut from the waterfront to the local deli on Williams Street. Physicians were unable to find any visible cause, but concluded after perplexed debate that some obscure gaseous agent, induced by the brisk ascent of so steep an irritable bowel was responsible for the end. At the time I saw no reason to dissent from this dictum, but latterly I am inclined to wonder--and more than wonder.

 As my great-uncle's agent, I am entitled to ten percent, so don't judge me; and for that purpose moved his entire set of files and boxes to my quarters in Boston to try and piece together a book deal while he parties in Vegas as he "recovers". Much of the material which I correlated will be later published by the American Inquiry Society, but there was one box which I found exceedingly puzzling, and which I feel I should have never let get out into the public. It had been locked and I did not find the way to open it till it occurred to me to use the key sticking out of it. Then, indeed, I succeeded in opening it, but when I did so seemed only to be confronted by a greater and more closely locked barrier. For what could be the meaning of the queer round vinyl disc which I found? Had my uncle, in his latter years become a DJ? I resolved to search out the eccentric sculptor responsible for this apparent disturbance of an old man's peace of mind. The remains of the contents included a brass tuba and a book.

The thing turned out to be called a record; obviously of human origin. Its recordings, however, were far from listenable in atmosphere or suggestion; for, although the vagaries of cubism and future techno pop are many and wild, they do not often reproduce that cryptic irregularity which lurks in prehistoric audibles. The other items, the brass tuba with bas relief etched into the side, and the odd manuscript were also highly peculiar.

I brought them both to a local expert at the pawn shop road show to see if they could be identified. After offering me thirty cents for the book and a buck twelve for the tuba, which I declined, he looked the strange writings over with a shrug.

"Above the apparent hieroglyphics is a figure of evident pictorial intent, though its impressionistic execution forbids a very clear idea of its nature. It seems to be a sort of monster, or symbol representing a monster, of a form which only a diseased yak could conceive. If I say that my somewhat extravagant imagination yields simultaneous pictures of an octagon, a squid, a pencil sharpener, and a human taco, I should not be unfaithful to the spirit of the thing. Here we see a pulpy, tentacled head surmounted a grotesque and scaly body with rudimentary wings; but it is the general outline of the whole which makes it most shockingly frightful. Behind the figure we see a vague suggestion of a Cyclopean architectural background very common in these early otherworldly alien horror reliefs. What makes this piece stand out is the fact that it's etched into a tuba. If it were to go to auction, I would say it would bring in ten to fifteen bucks."

"Is there anything else you can tell me about it?"

"It's a musical instrument. You play it. The writing accompanying this oddity however, aside from a stack of grass cuttings, is in Professor Ammell's most recent hand; and making no pretense to literary style, seems to be a main document headed:

"YODEL OF CTHULHU" in characters painstakingly printed to avoid the erroneous reading of a word so unheard-of. This manuscript is divided into two sections, the first of which is headed "2005--*Dream and Dream Work of H.A. Wilcox*, 7 Thomas St., Providence, R. I.", and the second, "*Narrative of Inspector John R. Le Asse*, 121 Bienville St., New Orleans, La., at 1998 A. A. S. Mtg.--Notes on Same, & Prof. Webb's Acct." The other manuscript papers are brief notes, some of them accounts of the queer dreams of different persons, some of them citations from theosophical books and magazines (notably W. Scott-Elliot's *Atlantis and the Lost Lemuria*), an ingredient list for ham salad, some coupons for borscht, and the rest comment on long-surviving secret recipes and hidden cults, with references to passages in such mythological and anthropological source-books such as Frazer's *Golden Booger* and Miss Murray's **All Witch Revue and Chorus line** in Western Europe. I've been to that review by the way, you have to see it to believe it, the little green witch on the end is cute as a button. A real heart breaker. Got her autograph and everything. I'll show it to you, I've got pictures. The cuttings largely allude to outré mental illness and outbreaks of group flatulence and uncontrollable break dancing in the spring of 2005. All in all it may be worth millions as your uncle is a famous reality show celeb now... I'll give you twenty bucks, final offer."

I left the pawn dealer with an armload of collectible paperweights and a sense of foreboding. The first half of the principal manuscript told a very strange tale. It appears that on March 1st, 2005, a fat, thin, darkly pale young man of neurotic and excited aspect had called upon Professor Ammell bearing the singular brass tuba with the bas-relief, which was then exceedingly damp and fresh. Apparently the spit valve had leaked and the saliva had etched the image into the brass. His card bore the name of Henry Anthony Wilcox, and my uncle had recognized him as the youngest son of an excellent family slightly unknown to him, who had latterly been studying tuba rock arias at the Rhode Island *School of music and living alone* at the Fleur-de-Lys Building near that institution. Wilcox was a precocious youth of unknowable genius but great eccentricity, and had from childhood excited attention through the strange dances and odd sounds he was in the habit of making. He called himself "psychically hyperundulative", but the staid folk of the ancient commercial city dismissed him as merely "stupid." Never mingling much with his kind, he had dropped gradually from social visibility, and was now known only to a small group of anesthesiologists from other towns. Even the Providence Art Club, anxious to preserve its liberal conservatism, had found him quite hopeless.

"Wait, he played an ass tuba?"

"Possibly, but for the record I said Brass tuba. Now stop interrupting me, I have to tell the rest of this story so we can get going and save the world."

On the occasion of the visit, ran the professor's manuscript, the sculptor abruptly asked for the benefit of his host's archeological knowledge in identifying the hieroglyphics of saliva etched bas-reliefs. He spoke in a dreamy, stilted manner which suggested pose and alienated sympathy; and my uncle showed some sharpness in replying, for the conspicuous freshness of the tuba implied kinship with anything but archeology. Young Wilcox's rejoinder, which impressed my uncle enough to make him recall and record it verbatim, was of a fantastically poetic cast which must have typified his whole conversation, and which I have since found highly characteristic of him. He said, "It is new, indeed, for I made it last night in a dream of strange cities; and dreams are older than brooding Tyre, or the contemplative Sphinx, or garden-gridled Babylon breakfasts."

It was then that he began blowing on the tuba. It made deep farting sounds and spit flew from its great horn like a garden sprinkler. The notes told a rambling tale which suddenly played upon a sleeping memory and won the fevered interest of my uncle. There had been a swinging dance contest the night before, the most considerable felt in New England for some years; and Wilcox's imagination had been keenly affected. Upon retiring, he had had an unprecedented dream of great Cyclopean cities of Titan blocks and sky-flung dung, all dripping with green road apples and sinister with latent horror. Fire hydrants and hieroglyphics had covered the walls and pillars, and from some undetermined point below had come a voice that was not a voice; a chaotic sensation which only fancy could transmute into sound, but which he attempted to render by the almost unpronounceable jumble of letters: "Yo da la-ay heee hooooo."

This verbalization was the key to the recollection which excited and horrified Professor Ammell. He questioned the tuba player with scientific minuteness; and studied with frantic intensity the bas-relief on which the youth had found himself creating, chilled and clad only in his night clothes, when dancing had stolen bewilderingly over him. He moonwalked in a cold sweated fury as hundreds of sleepwalking citizens joined him, matching him move for move as if compelled uncontrollably by his lead. My uncle blamed his secretary, Wilcox afterwards said, for his slowness in recognizing both hieroglyphics and pictorial design. Many of his questions seemed highly out of place to his visitor, especially those which tried to connect the latter with strange cults or societies; and Wilcox could not understand the repeated promises of silence which he was offered in exchange for an admission of membership in some widespread mystical or paganly religious body. When Professor Ammell became convinced that the sculptor was indeed ignorant, he besieged his visitor with demands for future reports of break dancing in the night. This bore regular fruit, for after the first interview the manuscript records daily calls of the young man, during which he related startling fragments of nocturnal getting down and moves being busted and with them always the burden of some terrible Cyclopean vista of a dark and dripping stone outhouse, with a subterranean voice or intelligence singing monstrously in enigmatical sense-impacts uninscribable save as gibberish. The two sounds frequently repeated are those rendered by the letters "yodalayhecthulhu" and "something about a lonely goat creature."

On March 23, the manuscript continued, Wilcox failed to appear; and inquiries at his quarters revealed that he had been stricken with an obscure sort of dance fever and taken to the home of his family in Waterman Street. He had cried out in the night, arousing several other artists in the building, and had manifested since then only alternations of uncontrollable tuba playing and delirious swing dancing. My uncle at once telephoned the family, and from that time forward kept close watch of the case; calling often at the Thayer Street office of Dr. Tobey, whom he learned to be in charge. The youth's febrile mind, apparently, was dwelling on strange audible expletives; and the doctor shuddered now and then as he spoke of them. They included not only a repetition of what he had formerly dreamed, but touched wildly on a gigantic thing "miles high", "yodeling" while it spun on its head and walked about doing the *robot*.

He at no time fully described this object but occasional frantic words, as repeated by Dr. Tobey, convinced the professor that it must be identical with the nameless monstrosity he had sought to depict in his saliva-etching. Reference to this object, the doctor added, was invariably a prelude to the young man's subsidence into energetic break dancing and "stepping up" while singing "*Dancing Cthulhu, young and sweet, only 17 million.*" His temperature, oddly enough, was not greatly above normal; but the whole condition was otherwise such as to suggest true fever rather than mental disorder.

On April 2 at about 3 P.M. every trace of Wilcox's malady suddenly ceased. He sat upright in bed, farted, and seemed astonished to find himself at home and completely ignorant. He also recollected nothing of what had happened in dream or reality since the night of March 22. Pronounced alive by his physician, he returned to his quarters in three days; but to Professor Ammell he was of no further assistance. All traces of strange screaming had vanished with his recovery, and my uncle kept no record of his night-thoughts after a week of pointless and irrelevant accounts of infomercial watching and thoroughly usual visions of pink elephants and clogging leprechauns.

Here the first part of the manuscript ends, but references to certain of the scattered notes give me much material for thought--so much, in fact, that only the ingrained reluctance to work too hard when not getting paid and scientific skepticism to the point of deliberate fact burying when the data doesn't do what I want it to can account for my continued distrust of the artist. The notes in question were those descriptive of the dreams of various persons covering the same period as that in which young Wilcox had had his strange visitations. My uncle, it seems, had quickly instituted a prodigiously far-flung body of inquiries amongst nearly all the friends whom he could question without impertinence, asking for nightly reports of their dreams, and the dates of any notable visions for some time past. The reception of his request seems to have varied; but he must, at the very least, have received more responses than any ordinary man could have handled without a dozen more secretaries. This original correspondence was not preserved, but his notes formed a thorough and totally insignificant digest. Average people in society and business--New England's traditional "salt of the earth"--gave an almost completely negative result, though scattered cases of uneasy but formless nocturnal impressions appear here and there, always between March 23 and April 2--the period of young Wilcox's delirium. Scientific men were little more affected, though four cases of vague description suggest fugitive glimpses of strange landscapes, and in one case there is mentioned a dread of something abnormally jaunty.

 It was from the trapeze artists and mime poets that the pertinent answers came, and I know that panic would have broken as loose as their stools had they been able to compare notes. As it was, lacking their original letters, I half suspect the compiler of having asked leading questions, or of having edited the correspondence in corroboration of what he had blatantly resolved to see. That is why I continued to feel that Wilcox, somehow cognizant of the old data which my uncle had possessed, had been imposing a type of flaccid will on the veteran scientist. These responses from esthetes told a disturbing tale. From February 28 to April 2 a large proportion of them had dreamed very bizarre things, the intensity of the dreams being immeasurably the stronger during the period of the sculptor's delirium. Over a fourth of those who reported anything, reported scenes and half-sounds not unlike those which Wilcox had described; and some of the dreamers confessed acute fear of the gigantic nameless thing visible toward the last. One case, which the note describes with emphasis, was very sad. The subject, a widely known architect with leanings toward theosophy and occultism, went violently insane on the date of young Wilcox's seizure, and created an apartment building somewhere in New York several months later. This all being done after incessant screamings to be saved from some escaped smell. He then started a cult of bulldozer worshipers bent on bringing about the end of the world. Had my uncle referred to these cases by name instead of merely by number, I should have attempted some corroboration and personal investigation; but as it is, I succeeded in tracing down only a few. All of these, however, bore out the notes in full. I have found myself wondering if all the the objects of the professor's questioning felt as puzzled as did this fraction. It is well that no explanation shall ever reach them. Unless they read the *Inquisitioner* newspaper report or see the movie that is...

The press cuttings, as I have intimated, touched on cases of panic, mania, and eccentric belly button lint collecting during the given period. Professor Ammell must have employed a grass cutting bureau, for the number of extracts was tremendous, and the sources scattered throughout the globe. He totally couldn't have had time to mow his lawn. Here was a nonfatal suicide in London, where a lone sleeper had leaped from a first story window after a dancing with a bunch of zombies. Here likewise a rambling letter to the editor of a paper in South America, where a fanatic deduces a dire future from visions he has seen. A dispatch from California describes a theosophist colony as donning white robes en mass for some "glorious fulfillment" which never arrives, whilst items from India speak guardedly of serious native indigestion and unrest toward the end of March 22-23

The west of Ireland, too, is full of wild rumor and legendry, and a fantastic painter named Ardois-Bonnot hangs a blasphemously Dreamy Landscape in the Paris spring salon of 2006. It is really really dreamy let me tell you. And so numerous are the recorded troubles in insane asylum toilets backing up that only a miracle can have stopped the medical fraternity from noting strange parallelisms and drawing mystified conclusions. A weird bunch of cuttings, all told; and I can at this date scarcely envisage the callous rationalism with which I set them aside. But I was then convinced that young Wilcox had known of the older matters mentioned by the professor.

We were barreling down the highway at nose bleeding speed as I bit into my soda and a pickled fuschia taco from Dumwich.

"Did they have any good silverware at the pawn shop. I'm looking for a new dinette set."

"I forgot to look. Sorry. But did you check out those paperweights?"

"Amazing! So what was you're uncle working on when this tuba player came to him?"

"Well, the older matters which had made the sculptor's dream and tuba bas-relief so significant to my uncle formed the subject of the second half of his long manuscript. Once before, it appears, Professor Ammell had seen the hellish outlines of the nameless monstrosity, puzzled over the unknown hieroglyphics, and heard the ominous syllables which can be rendered only as "Yodel lay hee Cthulhu"; and all this in so stirring and horrible a connection that it is small wonder he pursued young Wilcox with queries and demands for data."

This earlier experience had come in 1988, seventeen years before, when the American Archaeological Society held its annual meeting in St. Louis. Professor Ammell, as befitted one of his authority and attainments, had had a prominent part in all the deliberations; and was one of the first to be approached by the several outsiders who took advantage of the convocation to offer questions for correct answering and problems for expert solution.

The chief of these outsiders, and in a short time the focus of interest for the entire meeting, was a commonplace-looking middle-aged man who had traveled all the way from New Orleans for certain special information unobtainable from any local source. His name was John Raymond Le Asse, and he was by profession an Inspector of Police. With him he bore the subject of his visit, a grotesque, repulsive, and apparently very ancient stone statuette whose origin he was at a loss to determine. It must not be fancied that Inspector Le Asse had the least interest in archaeology. On the contrary, his wish for enlightenment was prompted by purely professional considerations. The statuette, idol, fetish, or whatever it was, had been captured some months before in the wooded swamps south of New Orleans during a raid on a supposed voodoo meeting; and so singular and hideous were the rites connected with it, that the police could not but realize that they had stumbled on a dark cult totally unknown to them, and infinitely more diabolic than even the worst of the heavy machinery worshiping circles. Of its origin, apart from the erratic and unbelievable tales extorted from the captured members, absolutely nothing was to be discovered; hence the anxiety of the police for any antiquarian lore which might help them to place the frightful symbol, and through it track down the cult to its fountain-head.

Inspector Le Asse was scarcely prepared for the sensation which his offering created. One sight of the thing had been enough to throw the assembled men of science into a state of tense excitement, and they lost no time in crowding around him to gaze at the diminutive figure whose utter strangeness and air of genuinely abysmal antiquity hinted so potently at unopened and archaic beer kegs. No recognized brewery or school of sculpture had animated this terrible object or claimed it as a mascot, yet centuries and even thousands of years seemed recorded in its dim and greenish surface of unplaceable stone.

The figure, which was finally passed slowly from man to man for close and careful study, was between seven and eight inches in height, and of exquisitely artistic workmanship. It represented a monster of vaguely anthropoid outline, but with an octopus-like head whose face was a mass of feelers, a scaly, rubbery-looking body, prodigious claws on hind and fore feet, and long, narrow wings behind. This thing, which seemed instinct with a fearsome and unnatural malignancy, was of a somewhat bloated corpulence, and squatted evilly on a rectangular block or pedestal covered with undecipherable characters. The tips of the wings touched the back edge of the block, the seat occupied the center, whilst the long, curved claws of the doubled-up, crouching hind legs gripped the front edge and extended a quarter of the way down toward the bottom of the pedestal. The cephalopod head was bent forward, so that the ends of the facial feelers brushed the backs of huge fore paws which clasped the croucher's elevated knees. The aspect of the whole was abnormally life-like, and the more subtly fearful because its source was so totally unknown. Its vast, awesome, and incalculable age was unmistakable; yet not one link did it shew with any known type of art belonging to civilization's youth--or indeed to any other time. Totally separate and apart, its very material was a mystery; for the soapy, greenish-black stone with its golden or iridescent flecks and striations resembled nothing familiar to geology or mineralogy. The characters along the base were equally baffling; "Made in China" what could it mean? No member present, despite a representation of half the world's expert learning in this field, could form the least notion of even their remotest linguistic kinship. They, like the subject and material, belonged to something horribly remote and distinct from mankind as we know it, something frightfully suggestive of old and unhallowed cycles of life in which our world and our conceptions have no part.

And yet, as the members severally shook their heads and confessed to a number of crimes including being part of some ancient cult, they also claimed defeat at the Inspector's problem, there was one man in that gathering who suspected a touch of bizarre familiarity in the monstrous shape and writing, and who presently told with some diffidence of the odd trifle he knew. This person was the late William Channing Webbslinger, Professor of Anthropomorphic spiders in Princeton University, and an explorer of no slight note. Professor Webbslinger had been engaged, forty-eight years before, in a tour of Greenland and Iceland in search of some Runic inscriptions which he failed to unearth; and whilst high up on the West Greenland coast had encountered a singular tribe or cult of degenerate Eskimo pies whose texture and filling, created through some curious form of devil-worship, chilled him with its deliberate bloodthirsty creaminess and repulsively good tastiness. It was a recipe of which other Eskimo pie creators knew little, and which they mentioned only with shudders, saying that it had come down from horribly ancient aeons before ever the world famous *Arctic bars* were made. Besides nameless rites and human sacrifices there were certain queer hereditary rituals addressed to a supreme power it had to get people to do things in order to get one; and of this Professor Webbslinger had taken a careful phonetic copy from an aged angecootch or wizard-priest, expressing the sounds in Roman letters as best he knew how. "Whut wud ya doo-ooo-ooooo for an Arctic barrrr?" But just now of prime significance was the fetish which this cult had cherished, and around which they danced when the aurora leaped high and dove over the ice cliffs. It was, the professor stated, a very crude saliva etched bas-relief of stone, comprising a hideous picture and some cryptic writing. And so far as he could tell, it was a rough parallel in all essential features of the bestial thing now lying before the meeting.

This data, received with suspense and astonishment by the assembled members, proved doubly exciting to Inspector Le Asse; and he began at once to ply his informant with liquor and questions. Having noted and copied an oral ritual among the swamp cult-worshipers his men had arrested, he besought the professor to remember as best he might the syllables taken down amongst the diabolist Eskimos. There then followed an exhaustive comparison of details, and a moment of really awed silence when both detective and scientist agreed on the virtual identity of the phrase common to two hellish rituals so many worlds of distance apart. What, in substance, both the Eskimo wizards and the

Louisiana swamp-priests had chanted to their kindred idols was something very like this: the word-divisions being guessed at from traditional breaks in the phrase as chanted aloud:

"Ph'nglui lu ai oh mglw'nafh we gotta go ai ai ai ai Cthulhu R'lyeh wagit'nagl fahrtagn."

Le Asse had one point in advance of Professor Webbslinger, for several among his mangled prisoners had repeated to him what older celebrants had told them the words meant. This text, as given, ran something like this:

"In his house at R'lyeh dead Cthulhu waits dreaming of a Broadway musical."And now, in response to a general and urgent demand, Inspector Le Asse related as fully as possible his experience with the swamp worshipers; telling a story to which I could see my uncle attached profound significance. It savored of the wildest dreams of myth-maker and theosophist, and disclosed an astonishing degree of cosmic imagination among such half-castes and pariahs as might be least expected to possess it."

On November 1st, 1987, there had come to the New Orleans police a frantic summons from the swamp and black lagoon country to the south. The squatters there, mostly advanced but good natured descendants of Lafitte's men, were in the grip of stark terror from an unknown thing which had stolen upon them in the night. It was voodoo, apparently, but voodoo of a more terrible sort than they had ever known; and some of their women and children had disappeared since the malevolent tom-toms and ann-anns had begun incessant beatings far within the black haunted woods where no dweller ventured. There were insane shouts and harrowing screams, soul-chilling chants and dancing devil-flames; and, the frightened messenger added, the people could stand it no more.

So a body of twenty police, six robots, and a dog, filling two carriages, an automobile, and a canoe had set out in the late afternoon with the shivering squatter as a guide. At the end of the passable road they alighted, and for miles splashed on in silence through the terrible cypress woods where day never came. Ugly roots and malignant hanging nooses of Spanish moss beset them, and now and then a pile of dank stones or fragment of a rotting wall intensified by its hint of morbid habitation a depression which every malformed tree and every fungous islet combined to create. At length the squatter settlement, a miserable huddle of huts, hove in sight; and hysterical dwellers ran out to cluster around the group of bobbing lanterns. The muffled beat of tom-toms was now faintly audible far, far ahead; and a curdling shriek came at infrequent intervals when the wind shifted. A reddish glare, too, seemed to filter through pale undergrowth beyond the endless avenues of forest night. Reluctant even to be left alone again, each one of the cowed squatters refused point-blank to advance another inch toward the scene of unholy worship, so Inspector Le Asse and his machine gun and RPG toting colleagues plunged on unguided into black arcades of horror that none of them had ever trod before.

The region now entered by the police was one of traditionally evil repute, substantially unknown and untraversed by ultra men. There were legends of a hidden lake unglimpsed by mortal sight, in which dwelt a huge, formless white polypous thing with luminous eyes; and squatters whispered that bat-winged devils flew up out of caverns in inner earth to worship it at midnight. They said it had been there before D'Iberville, before La Salle, before the Indians, and before even the wholesome beasts and birds of the woods. It was nightmare itself, and to see it was to throw up a little. But it made men dream, and so they knew enough to keep away. The present voodoo orgy was, indeed, on the merest fringe of this abhorred area, but that location was bad enough; hence perhaps the very place of the worship had terrified the squatters more than the shocking sounds and incidents.

Only poetry or madness could do justice to the noises heard by Le Asse's men as they plowed on through the black morass toward the red glare and muffled tom-toms. There are vocal qualities peculiar to men, and vocal qualities peculiar to beasts; and it is terrible to hear the one when the source should yield the other. Animal fury and orgiastic license here whipped themselves to daemoniac heights by howls and squawking ecstasies that tore and reverberated through those nighted woods like pestilential tempests from the gulfs of hell. Now and then the less organized ululation would cease, and from what seemed a well-drilled chorus of hoarse voices would rise in sing-song chant that hideous phrase or ritual:

*"Ph'nglui lu ai oh mglw'nafh we gotta go ai ai ai ai,
Cthulhu R'lyeh wagit'nagl fahrtagn."*

Then the men, having reached a spot where the trees were thinner, came suddenly in sight of the spectacle itself. Four of them reeled, one fainted, and two were shaken into a frantic type of square dance which the mad cacophony of the orgy fortunately deadened. Le Asse dashed swampy septic tank water on the face of the fainting man, and all stood trembling and nearly hypnotized with horror.

In a natural glade of the swamp stood a grassy island of perhaps an acre's extent, clear of trees and tolerably dry. On this now leaped and twisted a more indescribable horde of human abnormality than any but a Simean or an Angry Krayarola could paint. Void of clothing, this hybrid spawn were braying, bellowing, and writhing about a monstrous polyhexagonal ring-shaped bonfire; in the center of which, revealed by occasional rifts in space and the curtain of flame, stood a great granite monolith some eight feet in height; on top of which, incongruous in its diminutiveness, rested the noxious carven statuette. From a wide circle of ten scaffolds set up at regular intervals with the flame-girt monolith as a center hung, head downward, the oddly unharmed helpless squatters who had disappeared. It was inside this circle that the ring of worshipers jumped and roared, the general direction of the mass motion being from left to right in endless Bacchanal between the ring of snapping crocodiles and the ring of fire.

It may have been only imagination and it may have been only echoes which induced one of the men, an excitable Spaniard wearing a black mask and cape, to fancy he heard antiphonal responses to the ritual from some far and unillumined spot deeper within the wood of ancient legendry and horror. This man, Joseph D. Galvez, I later met and questioned; and he proved distractingly imaginative. He indeed went so far as to hint of the faint beating of great wings, and of a glimpse of shining eyes and a mountainous white bulk beyond the remotest trees but I suppose he had been hearing too much native superstition.

Actually, the horrified pause of the men was of comparatively brief duration. Duty came first; and although there must have been over a hundred mangie celebrants in the throng, the police relied on their firearms and the unimaginable strength of their robot helpers and plunged determinedly into the nauseous rout. For five minutes the resultant din and chaos were beyond description. Wild blows were struck, lasers were fired, and escapes were failed; but in the end Le Asse was able to count some forty-seven sullen prisoners, and ninety-two happy ones whom he forced to dress in haste and fall into line between two rows of policemen. Five of the worshipers lay dead, and two severely wounded ones were carried away on stretchers brought by their well prepared fellow-prisoners. The image on the monolith, of course, was carefully removed and carried back by Le Asse.

Examined at headquarters after a trip of intense strain and weariness, the prisoners all proved to be men of a very little attention, and of mentally absent type. Most were seamen, and a sprinkling of landmen and airmen, largely from the west coast of Brava Brava from the Cape Flapper Islands, and gave a colouring of voodooism to the heterogeneous cult. But before many questions were asked, it became manifest that something far deeper and older than foot fetishism was involved. Well educated and ignorant as they were, the creatures held with surprising consistency to the central idea of their loathsome faith.

They worshiped, so they said, the Great Old Ones who lived ages before there were any men, and who came to the young world out of the sky. Those Old Ones were gone now, inside the earth and under the sea, (they sang this last part); but their dead bodies had told their secrets in dreams to the first men, who formed a cult which had never died. Except that one time. This was that cult, and the prisoners said it had always existed and always would exist, hidden in distant wastes and dark places all over the world until the time when the great priest Cthulhu, from his dark house in the mighty city of R'lyeh under the waters, should rise and bring the earth again beneath his sway. Some day he would call, when the stars were ready, and the secret cult would always be waiting to liberate him.

Meanwhile no more must be told. There was a secret which even torture could not extract. Then Le Asse threatened to make them eat at the cafeteria and they cracked like eggs. Mankind was not absolutely alone among the conscious things of the earth, for shapes came out of the dark to visit the faithful few. But these were not the Great Old

Ones. No man had ever seen the Old Ones. The carven idol was great Cthulhu, but none might say whether or not the others were precisely like him. No one could read the old writing now, but things were told by word of mouth. The chanted ritual was not the secret--that was never spoken aloud, only whispered. They whispered. The chant meant only this:

"In his house at R'lyeh dead Cthulhu waits... dreaming of a Broadway musical."

Only all but two of the prisoners were found sane enough to be hanged, and the rest were committed to various institutions. All denied a part in the ritual singing, and averred that the singing had been done by Black Winged Ones which had come to them from their immemorial meeting-place in the haunted wood. But of those mysterious allies no coherent account could ever be gained. What the police did extract, came mainly from the immensely aged fishmonger named Castro, who claimed to have sailed to strange ports and talked with undying leaders of the cult in the mountains of China just before the Chinese commandos had killed them.

Old Castro remembered bits of hideous legend that paled the speculations of theosophists and made man and the world seem recent and transient indeed. There had been aeons when other Things ruled on the earth, and They had had great cities. Remains of Them, he said the deathless Chinamen had told him, were still to be found as Cyclopean stones on islands in the Pacific. They all died vast epochs of time before men came, but there were arts which could revive Them when the stars had come round again to the right positions in the cycle of eternity. They had, indeed, come themselves from the stars, and brought Their images with Them.

These Great Old Ones, Castro continued, were not composed altogether of flesh and blood. They had shape--for did not this star-fashioned image prove it?--but that shape was not made of matter. When the stars were right, They could plunge from world to world through the sky; but when the stars were wrong, They could not live. But although They no longer lived, They would never really die. They all lay in stone houses in Their great city of R'lyeh, preserved by the spells of mighty Cthulhu for a glorious resurrection when the stars and the earth might once more be ready for Them. But at that time some force from outside must serve to liberate Their bodies. The spells that preserved them intact likewise prevented Them from making an initial move, and They could only lie awake in the dark and think whilst uncounted millions of years rolled by. They knew all that was occurring in the universe, for Their mode of speech was transmitted thought. Even now They talked in Their tombs. When, after infinities of chaos, the first men came, the Great Old Ones spoke to the sensitive among them by molding their dreams; for only thus could Their language reach the fleshly minds of mammals.

Then, whispered Castro, those first men formed the cult around tall idols which the Great Ones showed them; idols brought in dim eras from dark stars. That cult would never die till the stars came right again, and the secret priests would take great Cthulhu from His tomb to revive His subjects and resume His rule of earth. The time would be easy to know, for then mankind would have become as the Great Old Ones; free and wild and beyond good and evil, with laws and morals thrown aside and all men shouting and drinking and singing and reveling in joy. Then the liberated Old Ones would teach them new ways to shout and dance and revel and enjoy themselves, and all the earth would light flames from their behinds with a holocaust of ecstasy and freedom. Meanwhile the cult, by appropriate rites, must keep alive the memory of those ancient ways and shadow forth the prophecy of their return.

In the elder time chosen men had talked with the entombed Old Ones in dreams, but then something happened. The great stone city R'lyeh, with its monoliths and sepulchres, had sunk beneath the waves; and the deep waters, full of the one primal mystery through which not even thought can pass, had cut off the spectral intercourse. But memory never died, and the high-priests said that the city would rise again when the stars were right. Then came out of the earth the black spirits of earth, moldy and shadowy, and full of dim rumors picked up in caverns beneath forgotten sea-bottoms. But of them old Castro dared not speak much. He cut himself off hurriedly, and no amount of persuasion or subtlety could elicit more in this direction. Le Asse offered an Arctic bar and asked what he would do for it. Castro readily agreed to tell him everything then. The size of the Old Ones, their locations, how to defeat them, the addresses of the surviving cult leaders. Of the cult, he said that he thought the center lay amid the pathless desert of Arabia, where Irem, the City of Pillars, dreams hidden and untouched areas lay. It was not allied to the European witch-cult, and was virtually unknown beyond its members. No book had ever really hinted of it, though the deathless Chinamen said that there were double meanings in the Necronomicon of the mad Arab Abdul Alhazred which the initiated might read as they chose, especially the much-discussed couplet:

That is not dead which can eternal lie,
And with strange aeons even death may die. So there.

Le Asse, deeply impressed and not at all bewildered, had inquired in vain concerning the historic affiliations of the cult. Castro, apparently, had told the truth when he said that it was wholly secret. The authorities at Tulane University could shed no light upon either cult or image, and now the detective had come to the highest authorities in the country and met with no more than the Greenland tale of Professor Webbslinger.

The feverish interest aroused at the meeting by Le Asse's tale, corroborated as it was by the statuette, is echoed in the subsequent correspondence of those who attended; although scant mention occurs in the formal publications of the society. Caution is the first care of those accustomed to face occasional charlatanry and imposture. Le Asse for some time lent the image to Professor Webbslinger, but at the latter's last knowledge it was returned to him by accident in a box of laundry he was sending and remains in his possession, where I viewed it not long ago. It is truly a terrible thing, and unmistakably akin to the dream-sculpture of young Wilcox.

That my uncle was excited by the tale of the sculptor I did not wonder, for what thoughts must arise upon hearing, after a knowledge of what Le Asse had learned of the cult, of a sensitive young man who had dreamed not only the figure and exact hieroglyphics of the swamp-found image and the Greenland devil tablet, but had come in his dreams upon at least three of the precise words of the formula uttered alike by Eskimox diabolists and monster Louisianans? Professor Ammell's instant start on an investigation of the utmost thoroughness was eminently natural; though privately I suspected young Wilcox of having heard of the cult in some indirect way, and of having invented a series of fever dance dreams to heighten and continue the mystery at my uncle's expense. The dream-narratives and cuttings collected by the professor were, of course, strong corroboration; but the rationalism of my mind and the extravagance of the whole subject leads me to adopt what I think is the most sensible conclusion. It was ancient freakin' aliens. The jerks! Nonetheless I made a trip to Providence to see the sculptor and give him the ass kicking I thought proper for so boldly imposing upon a learned and aged man.

Wilcox still lived alone in the Fleur-de-Lys Building in Thomas Street, a hideous Victorian imitation of seventeenth century Victorian Architecture which flaunts its Victorian front amidst the lovely Victorian houses on the ancient hill, and under the very shadow of the finest Georgian steeple in America, I found him at work in his rooms, and at once conceded from the specimens scattered about that his genius is indeed profound and authentic. He will, I believe, some time be heard from as one of the great decadents; for he has crystallized in clay and will one day mirror in marble those nightmares and phantasies which Arthur Machen evokes in prose, and Clark Ashton Smith makes visible in verse and in painting.

Dark, heavily muscular, and somewhat unkempt in aspect, he turned languidly at my knock and asked me my business without rising. Then he stopped me, told me who I was, and displayed some interest; for my uncle had excited his curiosity in probing his strange dreams, yet had never explained the reason for the study. I did not enlarge his knowledge in this regard, but sought with some subtlety to draw him out. Unfortunately he seemed to already know everything I did after examining my shoe with a magnifying glass. In a short time I became convinced of his absolute sincerity, for he spoke of the dreams in a manner none could mistake. They and their subconscious residuum had influenced his art profoundly, as had his uncle, a man named Shurluck, and he shewed me a morbid statue whose contours almost made me shake with the potency of its spicy suggestion. He could not recall having seen the original of this thing except in his own dream and a visit to a beach in Fort Lauderdale, but the outlines had formed themselves insensibly under his hands. It was, no doubt, the giant boobed shape he had raved of for weeks. That he really knew nothing of the hidden cult, save from what my uncle's relentless catechism had let fall, and his own almost psychic deductions revealed to him, and the whole of their plans for the next two years, he soon made clear; and again I strove to think of some way in which he could possibly have received the weird impressions.

' My dear friend,' He said then. ' If you were to find the truth of this tale, why not investigate it yourself. I have recently come across a note intercepted from a cult member, hinting at the location of the sunken city itself.'

"And that is what I set out to do."

III. The Madness from the Sea

"That evening, after a day of hurried internet surfing and arranging, I called you."

"Oh, ok. "

"I probably should have told you all this before we were almost to the dock where our ship is waiting to go to the ancient city. We really should try to save the world but we're probably gonna be eaten by ancient alien fish monsters."

"Meh, I wasn't doing anything this weekend anyway."

The *Vigilant* stood vigilantly in the harbor. A ship of fifty seven canon, twelve fifty millimeter machine guns, bristling with missle launchers and hulled with sixteen inches of ballistic reinforced armored steel. The ships captain, one Captain Scarred Johanson, a lusty pirate of a man with tattoos on his tattoos. The crew was a suicidally courageous lot of salty sea urchins.

We made our way with haste as a hurricane induced perfect earthquake thunderstorm was already turning the sea and the skies above into an impassable black swirl of horror. The crew sang pirate songs and scrubbed the deck mercilessly as we crashed headlong through the sea spray and salty air.

The great storm blew us like a fart in a tornado, the giant ship was tossed about on three hundred foot waves like it was a minnow. What should have been a simple three hour tour had became a fight for sea dominance. We faced it down, driving through the wind and rain and finally blasted through. Then on the second day of the cruise, in S. Latitude 49° 51' W. Longitude 128° 34', we encountered the *Inert*, manned by a queer and evil-looking crew of kayak pirates and half-wits. Being ordered peremptorily to turn back, Capt. Johanson refused; whereupon the strange crew began to fire savagely and without warning upon the battle schooner with a peculiarly heavy battery of brass cannon forming part of the yacht's equipment. The Vigilant's men laughed as the canon balls bounced off the steel armor, but eventually showed fight, and though the enemy ship began to sink from shots from our torpedoes beneath the water-line we managed to heave alongside the enemy and board her, grappling with the savage crew on the yacht's deck, and being forced to kill them all a lot, as they refused to let us rescue them. Despite their number being slightly superior to ours by a factor of fifty to one, we took them with little effort because of their particularly abhorrent and desperate, though rather clumsy mode of fighting, which involved spinning on their heads and trying to hit us with their feet. We shot them.

Five of the enemy men, including their Captain Samm Krunch and First Mate Jed Sogworthy, were captured; and the remaining eight, who formed into three people, proceeded to lead us through the captured yacht, giving us a grand tour just before it sank.

We then proceeded going ahead in our original direction to see if any reason for their ordering us back had existed. The next day the former enemies and now new members of the crew raised a yell and pointed to a weird looking shape rising out of the water.

It was a great stone pillar sticking out of the sea, and in S. Latitude 47° 9', W. Longitude 123° 43', we came upon a coastline of mingled mud, ooze, and weedy Cyclopean masonry which can be nothing less than the tangible substance of earth's supreme septic system--the nightmare corpse-city of R'lyeh, that was built in measureless aeons behind history by the vast, loathsome shapes that seeped down from the dark toilets of the stars. There lay great Cthulhu and his hordes, sunbathing, no longer hidden in green slimy vaults and sending out at last, after cycles incalculable, the thoughts that spread fear to the dreams of the sensitive and called imperiously to the faithful to come on a pilgrimage of liberation and restoration. All this we know only because there were giant neon signs saying it!

Only a single mountain-top, the hideous monolith-crowned citadel whereon great Cthulhu was fond of lounging, actually emerged from the waters. When I think of the extent of all that may be brooding down there I almost wish to dive down and do some treasure hunting forthwith. Johanson and his men were awed by the cosmic majesty of this dripping Babylon of elder daemons, and my companion quickly guessed without guidance that it was nothing of this or of any sane planet. Awe at the unbelievable size of the greenish stone blocks, at the dizzying height of the great carven monolith, and at the stupefying identity of the colossal statues and saliva etched bas-reliefs with the queer image found in the shrine on the sunken ship *Inert*, is poignantly visible in every line of the frightening karaoke that echoed over the waves from unseen speakers.

There wasn't really any definite structure or building, only broad impressions of vast angles and stone surfaces--surfaces too great to belong to anything right or proper for this earth, we always build properly crappy stuff. It was resplendently decorated with horrible images and hieroglyphs that we posed next to and took many pictures and vacation videos of. I mention the angles because it suggests something Wilcox had told me of his awesome dreams. He said that the geometry of the dream-place he saw was abnormal, non-Euclidean, and loathsomely redolent of spheres and dimensions apart from ours. Now an unlettered seaman named Al saw the same thing whilst gazing at the terrible reality in which he exclaimed. "Holy crap, this place is like weird, man."

We landed at a sloping mud-bank on this monstrous Acropolis, and clambered slipperily up over titan oozy blocks which could have been no mortal staircase. The very sun of heaven seemed distorted when viewed through the polarizing miasma welling out from this sea-soaked perversion, and twisted menace and suspense lurked leeringly in those crazily elusive angles of carven rock where a second glance showed concavity after the first showed convexity.

 Something very like excited anticipation had come over all of we explorers before anything more definite than rock and ooze and weed was seen. Each would have sang and danced had he not feared the scorn of the others, and it was only half heartedly that we fought off the urge from the catchy music that seemed to come from nowhere and searched--productively, as it proved--for some portable souvenir to bear away. (The gift shops were surprisingly well stocked and reasonably priced.)

 It was Rodriguez the Portuguese who climbed up the foot of the monolith and shouted of what he had found. The rest of us followed him, and looked curiously at the immense carved door with the now familiar squid-dragon-turd bas-relief. It was, Johanson said, like a great barn-door; and we all felt that it was a door because of the ornate lint covered threshold, and door jams around it, though we could not decide whether it lay flat like a trap-door or slantwise like an outside cellar-door. As Wilcox would have said, the geometry of the place was all wrong. One could not be sure that the sea and the ground were horizontal, hence the relative position of everything else seemed phantasmally variable.

 Briden pushed at himself in several places without result. Then Donovan felt over it delicately around the edge, pressing each point separately as he went. He climbed interminably along the grotesque stone molding--that is, one would call it climbing if the thing was not after all horizontal--and the men wondered how any door in the universe could be so vast. Then, very softly and slowly, the acre-great lint trap began to give inward at the top; and we saw that it was balanced.

 Donovan slid or somehow propelled himself down or along the edge and rejoined us, and everyone watched the queer recession of the monstrously carven portal. In this phantasy of prismatic distortion it moved anomalously in a diagonal way, so that all the rules of matter and perspective seemed upset.

 The aperture was black with a darkness almost material. That tenebrousness was indeed a positive quality; for it obscured such parts of the inner walls as ought to have been revealed, and actually burst forth like smoke from its aeon-long imprisonment, visibly darkening the sun as it slunk away into the shrunken and gibbous sky on flapping membranous wings. The odor rising from the newly opened depths was highly tolerable, something like honey suckle and fresh linens, and at length the quick-eared Hawkins thought he heard a nasty, slapping sound down there. Everyone listened, and everyone was listening still when It lumbered slobberingly into sight and gropingly squeezed Its gelatinous green immensity through the black doorway into the tainted outside air of that poison city of madness.

The Thing cannot be described--there is no language for such abysms of shrieking and immemorial lunacy, such eldritch contradictions of all matter, force, and cosmic order. A mountain walked or stumbled. GOD! What wonder that across the earth a great architect went dancing, and poor Wilcox hosted raves with dance fever in that telepathic instant? The Thing of the idols, the green, sticky spawn of the stars, had awaked to claim his own. The stars were right again, and what an age-old cult had failed to do by design, we had done by curiosity. After vigintillions of years great Cthulhu was loose again, and ravening for delight.

Three men were swept up by the rhythm before anybody turned. If there be any rest in the universe it wasn't in their feet as they jumped and spun with the music. They were Donovan, Guerrera, and Angstrom. Parker slipped as the other three were plunging frenziedly over endless vistas of green-crusted rock to the boat, and Johanson swears he was swallowed up and stopped in his tracks by a catchy vocal from an angle of masonry which shouldn't have been there; an angle which was cute, but behaved as if it were bad and needed a spanking. So only Briden and Johanson, myself and my companion reached the boat, and pulled desperately for the earplugs as the mountainous monstrosity flopped down the slimy stones and hesitated, floundering at the edge of the water.

The great horror was suddenly surrounded by a throng of hearty mermen and really cute mermaids from the sea. With an unseen accompaniment from some phantom instruments he began to sing!!!

[Cthulhu:]
High on a hill was a goat with a thousand young
Yodel lay ee yodel lay ee yodel lay hee hoo
Loud was the voice of the goat with a thousand young
Odl lay ee odl lay ee odl-oo

Folks in a port town that was quite remote heard
Lay ee yodel lay ee yodel lay hee hoo
Horrible and clear from the goat beast's throat heard
Lay ee odl lay ee odl-oo

[The Fishmen:]
O ho lay dee odl lee hee, o ho lay dee odl ay
O ho lay dee odl lee hee, o ho lay dee odl lay

[Cthulhu:]
A cultist on the bridge of an ancient moat heard
Lay ee yodel lay ee yodel lay hee hoo

[Mermaid:]
Men out at sea with a loaded boat heard
Lay ee odl lay hee odl-oo

[The Fishmen:]
Men in the midst of an ancient rote heard
Lay ee yodel lay hee yodel lay Cthul hoo

[Cthulhu:]
Men drinking beer in Sarnath afloat heard
Lay ee yodel lay hee odl-oo

One little girl in a kingly yellow coat heard

Lay ee yodel lay hee odl lay hee hoo

[Mermaid:]
She yodeled back to the goat with a thousand young
Lay ee odl lay hee odl-oo

[Cthulhu:]
Soon her Mom with a bleating bloat heard
Lay ee odl lay hee odl lay hee hoo
What a duet for a fish girl and goat with a thousand young!

[Cthulhu and all:]
Lay ee odl lay hee odl-oo

[Cthulhu and all]
Yodel lay ee (odl lay hee)
Yodel lay hee hee (odl lay hee hee)
Yodel lay hee . . .

[Mermaid:]
One little girl in a kingly yellow coat heard
[Cthulhu:]
Lay ee yodel lay hee yodel lay hoo hoo
[Mermaid:]
She yodeled back to the lonely goat with a thousand young
[Cthulhu:]
Lay ee odl lay hee odl-oo

[Cthulhu:]
Soon her Mom with a bleating bloat heard
Lay ee yodel lay hee yodel lay hoohoo
What a duet for a fish girl and goat with a thousand young
Lay ee odl lay hee odl-oo

[All:]
Happy are they all day dee olay dee lee ooo ooo

Soon the the stars will be just right...

[Cthulhu:]
Lay ee odl lay hee odl-oo

[All:]
Yodel lay ee, yodel lay hee
Yodel lay hee hee, odl lay ee
Yodel lay hee
Yodel lay heeeeeeeeeeee

[The Fishmen and Mermaids:]

CTHUL- HOO FHARTAGN!!!!!

 Steam had not been suffered to go down entirely, despite the departure of all hands but our former enemies and my companions' great dane for the shore; and it was the work of only a few moments of feverish rushing up and down between wheel and engines to get the ship under way. Slowly, amidst the distorted horrors of that indescribable scene, she began to churn the lethal waters; whilst on the masonry of that charnel shore that was not of earth the titan Thing from the stars slavered and gibbered like Polypheme cursing the fleeing ship of Odysseus. Then, bolder than the storied Cyclops, great Cthulhu slid greasily into the water like cosmic poop and began to pursue with vast wave-raising strokes of cosmic potency. I hummed along in spite of myself as I worked the moorings and the men hurried to raise anchor.

 Captain Johanson had the powerful diesel and steam combo engines running like a turbine. Knowing that the Thing could surely overtake us until our speed was fully up, he resolved on a desperate chance; and, setting the engine for full speed, ran lightning-like on deck and reversed the wheel. There was a mighty eddying and foaming in the noisome brine, and as the steam mounted higher and higher the brave Norwegian drove the vessel head on against the pursuing jelly which rose above the unclean froth like the stern of a daemon galleon, waving us back like a desperate shopkeeper who has not had a customer in too long. The awful squid-head with writhing feelers came nearly up to the bowsprit of the sturdy battle yacht, but Johanson drove on relentlessly. There was a bursting as of an exploding bladder, a slushy nastiness as of a cloven sunfish, a stench as of a thousand opened flowers, and a saying of words that can not be put on paper as the ship bottomed out on the shoal and we ran over Cthulhu's foot. For an instant the ship was befouled by an acrid and blinding green vapor cloud that bubbled up from below, and then there was only a venomous seething astern as the water seemed to boil with the green-crusted methane release; The great creature jumped up grabbing his foot and hopping on the other. Then he fell backwards, tripping over a ledge and falling with a crashing as if of plates and silverware and breaking dishes as it fell down its stairs back down the shaft into its unseen basement.

We did not try to navigate after the first bold flight, for we tried desperately to sing other songs to get the tune out of our heads. There was much drinking of beer and eating of rum flambayed tilapia tacos. Then came the perfect storm, the second that week and a gathering of the clouds about creating a spectral whirling through liquid gulfs of infinity, of dizzying rides through reeling universes on a comets tail, and of hysterical plunges from the pit to the moon and from the moon back again to the pit, all livened by a cachinnating chorus of the distorted, hilarious elder gods and the green, bat-winged mocking imps of Tartarus.

Three days later, the Vigilant, and its half sunburned crew and passengers, like a hung over sailor, sailed slowly into its home harbor.

That a book was to be written was inevitable. A three movie deal is already in the works. Don't blame me for the songs that are already circling the net and TV commercials everywhere. T-shirts and coffee mugs and day trips to R'lyeh are already in high demand. The horror of the songs echo on every radio station incessantly.

If the studios get their way we'll all be roped into playing ourselves on Broadway as well, standing on the great stage with the eldritch horror, singing along... to the ...

YODEL OF CTHULHU...

About the Author

Mike Oswald lives in Michigan, where he enjoys writing, ghost hunting, looking for buried treasure, and building haunted houses for Halloween. He is currently working on several new projects that will be coming out soon!

Be Sure to check out: WWW.WITCHHOUSEBOOKS.COM

Are you sure you lost your contact here?

www.ingramcontent.com/pod-product-compliance
Lightning Source LLC
Chambersburg PA
CBHW060540260626
47161CB00003B/992